BY H. E. BATES

LOVE FOR LYDIA

H. E. BATES

LOVE *for*

LYDIA

An Atlantic Monthly Press Book

LITTLE, BROWN AND COMPANY · *Boston*

ATLANTIC—LITTLE, BROWN BOOKS
ARE PUBLISHED BY
LITTLE, BROWN AND COMPANY
IN ASSOCIATION WITH
THE ATLANTIC MONTHLY PRESS

To Laurence

The "I" of this story is purely
fictitious, as are the characters
he describes.

PART ONE

I

Aﬤ the death of their elder brother the two Aspen
sisters came back to Evensford at the end of February, driving in the enormous brown coachwork Daimler with the
gilt monograms on the doors, through a sudden fall of
snow.

Across the valley the floods of January, frozen to wide lakes
of ice, were cut into enormous rectangular patterns by black
hedgerows that lay like a wreckage of logs washed down on
the broken river. A hard dark wind blew straight across the
ice from the northeast, beating in at that end of the town
where for a few hundred yards the High Street runs straight,
past what is now Johnson's car-wrecking yard, under the
railway arches, and then between the high causeways that
make it like a dry canal. It was so cold that solid ice seemed
to be whipped up from the valley on the wind, to explode
into whirlwinds of harsh and bitter dust that pranced about
in stinging clouds. Ice formed everywhere in dry black pools,
polished in sheltered places, ruckled with dark waves at street
corners or on sloping gutters where wind had flurried the
last falls of rain.

Frost had begun in the third week of January, and from
that date until the beginning of April it did not leave us for
a day. All the time the same dark wind came with it, blowing bitterly and savagely over long, flat meadows of frozen

[3]

floods. There was no snow with it until the afternoon the Aspen sisters came back; and then it began to fall lightly, in sudden flusters, no more than vapor, and then gritty and larger, like grains of rice.

It began falling almost exactly at the moment the heavy brown Daimler drove past the old Succoth Chapel, with its frozen steps like a waterfall of chipped glass, opposite the branch offices of the *County Examiner,* where the windows were partly glazed over with a pattern of starry fern. It came suddenly on a darkened whirl of wind that flowered into whiteness. The wind seemed to twist violently in the air and snatch from nowhere the snow that was like white vapor, catching the Daimler broadside at the same time. Through the windows of the *Examiner,* where I stood nursing the wrist I had sprained while skating, I saw the car shudder and swerve and twist itself into a skid and then out again. From a confusion of leopard rugs on the back seat the younger Miss Aspen, Juliana, seemed to shudder too and was swung forward, snatching at the silken window cord with her right hand. The elder one, Bertie, bounced like a rosy dumpling. They were still both in black. But round the neck of the younger one was pinned a violet woolen scarf, as if she had caught a cold, and it was when she jolted forward, clutching the scarf with one hand and the window cord with the other, that I saw Elliot Aspen's daughter sitting there, between her aunts, for the first time.

She had long coils of black hair that fell across her shoulders, so that she seemed to be wearing a hood. I saw only part of her face, jerked forward above her raised coat collar, startled but not frightened by the skid. She did not lift her hands. It was her eyes instead that seemed to stretch out, first to one window and then another in an effort to get her bearings, as if she did not know exactly where she was. And in that moment, before the car straightened and righted

[4]

itself and went on, she seemed, I thought, about fifteen. It was my first mistake about her.

In the back office the kettle was on the gas ring and Bretherton was asleep by the stove. On the table were the remains, set about on torn and greasy paper bags, of Bretherton's lunch, several pieces of bread and butter and a mauled pork pie.

When Bretherton woke, beer-flushed, with belches of discomfort, at the sound of the caddy spoon on the side of the teapot, he looked like one of those model porkers, fat and pinkish, squatting on its hindlegs with an advertisement for sausages in its lap, that you see in butchers' windows. The sausages were his fingers. They glistened, a pink-gray color, as they grasped tremulously at each other and then at his tobacco-yellow moustache. They were tipped with black moons of dirt that presently scraped at the forefront of his thinning scalp, while in the first startling unpleasantness of waking he banged his squat, scrubby elbows on the desk, his thick white fingers flapping.

"Tea," I said, setting the big white cup on the blotter in front of him. He attacked it where it stood, in a stooping gurgle of his mouth, sucking at it in piglike fashion. Tea dribbled brownly over desk and blotter and down his shirt front and over his ready-made bow tie that clipped into the shirt with a brass stud, leaving on his Adam's apple a bright green stain.

And then, in this slopping stupor, he remembered his favorite word for me.

"Come here, Clutterhead!"

I stood before him at the desk, waiting while, for the second time, he soaked his lips in tea.

"Didn't you have something on, Clutterhead? Don't I seem to remember — "

[5]

"Bazaar," I said. "Four o'clock. Congregational Rebuilding Fund."

"Then for Jesus' sake get there!"

"It's just past three," I said.

"Three, two, four, eight, bloody midnight — what does it matter? Be there, never mind — be there, get there — "

"They're all the same," I said. There were times when it seemed to me I had written up a million bazaars. "One bazaar is like another — "

He sucked incoherently at the cup again. I knew that he was incapable of answering because he began grating his teeth. Brown tea seemed to pour back through his eyes, filtering and dribbling down to his moustache. It poured out of his mouth in pale and sticky spit that he sucked swiftly back again.

At this moment I could not look at him any longer and I turned instead to stare through the back window of the office. Snow was falling now in softer, larger flakes, covering already the steel-blue roofs of tanneries and factories, lining the frost-dark corrugations of back-yard henhouses and coal sheds. I saw it already beginning to transform, with wonderful delicacy, the harsh flat lid of the town broken only, in the middle distance, by the iron-stone church spire, and farther away, in the south, by the great chestnuts of the Aspen park.

"Look at me, Clutterhead," he said. "Could you? For one moment. Does it strain you?"

I turned and looked at him, nursing my sprained wrist, not speaking.

"Tell me if the strain is too great for you."

Rage and tears of tea-brown moisture had left the eyes brighter and narrower. They pierced me as the thick little fingers repulsively waved again like tied sausages.

"It must be so interesting out of the window," he said.

I did not speak.

"Tell me what you see," he said. "Could you? Tell me what interests you."

There was nothing to see but roofs and the corrugated tops of henhouses and coal sheds and snow falling across them, obliquely, thickening, borne on a dark wind from a dark sky.

"I was watching the snow," I said. "It started ten minutes ago."

"And from the front window?"

There was nothing to see from the front window except the Succoth Chapel with its wind-torn list of preachers and Dancy's Furniture Shop and Jimmy Thompson's Barbershop.

"You must have stood there an hour," he said. "Tell me about that."

There was nothing to tell.

"It's Thursday afternoon," I said. All through the street the blue and green and yellow blinds of the shops were down. "It's always the same on Thursday afternoons."

"Always the same," he said.

"Yes."

"Nothing happening. Always the same." He picked with a black-nailed finger at one of his teeth, staring at whatever he had found embedded there.

"Nobody in trouble?" he said. "No suicides?"

I did not answer. Suicide was an unkind, embittering, excruciating point between us. A week before a girl had leapt from the fifth floor window of a factory; she had quarreled first with her foreman lover and then had jumped from the crane doors on to frozen concrete below. It ought to have been my business to have discovered these things about her long before I did. Negligently, instead, that same afternoon, I had sprained my wrist while skating.

Remembering it and staring at the snow again, I remembered too, suddenly and uneasily, the big Aspen Daimler coming up the street, skidding in the first fluster of snow. Bretherton seemed sharply aware of my new uneasiness. He flicked a finger in the air. "Nothing?" he said, and looked sideways with a drab yellow smile at the falling snow and then at my face again.

"There's nobody out," I said. "The only people I saw were the Aspen sisters. They came by in the Daimler. The two of them, with a girl — "

He lay for some time across the desk, swaying slightly, saying nothing, beating his elbows mournfully on the blotter so that the teacup rattled. An occasional incoherent sound was sucked in through his teeth and then exhaled. I felt a dry sickening rawness in my upper throat liquefy into bile that drained down into my stomach with scalding bitterness.

"Get your hat," he said at last. "Put your hat on."

Bretherton always forgot that I did not wear a hat. Snow was now falling in such large, easy-blowing flakes that it created a mist in the air behind which the town had disappeared.

"You will need your hat," he said. "Because it's polite for a young man to have a hat. And you are going to be polite to the two Miss Aspens."

He spoke quietly now, with restraint that terrified.

"You are going to get a story from them," he said. "Perhaps there is a story about the girl — she's the niece, she's the one who will come into the money — you never know. Get your hat and go up there now."

"Now?" I said. "They'll hardly have arrived. They'll hardly be there themselves — "

"For the Good Jesus!" he shouted.

He flung his short squabby arms sideways and then sideways across his neck, tearing at the shoulders of his jacket with clawing movements of rage, his eyes expanding like intolerable yellow bubbles moist with tears.

"They'll hardly be there themselves!" he said. "But you will — you will — you will. For once you will."

He threw back his face and I thought for a moment he would spit into the cold milk-skinned tea that stood before him on the desk.

"You will — for once. For the first time. Perhaps," he yelled at me brokenly, "for the last time — "

As he turned and prepared to spit at the stove I found my coat and walked out into the street. Broad, featherlike flakes of snow blotted out the distances of the street of closed shops, bringing to the afternoon an air of relief, a wonderful softening, after weeks of snowless frozen wind. In the shop windows with their drawn blinds the reflection of snow had an effect of scintillation. It began to transfigure them all. The gauze-windowed offices of solicitors, the club where local gentlemen met and played billiards over tots of whisky, the Succoth Chapel with its narrow windows of stained glass, the piano shop where Miss Scholes gave music lessons, Thompson's Barbershop with the umbrellas in the windows, the shuttered banks and the Temperance Hotel with its tearoom on the side and its copper tea urn, boiling under blue gas flames, on the marble slab on the counter: curtained by falling snow, it grew more delicate and unreal and transfigured as I walked through it, sick and nervous and nursing my sprained wrist, to call for the first time on the Aspen sisters, Bertie and Juliana, and their niece, whose name I did not know.

II

My father was a man of gentle and unargumentative temperament who loved music and spoke sometimes of the sin of pride. He was most anxious, as he said, that I should not get above myself.

We lived, intensely respectable, behind drawn lace curtains, in the end house of a row of six, adjoining a factory from which the thump of presses shivered the crockery on the table and fluttered the artificial flowers in the ornaments on the mantelpiece. At the back was a little garden bounded by a tarred fence on two sides and part of the factory wall on the other. In summer there were lilies in bloom by the factory wall and a pure-white Frau Karl Drushki rose by the water butt, and along the fence a row of sunflowers and shrubs of pale yellow flowers whose name I did not know. We had no light upstairs. I went to bed either in darkness or by candle-light and then in the afterdarkness watched the glow of furnace lights across the valley. On Saturday nights I heard Joe Pendleton, our neighbor, quarreling with Clem Robinson, his neighbor on the other side. Everybody seemed to get drunk on Saturdays; neighbors threw buckets of water on each other and violently against back doors. The days were filled with the beating of ragged bits of matting on back-yard fences and the chant of women gossiping in curling pins and sackcloth aprons and men's caps. I had a text on my bedroom wall which told me that God was the unseen listener to every conversation; but the walls were so thin that we could hear the conversations of the Pendletons too and the sizzle of kippers in their frying pan. Joe Pendleton played the euphonium in the Rifle Band and practiced sometimes in the bedroom next to mine, so that I could hear the metallic clatter of valves between the notes of music. Clem Robinson kept homing pigeons in a gas-tarred dovecot made from orange boxes at the end of the garden, and in the evenings and on Saturdays and Sundays the birds circled gracefully over a world of other little gardens, other back jetties lined by gas-tarred fences and other factories, gaunt and silent and covered with a snuff-brown bloom of leather dust that was sometimes blown, too, on gritty little winds down the streets outside.

"The trouble with you is you're too damn shy," Bretherton said to me. It was six o'clock the following evening before I could in fact bring myself to walk up to the lodge of the Aspen house, where the lodgekeeper came out with an old-fashioned hurricane lamp and let me in. I had pleaded the sprained wrist and a doctor's surgery as excuses to Bretherton for not going before, and that morning he had yelled at me about my damned shyness — "That's what you've got to get over," he said, "that's what you've got to conquer. Yourself!"

As I walked through the gates of the Aspen house and up the avenue of limes on the other side no snow was falling, but sometimes from the trees a few wind-feathered flakes detached themselves and floated slowly down, and it was quite quiet except for the clip of high ash boughs swinging stiff and frozen against each other in the darkening air. Under snow the avenue, the trees and the park looked larger than perhaps they really were, and the house seemed more impressive and more secluded and farther away.

In Evensford's world of steep back alleys and whining stitching machines and clattering dray horses pulling loads of belly leather into granite factory yards there were no aristocrats except the Aspens; there was no possible suspicion of any monogram but theirs. Everyone else in the town had climbed up, self-made, self-projected, sometimes self-taught, to whatever he was, and if he could not climb he remained whatever he had been.

The town had grown swiftly from a long stone street and eight hundred people and an open brook in 1820 to a place of fifty boot factories, ten chapels, a staunch liberalism and ten thousand people in 1880; and to a town of Rotarian and Masonic circles, many gleaming fish-and-chip shops and a public library, of golf clubs and evening classes, of amateur operatics on winter evenings and sacred concerts on Sunday afternoons, in 1929. Long rows of bright red brick, of houses roofed with slate shining like blue steel, had rapidly eaten their way beyond the shabby confines of what had been a village, beyond new railway tracks and gasworks, obliterating pleasant outlying farms and hedgerows of hawthorn and wild rose, to stop only where the river valley took its steep dip to wide flat meadows that were crowned in turn by the iron-ore furnaces I could see flaring at night along the escarpment beyond. Gauntly, in a few generations, a valleyside had been transformed; a skyline of factory chimneys and railway viaducts, gasometers and chapel cupolas, temperance hotels and bus depots had marched in, replacing old horizons of cornstack and farm and elm. Continually new roofs spawned along clay hillsides, encrusting new land, settling down on the landscape in a year or two with the grayness of old ash heaps under rain.

In the center of all this the Aspen stood in a circle of land diametrically split by great avenues of lime and chestnut and elm. The town had been kept away from it by the barricade of a stone wall a mile long and a perimeter of great trees. Outside the barrier men crawled with despondence into and fled with a sort of hungry distraction out of opaque-window factories and their dark bloom of leather dust. Odors of burning leather hung on all Evensford streets, in sultry clouds, on windless afternoons, after waste had stoked the fires. Men like Clem Robinson kept homing pigeons in stunted cots in back gardens and watched them, mostly on Sunday mornings, with a sort of forlorn possessiveness, carving patterns of gray and pearl and white on Evensford's sky. Life in Evensford and life behind the long Aspen walls were not merely different. It was possible to live in Evensford for a long time, even for a generation, and not see the Aspen house, the Aspen garden or the Aspens themselves. It was possible to drive through it and never know that behind the factories and their alleyways the streets that were like parallels of smoky ash heaps, desolate under rain and transfigured only under snow, a great house remained.

The only house of comparable size in all Evensford was the Sanatorium. It stood high up, almost within sight of the Aspen house, behind a barricade of trees, on the south side of the town. It was always full, and there seems to be no doubt that it was more healthy there.

When the maid let me in at the high rounded front door and said to me, "If you'll wait a minute I'll tell Miss Aspen you're here. The press, is it?" the fingers of my sprained hand were so cold and shaking that I held them inside the overcoat, trying to warm them with the other hand. I could feel a draft of east wind clear as a knife as it whipped under the door, and then with something of the same level steeliness a voice called in a piercing accent from a room at the end of the hall:

"Mr. Bretherton, is it? Is it Mr. Bretherton there?"

"It's Mr. Richardson," I said.

"Mr. who?"

"Mr. Richardson."

"Mr. Richardson? What Mr. Richardson is that?"

"I'm Mr. Bretherton's assistant," I said.

"What is it you wish to speak to me about?"

"The late Mr. Aspen," I said, "if you would be so kind."

She did not answer. A moment later the maid came out of the room, into the long cold hall, and beckoned me in. The voice pierced the air loudly again as I went over the threshold into a room draped everywhere, it seemed, with curtains of plum-red chenille.

"What is the matter with Mr. Bretherton?"

"Nothing," I said.

"He doesn't like me," she said. "He sent you instead."

The two sisters were sitting by the fire, one on either side, Juliana still wearing the high mauve scarf pinned round her neck, and Miss Bertie still sitting, as she had done in the Daimler, like a pale round dumpling. I began to say something about not disturbing them when I saw, or rather heard, Juliana eating soup from a bowl. She took it in with deep, broad sucks from a spoon. There were large pieces of bread in the soup and each piece of bread was a suck, short and determined and ferocious.

When she stopped sucking to speak to me, to turn on me a pair of remarkably blue assertive eyes, she said:

"How do you get on with Bretherton? What are you doing there?"

"I'm supposed to be a reporter."

"Supposed? Don't you like it?"

"No," I said.

She seemed, I thought, to like the candor of this.

In the moment before taking another suck at the bread she smiled, showing her teeth. They were very long, fanglike, unfortunate teeth. Her lips could not cover them. They were prominent and ugly and yet, whenever she smiled, swiftly, spontaneously, they made her attractive.

"You needn't stand up. This is my sister. Does it snow?"

Miss Bertie nodded her head to me. It was not until afterwards that I knew she was the elder. Her skin, distended and

[14]

gentle and rosy, had a curious bloom of preservation on it that misled me. She had a sort of dampness about her round, soft face, a certain dewiness, that made her seem self-effacing, without power. She was not eating soup. She sat poised instead, rotund and gentle and as if watchfully expectant about something, on the edge of a low chair, her skirts up, so that I could see a pair of soft elephantine calves encased in thick fire-colored stockings, with sometimes a glimpse of pale brown bloomers falling from above.

No, I said, it was not snowing any longer, and Miss Juliana took a passionate suck at her soup and said:

"What have you done to your hand?"

I told her about the skating. The division of heat and cold in the room was so sharp that when I sat down I felt as if I were perching on a knife. I gave an involuntary excruciating shudder, my face hot from the fire, the back of me iced by the steady whipped draft that came in somewhere through the thick curtains behind.

"You had better slip off your overcoat," she said. "You'll feel the benefit when you go out again." She sucked passionately and ferociously at bread and soup as I took off my overcoat and laid it on the back of the chair. "You look awfully thin. You ought to have hound's-tongue for your hand."

As she stood up to take more soup from the tureen keeping hot in the hearth, I saw that she was very tall. She stood bony and large and monolithic, the mauve scarf round her long neck, her long teeth ugly and attractive and glinting. She belched once or twice with genteel reservation into the fire as she ladled her soup, saying between each belch and its suppression: "We both of us caught our deaths yesterday." Her angular body rumbled again as she sat down. "We are going to have a glass of port when Lydia comes down," she said. "It will probably do you good to have one too."

It struck me several times that she had not the faintest

idea what I had come there for; and I hoped she would not ask me. I had some sort of story to make up about Elliot, the dead brother, and in the morning Bretherton would either rage, in jaundiced ironies, because the facts were wrong, or forget it altogether. I need not have worried about these things. Passionately sucking, blowing and belching, monolithic and almost masculine, Miss Juliana failed to let any word of Elliot come between us as we sat there.

"If you are not going to work with Bretherton," she said, "what are you going to do?"

"I'm not sure."

"Does he drink as much as ever?"

"About as much."

"You're frightfully thin," she said again. "You ought to live in the country. You need country air. You'll be better when you're twenty-eight — that's the fourth cycle of seven, and if one can get over it it's all right. All men go through that. How old are you now?"

"Nineteen," I said.

"Just Lydia's age," she said.

"Oh! No," Miss Bertie said. She spoke for the first time, and I caught in her voice an irresistible precision, calm and firm and so unlike the rosy gentleness of her dumpling face. "Lydia's nineteen and eight months. She'll be twenty-one next year."

"Ah, yes," Juliana said; and for a single moment, for the first and only time, her charging enthusiasms were stopped and subdued.

At once there was an awkward silence, the smallest touch of antagonism in the air. I became aware, after a moment or two, of the scent of hyacinths. Until then I had not noticed deep Chinese bowls of them, pale mauve and pink, in full flower, in the far corner of the room. Now I saw them and said:

"The hyacinths are very beautiful — "

"They are Bertie's. It's Bertie who's the one for flowers. Aren't you, Bertie?"

"You like flowers?" Miss Bertie said. "Oh! I can see you do. How nice — it's not often men like flowers."

"I am very fond of them," I said. I felt the conversation, through flowers, spring a little further out of formality. "It's one of the things in our family. We all like them. My father especially."

"Do I know your father?" she said.

I said I did not think so; I said he sang — it was the first thing I could think of in possible identification — in the Orpheus Choir.

"Is that the choir that sang at the Coronation?" Miss Bertie said; but because the Coronation had been in 1911 and myself a baby at the time, I said I did not remember. Miss Bertie declared at once, assertively:

"I rather think it must have been. I feel quite sure. They sang on the terrace here. I thought they sang most beautifully. I remember it very well. It was quite lovely — there is something so beautiful about the sound of men's voices in the air."

For a few moments she seemed to consider all this, and I wondered if she were satisfied.

"You are church?" she said.

"Chapel."

"I see."

She seemed to weigh it all up, the skating, the flowers, the singing, the chapel, my father and last of all myself. She seemed to be on the point of deciding whether I was a satisfactory person or a dubious person. She looked hard at me for some seconds and I looked steadily at her in return. A breath of ice crept across the room from under the chenille door curtains, which shuddered distinctly. The scent of hyacinths faded perceptibly. I could hear the whine of wind through tree boughs in the frozen darkness outside, and then it was Miss Juliana who said:

"We ought to get the port. We ought to have Lydia down," and Miss Bertie cut in, crosswise:

"I find it rather a refreshing manifestation in a young man to like flowers. I find that something of a phenomenon these days," and I felt she had gone a great way towards accepting me. She seemed to have decided, above all, that I was intensely respectable.

"Pull the bell," she said.

Two great enameled bellpulls, like the lids of enormous soup dishes, were let into the wall on either side of the fire that scorched us and yet left us icy, and when Juliana pulled one of them I heard the bell jangling down long cold passages through the house.

"We must tell Lydia about your skating," she said. "I don't think she skates. You ought to teach her. Where can one skate in Evensford?"

"On the old marsh," I said. "Anywhere on the flood water."

"Where is that?" she said. I caught in the words the mark of her isolation. She did not know that for forty miles the floods were frozen, as they had not been frozen for many years, in a mile-wide lake. Her life behind the stone walls, in the island of trees, shut her away from such things. But she startled me at once by saying:

"That's the trouble with us. We stew. They say Evensford is getting quite big. They even have Woolworths or something. Do they have Woolworths? I never go down there now." The large, assertive blue eyes seemed to make an appeal to me, above the long, ugly attractive teeth, for my feelings about this. "That's what I don't want to happen to Lydia. To be cut off. What do you feel? Would you want a young girl to grow up like that? We don't want her to stew. We want her to have friends."

I did not know what to say to all this; I had not yet learned that her questions, almost all of them, were simply rhetorical bullets fired off in mid-air out of a fine-drawn nervousness. It was some time before I noticed the fluttering weakness of her colorless hands.

But now I was saved from answering by a voice at the door, a man's voice, saying:

"Was that the bell for dinner? Are you coming in?"

"No, I don't think so. Unless Bertie is. Are we, Bertie? Mr. Richardson, this is my brother," she said to me, "Captain Rollo Aspen."

The Captain was a thinnish, hooked man of six feet with a pronounced weakness of chest and loose inbred lips that seemed to dribble. From the tip of his hollow, stooping body his hair, long and black, was constantly drooping down.

"Foul day," he said, "don't you think so? Plum awful."

He was dressed for dinner in a velvet smoking jacket with large corded frogs across the chest that seemed only to accentuate his narrowness. He said several times that the weather, the snow, or something or other, was plum awful, and I noticed that neither Miss Juliana nor Miss Bertie bothered to reply.

He stood there for a few moments longer, weakly fingering the lapels of his jacket, the thickish, too-red lips wavering in a search for something else to say. He gave a clipped laugh or two, half to himself, and then said at last: "Mackness says there's a lime down in the avenue" — and Miss Bertie stirred uneasily by the fire.

When I looked to the door again, some moments later, he was no longer there. Miss Juliana had finished her soup, and now a maid, a woman in her scrawny fifties in all the appropriate getup of fanning bows and cap and apron, came in to take tureen and plate away.

"We'll have the port now," Miss Juliana said. "Four glasses. I think Lydia will have a glass" — and presently I was sitting with a glass of port wine in my hands. It too was dead cold, and while I waited for some signal to drink it Miss Juliana pronounced:

"I think things are changing for girls. I mean to say there's no longer — "

At that moment she broke off with restless and brittle suddenness to look behind me, at the door. Her large teeth woke and leapt into the disarming smile that ought to have been so ugly but that was now more than ever affectionate and attractive and beautiful.

I turned too, and for the swiftest moment I thought the Captain had come back. I felt I was the victim of a mesmeric sort of trick. The tall figure of the girl I saw there, as tall as Miss Juliana but not quite so tall as the Captain, had the same full lips and drooping hair. The angularity of her body was startling in the long black dinner dress that hung from her shoulders with the straight flatness of something suspended from a coat hanger of curved white bone.

"This is Lydia," Miss Juliana said.

As I stood up she came over to shake hands with me. Her own awful shyness, clear in the startled black eyes and the slightly retracted mouth, had the effect of doubling my own. I think I was more sorry for her than anything, draped in the long, low-waisted dress that was too old for her, and I could not say a word. The dress might have belonged to Juliana. It gave her the effect not only of being lost and unawakened but, as she lumbered to snatch my hand, of pitiful clumsiness.

The effect vanished when she sat down. At first she did not smile; but her body, in its sitting position, seemed to soften and fold over. She took the glass of port and held it under her face. I saw her looking through it at the fire. For some minutes I heard Miss Juliana, really without listening to her properly, prattling on with masterful nervousness about "Mr. Richardson says there is skating, Lydia dear. I've been telling him he ought to teach you. I think we have skates somewhere — I know I used to have skates — " and sometimes the girl, rounded to girlishness in her sitting position, the tips of her long white fingers and the receding pale bone of her cheek made rose-clouded by reflections of firelight through the wineglass she was holding, would smile. Her smile was always of the same kind, and it always had the same effect on me; it was one of those smiles that are not directed at anyone; it was not even directed at something undisclosed, a thought or an emotion, inside herself. It was not reflection at all. It was directed outwards: not to the two women or to me or the things that were being said in the too-large, half-freezing, half-scorching room, but to some unspecified moment of delicate and nebulous attraction, like a dream, something remotely projected, in the future. And the effect on me was exactly the effect made by the smile of the older woman: the sudden flash of plainness flowering impossibly, almost sensationally, and yet softly, into something beautiful.

"Would you think it a great bore to take Lydia skating with you?" Miss Juliana said. "You wouldn't, would you? It would be such fun for her."

"Not at all."

"Would you like that, Lydia dear?"

"I don't skate," she said.

"Opportunity comes with Mr. Richardson," Miss Juliana said, and I thought Miss Bertie stirred by the fire with noises of approval.

"And what about the impossible Mr. Bretherton? Can that be arranged?"

"I think so. There's the police court tomorrow — "

[21]

"Police court? Evensford has a police court now? You go to police courts?"

"Not Evensford," I said. Evensford had risen too late in civic expansion to be favored with the importance of petty sessions; the court was at Nenborough, a market town of iron ore and railway yards, up the valley.

At this moment Miss Bertie made a pronouncement.

"You know Evensford is not even a postal entity," she said. "It is still a subdistrict." The voice had a clear, informative asperity, contrasting with a cold and surprising severity with Juliana's nervous ripplings. "By standards of Ordnance Survey it is still a village."

As she spoke she ruffled up in her chair and, no longer dumplinglike and rotund, seemed to be going through a process of an almost grotesque enlargement, fluffing herself out, sprouting wings. Like a hen about to spring up on a perch after laying an egg, she said:

"If you look on the Ordnance Survey of even thirty years ago you will see that nothing of Evensford is shown but the church and this house. It is still a subdistrict of Nenborough. It is still not even on the map."

"The town has grown all along the valley," I said.

"Possibly so. But it is not *shown*."

"It is there," I said.

"Possibly so. But for our part we don't *see* it. It is not the Evensford we *like*. It is not the Evensford we *knew*."

For a moment I was aware of a small clash, a grating of temperaments, hers and my own, hers and that of Miss Juliana, who was quiet now for the first time; but to my surprise she said, again in a most informatively level voice:

"However, that isn't what we wish for Lydia. We wish Lydia to be of Evensford. We wish her to know young people. We have grown up in our own way, and this is how we are. But we feel it would not be right for her. Do you think so?"

[22]

"Yes," I said.

"I think it is most extraordinarily considerate of you to take her skating," she said. "She will be busy tomorrow unpacking, and you will be busy at the court. Then there's your hand." Miss Juliana had forgotten my hand.

"My hand makes no difference," I said.

"Then you could take her on Saturday?"

"Yes," I said. I began to say something too about the means of getting there, about the marshes being nearly two miles away, but Miss Juliana, absolutely silenced for so long, set down her empty port glass and said:

"There is the Daimler. They can go in that."

"I really don't think so, Juley." It was again the clear, deliberate voice, startling in firmness and incision. "I see absolutely no point in that. Is there a bus?" she said to me.

Yes, I said, there was a bus.

"Then I suggest you go by bus. Shall we say at two o'clock?" she said.

With a swift and flapping sort of movement of her hands, exactly like the beating of a pair of peremptory wings against the arms of the chair, she got up. Her skirt fell ruckled over squabby woolen legs and a last glimpse of slipping bloomers.

"Good night," she said. She crossed to Miss Juliana, who had run down into silence like a galloping clock, and kissed her on both cheeks, and then to the girl, who had not spoken once, and then kissed her too. In that moment the girl stretched up her hands, at the same time uplifting her face, pressing her lips upward and outward in the act of kissing. Her arms emerged from the loose-cut sleeves with a roundness not distinguishable before. The lips, full and rather loose but not so weak as the Captain's, suddenly produced in me a sensation more abrupt and startling than her smile. I felt as I had when I first came into the room: poised on the edge of a knife, in a queer excruciating quiver of heat and cold,

[23]

the blood pricking and thumping in my throat, my mind all the time frozen and yet excited.

"I ought to go too," I said.

"Have you no hat?" Miss Juliana said. "You will catch your death without a hat."

I had no hat. I shook her hand. The girl got up from the chair and shook hands with me too. All her tall angularity, undispelled even by the candle-shaped coils of black hair falling down to the shoulders of her black dress, was suddenly there at its most awkward again. She did not speak to me. With a dry and ghastly shyness I could hardly even look at her, and I realized, fumbling among the draperies of heavy chenille to find a door that did not seem to be there, that all evening we had not exchanged a word.

"Tell your Mr. Bretherton I will deal with him myself," Miss Juliana said.

I heard the clang of the bellpull and the jangling of the bell as she rang for the maid to let me out; but in the corridor, with its odor of ancient paraffin, its oil light falling from the stairhead through a single chandelier of diffusing crystal on a path of molting leopard rugs, the Captain suddenly appeared and called to me:

"Hullo there, I'll let you out."

In friendly, drooping attitudes, he escorted me along the hall, pulling back in a hearty and rather too powerful gesture the heavy iron bolt of the door. I could see his breath and my own vaporing in almost solid bladders of white in the freezing air. When the door opened the air from outside was no colder. Beyond the porch a great expanse of snow whiteness, still and sparkling and smoothly settled, clothed the terraces and steps and slopes of the silent park. I stood for a second or two looking at it. A drowsy and almost fungoid whiff of whisky on an air savage in its starry and brittle frostiness floated past me as the Captain said:

"God, it's plum awful. Enough to freeze brass monkeys."

In a weak, high-toned voice he laughed at the joke he made, and then, for want of something to say in farewell, asked me if I did any shooting. Before I could answer I remembered suddenly, in brief panic, what I had come for. By this time he must have wondered too.

"I'm very sorry about the elder Mr. Aspen," I said.

"Oh yes, you're the *Messenger* chappie. Yes: bad blow."

"*County Examiner*," I said.

He took no notice of this and went on: "He died at his place in Leicestershire. He really liked it better there."

"Could you — "

"It'll be rather dull for Lydia here," he said. "Have to keep her amused somehow. Plum-awful town, I think, Evensford. God, it's cold."

"I'm sorry: I don't want to keep you," I said. "But is there a Mrs. Aspen?"

"No," he said. "No. No." He slipped slightly on the frozen snowy steps as he backed towards the door. "No — well, in a way I suppose there was."

"It really doesn't matter," I said. I knew Bretherton would say it did matter; and thinking of his rage I waited. "It was just — "

"Well, you know how it is. It's bloody delicate, and I know the girls would prefer — " I supposed the girls were Miss Juliana and Miss Bertie, but I said nothing and his hand was already on the door as he went on: "She was a Miss Crawford. They sort of never hit it off together. She was a good deal younger. She's — well, we assume — "

"Thank you," I said. "I won't keep you. Good night."

"Not at all, old boy. Pleasure. Good night."

In the moment before he shut the door I heard him give a curious sound between a grunt and a shiver, saying at the same time that everything was plum awful and didn't I think

[25]

so? The door closed before I could answer; and then a moment later I was walking across the snow-covered terrace and down the steps to where, between two great clumps of yew and cypress, the carriage drive ought to have cut across to the long avenue of lime, to a stream, and then copses of hazel and hornbeam and ash below. But snow, in its quiet level fall, had obliterated everything in a shining crust, and I could not find the way.

I stood for some moments looking for the path. There was no wind, and snow had frozen in stiff flowerlike panicles to the great mass of branches that hid all of Evensford, even the church spire, with complete extinction, from the house. Above the trees a mass of winter stars, glittering with crystal flashes of vivid green, then white, then ice-clear blue, flashed down through a wide and wonderful silence that seemed to splinter every now and then with a crack of frost-taut boughs in the copses, down where the drive went, above the frozen stream.

After a few minutes I found the path. I felt suddenly very hungry. I had not eaten since midday, and in a curious light-headed sort of fashion, from the tension of hunger and snow and frost and starlight, I began to run.

Two days later it all began.

III

THE southern escarpment of the valley sweeps down beyond old railway tracks through allotment fields bordered by brickworks and stuck about with tool huts of corrugated iron and past rows of tanneries that break from an otherwise bald, low-toned landscape like eruptions of crimson brick. At the broken curve of the slope there is a sudden redness in the soil, the strata of ore emerging in warm brown tones, something of the ginger-brown of iron mold. The last farmhouse, half stone, half brick, looks down on giant dredgers scooping a dripping sugar-brown gravel from pits in what once were green meadows and then farther on to the last bargehouse, empty and abandoned and overgrown with nettle and elder, like the bargepath that weaves across the marshes with the river. It was on these marshes that I taught Lydia skating on the following Saturday afternoon.

She appeared that day in a sort of black cloak that was half a mackintosh, half like the kind of garment, cowled over the head, that nuns or nurses wear. She brought her skates in a leather case with interior linings of green plush into which the skates and the skating boots of white buckskin fitted with snug perfection. The skates, old-fashioned, with undersupports of polished wood, had belonged to Miss Juliana, and the Aspen monogram was embossed on the case outside.

There were two ways down to the river. You could keep in the bus to the very end of the lower town, and then walk through a hundred yards of street to where, at the bottom, the old bargehouse stood. Almost everybody went that way. A potato oven still stood there in those days at the end of the road where the ice began, and men screwed your skates on for twopence a time. But you could leave the bus earlier, at the top of the hill, and walk down by footpath, between hedges of sloe smothered all winter in reeds of partridge-brown, coming on to the marsh where floodwater ran thin between islands of sedge and froze to salt-white cat ice along the riverside.

That afternoon I took her the second, isolated way, because of a growing terrible shyness of her. She did not speak to me in the bus. Down the footpath there was no room for us to walk abreast, and I felt it polite to walk ahead of her because she did not know the way. She was so quiet that several times I turned round to make sure that she was there, and the third or fourth time her face expanded, exactly as Juliana's did, into a grave and beautifully friendly smile.

"I'm here," she said. "Don't worry about me."

Her voice was one of those deep, rather heavy voices that frame their syllables with odd hesitation. Time after time it seemed as if she were going to speak with the slightest stutter. But the words always came, at last, from deep in the throat, heavy and thick, as if the blood in her was sleepy.

When she took off her cloak that afternoon she was wearing an old scarlet polo sweater underneath and a long black skirt that was too tight for her because she had grown out of it. When she took off the cowl of her cloak I was horrified to see her hair emerge from it in the stiff candle-straight clusters that had first made me think she was only fifteen. She must have caught that look on my face because, a second later, she took a wide strip of vermilion ribbon from her skirt pocket and held it in her mouth for a moment and then looped it through the mass of her hair. It bunched up the hair in a tight-drawn coil, something like a horse's tail at a fair, and the red of the ribbon did not quite match the red of the sweater. But when the hair was drawn away from her face, leaving it clear, rounded and not girlish any more, she looked at me and smiled and said:

"There. Is that any better?"

"I like it better," I said, and when she gave her hair a final shake it shone, blue-black, rather wiry in the sun.

"It makes me look older, doesn't it?" she said.

"Yes."

"It's rather silly not to be able to cut it or do it up or anything, don't you think?" she said.

"Yes," I said.

"Don't always say yes," she said. "You don't have to."

"No," I said.

The word mocked her a little and we both laughed, the tension gone.

Across the ice, all that afternoon, the sunlight was a wintry apricot, deep and fiery above the edges of flat horizons smoky-blue with frost. Skates sang shrill and then deep and thrilling across empty meadows in the lovely air. There were a lot of people there that I knew that day, and whenever I passed them they stared at me, not speaking, because of the strange new girl I had with me.

She moved through all the early afternoons like a girl whose limbs had never been used. Her hands were quite fierce and terrified as they clutched at me. She held her head too high, too stiff and too far backwards, and her body went forward as if on stilts. All her inbreeding, her seclusion and what I took to be a genteel physical frustration came out that afternoon in a painful wooden awkwardness that made her more clumsy than ever. We fell down every ten yards or so. Everywhere people were falling down in the same way, shrieking and laughing, but she did not laugh when she fell down. She got to her feet every time with a look of remarkable intensity, with dark eyes fixed ahead.

She did not speak much during all this, and she did not tire. We went round and round the long marsh twenty or thirty times without a stop except for the pauses when we fell down. A small wind, touched with keenness, the old wind that always came in from the direction of the sea, sprang up about midafternoon and blew into our faces whenever we turned and skated east to north. But she did not mind the wind. It seemed simply to stiffen her face into fresh determination. It did not even appear to chill her. Instead it seemed to drive the blood through her body with pulsations of heavier excitement, so that I could feel the heat of it through her sweater and the warm moisture of it on her hands.

In the middle of all this a voice began hailing me, and I saw Tom Holland come skating across from the bargehouse. Tom was a big, gentle boy with heavy masses of fair hair, rather a slow-speaking boy, a farmer's son, warm and friendly and earnest, with large pale-blue eyes.

As I introduced them Tom raised his brown tweed cap and said "Good afternoon," holding out his hand. She did not take it, and I thought her shyness seemed to come back. There was some sort of half-acknowledgment of him, for a second, in a sideways twist of her head, but it was like something coming from beyond a screen. A sort of gauze, something of her own veiled intensity and distraction, seemed to drop down in front of her eyes, blinding her, so that it was as if she simply did not see him there.

"I think people get on better when they go alone," Tom said.

"I think she's getting it gradually," I said. "I think she's beginning to feel her way a bit — "

"Take me again," she said. "Once more — "

I took her by the hands and this time we skated for forty yards across the marsh without falling down. Then we turned and I let go her hands, holding her only by the tip of a single finger. In the distance I saw Tom Holland, his head more coppery than yellow in the bronzy setting sun, framed handsome and very fair, blue-shadowed, against slopes of snow. I have no idea if he was really waiting for her or if she, in turn, had a sort of snow-blinded, half-conscious feeling that he was there. But all at once she began skating. She went forward in a flash of release, suddenly, as everyone does, all alone, clear and confident at last and free.

Like this, tentative but balanced and feeling her way, she skated for about twenty yards. And then, in a freer, wider swing of her arms, she lost her balance, but she regained it, bringing her feet together so that she could glide. In this moment I heard her laughing. The impetus of her strokes had taken her rather fast from thin, unbrushed snow into ice that had been swept clear. She was going too fast to stop. Then I saw Tom Holland laughing too, holding up his large hands, ready to stop her. In another moment he was holding her by the red sweater and she was laughing on his shoulder.

"Wonderful! It's wonderful!" she screamed. "I can do it! I can stand!"

She flung out her arms, grabbing wildly at air. For a moment she lost balance again, but Tom caught her and held her with large hands until she regained it and could stand.

What emotion there was on his face as he stood there grasping her with his large, golden-haired hands, still dark brown from summer, I did not really know at that moment, though I thought of it often afterwards. The color of the frozen afternoon, all apricot and bronze, came levelly across the ice in a startling horizontal fire, full into his large pale-blue eyes. My impression was that it was this that dazzled him. All the life of the very pale retina seemed to vanish, leaving them transparent, so that he stood staring exactly like a big muscular statue into which the eyes have not been carved.

When he recovered he shook his head slightly and his sight came back. It was all over in a second or two, and he said:

"You're all right now. You won't need anybody now. Once you've got the feeling of it — once you know — "

He let her go without finishing his sentence into the big rushing outer wheel of skaters. We watched for a few moments the slow red sweater as it joined them and revolved too. "She'll be all right now — she's got the feeling," I heard him say — and the sweater, like a blob of scarlet paint, went slowly round, not falling, on the outer wheel.

The sun went down a moment later in a plunge of wintry

magnified fire that left on the ice, the snowy meadows and the cold sky a wonderful afterglow. A lichenlike green hung above the sunset, and the shadows, all across the snow, became of indigo brilliance before finally dissolving. A biting moment of dispersing day, exhilarating and almost cruel, hung in the pure stark air before the first star sparked into green sky above the sunset.

I turned to say something about this and found that Tom had gone. I saw him skating across to the bargehouse — big and easy, as he was at everything, a beautiful swimmer and a good tennis player, heavy but never rough, immensely healthy and shy and warmhearted: my oldest friend, as decent and solid and lovable as earth.

When I joined Lydia, two minutes later, she had nothing to say of Tom. It is very probable, almost certain, that she was less than half-aware of him as a person that afternoon. Somebody had stretched out a pair of supporting hands to stop her from falling, and this was as much as she knew. She had no name, at least I think until much later, for whoever it was. She simply laughed at me:

"It's wonderful! I can do it! Oh! It's the most marvelous thing!"

And then, as we skated, something happened that I knew was bound to happen sooner or later. Miss Juliana's skates, with their old-fashioned runners set in boxwood and unoiled probably for a quarter of a century, could not stand the strain. A screw rusted to the thinness of wire snapped suddenly, throwing one skate so that it flapped like a slipper.

On the riverbank, under the curling line of doddled willow trees growing opposite the towpath, Lydia sat down while I took the skate off and looked at it. The air was growing very cold, and her lips were rather more tightly set as she said:

"What is it? Can't you mend it? Can't you hurry? I want to *skate* again — "

"You'll have to have new screws — probably new skates," I said.

"But I want to go *now*."

"There might be somebody over at the bargehouse with a screwdriver and an odd screw or two," I said. "It's getting late, but — "

"All right, all right, all right," she said.

I did not say anything and she seemed, all at once, to become aware of my resentment about this. I looked up and she smiled. I suppose I was to see her smile in exactly that way, engaging and disarming and transforming, hundreds of times afterwards, but it never failed to have the same effect on me. It had some curious quality of combining tenderness with a flash of compelling uneasiness. It was like sunlight on the surface of a knife.

As I skated over to the bargehouse she ran with me, in her eagerness to get there. The skaters were thinning out a lot by now and out of the half-dozen men who had been screwing on skates only one, an old nightwatchman named Hoylake, was still sitting there.

"Screws are rotten," he said. "Old as Adam — "

"It's a simple thing to put new ones in, isn't it?" she said.

"Not tonight, miss."

"I want them tonight. Now," she said.

"Well then, miss, you'll have to want on," he said. "You can't have everything you want — "

She stood glaring at him with impatient anger. She had come up for the first time against a true downright Evensford character who, in his droll dry way did not care a damn for her or anyone else. She did not know at all what to make of him, and suddenly he said:

"You'll git plenty o' skating, miss. Weeks on it yit. Don't whittle your breeches out — the skates'll be here tomorrow morning as soon as you are."

[33]

I saw her face soften a little; I found myself almost eagerly waiting for it to break into a smile.

"What time'll you be down, miss?" he said.

"Oh! early — early," she said. "Won't we?" she said to me. "We will, won't we?"

"Yes," I said. I watched her face, excited, framed in the folded cowl of the cloak. Suddenly the smile I had been waiting for, swift and disarming, spread over it softly, transforming it completely.

It charmed even old Hoylake, who actually got up and touched his cap to her.

The skates were ready next morning by ten o'clock. She gave the astonished Hoylake ten shillings without asking, and we skated all day.

It was something of a triumph for her to have escaped in order to come with me. Every Sunday the Aspens drove down twice to church in the big, closed Daimler, transferring themselves to the big closed pew that was theirs by three or four centuries of tradition. They worshiped apart; and then drove back, both at noon and in the evening, to meals religiously served cold in the interests of parallel devotions in the servants' quarters. Four fifths of the rest of Evensford prayed in its pine pews, offering strong devotion through five sorts of Methodism, three of Baptist, two of an obscure Adventism, and one, in the oldest of chapels, the Succoth, a powerful Calvinism that at least two Scots families accepted as the nearest joyless substitute to a Presbyterianism the town could not otherwise provide.

Because of all this an embalmed hush, once the church bells had finished, settled on the town, casting a gray anaesthetizing skein over the shuttered shops, the factories, the unopened pubs, the long cabinlike rows of houses where men pottered on gray ash paths in carpet slippers. It brought down on the noon streets an after-church emptiness that was like a suspension of living, the last husband trotting home from the bake-house with his steaming baking tin of beef and Yorkshire pudding, the last drunks turning out and arguing at street corners before staggering home, the last young girl hurrying through empty streets with shining agitation and a prayer book in her white-gloved hands.

From this strange, embalming griping vacuum there was no escape except through long walks into a shabby, windy coun-tryside, into clay lands where spring came late and very re-luctantly. There was still a feeling that Sunday ought not to be violated by anything more active than eating roast beef and Yorkshire pudding — separately, pudding first, beef after-wards — at midday, and vast teas, such as I used to eat at the Hollands' farm, Busketts, at four o'clock. There was still a feeling that things like skating on Sundays were, if not wrong in themselves, rather like laughter at a funeral service — something the right people did not do.

So as we skated all that Sunday, on into the evening by the light of fires and the headlamps of cars and lastly by a white bitter moon, she could not have suspected anything of the feeling of escape I knew. What she felt was simply the joy of the first mastery over something that was new to her. She was thrilled by the first steps of her growing up.

By afternoon she was beginning to skate quite well, and we stopped once, over a Thermos flask of tea I had brought, to drink and rest and gaze at the freezing river. The wind had dropped, but the air was so still and bitter that I could hear the river creaking as it froze. It was only once in twenty years, perhaps longer, that the river froze, but that day we watched the ice joining and hardening across the narrow central pas-sage of water that snow had stained a deep, smoky yellow.

"Shall we go on?"

As she spoke she slid down the snowy, frost-smooth bank on her skates and stood at the edge of river ice, looking across.

She could do even this without falling. She was full of confidence in herself.

I did not follow her. "It's eighteen feet deep," I said.

"Shall we?" She turned her body with suppleness, looking back at me, keeping her balance, smoothing her hair back with her hands. "Dare you?"

"No," I said.

"I can put my foot on it. It bears."

"Come away," I said.

I made a snowball and threw it into the stream. It hit the central core of half-formed ice and sank slowly in like a pill.

She turned and laughed at me. "Did I scare you? Did you think I meant it?"

She began to climb up the bank, her face shining with rosy brilliance under the black hair. "You did think I meant it. You really did."

"No."

"I believe you did — the way you stood there. I really believe you did."

I caught her hand and dragged her up the last few feet of the bank. I had grown up with the river. It was the grave of too many suicides, half-swimmers and small careless boys for me ever to trust it too much. It flowed deep, on rapid currents, on dark whirlpools beyond millraces. I was frightened of it. I was afraid too that she would see that I was frightened, and I said joking:

"We'll let Tom Holland try it. If it bears him it'll bear us."

"Tom who?"

"Tom Holland. The boy you saw yesterday."

"Oh," she said, and it was clear that she did not even remember his name.

"Let's skate again," she said, "shall we? With crossed hands."

I took her hands in mine; she held my sprained wrist gently.

She was wearing big fur gloves so that I could not feel her hands properly and they gave me a feeling that she was wrapping me snugly into herself. I felt glad about it and we skated some distance, into an afternoon of blue harshness, against a coldness growing deathly towards sunset, before she spoke again.

"If it freezes — will you? Dare you come on?"

"We'll see," I said.

She laughed and began to skate a little faster, dragging me along.

"I shall make you," she said.

After that we skated every afternoon. Overnight I left my skates at the bargehouse, and if there were assignments from Bretherton I did them quickly or did not do them at all. I suddenly did not care about anything but the marsh, the skating, the frost, the freezing river and the girl in the cloak and the scarlet sweater.

Every evening we walked home through the town. Sometimes a little light brief snow came floating out of the upper darkness, through the green light of street lamps, and then lacily, in crossed white knots, about her face. I carried her skates for her and she would be muffled up, warm and dark, with the hood over her head. Because of the skating she began to lose some of the stiffness of her body; she began to be easier as she walked, with the big cloak-folds giving her a swinging and plushy appearance on the streets of snow.

Whenever we came up from the river we walked slowly. I was always tired after skating and she brought an excitement to the town that at first I could not share. She wanted to stop for a cup of coffee at dreary little places like the Geisha Café, by the station, or Porter's Dining Rooms farther up, or at the Temperance Hotel, where there was a hot twang of naked gas and frying cod in the air among the aspidistras. She was

[37]

thrilled by these things. All the lights in the shops would still be burning and one by one she would make me stop by them, telling her which was which and who was who, and she was thrilled again because I knew them all.

That winter everything in the town was new and strange and exciting to her. I had grown up with it, and I could not see it that way. To me it was ugly, and I was locked in it. It was a shabby little prison, and there was nothing in it I wanted. It took me some time to grasp that she had been in a prison of her own.

The house in Leicestershire had been a mid-Victorian so-called shooting lodge set in a grim, clay countryside of elm and grass over which hounds wailed with big hunts, on long unbroken runs, in wintertime. She had been brought up in a world of barracklike stables and bowlegged grooms and stableboys and horses chocking out to exercise across granite stableyards. She was frightened of horses. She had been thrown very badly as a child and after that her father had been frightened too. He replaced the horses by a governess, a Miss Crouch, a fragile yes-woman who taught simple subjects and saw that Lydia kept her hair in pigtails. By means of a curriculum of appalling unadventurousness they went stiffly hand in hand through primary mathematics and restricted history and feebler French and a few exercises in simple sonatas on the piano. Her father hunted or rode inexhaustibly. She sometimes did not see him for a day or two or an entire week end.

At sixteen she was still dressed in the kind of dark-blue garment, hardly a dress, that in its entire absence of waistline or frill concealed the fact that she was a girl. It was not surprising that she had seemed to me, nearly four years later, like a child of fifteen, and on that first afternoon on the ice like a person who had never used her body. She had never been aware of having a body in the sense of being curious or surprised or excited about it. Miss Crouch had hinted heavily once or twice that there were circumstances or experiences or trials or shocks or even pleasures that awaited girls, for unspecified reasons, in later years, but there was never any fuller explanation. Her father — I took him to be rather like an elder, more assertive Rollo, fanatical in a desire for frequent exercise, so wholly insensitive to a motherless daughter that he developed a sort of highly refined absent-mindedness about her — had been a man of fifty when she was born. He never seemed to grasp that she might need the company of other girls, except at her birthday and at Christmastime, when he arranged a schoolroom party for the children of neighboring houses: a party at which she invariably broke down and wept hysterically in sheer frustration at having so many to share in what she wanted.

It was quite by accident that her father supplied the means of putting an end to this protracted childhood of hers. One summer afternoon, when she was seventeen, she saw her father ride home with a woman.

"I knew she was married, too," she said. The July afternoon was hot and still and Lydia had been sent upstairs, exactly like a child, to rest. But it was too hot to sleep, and she sat at the open window, staring into the quivering afternoon. Then her father and the woman rode up. The woman had on a soft white silk riding skirt. Her father dismounted first and tethered his horse under a cedar tree that fringed the lawn between the house and the outer fields. The woman sat there and waited for him to come back. When he came back he held up his hands and she smiled and slipped slowly down the flank of the horse and into his arms.

The sight of her elderly father kissing the woman stung her into an amazed spasm of something between jealousy and pure excitement. She had actually never seen two adult people kissing each other in anything but the most formal fashion;

she had never even seen it at a cinema or in a play. She heard the woman laughing as her father kissed her again and ruffled her hair. She saw her brushing his face with her lips, teasing him and waiting to be kissed again. A confusion of bewildered and vaguely exultant ideas that what she saw might be something to give great pleasure to a woman poured through her, fantastic in an intricate and delayed effect of waking.

It was still only a half-awakening. Even to make it a little fuller she found herself grow cunning. She tricked the nervous Miss Crouch into accepting a ten shilling note so that she might go out for the day; and then retricked her by threatening exposure. Her idea of going out was to take long walks through neighboring fox coverts with the gardener's daughter, a restless heavy-bodied girl of her own age with reddish-golden hair and a head full of spun-out stories about the delicious variations of masculine betrayal. The girls sometimes took food and lay on hot days under dark spruce boughs, talking of love and their idea of how you did it and what it did to you. It awoke in Lydia a startling hunger, of which she was, in turn, startlingly afraid. She had hardly ever had an intimate conversation on any sort of subject with a single soul; and it was not surprising that all her life suddenly began to be a long passionate adventure in curiosity, with the amorous gardener's daughter and her restless blonde body as the focal centre of it all.

Two years later her father was thrown from his horse; he died as the grooms carried him home. Miss Bertie and Miss Juliana came to fetch her.

"I didn't know my father. He was never there. It made no difference," she said.

Miss Bertie was appalled. She found a girl so lamentably backward in physical behavior that she still looked and dressed like a child of fourteen and so shy that she did not speak more than half a dozen words on the long, icy drive down from Leicestershire. Miss Bertie had evidently done a great deal of thinking on that freezing journey among the leopard rugs. She must have been a little frightened herself by the problem of how to break down that special shyness that had all the frigidity of glass outside and yet was evidently seething madly within. I had drawn what I thought were all the correct conclusions that first evening among the passionate soup-suckings of Miss Juliana and the sippings of port and the assertive pronouncements of Miss Bertie. It was impossible not to detect the ghastly shyness, the frigid, rigid awkwardness, the bony undevelopment. It took me some time longer to reach Miss Bertie's first intuitive conclusion that there was something molten underneath it all.

So we were, in several ways, an oddly opposite pair as we walked home through the snow from the river after skating, with almost nothing in common except sheer youth and an exchangeable shyness that we were slowly breaking down; myself intolerably overproud and with my head up because I was walking with a strange girl from a family I pitifully imagined was the last word in ancient lineage, Lydia almost as pathetic in a hunger to get down into Evensford's gutters and lap up the life she found there simply because she had never known any life at all.

"Let's go to the Geisha. Let's stop at Porter's. Whose shop is this? Cartwright? Tell me about Cartwright. Who is he? How long has he been here? You know everybody, don't you? I want to go everywhere — I want to know everybody like you do."

Every evening she kept up that same tireless kind of catechism; and I would tell her about Cartwright, the draper, or Meadows, the tailor and hatter who drank all day in the back of the shop, or Avery, the seedsman, or the two Miss Quincys, the confectioners, peering out like a pair of keen binoculars from behind the marshmallows, under piled Edwardian coiffures that were themselves like dark brown chocolate whirls.

But I drew the line, one evening, at Jerry O'Keefe's, the fish shop where people crammed in late for hot plates of peas and chips and yellow-battered fish, in a kind of boilerhouse of steaming fat, after the last cinema show or the old theater.

"But why?" she said. "Why? It looks fun in there."

I said I did not think it the place for her, and she said:

"You talk like a parson or something. You talk just like old Miss Crouch."

"I'm not taking you," I said.

"Why? If it's good enough for these people it's good enough for us, isn't it?"

"No."

"That's because you're really an awful snob," she said. "You're too uppish to be seen in there."

"It's not myself," I said. "It's you."

"Are you going to take me or aren't you?" she said.

"No," I said. "I'm not."

She turned and walked down the street. I stood for a moment alone, stubbornly, watching her swinging away into darkness out of the steamy, glowing gaslight. Then I had a moment of sickness when I felt she was walking out of my life, that I had given her impossible offense and that I should never see her again.

"Wait," I said, "wait. Don't go like that. I'll take you."

Coming back, on the half-dark glassy pavement, she turned on me the sudden disarming smile that was always so irresistible and so compelling, and we went in.

The curious thing is that I was glad we went in. Inside the shop the old gaslight sang warmly and I knew that I was irritable simply because I was cold and tired and hungry. We sat at the counter and ate fish and chips and separate saucers of scalding stewed peas, seasoning them from great tin salt and pepper dredgers that were like pint pots. Mrs. O'Keefe tossed the frizzling chips in the gleaming fryers and wiped her fat hands on her hips and asked me how my father was. Steam hung thick and hot against the ceiling and there was a glow on Lydia's face and patches of glowing grease on her lips that made them more red, more shining and more tender.

"You see, you like it now, don't you?" she said. "It just shows it's better to do the things I want to."

She put her mouth against my ear to whisper the last words, and I was full of intolerable pride again because Mrs. O'Keefe stared at us through the steam of the fryers and wondered who the lady was; I was large with vanity.

Another evening we stopped at the potato oven that used to stand in those days on the corner by "The Rose and Miter," opposite the post office, halfway down High Street. We ate hot baked potatoes with our fingers, juggling them up and down, and presently snow began to fall in slow, fat flakes that hissed on the hot oven. In the bitter night we stood close by the fire, talking to old Sportsman Jennings, the man who kept it — a small man with black side whiskers and a square bowler that he wore on the back of his head — and every time the shutter was opened the glow of fire sprang into the night, turning the snow, the ice-bound pavement and her face a quivering rosy orange. The fresh potatoes as they came from the oven were too hot to hold. We blew on them, making steam against an air already clotted with dancing snow. The winter, as I stood there watching her bite at the hot potatoes and laugh with her mouth against the burnt, black skin and the white flesh of them, did not seem like winter. Evensford was not like Evensford any longer. I did not think I had ever been so happy. I felt exalted by the transfiguration of snow and cold and fire, each of them turning the world to something it was not, and because I felt she was free and exalted too.

And when the voice of a young police constable said, "I've

a good mind to take the three of you in charge for loitering," I could only laugh and then laugh again as I saw her face, horrified at what I had done.

The constable, a man named Arthur Peck, laughed too as he saw the frightened stare of her face.

"It's all right, miss. Mr. Richardson and I were at school together," he said.

Then we all laughed and Sportsman Jennings opened the oven and said, "What about a nice 'ot tater, Muster Peck?" But Arthur stood solidly in the snow and murmured about duty and what a night it was for it too. Then I said:

"Arthur, I'd like to introduce you. This is Miss Aspen," and I saw a stupefied look of startled respect on his face that made me feel again the intolerable, superior, condescending pride of knowing her. He was so impressed that I thought he would so far forget himself as to take off his helmet. Like me — and in fact like the rest of Evensford — he had grown up to think of the Aspens as a legend, to associate them with hereditary wealth and position, a high and distant aura, the rest of us did not share.

I do not know how long we stood there, eating potatoes in the snow, warming our hands by the opened fire, talking and laughing to Sportsman Jennings and Arthur Peck, exalted and happy in the dancing, sizzling snow, but suddenly she remembered how late it was. She gave a little cry and said, "Good night, Mr. Peck," and "Thank you for the potatoes," and then we began to run.

Snow was still falling heavily, the wind sweeping it already into smooth drifts on dry pavement, as we reached the gates of the park and stood under the street lamp there.

"You'll come tomorrow," she said, "won't you?"

"It depends on Bretherton — "

"Oh! Who cares about Bretherton?" She laughed: "Don't be so serious about him. If you don't like him walk out."

[44]

"It isn't so easy as that."

"Of course it is. You're too serious about things. What about the river tomorrow? Shall we try it?"

"It depends on the snow — "

"It depends on Bretherton, it depends on the snow — don't keep saying it depends," she said. "If we want to do it we just do it, don't we? I think it's awfully silly to weigh up things. Let's just do them when we want to."

"All right," I said, "if the snow stops — "

"There you go again. It's simply got to stop. And I shall hate it if you're late. You won't be late, will you? You won't let old Bretherton keep you?"

"No," I said.

"The next time he does you're going to walk out on him," she said.

The world beyond the gaslight was drowned in a wild blizzard that seemed to have put an end to the long dry and bitter spell.

"It's snowing awfully fast," I said. "I'll come to the house with you."

"No," she said. "I'll run." Without taking her hands from under the cloak she made a shy grab at one of my own. "I'll run to the end of the avenue and then shout. You answer. Say good-by."

"All right," I said.

"Shout hard," she said. "Then I'll hear you and be all right. You will, won't you?"

"Yes," I said.

The gate had been kept unlocked for her. I opened it and let her through. For perhaps a minute I stood under the gas lamp outside, listening to her padded footsteps running up the avenue in the snow. It seemed a long time that I waited and nothing happened. Then presently I got the odd feeling that nothing was going to happen, that she was not going to

[45]

shout, and then again the sickening feeling that I was not going to see her again. Her naïve idea of shouting good night at that distance seemed all at once like a silly little trick to fool me. I stood there with a growing gnawing sensation of wretchedness, of being tricked and laughed at and let down. Then suddenly I knew that I wanted to see her more than anything else that could happen to me. Snow was coming down in swirling, buffeting rings of white wind that I thought would blow out the gas lamp above my head, and from the avenue I could hear nothing but the empty clap of frozen ash boughs. I had never realized before how long that avenue was; and it still seemed like another five minutes before I heard a voice, deep and clear and wonderfully alive, calling through the snow:

"Good-by!"

"Good-by," I shouted.

After a pause of a moment or two her voice came back for the second time, like an echo:

"Good-by!"

"Good-by," I shouted.

I waited for a moment or two longer but she did not call again. The gas lamp shook under a gust of snowy wind. The noise of it woke me with a quiver, almost a shudder, of exhilaration, and as I walked away I came to myself with final reality to see, across the street, the peering, astonished faces of a man and his wife watching me as if I had been calling a snow-ghost. They stood staring at me through the snow long after I had walked past them; and I knew they would go home to speak of the queerest thing they had ever seen, perhaps, in Evensford: a young man standing in a blizzard, in an empty street, under a gas lamp, calling good-by at the top of his voice to no one at all.

*　　*　　*

Next morning Bretherton began to upbraid me for what he called my "inexactitudes." From time to time he spat at the stove. It was always a bad sign when Bretherton spat at the stove, and soon I knew that much was not right with my note, written a week before, on the late Charles Elliot Aspen.

"Sixty, you say he was. How did that get in? What inspired that particular perpetration?"

I did not answer, and Bretherton spat at the stove.

"You guessed!" he shouted. Waving a copy in air, he raved: "He was the elder brother! The old fire-horses are seventy if they're a day."

He calmed a little, and then read out:

" 'It is understood that Mrs. Aspen predeceased her husband by some years.' Predeceased for Christ's sake!" he yelled. "Who told you that?"

"I was given to understand — "

"She's alive! She lives in London!" he bawled at me.

I stood sickly by his chair.

"We then come to a further masterpiece," he said. He spoke with flourishes: " 'It is understood that the deceased, after a sudden collapse, died of heart failure.' Understood, understood, understood!" he raved. "Every bloody thing in this piece is understood! Didn't you know he was thrown from a horse?"

"I know now," I said; I was wretched and sick with the embarrassment of my inaccurate stilted phrases.

"In the future don't try to understand things. Get the facts. Where were you yesterday?"

"Skating."

"And the day before that?"

"Skating."

"Now we get to the truth," he said. "And today?"

I did not answer. He raged for some moments about the importance of being on hand when citizens shot themselves, when lovers threw themselves from fifth-floor factory windows, and then he leapt for his hat.

"In future for Christ's sake stay here. Sit by the telephone. Wear your sensitive refined arse out waiting until something does come to you!"

He spat again across the desk at the stove, missing it. He raved incoherently, lifting his short stubby arms in new despair.

"Stay in this office!" he yelled, and stumbled out, at last, into a street where workmen were chipping at snow and ice with pickaxes, in a strange, flat monotone of steel.

I stayed in the office for half an hour. I stared out of the back window to a world of corrugated hen huts in back gardens, of frozen washing lines, of factory yards where drays had dumped piles of belly-leather on thin layers of snow. The blizzard had not come in the night after all. Wind was blowing fine snow from the roofs of hen huts and whipping up small clouds of frozen yellow dust where traffic had powdered snow and ice on the roads.

Suddenly I knew that I hated this view more than anything in the world. I stared at it a little longer, remembering Lydia. I remembered her voice calling good-by in the avenue, and how, a moment or two before it came, I had had the queer, pained notion of not seeing her again. I remembered what she had said of Bretherton. I thought of that too a little longer. Then I closed the damper on the stove, put on my coat and walked out.

We skated again that afternoon. It was a keen, glassy day with ice in the wind, and as we came down to the bargehouse I could see the black ring of swept snow almost empty of skaters. And then someone shouted:

"They're skating on the river!"

"Now we don't have to get that boy to try it for us," she said. "What's his name?"

"Tom Holland."

"I'm going to race you!" she said.

Because the river flows across the marshes and meadows in long ox-bow curves, making heavy currents at the bends, I had never believed it would freeze at these places; but that afternoon it was a single, long block of ice, a white-yellow glacier with smoky shadows of half-frozen strips only under the arches of the railway bridge.

A few dozen people were skating on it; one man, two meadows away, was skating, almost sailing, upstream with the wind.

I stood on the bank watching him come along. Lydia laughed at me from the ice and presently the man came skating in, fast, and I heard him say:

"Safe as houses. Must be three inches all the way."

She heard it too, and began to skate downstream without waiting for me.

I went after her without any feeling of insecurity; I was not afraid. All along the raised riverbanks the ice split under pressure with sounds like whining and cracking gunshot. The sounds sang away in the wind, far across the empty meadows, with strange moaning, twanging echoes, like broken wires. Perhaps because I had walked out at last on Bretherton and was free, perhaps because I had again the feeling that as she skated ahead of me she was running away from me — for some sort of reason I went after her only with exhilaration and not fear. She turned several times and laughed at me. Then once I shouted for her to be careful and not fall down and she simply laughed back at me again.

We skated in this way across two meadows. The wind had nothing to stop it in its long, savage lick across the valley, and by the time we came down towards the railway arches, over the old Queen's meadow, I was taking deep gulps of bitter air, like a swimmer. Against the thrust of wind I started to skate with my head down.

I suppose I skated like this for half a minute. Then I looked up to see her twenty yards from the bridge. I started shouting. I felt anxiety, then fear, then pure cold horror hit me more savagely than the wind, and in another moment, trying to skate faster, I fell down.

In the moment before falling down I remembered seeing her bright scarlet sweater flashing into the left of the three archways of the bridge. When I got up again it was no longer there. I skated wildly forward, yelling her name. Then I hit the bank just in front of the bridge, fell half-forward on my hands and began to scramble like a sort of frozen spider along the towpath, still yelling her name in shouts that hit ice and bridge in hollow slapping sounds that echoed and re-echoed back at me.

The bridge was supported with round iron pillars, under which the concrete towpath ran. When I half-skated, half-fell underneath it she was leaning against one of the pillars, waiting for me. Her body was pressed back, its lower shape in the too-tight skirt thrust outward, so that the long line of her thighs was hollowed and clear. She stood there very quiet for a moment, looking at me with amused dark eyes. Then she began laughing, with a flash of white teeth, because she saw that I was frightened. I was so relieved and shaken that for a second I staggered about, half-losing my balance, so that she had to put out her hands to stop me.

"Lydia," I said. "Oh! Lydia, for God's sake — "

A moment later she stretched out her arms and drew me slowly towards her. I wanted to ask her what had happened and how she escaped, but I did not say another word. I could hear a small continuous lapping of loose water over thin ice under the bridge behind her and I listened to it, in fear, all the time she kissed me. Her stretched, long body tautened itself in a curious curve as she kept her balance and folded me against her, kissing me at the same time.

"Did you think I'd gone?" she said. "Did you think I'd run away?"

I pressed my mouth against her cold fresh skin and could not answer.

"Not yet, my darling," she said, and again I could not speak for happiness.

Spring came to Evensford about the end of April with shabby flowerings of brown wallflowers on allotment grounds, with dusty daffodils behind the iron railings of street-front gardens. Earth everywhere had been pulverized by black frost to a saltiness that blew grittily about on dry spring winds, cornering fish-and-chip papers in Evensford's many alleyways. In the town there was hardly anything to distinguish what was now the spring from what had been the winter except that the days were longer and not so cold and that the view across the valley showed ice no longer. There were now only broken lakes of receding water to which swans returned for a last few days in great white flocks, before they too broke up and paired for summer nesting.

Behind the walls of the Aspen ground, all across the park, spring came so differently that it was another world. Rooks did not begin nesting in the old chestnut trees behind the lime avenue and in the big elms above the gatehouse until the middle of April, cawing all day in slow-greening branches. Everything was late that year. The brook thawed and all along its wet banks white anemones came fluttering into bloom, together with big, soft, white violets, pure as snowdrops, and primroses among blobby islands of kingcup under yellow hazel boughs. Whenever I went through the gates and along the avenue there was a wonderful belling chorus of thrushes that expanded under a closing framework of branches, madly and most wonderfully in the long pale twilights when the air was green with young leaves and the acid of new grass after sunset and spring rain. Nearer the house there were random drifts of pale blue anemone, bright as clippings of sky among black clusters of butcher's broom, and then, under limes and in grass along every slope leading up to the house, daffodils in thousands, in crowds of shaking yellow flame. Some earlier, farsighted Aspen had planted great groups of blue cedar about the place and they rose in high, conical groups, grayish after winter, to be touched, as spring came, with young delicate sprouts of blue-green fire. Acres of grass flowed away under plantings of horse chestnut that flared, by the end of April, into thick blossom that soon became scattered by wind into rose-white drifts on paths and terraces and even as far as the elm avenue that led to more spinneys of primrose and hazel and white violet on the western side.

By May the spinneys were thick with bluebells. The air all day long was soaked heavy and sweet and almost too rich with the scent of them and the juiciness of rising grass. The earlier Aspen who had planted the cedars had also planted great shrubberies of lilacs that by now had grown into old rambling woodlands heavy with white and rose-pink flower. He had planted many white acacias too, and it was he also who had built a small, two-storied summerhouse on the south side of the park, at the crest of a walk of yellow wild azaleas. They too broke into flower about the time of the bluebells, the lilac and the chestnut flower, clogging the air with a haunting drowsy perfume that still rises, above all the smell of grass and bluebell and lilac and primrose, to mark the spring and summer that I spent there.

By this time I had stopped using the main gate that led into the park from the center of the town. I used to walk round the long wall and come instead through the spinneys on the south side. The spinneys are all gone now. New streets of houses built of prefabricated slabs of stucco-concrete, with concrete paths and concrete line posts and concrete coal sheds, with television aerials sprouting everywhere like bare steel boughs, have taken their places; but in those days there was a carriage gate to the spinneys and a riding that went down through them until it forked one way to the house, down the long avenue of elms that concrete tank emplacements killed as sure as a poison twenty-three years later.

It is very hard to say exactly what happened to us that summer, to express in terms that do not seem foolish how for a long time we did nothing but meet in the summerhouse and lie on the old cane, long chairs in the small upstairs room and look through the little, arched, diamond windows down on the path of azalea flowers, where it was so quiet that we could watch pheasants feeding a yard or two away on the corn we put down and see a partridge bring up her brood of thirteen there, fussing about with her own small, brown circus under her wings.

That summer was very hot, and I remember the thick, dry, strawy heat stifling under the little roof. I remember the scent of azaleas and the hot feeling of tension when Rollo, walking up with his gun one afternoon, tried the door of the summerhouse down below us with twenty or thirty or even forty keys, as it then seemed, rattling them one by one in the lock. I remember the thundering bump of my own heart as Rollo tried the keys and how every beat of it got bigger and hotter and more choking with every key. I can see Lydia, lying back in the chair, her chest leaping up in deep gasps that seemed to lift her breasts painfully, and I can feel the grip of her hand on the wrist I had sprained while skating. The grip was so tight that the blood, held back, stopped flowing to the fingers, and I could feel them gradually grow colder, until they seemed frozen again with their old familiar winter pain.

When Rollo had gone I sat on the edge of the chair, dangling my dead, bloodless hand, pained by the flow of blood coming back to it.

"Did I hold you too tightly?" she said. "Did I really? I didn't know — "

"It's the wrist I sprained — "

"I'm sorry," she said. "Let me hold it for you."

"Gently," I said.

I sat there watching her for some time while she gently held my fingers. Her body, flat in the chair, was still heaving with excitement. She had grown up very rapidly since the first evening I had seen her in the black dinner dress. The girl I had taken skating, with the low waist, gawkily throwing all the angular body out of proportion, with the almost monolithic straightness of Juliana herself, was not there any longer. Flesh had begun to spread on her bones with the effect of making her seem much less tall. She was warmer, rounder, softer, lovely in a way of which there had been no hint on the days of her scrawny skating in the winter. Her mouth, too, was firmer. Its fleshiness and breadth were still there, but it was soft now without being loose, and it revealed, even more than the rounding breasts, how quickly she had grown.

"Dare we open the window?" she said. "It's so hot in here."

"I'll open the back window," I said.

"I'm stifled — let's have some air." She let go my hand. "Why don't you take off your shirt? The sweat's pouring from you like water — "

The back window looked out from a tiny landing where the stairs came up. I went through to open it. Through the small casement, as I threw it back, came the heat of July, clear and fierce, sweet with light undertones of hay still being turned in fields outside the park. I stood breathing it for a moment, listening to the beat of a hay-turner, undoing the front of my shirt so that air could cool my chest.

When I went back to her she had taken off her dress. She was sitting up in the long chair, unrolling her stockings. They peeled from her thighs like another skin, leaving the flesh wonderfully white and without blemishes.

She lay back in the chair. I touched her thighs with light tips of my fingers and began to say something about how much I had wanted to touch her and how —

"I wondered if you ever would," she said. "If you ever wanted — "

She was smiling a little, her lips parted. I could hear the hay-turner beating somewhere across the park. Then my heart started thundering again as it had done when Rollo had tried the keys in the lock.

"Don't be shy," she said. "I'm not shy — "

She rolled her body sideways in the chair, tenderly and heavily, pulling me towards her with both hands. One of the straps of her slip fell from her shoulders and she let go of me for a moment to pull the other one down. Her skin had begun to mature with the waxen stiff whiteness that goes sometimes with deep black hair and it seemed to melt as I touched it with my hands.

"Oh! darling — don't stop loving me — " she said. "Don't ever stop loving me — "

I promised I would never stop loving her. "I promise I never will," I said. "Never. I promise I never will."

Some time later she lay in a sort of daydream, quieter, looking at the sky. The hay-turner spun softly across the hot afternoon. The scent of her hair had something strong and aromatic about it, and I remember that too as I think of her suddenly sitting up in the chair and bending over me and saying a most curious thing to me:

"Even if I'm bad to you?" she said.

"You won't be bad to me."

"Even if I were bad to you — would you? — will you always?"

"Yes," I said.

"Do you want to go on like this — always? Forever and ever?"

"Forever," I said.

"I wonder if we shall," she said.

I stretched up my hands and put them against her body. Its roundness, I felt, was all mine; it was I, in a sense, who had made it grow up; I was quite sure it was I who had woken her.

"Do you like my body?" she said. "Did you think I'd grown like this? Is it the first time you've seen a girl?"

"Yes," I said.

She laughed and said: "I'm growing up and it feels queer — it feels terribly queer — it goes pounding and pounding through me."

She laughed again, lying with her mouth across my face, her voice warm with tenderness and rather hoarse, and I felt all summer spin together, through the sound of the hay-turner, the warmth of her voice and the heavy repeated turn of her body, into a deep and delicate wonder, into what was really for me a monstrously simple, monstrously complex web of happiness.

By this time I had got another job. My father more than anyone was disappointed at my failure with Bretherton. "But it's no use if you're not happy," he said. "Better to take a job in the trade and be happy than get above yourself and be miserable."

It was he who got me the job of clerk to a one-man leather factor's business run by a man named Arthur Sprague. "Arthur's a very sound fellow," my father said. "He'll treat you well." Trade had begun to decline with the seasonal slackness of summer. "You're lucky to fall into a job like that too," he added. "There are a lot of unemployed. All you have to do is keep the books in order and unpack the leather as it comes in and answer the telephone. You'll be done every day by four."

In this way Lydia and I were able to meet in the summer-house almost every hot afternoon of that summer except Sundays.

On Sundays Miss Bertie and Miss Juliana, true to the Evensford tradition, invited me to tea. It used to be part of the sanctity of Sunday for Evensford to meet over heavily laden tables at four o'clock, after a sort of High Street fashion parade, talking of what anthem was going to be sung at chapel, listening perhaps for the voice, crying drably through the streets, of a late watercress man — "water-cree-ee-ee-es! — water-cree-ee-ee-es! — fine water-cree-ee-ee-ses!" — and the sound of an early brass band battling with discord against the sound of pianos played near open parlor windows.

We always had tea in a small, bay-windowed, overcrowded room on the south side of the house, adjoining the conservatory. Its walls were papered in patterns of pink and silver roses and its furniture was in a style of ponderous cabriole, touched with ecclesiastical. The legs of chairs and tables, in the shape of claws, grasped everywhere at balls that were like mahogany cannon shot. The upholsterings were mostly of a bright prawn pink unfaded by sun because at the slightest touch of it all blinds and shutters were drawn. The Aspens were not Catholics, but there was a *prie-dieu* in blue beaded petit point in one corner; nor were they very musical, but in another corner was a grand piano, a rosewood music stand inlaid with strips of ivory, and a cello in a case by the wall. Sometimes if the afternoon was very warm we sat at open French windows, through which all the scents of the park and

[57]

the gardens came to us in exquisite waves, rose with azalea, pink with hawthorn, some wonderfully indeterminate breath of high summer and strawberry with a drowsy flavor of hay.

There were rarely, I think, more than the five of us there: the two Aspen sisters, Rollo and Lydia and myself; and it suited my vanity to be so very privileged. A maid with her appropriate dragonflies of starched apron strings brought tea at four o'clock and Rollo lit the burner under a small silver methylated spirit kettle. Either Miss Juliana or Miss Bertie poured tea, one on one Sunday, one on another. "It's Juley's Sunday," they would say, or "it's Bertie's Sunday." Rollo and I had round plates of thinniest triangular bread and butter in three varieties of white and brown and a pleasant sugar-browned loaf of currant bread. Sometimes Rollo called me "Old fellow" or made a remark about pheasants or spoke of how plum awful something was. Miss Juliana, in her assertive jolly way, rattled on about this and that until arrested with firmness by Miss Bertie on some point of dry, irrefutable fact about the nature or history of the town. Most of the time Lydia and I sat looking at each other.

There was an amazing, beautiful frenzy about these quiet teatimes. There was a sort of suspended inner fieriness about us both that was painful and lovely. Sometimes we could not bear any longer to look at each other, and I felt myself caught up again in a sort of entangling web, enraptured and baffled. She always wore dresses of silk on Sunday and their smooth peel-like softness, growing tighter all summer as her body filled out, was drawn over her breasts with startling clearness whenever she moved.

Tea was always over by five o'clock. There would then be half an hour of latitude, in the garden perhaps, or on the terrace outside, before Miss Juliana and Miss Bertie and Lydia went to dress for church and I said good-by and thanked them for having me. During this time Rollo drew himself off and smoked a cigarette in the conservatory. Then he got ready for church. Then the servants got ready for church. As he smoked that cigarette in the conservatory Rollo always had about him something of the uneasy and chained-up look of a dog that has had no run all day. It was not until late summer that I discovered why. There was a look of unhappy costive strain about him as he paced up and down among the ferns and begonias and dracaenas with his long amber-green cigarette holder, in his two-inch collars and his cravat of dark blue, with horseshoe tiepin, in the style of twenty or thirty years earlier. He always looked rather like some advertisement for Edwardian bicycles, a dried-out dandy waiting, doglike, abject and eager, for a girl.

Punctually at ten minutes to six the Daimler came to the front door to take the three women to church. Rollo, even when it was raining, preferred to walk. It was not until the third Sunday in July of that summer that I discovered he did not go to church at all.

That Sunday was a week after Rollo had tried the door of the summerhouse and Lydia had said that curious, disturbing thing to me: "Not even if I'm bad to you?"

It had been very hard to look at each other during tea that day. Summer had burned up into hard flaming heat, into a torrid afternoon of white reflections springing back from the stones of the terrace and the glass panes of the conservatory outside. Twice during tea Lydia complained about the heat and finally she got up and said, "I feel rather queer," and went outside.

When she came back, five minutes later, she did not sit down. She ran one of her hands backwards and forwards across her face. Her white dress was pulled, as it always was, tight across her figure, which seemed flushed and swollen by the heat of the day.

"I think I'll lie down," she said. "I've been rather sick."

Anxiously Miss Juliana said, "Oh! my dear child," and I got up to open the door. The necessity of opening doors for ladies on all possible occasions had been brought acidly home to me on an earlier Sunday by Miss Bertie. "Young men do not seem to be very well trained nowadays," she said, "I suppose it's part of the general decay."

So now I had the trained promptitude of a dog in opening doors. I rushed forward to hold the door for Lydia and she seemed to sway slightly, I thought, as she went through it into the hall outside. I said something about her being able to manage by herself and then she swayed out into the hall and I went after her.

"I haven't been sick," she said.

She stood there staring at me with a curious, rigid sort of smile.

"I'm not going to church," she said. "Come back to the house."

She framed the words with her big wide lips soundlessly, in a sort of speaking smile, and before I could answer she went upstairs.

At a quarter to six I said good-by to the Aspen sisters and Rollo and walked across the park. A footpath led out to the southeast side of it through a plantation of old birch trees and to a keeper's house at the far end — twenty years later a tank brigade put a camp of cylindrical corrugated huts on it and later squatters moved in and hung from the few remaining birch trees their lines of frowsy washing — and I waited there until the church bells stopped and six o'clock struck and then I walked back to the house.

She must have watched me all the way across the park and all the way back again. Coming up the steps of the south terrace I saw her wave from an upstairs window, and then she opened it and said:

"There's no one here, darling. Come up."

I had never been upstairs in the house before. A wide mahogany staircase wound up in a central coil of ponderous chocolate-red banisters to an amber skylight at the top. She was there leaning over the upper rail, waiting for me.

When I ran up to her she ran a little way down the top flight of stairs to meet me. She could not wait for me. We fell against the banister rail in a frenzy of kissing. I could feel all the heat of the afternoon compressing and narrowing and refining itself until it was a needle that jabbed down through the two of us and held us together. "Oh, darling!" she kept saying to me. "Darling, darling."

She held me there in this refined needlelike trap for some moments longer. We came out of it in an ecstatic daze. I remember thinking that the bedroom where we went was not even her own bedroom, but only some spare servant's room in which a brass-railed monster of a bed glittered among piles of varnished traveling boxes. On the bed she begged me several times, in a dry, tearless sort of crying: "Kiss me harder," and I heard her fingers running with regular, frantic scratching across the old-fashioned cotton counterpane until she drew it up to her thighs and then let it go again with a sigh. I felt the impact of all this through the confusing softening complex of my web of feelings about her. I felt her voice struggling to free itself with the frenzied panic of an insect torturously trapped. Her fingers scratched at the counterpane over and over again and her voice beat at me the same dry harshness that had shed all tenderness, begging me to hurt her, until I could only break into half-sobbing against her body and tell her I could hurt her no longer.

Some moments later her tenderness came back. Her hand, dry and slow, began smoothing my forehead in a continuous movement of great softness, calming me down. My web of feeling about her seemed to respin itself. Her harshness receded completely, and I could not think it had ever been there, crying for me to hurt her.

Later she shut her eyes. The lids, a deep olive color, had a sort of smoldering look, and then as I lay there watching them they opened, sharp and black, and she said:

"There's someone walking about on the terrace outside."

She got off the bed, just as she was, and went to the window. She stood there in the light of the old-fashioned yellow window-blind like an amber silhouette, the fringes of her hair fiery as she pulled back the blind and looked down.

"It's Rollo."

"He went to church," I said. I could feel my heart thundering with fear.

"He never goes to church." She went over to the door and locked it. She had forgotten even that as we came in. "Didn't you know?" And then: "You're just as innocent as I used to be sometimes."

I did not think I was awfully innocent and it hurt me, with one of those minute touches of anger I always felt when she spoke to me so peremptorily, to hear her say so.

"You poor dear," she said. "He never goes."

She came back to lie on the bed. She curled her body and lay sideways, looking at me. All her tenderness had come back into the deep, dark eyes.

"I could lie here all day with you," she began saying. "All day and all night — all tonight and all tomorrow —"

"Yes, but for God's sake what about Rollo?" I said. I was astonished to see she was not afraid.

"He's spying on us. He's always spying on us. He knows about the summerhouse. I thought he did, that day."

I could not speak.

"I loathe him," she said.

She began to slide her body nearer to me; she started to spread out her hands to touch me.

[62]

"I ought to go," I said. "How the hell am I going to get out with Rollo there?"

She came nearer, smiling: "I don't think I'm going to let you go," she said.

I said something about being sensible and she said:

"Hold me. Who wants to be sensible?"

As I held her she brushed her mouth across my face.

"There's no need to worry," she said. "Rollo has a woman down in Corporation Street."

"What?" I said. Corporation Street ran squalidly down by the brook, its rows of smoky brick and slate backing onto old culverts. "There? How did you know?"

"Don't sound so outraged," she said. "I found out."

"It's just a tale," I said.

"She's one of the keeper's daughters. She married and then he died. Rollo keeps her. He's been doing it for years — "

"I suppose some people would believe that."

"Her name's Flo Welch," she said. "You see, you've lived in the town all your life and you know nothing about it. He calls her Boodles. Everybody knows."

I was reminded painfully of all my incompetence with Bretherton. It was true, in a way, that I had lived there all my life and that, after all, I knew nothing about it. It was perfectly true that there was a sort of innocence about me. Perhaps my awareness of this put a touch of anxiety into my face that I did not really feel, because the next moment she said:

"Don't look worried. Nobody's afraid of Rollo."

"I didn't say I was afraid of Rollo." I felt a stab of annoyance and I tried to get off the bed. She smiled and held me back.

"Anyway, next year I'm twenty-one. I shall do what I like then."

She gave an odd sideways reflective glance into the air.

[63]

"That'll make him sit up," she said. "Until then he's one of my guardians — that's what makes him spy round on us all the time." She flattened her body suddenly, flexing her legs downwards with a long, quiet sigh. "Poor dear, he hasn't any money of his own. That's what makes it so funny."

I began to see, now, that her mind was growing too.

"He put all his money into some wretched rubber shares or something," she said, "and all he can show for it is a drawer full of papers. He knows he has to behave himself with me."

I still had no particular wish to meet Rollo on the stairs, and I said so.

"You really are frightened, aren't you?" she said. "You're as nervous as a kitten because we're up here." Her power to hurt me with sentences like that was so sharp that the words would cut into me with jabs of physical pain. "Don't worry — I'll go down and look."

She stirred again and then lay still.

"I don't want to go — it's so nice up here. We had such a lovely time, didn't we? You wouldn't have thought of it, would you?"

I did not answer. She laughed, asking me to hold her. I held her and she said:

"It takes me to think of things like that. I thought of the summerhouse, too — do you remember?"

I remembered how she had thought of the summerhouse. She bent over me, kissing me several times on my face, her body ripely warm and taut where it touched me. "You're like someone half-asleep," she said. "Wake up, you old dreamer. Do I have to do all the love-making? Hold me a little while longer before I run down and see where Rollo is — "

She kissed me again several times, mocking me about Rollo. Nervously I thought of the Aspen sisters coming out of church, a short sermon, a parlormaid running home to lay supper; and at last, after about ten minutes, hot and driven by fear, I went downstairs. Before I went she begged me several times, in a voice growing slightly hoarse again with excitement, not to be the old dreamer — "Love me, darling, make the most of it while we can" — while outside, beyond the yellow blinds, the hot evening flamed in pure white-golden light, in a singing summer silence, without a breath of wind. I said several times how late I thought it was and how I ought to go, but she did not mock me again. "I'll save it all for tomorrow," she said, and her mouth began searching my face in probing, eager stabs of excitement, "only sometimes I can't wait for you — I can't wait — I feel I'll go mad with waiting — "

In the moment before I went out of the room she lay there looking at me with restless, tender eyes that were the only moving things in the golden body laid centrally taut on the monster, glittering bed.

"You know what to say to Rollo if you see him?" she said.

I had no idea at all what to say to Rollo; I felt I could do no better than turn and run.

"Ask him how the sermon was," she said. Her face broke for the last time into an abrupt, transfiguring smile. It made her suddenly into a very young and girlish person of infinitely simple and tender feeling, all light and sublimation, all lovable, completely happy.

"Say you love me," she said.

"I love you."

"Near and far and always and everywhere and everything — "

"Yes," I said.

"You've got to say it," she said. "If you don't, I'll hate you."

I said it. It seems unreal and embarrassing and stupid now, but there were tears in my eyes as I repeated it all. There was a breaking of the unbreakable tension of young agonies across my chest as I spoke the words she made me repeat to her, and I trembled with a joy that now seems unreal too as she turned her body for the last time, holding the pillows against her big, young breasts, saying:

"That's how I want to be loved — near and far and always and everywhere — "

It was striking seven by one of the French mantel clocks in the big sitting room as I went downstairs. I went through the small drawing room and onto the terrace outside. It was in my mind to say to Rollo that I had forgotten a book and had come back for it, but Rollo was not there.

Five minutes later I met him coming out of the spinney path across the park — exactly as if he had been waiting for me.

"Hullo," he said, "I thought you'd gone."

"I thought you'd gone," I said.

We stood staring at each other. I noticed, I think really for the first time, how very small his eyes were. They stared out brown and retracted and petrified as the brain behind them tried to work out some kind of answer to what I said. His two-inch choker collar lifted up in a startled way the face that was grossly scribbled with many small cabbage veins of purple-rose, the lips like a bloated central vein.

"How was the sermon?" I said.

He made no pretence of answering. The small eyes were cast downwards.

A moment later I saw that he was looking at my feet.

"Did you know," he said, "that you have a shoelace undone?"

It was perhaps not a coincidence that Miss Bertie spoke to me on the following Sunday. "You are the great one with flowers, Mr. Richardson," she said. "I want you to give me your opinion on the winter irises. It's my belief they're dead."

We walked, after tea, into the great square of box-hedged garden that ran southward from the house. It extended from walls draped with trees of Maréchal Niel down to long stone pergolas of dripping rambler rose, hot crimson above urns of pale blue agapanthus lilies on paths of sun-baked stone. The gardens were very large. In those easy, undistressful days, opulence and amplitude and calm loveliness spread with lushness everywhere about long lawns broken by cedar-shade pools of intense blackness; it was part of the air you breathed in wide rose gardens, in hot walled compounds filled with peach and nectarine and vine, along terraces illuminated with spires of ivory yucca bells.

That afternoon the leaves of the stylosa irises lay like withered whips under a long south wall.

"I shall be most intensely grieved if they're dead," she said. "They're so beautiful — you know them, don't you?"

"Like orchids," I said.

"Could they be dead? Do you think so? what do you feel?"

I told her how I thought they were not dead and how beautifully, because of the long summer baking, I thought they would flower again in the early year.

"I am intensely relieved to hear you say so," she said. "And now there's another thing — " she began to walk away from the house, across the hot, springy lawn, beyond blossoming yucca spires — "there's a tree over here of which nobody seems to know the name — "

We walked in hot sunlight. One of the reasons, perhaps the chief reason, for her acceptance of me was because, as she said, "You like flowers — you have a feeling for these things." I could smell all the drowsy opulence of July, as we walked there, in a deep cloud of lily scent floating across the lawns. She caught it at the same time and said:

"The summer has been very beautiful."

"Yes," I said.

"It's so often the way — after the long hard winter the lovely long summer."

"I've never enjoyed a summer so much," I said.

In this rather formal fashion, through a sort of gently stepped conversation on weather and flowers and the general beauty of things, we reached the far side of the lawn. Suddenly she turned to me and said:

"You've seen a lot of Lydia this summer."

"Yes," I said.

"I think perhaps you're fond of her, aren't you? Very fond of her — would that be right?"

"Yes," I said.

"I'm not sure you ought to get too fond of her." I felt miserably sick and embarrassed; I knew suddenly that the talk of flowers and weather and summer beauty was all a blind. I remembered Rollo and my shoelaces and the hot evening in the bedroom. "There are ways of being too fond, and ways of being not too fond."

I said nothing; she went on:

"She's rather excitable. You know that."

"Yes."

"Quite often she doesn't stop to think. And then quite often she has the sort of thoughts that run away with her."

"Perhaps," I said.

"Of course she'll be twenty-one next year."

I could not understand, for a moment, what that had to do with it. We had reached borders where, in full hot sun, seed pods of Peruvian lilies were cracking off like miniature artillery, shooting golden seed. Her dumpy body, bouncing past regiments of phlox and petunia and summer daisy and delphinium, all flabby with heat, distended itself and puffed before she spoke again.

"She comes into — well, her legacy."

I did not answer. Heat stung the crown of my head and there was no sign of the tree whose name, as she said, no one knew.

"We have to think of that," she said. "Of course she will have good advice and all that sort of thing. That is taken care of. But it will be a time of difficulty for her and added responsibility and all that sort of thing."

"Yes," I said.

"You probably think I am being a fussy old windbag and so on and so forth — do you?"

I said I did not think so.

"You have been very sweet to her," she said. "We liked you from the first. You have been just the person for her." Uneasiness took her bouncing on, always a yard or two in front of me — "You see until we met you we were in a way handicapped. We didn't know young people. We've rather got out of the run of things. We didn't want her to live a life of absolute stuffiness with us, and we didn't want her to know nobody but people like the Orme-Smyths" — the Orme-Smyths lived five miles away with crested and shabby hauteur in a square mansion lost in derelict parkland, too poor for the rich and too gilded for the poor — "who are such fatuous snobs, taken all in all. Don't you think so?"

I said I did not know the Orme-Smyths.

"Well, thank Heaven," she said. "Young Beauchamp would have been certified long ago if his father had a brain in his head. Florence I knew, forty years ago — *her* brain never developed after she was fourteen."

We stood looking across from where yew hedges had been clipped into curved saddlebacks to reveal, beyond, blistered slopes of parkland. There was no sign of the tree that had been her excuse for coming there, and she said:

"It isn't easy to have a young girl thrust on you like that — we wanted to save her from having one of that sort of awfully

[69]

circumscribed existences" — she hesitated — "of course it would have been different if her mother hadn't died — "

In a moment of intense stupidity, before I could stop myself, I said:

"I thought her mother was still alive?"

"Oh, no, no." She turned startled eyes on me, the pupils blobbing and frightened. "Oh, no, no, no. That's quite a mistaken idea. No, no. No." And then still again: "Oh, no, no, no."

I said something, hurriedly and awkwardly, about being sorry I had had a wrong impression about a painful thing like that, and she snapped:

"It was not a painful thing. It was one of those happy releases."

I said I understood. I did not really understand, and she said:

"What I really wanted to ask you about was dancing. Do you care for dancing?"

"Yes," I said.

"We thought it would be nice for her if you would take her dancing. The skating was such a tremendous success in every way. We thought, too, if you had friends — when the autumn comes you could begin to make up parties."

I said I should love to do that, and she smiled. Like a person in an obstacle race she had floundered through her traps and hazards and difficulties and had begun to emerge, triumphant, on the other side.

"What about your friends?"

I stood thinking. I could hear the startling artillery noises of lily seeds shooting into the hot, breathless Sunday air, and my thoughts seemed something like them, brittle and scattered and difficult to collect.

"We have tickets for a Red Cross Ball at Nenborough in September," she said. "They're rather expensive, but you needn't worry about that. On the other hand, there are your friends — what about your friends?"

I thought of Tom Holland, and I said that perhaps Tom Holland and his sister, Nancy, might come. I had not seen them all summer.

"Holland? Who are they? — Are they nice people?" And then she remembered: "Oh! the farmers — Will Holland — it's one of our farms, of course it is. The mother is such a delicate-looking person — like eggshell — "

I thought for a moment of saying something about Mrs. Holland having twelve children — the family was big and spaced-out and fair-haired, so that for a long time I had never been able to tell if the elder sons were brothers or uncles or fathers to the younger generation, Tom and Nancy, the children of my own age — but she was too quick for me:

"I'm sure they would be nice. What I call a real Evensford family. A real yeoman family — there aren't many of them left. Who else is there?"

I thought for a moment and then said:

"Alex Sanderson."

"Who is he?" she said.

"His father is in leather," I said.

She thought, too, and said:

"Not that heavy Baptist family who got involved in some sort of profiteering scandal during the war? Didn't the father and one of the sons get sentences — "

"Not that family," I said. Evensford was full of Sandersons. Like leather they were everywhere, branching out, making money, dedicating chapel foundation stones, strong in Rotarian and golfing and Masonic and bridge-playing circles, living in red-gabled villas having conservatories filled with scarlet geraniums and drawing rooms with Tudor radio sets. Their wives began by being sleek and good-looking and ended up, in a few years, wadded with corsets that revealed pimpled suspender buttons, frothy with fox furs whose bony skulls were chained under chins of mauve-powdered flesh, healthy and puffed and in a rubbery way voluptuous.

But every family has a branch that does not run to rule; and Robert Sanderson, Alex's father, had married a girl of taste who came from somewhere in the West country. She was dark and compact, with a small, bright-eyed head, like a black-bird's. She wore earrings that made her look slightly foreign and immensely distinguished and always young, and as the years went by she did not grow fat. Her figure kept a wonder-ful tautness, and Alex once said to me: "My God, I barged into the bedroom and saw my mother dressing. She's like a girl." She was one of those women who develop, in the late forties, an elegance and a gaiety, an almost impulsive refiring of youth that is more beautiful than youthfulness. I had kissed her once in a party game at the Sanderson house, in one of those room-to-room scrambles where people rush out of light into darkness and disappear into pantries and hatstands, and I remember how I pecked at her mouth as we passed on the dark stairs. For a second or two she held me back with slender fingers, laughing delicately against my ear: "You can do better than that, surely — try again. Come on, once more."

There was nothing in bad taste about that; it was a little moment of impetuous gaiety that I daresay she forgot, three minutes later, over the pineapple trifle downstairs. It was real and warm and delightful and infectious: and all of it, including her looks, her deep black hair and eyelashes and her delicate hands, she had given to Alex, who was not merely like her in looks and ways and a tendency to sudden and affec-tionate impulsiveness but closer to her, I often thought, than his father. So much so that he even brought her, sometimes, to dances.

I could not explain all this to Miss Bertie, but I said:

[72]

"This is quite a different family. Only cousins or something to the others."

"I see." I thought she seemed dubious and reserved and not satisfied. We turned and began to walk back. The sun stabbed down on the back of my neck and I suddenly wondered if Lydia dare try again the Sunday trick of making herself sick. Then Miss Bertie said:

"I don't want her mixed up in that awful sort of golfing-Rotarian rubbish that always goes on in towns like Evensford."

"Alex hates golf," I said. "He's never liked sport. He doesn't even swim. He's all for music and that sort of thing — he's a gay and friendly fellow. I think you'd like him."

"What sort of girls does he know?"

She said it almost tartly, with a touch of wry catechism.

"He doesn't like them if they don't dance well," I said. "If he can't get one that dances well, he'll bring his mother."

It was that remark that seemed to change her; she seemed suddenly happier about all I had said.

"Do you suppose it would bore his mother to come along and keep an eye on you young people sometimes?"

"She'd love it. She loves young people. She's young herself," I said.

The last of whatever fears had troubled her suddenly vanished — I could tell it by the way she lifted her face all at once and caught, in deep, lip-closed breaths, all the honeyed drenching odor of lime and lily and pure heat that rose from the stilled gardens — and as we came back to the terraces of white yucca bells she smiled:

"It's very sweet of you to do all this, and I hope you don't mind." Before I could answer I saw her look towards the house. "Oh! They're ready and waiting for me." I looked too, and saw Lydia, standing side by side with Miss Juliana against the French windows on the terrace, slowly drawing on her long white gloves for church.

"Have we been long? Shall we be late?" Miss Bertie called.

"I've nothing to do but put on my gloves and hat."

She trotted bumpily into the house. Miss Juliana, who was holding a buttonhole of a single Maréchal Niel rose sprigged with fans of maidenhair, followed her through the French windows a moment later, calling:

"You need a pin for your buttonhole, dear — "

I stood looking at Lydia. Something about the long white gloves, about the gap of smooth, supple flesh above the elbow between the gloves and the sleeve of white silk, filled me with sickness. A wave of pure nausea, a swamping ache of wanting to touch her, ebbed over me, quivering centrally down through my body. I thought of the hot Sunday evening in the room with the great brass bedstead, and I knew that she was thinking of it too. There was a curious, voluptuous primness about the Sundayfied white gloves, leaving their gap of white flesh, that was more startling than if I'd seen her naked, and in a flat voice that I knew she was flattening purposely she said:

"Where are you going? What are you going to do?"

"I was going — "

"Go home and write to me," she said. "Please, darling. I'll have a letter in the morning then. Tell me you love me and tell me what Auntie Bertie said."

"All right," I said.

"Where were you going really?" she said.

"To see Tom Holland," I said. "I was going to — "

"Who's he?" she said.

"He's the boy we met skating," I said, but once again, I think for the third time, she did not remember.

"Write to me," she said. "You will, won't you?" All she felt for me was fused into bright and narrowed eyes shining

[74]

back at me in full sunlight. "If you don't, I shan't love you."

"I'll write," I said. "I'll tell you everything in a letter."

Two minutes later the Daimler drove away from the front door and down the avenue, under the too-sweet dripping limes. I walked home across the park and wrote to Lydia, trying to tell her, in phrases that were warm and clogged and indecisive, how much I loved her. Then I walked across the fields to Buskett's farm and saw the Hollands for the first time that summer, telling Tom what had happened and what I wanted him to do.

"Love," they teased me. "That's how it is — that's what. Nobody has seen him all summer. Love," they laughed at me, *"now* we know — "

In this way began the autumn and winter when we first took Lydia dancing: myself and Alex Sanderson, who knew all the girls; Tom Holland, who knew none of them and was too shy to know; Tom's sister Nancy, and Mrs. Sanderson, with her elegant vivacious manners, her affection and experience, and her eyes like a bird's.

And also a man named Blackie Johnson.

PART TWO

I

THE weather was very beautiful that autumn when we first began dancing. The valley seemed always to be dreamy with light mists, sometimes a smoke-straw color, sometimes pale amber-rose, that broke into October days of tender, fly-drowsy sunshine. We used to go to the dances in an old black Chrysler limousine with a glass division and occasional seats at the back, that I hired in the first place, and almost by chance, from Johnson's garage down beyond the station.

Johnson was a tall, craggy man of old-fashioned Gothic appearance, with a voice like a crow. He wore narrow trousers that fitted his legs like black gloves, and a flat, black-peaked chauffeur's cap that scotched on the left side of his gray head like an oily frying pan. When the wagonette-and-brake business began to fail under pressure of the internal combustion engine, about 1912, Johnson took gradually to cars, but I thought the conversion left him with a sort of bemused and lingering regret. You rarely saw him unless he was chewing a straw, nor could I ever quite rid myself of the idea that the old slow, plushy limousine would break suddenly into trotting, and that if it did so Johnson would know very well how to deal with such a situation. Perhaps that is why we liked it so much. Certainly we liked Johnson, who treated us with something of the leisured respect of an old coachman and tucked us up, after dances, with thick, checkered and velvety coach rugs, so that we would come home warm and snoozy and wonderfully intimate and fugged up, like six people half-asleep in a big, crawling, hearselike bed.

Perhaps another reason why we traveled in such slow, easy comfort was that Johnson did funeral arrangements too. When I first went down to order the taxi — it was purely by chance that I did so, because Alex Sanderson's Humber, in which we were to have traveled, had blown a gasket that day and would not have been ready in time — the yard behind the garage was still full of horse-cabs, station flies, a landau, a number of black horse-hearses, and two old yellow wagonettes with copper-and-brass carriage lamps and shining mudguards picked out with scarlet lines. The old world had not quite departed. There were still black horses in the stables in the back yards and only two cars, and a single hand petrol pump in the yard at the front. But these were signs of the times. One of the station flies had a wheel off, and Johnson's first car, an old brass-lamped Schneider, a beautiful, high, ornate affair I always felt ought to have played fairground tunes out of its elegant sloping-bonnet grille, lay already cast aside under a cartshed, spattered white with the droppings of house martins that had built above it that summer.

Another sign of the times was Blackie, Johnson's son.

That day when I walked into the yard to order the taxi, Old Johnson had gone down to Nenborough to meet an express, and it was Blackie, lying half under the Chrysler limousine in the yard, who dealt with me.

"Yes, mister?" he said.

I told him I wanted to order the car.

"Yeh?" he said. He did not come out from under the car. "When for?"

"Tonight," I said.

"How many?"

"Six," I said.

He still did not come out from under the car, and I could not see his face. I could see only the big pack of chest muscles, hairy and brown and oiled, heaving themselves as he shifted to new positions under the axle.

"Where to?" he said. "What time?"

I told him. The chest muscles heaved and the legs lifted, pushing him farther under the car. He did not speak again for more than a minute, and somehow, I don't know why, I began to get an ugly, disconcerting impression of someone disliking me.

Then he said: "What time back?" and again I told him, and again he did not come out from under the car. His shirt was undone as far as the trouser-top, and I remember standing there looking down at the big, rippling belly muscles cramping and heaving themselves above the stiffened thighs, and all the time, I still did not know why, disliking them as if they had been his face, and all the time feeling that queer, ugly sensation of counterhatred.

He started to repeat, after a moment or two, what I had said to him. His voice gave the effect, somehow, of being forced through a narrow tube.

"Six people, nine o'clock, back at three," he said. He hit the wrench, under the car, against the leaf of a spring, and I heard him draw stringy phlegm, nasally and then down through the mouth, before hacking it out in spit.

"Well, you'll be unlucky, mister," he said.

He might just as well have slung the wrench at me. I still hadn't seen his face, but all the time, somehow, the impression of being hated grew on me. I didn't like the way he called me "mister" — perhaps it had something to do with that — and I didn't like the way he held conversation, as it were, at long range. It was that which made me stoop down, at last, and glare under the car, seeing his face, and his eyes especially, for the first time. It was a remarkably dark, swarthy, partially flattened face, with a heavy crop of oiled black hair. In a way it was a handsome face, and the eyes, contrasting with the blackness of hair and eyebrows, were a most surprising brilliant blue.

"What's up?" I said. "Car in dock?"

"Well, it looks like it, mister, don't it?" he said.

I asked him if he hadn't another car, and he said, rolling half over on his belly, away from me:

"No."

"Won't this be ready in time?"

"No."

"What about coming down again this afternoon," I said. "Any chance you'll have it done?"

"No."

Taxis were not very easy to get in Evensford in those days; taxis and places to eat — the young, raw town seemed, for some reason, to regard them suspiciously.

"Are you sure?" I said. "I don't mind coming down again."

I saw his body muscles squirm, giving a faintly perceptible sort of leer.

"How many more times've I gotta tell you the car won't be ready, mister?"

"All right," I said.

I stood up and he reached out a long black hand for another tool.

"Sorry you can't oblige," I said.

I walked past the old Schneider under its cartshed of martins' nests, past the old wagonettes and station flies and hearses, and into the street. I was walking blind with anger when I suddenly came to myself and saw, driving into the garage front, Old Johnson in his other car.

He stopped the car and spoke in his friendly, craggy way through the window.

"You wanna look where you're gooin', Muster Richardson,"

[82]

he said. He always called me "muster," in the old, now almost forgotten Evensford way. He had several bad teeth that showed up, tobacco-brown, when he grinned. "Is there anythink I can do for you?"

"I wanted a car," I said. "But your man says it's no go. It's for young Miss Aspen and myself and — "

"Man?" he said. "That's Blackie."

He stopped the engine and got out of the car. "You come along o' me," he said — men of his generation used to talk with a droll, rolling, soothing softness of accent that has almost gone now — "we'll see if we can git y' fixed up." He walked a yard or two before me on thin horse-bowed legs, and shouted:

"Blackie!"

And Blackie came out from under the car.

"How long you gooin' a-be on the spring?" Johnson said.

"Job to say."

"There's a gentleman here wants a car for tonight," he said, but Blackie looked at me and did not say a word.

"Thought you'd git done be midday," Johnson said.

Blackie wiped an oil rag over his hands and then across his chest and then put it into his hip pocket. Now, when he stood up, I could see how thick and tall he was, the big, packed muscles of his chest sewn tight and hard and curved like a blown football.

"All right, if you say so," he said.

"I do say so."

"All right, you say so."

There was something absolutely firm and quiet and final as a clenched fist about Old Johnson at that moment that I liked very much. He said, "Yes, and when I say so, I say so. Get that into your thick head," and once again Blackie did not say a word. "You come on into the office, Muster Richardson," Old Johnson said, "and I'll book it down."

[83]

In the dusty pine-paneled office, hung with advertisements for Michelin tires and oil and pictures of ladies in veils traveling in open coupés, I watched him put on his steel-rimmed spectacles and wet his pencil with his tongue and then take down the times and places at which I wanted him to call. As he stood writing, I had a sensation of uneasiness about something, and said:

"Will you be driving, Mr. Johnson? or Blackie?"

"I'll tek you meself," he said. "Him? Nothing ain't fast enough for him. Motor-bike hog."

He closed his order book and took off his spectacles. "Git 'isself killed afore he's much older. Does a bit o' racing." He sighed — I think he must have seen how, clear and inescapable, the forces of change were bearing down on the place and himself and the ways he cherished, but I thought he had wonderfully likable and craggy stubbornness as he stood staring out of the window, saying at last: "All right, Muster Richardson, I'll pick you and Miss Aspen up at nine o'clock. Don't you worry — you enjoy yourselves and come back when you're ready."

Out in the yard, by the Chrysler under which Blackie was at last wheeling and lifting a jack, Johnson paused in his slow way and said:

"Is she Elliot's gal?"

"Yes," I said.

"Bad job about her father," he said. "How old would she be?"

"She'll be twenty-one in the new year," I said.

"Will she? Lucky gal," he said.

That night the six of us danced together for the first time, and I was bloated with pride and happiness. I think the quietest person among us, quiet in a folded, watchful sort of way, was not Lydia, as I had rather fancied she would be, but Tom's sister, Nancy. Her face was bland and soft, and her arms were covered with glinting golden hairs that gave them the appearance of being covered with velvety down. She had clear, very English blue eyes of pronounced steadiness, but whenever I looked at her I always felt the faintest uneasiness, as if the eyes were watching me too closely.

But that evening she did not watch me quite so much. She was always looking, with that puzzled, curious reticence of hers, at Lydia. As the evening went on, I remember it developed into a kind of shyness, almost a mask of inferiority. I remember too how Lydia was dressed, and when I look back now I rather think it was her dress that evening that made Nancy, in her simplified way, uneasy.

Lydia arrived, that night, rather as she had done for the skating. Her dress was a long affair of gray-pink, with a heavy lace attachment of oyster color over the skirt. The bodice was very low, but there was something shrunken about the whole affair that made me think it was one of Miss Juliana's, dolled up and revived. Her figure sprang from its tightness in full curves that were not possible in dresses where the cut was so straight, as it was then, and the waist so low. Her breasts seemed high and startling, in a way that was almost aggressive under the tight, old-fashioned cut of the neck. She had also brought a fan — it was of white and black lace, and I remember she opened it once as we sat out a dance and how a woman gave a little giggling yap of astonishment at seeing such a thing — and one of those little corded booklets in which, at one time, dances and partners used to be written down with a silver pencil on a cord.

After I had danced twice with her I danced with Mrs. Sanderson — she was the lightest, most delicate person I have ever danced with, and she had a way of giving a tingling, floating exquisiteness to everything she did — and then I danced with Nancy.

After Mrs. Sanderson, it was a little like dancing with a comfortable, half-grown lamb.

"Where have you been all summer?" she said.

I felt she knew where I had been all summer, and I did not answer.

"You never came to see us. Once," she said.

I felt Nancy was being a bore.

"Anyway, here we are again," she said. I could feel that she had large, boned corsets under her pale duck-blue taffeta dress. They made her unsupple and slow and hard to lead. "And I might as well tell you I think she's very nice," she said.

"I never go with girls who are not nice," I said.

"You're always too clever for me."

"Nobody can be too clever for a woman," I said; and I thought this was rather clever too.

"Well," she said, "I think you might have to be very clever for this one."

Before I could speak again Alex Sanderson passed us, dancing with Lydia. As he passed, he stretched out one hand and ruffled, very lightly, the top of my hair. Then he swung Lydia round and round in a pirouette, making her dress fly in a whirl, and said:

"Cheer up, old boy. Don't look so damn serious. Some people are having a *wonderful* time!"

"She's got you all running round like little boys," Nancy said.

"I'm glad you think so."

"The three of you," she said. "You can't deny it, either."

I did not deny it. The room was now very crowded and warm, and I could feel my right hand making a sticky fan of sweat where I held the hollow of Nancy's corsets.

"Would you like an ice?" I said. "Alex says they're strawberry and very good."

"Now you're being very nice to me," she said.

We had pink-colored ices that tasted of borax or something just as indefinably unpleasant. They slid about, melting rapidly, on glass dishes that were too small for them.

"Do you know it's been a year since we found the violets?" she said.

"Violets? Oh! Yes," I said, and I remembered the violets.

On the edge of a spinney at the farm — ghostly and lovely butterfly orchis with lacy green-white wings grew there in July, and once I had taken her to see them too — we had found one of those late freak patches of violets, in black-purple bud, that flower sometimes in favorable autumns, giving a second spring. I had pinned a small bunch of them on her dress. It was about the time I had gone into Bretherton's office, a month or two before the great frost began, and it seemed like a million years away.

"They kept for weeks," she said.

I felt it embarrassing to talk of them, and I took another mouthful of flat ice cream.

"When are you coming up again?" she said. "Tom would love it."

"Some time," I said.

"Come on Sunday. It doesn't seem the same if you're not there," she said. "We got sort of used to you coming up there, and you know how it is."

"Yes," I said. I felt that Nancy was exactly like a drink of milk that we used sometimes to take straight from one of the cooling pans in the stone, whitewashed dairy at Busketts, on a warm summer evening, after a walk across fields of eggs-and-bacon flower. She was fresh and clean and smooth, neither warm nor cool, neither flat nor exciting. She would turn, some day, into a buttery and solid woman with light golden hair, brown and shining every summer from work in harvest fields. She would have children with straw-colored hair, like Tom, or else not marry at all, and grow more buttery and firm and plump every year, into an uncurdled, kindly and clovered middle-age.

"Come up on Sunday," she said again. "You can bring Lydia. We'd love to have her."

"Perhaps I might," I said.

"Oh! good," she said. "We'll have curd tarts. I know you like them."

When we went back to dancing, Tom was dancing with Lydia. As we passed them, Nancy leaned back and said over her shoulder:

"Tom. I say, listen. He's going to bring Lydia up to tea on Sunday."

"Oh! good," Tom said, and his voice and manner, and the sweetness of his surprise, were identical with hers, "we must have a bang at the wild duck one day. Crowds of them down at the brook."

"Will it be all right, Lydia?" I said.

"I would love to," she said. "I can escape from church," and I saw her smile up at Tom with that sudden expansion of the mouth that always revealed, in a curious and disarming way, her rather large, shining teeth, and I saw him stare back at her, transfixed, almost blank, his pale blue eyes almost fierce with wonder, as he had done on the marshes when she first skated there.

"He looks tired," Nancy said. "Don't you think so?"

"I hadn't noticed it."

"He's going to sit for an exam," she said. "He's taking one of those correspondence courses in bookkeeping and that sort of thing."

"Tom? — bookkeeping? — he hates things like that."

"He wants to have a farm of his own," she said.

As we drove home, after that first dance, at three in the morning, a large, blown golden moon was setting across the valley through low cylindrical mists that charged the car in puffs of pale ocher. Old Johnson had tucked us up, like the coachman he really was, and as he always did afterwards, with many checkered horse rugs, and we sat snuggled and fuggled together, warm and intimate, arms about each other. The evening had been very happy.

"I think we all should send a vote of thanks to the Miss Aspens," Mrs. Sanderson said. It was exactly the gracious and correct thing she would think of saying and which we should probably have forgotten. "It was their idea, and it's been wonderful — "

"Hear, hear," we all said.

"Hear jolly well hear," Tom said loudly.

"Will you thank them, Lydia, please?" Mrs. Sanderson said. I could see the flash of her earrings as she turned next to me in the misty, ocherous light of headlamps, her face pale and distinguished. "Tell them what a lovely time we had."

"I will," she said.

"All I should like to say," Tom said, and again it was rather loud, almost as if he were forcing himself, "is that next time *we* take Lydia. It's on us. There's a Hunt Ball at Grafton on the third of next month, and I vote we go. Agreed?"

"Agreed," we all said. "Hear, hear."

"May we have the pleasure, Miss Aspen?" Tom said.

"Thank you very much," she said.

"Cheers," Tom said. "That'll be the great day."

We all laughed. Mrs. Sanderson snuggled among the rugs and said: "Oh! it's just like a bed in here — here I am in bed with three men, and my husband at home and hungry and waiting, and I don't know what — I really don't know — "

Everyone burst out laughing again, and the car, swerving heavily on a misty corner, threw us together in a warm and joyous entanglement of dresses and brushing silken legs and bare smooth arms and laughing mouths, and I felt suspended and elevated and half-lightheaded with happiness.

When we dropped Nancy and Tom at the farm they shouted, "Sunday — don't forget Sunday." We called back that we wouldn't forget, and then, several times, "Square up later — settle up later," and I said, "I'll pay the cab, Tom, don't worry, good night," and then, "Good night, Nancy," I called.

"She's gone," he said. "Good night."

Afterwards we dropped Alex Sanderson and his mother. At the last moment Alex mischievously put his dark face into the car window and said, "Give her one for me, old boy. If you don't, I'll take one myself," and Lydia said:

"Oh! If you feel like that about it — "

An odd spasm of resentment, the minutest shock-wave of jealousy, shot through me as she said this, only to be quietened a moment later by Mrs. Sanderson, who stood waiting by the other open door.

"Oh! well — if there's going to be kissing of good nights," she said.

She leaned into the car, and in the darkness found my face with her mouth. She laughed, touching my lips in a brief, warm flicker. "Good night," she whispered. "It's been lovely — we must do it again."

After that we drove on alone, up through Evensford High Street, to the park. All the street lights were out; the deep yellow moon was down below the houses. There was now only a refracted amber glow of it, tender and transfiguring as snow, in the sky, on the gray church spire with its facings of ironstone, and on the toast-brown October chestnut leaves falling along the wall of the park.

"Ask him to put us down at the lodge," Lydia said. "We can walk up."

At the lodge gates, while I stood paying for the car, Lydia stood beside me, and although it was a soft, sultry night, I thought I heard her shiver.

Old Johnson heard it to, and said: "Don't you git cold, miss. Easiest thing in the world to git cold after dancing."

"No, don't get cold," I said. I took her arm, but she was not cold.

"Take a rug," Johnson said. "Put it round your shoulders. Muster Richardson can bring it back."

"I think I will," she said.

He opened the door of the car, took out a rug and draped it round her shoulders. "You better have one too, Muster Richardson," he said.

"Oh no," I said.

"Yes, have one," she said.

"You git sweatin' and afore you know where you are you got a chill round your backbone." He put another rug round my shoulders. "That's all right. You can bring 'em back."

"Well, I don't need it, but thanks," I said.

As we walked up the avenue she stopped, listening for the sound of the old Chrysler dying away in the empty street beyond the church, and stood close to me.

"You very nearly spoiled it," she said.

"Spoiled what?"

"The rugs," she said. "You're very simple sometimes."

We spread one of the rugs on dry chestnut leaves and lay down on it, drawing the other one over us. The moon had vanished, leaving the sky above the half-leaved branches orange-green, without a trace of blue, warm and lucent with the dying glow. Then it turned paler, whiter, and finally a clear salt-blue, with pure white stars, like a touch of winter. But under the rug it was quite warm, and she pressed herself so close to me that I could feel the bone of her hip round and hard against me through the flesh.

As we lay there she said several times how beautiful the evening had been and how much she had enjoyed it, and how much she had wanted me. Underneath the rug I found her

[91]

body in clean, long curves, and held it there while I watched the stars. I felt there was probably no one else awake in all Evensford except perhaps Old Johnson and Alex and his mother, and I pitied everybody because they were not awake and with her and as happy as I was.

Then I remembered how Alex had kissed her; I remembered the keen stab of jealousy, the sudden slitting through of all my puffed vanity; and I was sick because I did not want another person to touch her, and because I did not want to share her with another soul.

"Don't let Alex kiss you again," I said.

"Oh, that was just fun," she said. She laughed at me from deep in her throat, and the sound danced a long way through the already baring trees. "There was nothing in that at all."

II

SUNDAY would not have been remarkable in any way if it had not been for something that happened after all of us — fourteen I counted when we sat down to table at Busketts, and then sixteen as two brothers came in, rather late, in shirt-sleeves, from milking — had had tea in the long white parlor. Even now I cannot remember clearly — I never could — if there were six Holland sons and five daughters, or six daughters and five sons. One son had been killed during the war; two sons and three daughters were married, and already a new generation of fair, chaste-looking, golden-skinned Hollands was springing up, all alike, all clean and fresh as sheaves in a wheat field. You were never expected to hold conversation at Busketts; meals had the pleasant discordance of a disorganized and hungry choir. Brown arms passed and exchanged and repassed across the table buttery masses of scones and bread and currant loaf, plates of ham and watercress and pork pie, and in winter toasted crumpets and apples baked and stuffed to a sugary glitter with walnuts and figs. Tarts of lemon curd and Mrs. Holland's specialty, cheese curd, a tart of greenish, melting softness with fat brown plums in it, were wolfed down by mouths that seemed to be laughing whenever they were not eating. Mrs. Holland, pale, of delicate semi-transparence, exactly like eggshell, as Juliana Aspen had said, sat at one end of the table, watching it all with the brightest small violet eyes, staring sometimes with bemusement at Will Holland, the father, who sat at the other. Masses of reddish-gold hair grew out of his ears, and perhaps it was these that attracted her.

If you did not eat at Busketts, it was held that there was something wrong with you. If you did not help to finish up, with second and third helpings and large washes of thick brown tea, the plates of ham and pie and fruit and tart, there was something equally wrong with the food. Neither of these things, in my experience, had ever really happened there.

Only Lydia did not eat much that day.

At first the Hollands, in their own honest way, were shy of her. They stood, as it were, a little away from her, in respect, almost with delicacy, briefly formal; they looked on her as the aristocrat — there had been Hollands in Evensford as long as Aspens, for probably five hundred years, and there are Hollands there now, although there are no Aspens — and it was, I think, ingrained in them to stand away and look up, seeing her, as their forefathers had seen her forefathers, as someone from the great house, a lady growing up, a little unreal, detached from them. Her coloring had something to do with it, too. Her darkness was glossy and almost foreign, a little smoldering, against their clear, blue-eyed Englishness. It made them seem like touchingly simple, most uncomplicated people.

It was this that made them press on her, in their customary way, as the meal began, everything that the table bore under its arching glass vases of scarlet dahlia and late curled pink and purple aster. They could not understand a person who did not share with them their staunch and mountainous hunger.

Then all at once they grasped it and understood it. They stood away from her at once, shy again. Even Mrs. Holland left off asking, in her rather prim, distant manner, if Lydia was off-color or anything of that kind?

Suddenly Harry, who had eyes and hair some shades less pale than the rest, so that there was almost a shadow on them, a glint of something slightly richer, livelier and more full-blooded, leaned gravely across the table and spoke to her. He was in his shirtsleeves, fresh from milking. Sweat under his darker eyes made them flushed and glittering.

"Miss Aspen," he said, "is there anything you fancy that you *don't* see on this table, because — "

We broke into the first shouts of laughter. Lydia laughed too; and Harry, a little mocking, said:

"Miss Aspen, I implore you to eat. I can't *bear* it. If *you* don't eat, how can I?" — and we all laughed again.

"Let me fetch you something," Harry said. "Let me go to the pantry and *see* if I can find a titty-bit of something to tempt you — "

"Harry!" his mother said. "You great fool-jabey!"

"Girls have to eat," Harry said. He got up with a touch of solemn mockery.

"You great fool-jabey!" his mother said. "Sit down!"

"Got to find something to *tempt* Miss Aspen," Harry said. "Eh, Mister Richardson? — Mister Richardson knows, don't you, Mister Richardson? — like to be *tempted,* don't they?"

Harry gave me a grave wink, and his mother called that if he didn't sit down she'd warm his backside, big as he was, and all of us laughed again. One of the elder sisters began to say how Harry had always been the fool of the family, and another said he'd never grow up. Mr. Holland sat eating without a word, grasping a piece of celery as large as a hambone in one hand and a wedge of cheesecake in the other. The celery cracked and crunched, and Mrs. Holland shouted over her shoulder that if Harry didn't keep his fingers out of the pantry she'd burn him. Even Nancy, who had begun by being correct and formal as a window model, in order, I suppose, to impress on Lydia some idea that they were as good as she was, began trying not to laugh into a squeezed lace handkerchief.

When Harry came out of the kitchen with an unplucked wild duck on a dish, George, the elder brother, put his head down and started shrieking into his plate.

"Our Harry, you big wet thing," Edith said, and Mrs. Holland got up, tears running down her face, and began beating him about the shoulders.

When Harry started running round the room the duck did a lively, stiffish dance on the plate. The blows from Mrs. Holland went thumping into Harry's back. The duck, with a rubbery, brilliant leap, sprang into the air. Mr. Holland sat transfixed, celery and cakes suspended, and Harry, trying to catch the duck, dropped the dish instead.

"You great fool!" Mrs. Holland said, and picked up the dish, unbroken. Harry dived again for the duck, and Mrs. Holland — I see clearly now why, more like a little hawk than any eggshell, she was really the soul and master of the house — hit him squarely on the back of the head with the dish. It was the sort of smart, playful tap that breaks things more easily than more substantial blows, and the dish snapped into two pieces.

"It won't hurt him!" we shouted. "It's hard! It can stand

it! Hard as iron," we said, "he'll never feel it!" And Mrs. Holland said, "He'll feel it next time, I'll warrant," and chased him from the parlor into the kitchen, where we could hear her, in some final scuffle of motherly horseplay, giggling like a girl.

"Loves it! Just as bad," we said. "*Makes* him worse!"

"I remember the time she poured milk down his neck — I'll never forget that time," George said, and only Nancy looked embarrassed, murmuring something about a bad example and how lucky it was that Arthur's children were not there.

When it was all over, Mrs. Holland sat at the head of the table again, trying to pat solemnity into her bright, laughing violet eyes with a fresh and respectable handkerchief still folded into a square.

"I don't know what you think of your first visit to Busketts, Miss Aspen," she said, and before Lydia could answer, Harry said, with the old solemnity:

"Good Lord, hasn't she *heard* of us — the Holland circus? I thought everybody in Evensford had *heard* of us. *Me* — at any rate — "

"She hasn't been in Evensford so very long yet," Nancy said.

"Well, now show that Busketts *can* behave," Mrs. Holland said, and Harry said, gravely:

"She should come at Christmas — that's a time — *will* you come at Christmas, Miss Aspen?" he begged her.

"Oh! Perhaps," Lydia said. She laughed, and I could see that she was happy and liked it all. "It's a nice name, Busketts — it's very English and very like you."

Nancy saw her chance and said:

"It's really French. That's where it comes from — "

"I never understood that," her father said. "I never heard of that."

"It's a corruption," Nancy said. "It's the same word as bosky — there was probably a wood here once — "

"There's wood here now!" Tom said. He tapped the top of Harry's head, so that we all began laughing again. "Ah! That's wood, if you like. That's wood."

"In the French it's probably *bosquet* — and you get another word, *bocage,* meaning a sort of wooded place, too — "

"Harry again!" we said. "Wooded place — "

"*Now* we know," Tom said. "All this time we *wondered* — so that's it, wooded place."

"Good old Harry," we said. "Busketts for wood! Plenty of wood. A good wooded place."

Nancy did not know quite what to do about this nonsense. She sat for some time afterwards taking the plums carefully from a piece of cheese-curd, pushing them, in finicky embarrassment, to the side of her plate. When she had carefully removed them all there was not much left of the cheese-curd, and Harry said, in a sly way:

"Some time, never. Probably never."

"Oh, phoo! to you," she said. "You never miss a chance, do you?"

"Now, now," her mother said. "You two."

All the time Mr. Holland crunched celery in steady, crackling bites, in crisp splinterings, like the crushing of match-boxes.

When tea was over, the four of us, Tom and Nancy, Lydia and myself, stood in the garden. Warm in the sun, leaves were turning on the apricot trees along the limestone walls, and one tree of pears, half fruit, half leaf, burnt like a fiery, bronzy column on the lawn.

"What would you like to do?" Tom said.

"Didn't you say you'd shoot wild duck?" Lydia said.

"Oh! No," he said. "Did I? Not today."

"It's Sunday," Nancy said. "Nobody's supposed to shoot on Sundays. It's a rule. Let's walk."

"Oh! I looked forward to that" — Lydia turned up to Tom the flashing, disarming mouth — "couldn't we? I wanted to see you shoot — you two. We could, couldn't we?"

"Well, nobody does on Sundays," Tom said. "Dad doesn't like it — nobody really does on Sundays — "

"Oh! Tom," she said.

That was the second time — the first had been when she skated and fell against him on the ice — that I saw a flat, almost frozen immobility spread so completely over his face that I knew he could not see her. She had never called him Tom before. Twice or three times she had not even remembered his name. His transfixion was not only of pure shyness. He had a look of being partially stunned.

By this time Nancy had walked away a yard or two, and I said: "Oh, get the gun, Tom. You'll see a jackdaw or a maggy or something" — and the words brought him out of himself, so that he turned and went back into the house to fetch the gun.

"I thought the duck on the plate was so funny," Lydia said. "And the way she hit him — "

"Killing," I said.

"I didn't think it was very funny," Nancy said.

"Oh, killing," I said.

We walked across the meadows that slope away, southwestward, at Busketts, to the brook that finally finds its way through Evensford, flowing there through culverts that are always thick and scummy, except at floodtime, with floating fish-and-chip papers and the oily dust of streets. Up in the meadows and along the brook, where it winds through Busketts, a long marshy segment of the old pure country remains. Iron-brown bogs of sedge and belts of fawn-feathered reed grow about islands of sallow that are gold-crested in spring. A good number of wild duck collect to feed there, and often a few snipe that go whistling across cold twilights on winter afternoons. We used to fish there, Tom and myself, and I remember how once, as boys, we caught a good roach there, under a pink crab tree, out of season, with a piece of marmalade pudding his mother had given him, and how we toasted the roach on a fire of sticks and ate the remainder of the pudding with it for bread. It was a favorite place of ours, and if ever I arrived at Busketts and Tom could not be found, somebody would always say "Try the brook — he's probably fallen in it again." I had fallen in it several times myself, and the curious thing is that I liked falling in.

"This is the place we found the violets," Nancy said. We were passing the small triangular spinney where, in summer, butterfly orchis grew. "Let's stop and look — there might be some — Tom, stop with us."

"You two stop," Lydia said.

I did not want to go into the spinneys with Nancy, and I leaned against the fence while she climbed in and looked for violets. There were no violets, and presently she came back.

"It's perfectly true about *bosquet* and Busketts and the wood," she said. "I looked it up in the *Dictionary of Place Names*. This is probably the last piece of all the woodland — "

"It could be Middle English," I said. "Bosky. It means drunk, too."

"Oh! You're clever, aren't you?" she said.

A sudden shot came from the meadow below us. I felt uneasy and we went down, two minutes later, to find Tom reloading after firing a second shot at a straggling formation of rooks loping across from the high fields where the stubbles were still not ploughed.

Tom had missed with both barrels, and once more he stood there with the paralyzed, frozen look on his face.

"I never like Sunday shooting," Nancy said. For the first time I agreed with her. I did not like it either. "Let's get watercress," she said. "There ought to be beautiful watercress."

"Tom's going to shoot me a duck," Lydia said. "Aren't you, Tom?"

Tom nodded. Blindly, with the pale-blue eyes fixed somewhere on distances beyond the brook, he began to walk with Lydia across the field. Dew was beginning to fall already in a pure white nap on the grass, and Nancy said:

"Let's go back. It'll be dark by the time you get there."

The four of us went down the field. I remember making a few pointless remarks about legality. Some rain had fallen during the previous night and the lower strip of marsh was wet and muddy. We picked our way over sedge islands that gave way to red-brown pools of brackish water. A few old nests of moorhens remained here and there about the empty sedge, and at last a heron, ghostly and straggling and yet climbing fast, rose from a reeded waterhole and flapped away.

Lydia gave a short, throaty, metallic yell, not really a scream, but a sort of command, saying: "Fire at it, Tom! Hit it — kill it!" and Tom fired, missing again with two barrels.

The second barrel disturbed, in a wheeling, dark-blue cloud, perhaps twenty or thirty ducks that had gathered on the far end of the marsh. It was all over, I thought, as I saw them rise and circle and climb and circle again, and I was glad. But it was not quite over. In a painful moment Lydia turned on him sharply, in that peremptory, commanding way that simply made me angry, but that had on Tom only a more stunning and stupefying effect.

"You promised — you said you could. Didn't you, Tom, didn't you?"

Then, in the most confused moment of his awful stupefaction, she smiled. I know now — though I did not know then

— how much that sudden sweetness of hers affected him. Her face sprang with delightful friendliness and she took his arm. I knew then that one day he would shoot ducks for her, by the million if necessary. He would shoot wild geese or herons or swans or whatever she wanted. He would, in fact, do anything for her, perhaps almost without the grasp of full consciousness, if only she asked him and asked him long enough, with that particular insistence of hers and that particular smile.

I walked back with Nancy. Perhaps I had not been fair with Nancy. But if I was peremptory and impatient with her it was not only out of vanity but because I had grown beyond whatever she may have felt there had been between us. I wished, very often afterwards, that I had been fairer, less unreasonable, less obtusely self-centered towards her than I was that day. But I was not; I liked to show how proud I was, how vain and how clever, and even to give her, now and then, a touch of pain; I liked to wound her by taunting her, obliquely, my having risen beyond her simplicity into a world that I thought was golden and lofty and too complicated for her to understand. It was very stupid; but I could not tell, then, what was going to happen and how great, as someone has said, the confusion of simplicity can be. But long afterwards she said to me:

"If you'd hit me that day it couldn't have hurt more, and it might have been better. Then Tom would have hit you and the other might not have happened."

Perhaps the most curious thing of all is that, all that autumn, nothing did happen. Lydia had nothing for Tom, and over and over again she would display only that cool and surprised indifference of hers when I mentioned his name. He was there; but for all she seemed to care he was a doll wrapped away in a nursery cupboard, forgotten.

And in this way we danced to Christmas.

Christmas came with a touch of snow that transfigured Evensford as I loved to see it transfigured, with a penciling of unendurable delicacy on the streets of gray-red houses and, most lovely of all, on the bare trees about Busketts and the park.

There were many dances that year, and the nights were black and frosty. We drove from place to place in the big limousine, tucked under the many rugs Old Johnson brought for us, and every night through the old year we were very happy with each other and very gay. Old Johnson always brought the car early to fetch us, steady and decent and gentle as an old lady, and we always had plenty of time to get to the places where we danced, up and down the river.

But on the night of New Year's Eve, the car was not early. It did not come at nine o'clock, as we had asked for it. As I stood at the gate of the park with Lydia, waiting for it, the air was compressed and cold, darting into my nostrils with freezing stabs. The road was dark with patches of bitter ice, where irregular pools had frozen in hollow places.

"You're so wonderful when things go wrong," Lydia said. "You're absolutely comic when things don't go smoothly. You start stamping up and down."

"Old Johnson is never late," I said. "There must have been an accident."

"I don't suppose there has been," she said, "and in any case, stamping your feet wouldn't help it." Then she laughed at me again and said:

"Anyway, isn't that the car? Isn't that something coming now?"

A car came very fast round the long bend of the park wall, dipping and raising its headlights. It made a long, skewing swerve across patches of dark ice, brakes whistling, and then screamed to a stop beside us. The door flew open at the back, and Alex pushed his head out to say:

"Murder. Hop in."

"What made you so late?" I said, and then I looked at the driving seat. At the wheel was Blackie.

"Hang on to your hair," Alex said, and the car roared off with a skid of back tires, throwing me on the floor. I groped about on all-fours for a few moments, and everybody laughed. The car was traveling so fast that I could not get balance enough to stand up, and suddenly the entire chassis of Johnson's respectable old limousine seemed to take to air, lifting me bodily in a horrible jerk so that I struck my head on the roof and at once fell back on the floor again, dazed.

I was so dazed that I was not even angry. When I recovered, Alex and Tom pulled me back on the seat. There was some disentanglement of bodies, and Alex said:

"This is a damn nightmare — no rugs, nothing — God, we'll be lucky if we see another year — "

"Not long now," Tom said. I noticed Nancy and Mrs. Sanderson were both very quiet. We were traveling beyond the last houses of the town at something between fifty and sixty, and in that old, high chassis it seemed like nearer eighty or ninety. I could hear the exhaust roaring hoarsely behind us, and now and then a skidding crunch as we lashed through ice pools.

As we did a switchback over the last brook-bridge that marks the end of the town, I turned to see Mrs. Sanderson holding her handkerchief to her mouth, looking very pale. After the blow on the head I felt stunned and sick myself, and Nancy said:

"Tom, tell him to slow down. Mrs. Sanderson feels queer already — "

"This is bloody impossible," Alex said.

He pushed the glass partition back and said:

"Steady her down a bit, Johnson — "

"You want to get there, don't you?" Blackie said. I saw him

full-face as he turned completely round to answer. He had one hand on the wheel and he was driving, as it were, out of the back of his head.

"We want to get there," Alex said, "all in one piece."

"You'll get there."

"Steady her down — there's a lady feels ill."

"Where's Old Johnson?" I said.

"He broke his arm," Blackie said. The whites of his eyes were remarkably prominent. They flashed in the dashboard light as he flung his head round at us. "It's New Year's Eve. We only got one driver — I got seven jobs on and only one pair of hands and one car. I'm late now — "

We went over a long section of ice that did not break under us, and the car curled in a sickening slide.

"Here — that's enough," Alex said. "Slow her down!" Nancy began to clasp Mrs. Sanderson, who was either weeping, or trying not to be sick, into her handkerchief. Lydia had not spoken a word. "Slow her down — Stop her!" Alex said.

Blackie pushed back the glass partition with a flick of his hand, and then I heard the hoarse, rising roar of the exhaust as he put his foot down.

"Oh! Please," Nancy said.

I could hear Mrs. Sanderson suppressing sickness with small moans.

"This isn't what we pay for," I said, and anger leapt out at last through my own dazed mind. "Let me get at the damn window — " And then Lydia spoke for the first time.

"I'll do it," she said.

She leaned forward and opened the window. She put her head through the aperture to the driving seat, so far that Blackie must have felt the warmth of her mouth on his neck.

"Stop the car," she said.

I could hear her voice, level, slightly imperious, not angry or even rising, but with that particular compelling throatiness that always sounded, really, much older than herself.

"That's it — stop it," she said.

In twenty yards Blackie stopped the car. I noticed he did not speak at all or even turn his head.

Mrs. Sanderson moaned a little with relief. Tom said something about getting things organized properly now, and then Lydia opened the door of the car.

"What are you doing?" I said. "Lydia, where are you going — ?"

"I'm riding in front," she said.

All the rest of the journey — we went a little slower, perhaps, but not much, with Alex swearing bloody murder all the way, his mother too dazed and sick to listen or utter a sound of reprimand — I watched her, through the glass, talking to Blackie. I saw her face turning, white above the brown ruffle of fur collar in the upward dashboard light, remote and disturbing and cut off from me, in continual conversation. She seemed to be making a sort of speech to him, but whether it was annoyed or kindly or categorical or explanatory I never knew. I only know that he did not turn his head, once, in answer.

It was very gay at the hotel when we arrived. Strings of colored lights, red and blue and yellow and green, had been looped in chains between rows of dipped limes in front of the big white-columned hotel porch, and I could see the naked twigs glistening as if coated with soft burgundy-colored paint in the dry night air.

We were all a little shaken by the journey, and by the time we were out of the car, stiffish and groping under the dazzling lights, Lydia was already standing by the driving wheel, talking to Blackie.

"You can get supper and drink for yourself and put it down to us," she said.

"I got seven more jobs," Blackie said.

"We want you to stay here," she said. "That's the way your father does."

The engine was still running, and I heard Blackie move the lever into first gear with a slight, purposely grated push.

"Your father always waits for us," she said. "It's always been like that."

"I'll be back at three," Blackie said.

He revved the engine. Tom and Nancy and Mrs. Sanderson had gone into the hotel. Alex and I went over to Lydia and Alex said:

"Is there some argument? Because if there is — "

"Get yourself some drinks and supper, and wait for us here," Lydia was saying.

"I got seven jobs," he said. "I told you."

Her voice had no anger in it, nor had her face. It seemed to me only rather curiously set, not at all unlike that set and confused expression of Tom's.

Then she took a pound note from her handbag.

"Does that help?" she said.

She held it up for a moment, bluish, crisp, in front of his dark face. He said, "I'll be back at three. I got jobs," in the flattest, most arrogantly neutral sort of way. The car began to move slightly forward, and her insistence — I had seen her clumsy and excited and selfish before, but never quite like this — reached a point of embarrassment and panic as the car actually gathered a little speed and moved past her.

At that moment she suddenly threw the pound note into the driving seat, and called:

"Get yourself a drink with that, and park at the back — "

The car moved away under the limes. It did not strike me until long afterwards how curious it was that she did not ask for Alex's and my own support. I was preoccupied with the look on her face. As she stood watching the car turn at the end of the hotel drive, I saw in her eyes a flat, perplexed but still not angered look, not really pained or stunned, but full of bewilderment and hurt. She must have known, I think, that she had hurt herself and she did not know why.

At last I took her arm and Alex said: "I could have hit the bastard — and probably some day I will," but she did not hear, and Alex took her other arm and we went into the hotel.

The dance band had come from London that night and everything was exactly right. I do not think we missed a single dance before suppertime, and I thought there was a kind of fine-drawn exhilaration about everything in the big, white color-streamered hotel room under the exquisite chandeliers. Mrs. Sanderson was one of those women who imprint charm and taste on everyone about her, and very soon there was nothing about her to tell that she had been so miserably sick in the car, and soon the whole affair, except for Lydia, faded out of our minds.

At twelve o'clock we drank champagne in an *annexe* supperroom and toasted each other.

"First time I ever drank champagne," Tom said.

"How does it strike you?" Alex said to me, and I said with vanity: "Slightly on the dry side, perhaps," and Alex said, "I was going to say the same. But we shall bear up — " And we all laughed and drank and said things like "Happy New Year" and "Many of them" and "Bless you all."

"Oh! This isn't a toast list, is it?" Mrs. Sanderson said. "This calls for something better, doesn't it?" and she held my face in her hands and kissed me.

Then Alex kissed Lydia, setting down his champagne glass in order to do so, and then kissing her in his gay-dog, slightly ironic, debonair fashion. Then I kissed Nancy. Someone began at that moment to sing "Auld Lang Syne," and we joined hands together and sang it too. Several women, as they always do, had tears in their eyes, and Nancy, as we went back to have supper, was one of them.

"It's been a wonderful year," she said. "I hope there'll be another one."

"Tom didn't kiss Lydia," Alex said, and we all agreed that that was right.

"Kiss her," Alex said. "Or may I have your turn?"

"We ought to get some grub before there's a rush at the tables," Tom said, and we all said no, no, he was not going to get out of it like that.

"Take a long drink of champagne and close your eyes, Tom," Mrs. Sanderson said, and we all split our champagne, laughing. All the time Tom stood smiling, awkward and very sweet in his large shyness, and then suddenly Lydia took his arm and said:

"Come on, Tom. Let's go down and see if the driver has had his supper."

"Oh! cowards," we said. "He's not there, anyway. It's a rotten excuse to be alone."

"Oh! he'll be there," she said.

But he was not there; and it was only long afterwards that I understood why she had taken Tom down with her to see.

As the night went on, all of us, except Mrs. Sanderson, drank the cold champagne too quickly, and it must have been nearly two o'clock when Alex came sliding across the floor to me, sideways, his mouth springing about elastically to frame his words, and said:

"Let's go and find that bastard Johnson. Let's give him a bloody good do —"

"Good," I said. "The two of us."

As we went downstairs and outside and began to grope about, starrily, in the fierce air of the winter night, looking for Blackie Johnson, Alex kept shouting:

"Johnson! Come on out, you rotten bastard."

We walked several times up and down the lines of parked cars and then down a side avenue to where, at the bottom of the hotel gardens, the river ran, but Blackie had not come back.

"Anyway, we know one thing," Alex said. "We'll never have *him* as a driver again. That's certain."

"Never in your life," I said.

Then we stood under a tree, looking at the sky, the dark branches, the stars, and the fallen crispness of their frosty reflections in the river below us, and Alex said:

"God, it's so beautiful. Look at it, old boy — it's so beautiful."

I stood looking across the river. There was a wonderful unblemished purity of winter starlight over the dark water, and the air, I thought, was full of a strange distant frosty singing. I thought of Lydia and Johnson again. For a second I was ripped by spasmodic hatred of Johnson. Then Alex fell over and said, still sitting on the frozen ground:

"Damn. That comes of thinking too much of her."

"I was thinking of her too," I said. "What were you thinking?"

"I was thinking — Oh! God, never mind."

Starlight and frost and champagne and affection swam together in my head and I said:

"She's beautiful, isn't she?"

"No," he said. "That's where you're wrong. She isn't. Haven't you ever looked at her face — ?"

"You only know her face," I said.

"I doubt if any one of us knows her," he said.

Solemnly he got to his feet and we linked arms, winding back to the hotel through the lovely, bitter starlight air.

"She always does the things you don't expect of her," Alex said, and we stumbled back into the hotel, laughing in a sudden gay hysteria of friendship, slightly forced, perhaps, because I had nothing else to say in answer.

Blackie Johnson came back, as he had said he would, at three o'clock. Alex was three-parts asleep when we put him into the car. Mrs. Sanderson had a lovely drowsy suspense about her, saying over and over again: "Tom, I'm going to put my head on your shoulder." Nancy and I had floated out of the champagne into a period of second wakefulness; and Lydia, without asking or saying a word, got into the front of the car again with Blackie.

"She's tamed him down a bit," Nancy said. She moved her body and slipped down beside me on the seat. "He's not driving so fast this time."

As we drove along, I stared dully at fences and hedges, wraithed in pale frozen grasses and wands of old meadowsweet and willow herb and thistle flowing past like things stark in salt wastes. I could hear the crunch of ice as we slid over it and I remember thinking that soon there would be skating again. I saw Lydia's face turning pale, fur-framed, in the dashlight, and once a movement of Blackie's in answer.

"Perhaps next time she can get him to remember the rugs," Nancy said. "It's much cozier — it's awfully cold without them," and she put her arms round me, curling her body and holding it down against me.

"Oh! I'm so cold," she said. "Hold me — bring my coat over my shoulders."

I held her, bringing her coat over her shoulders.

She was not cold; but something inside myself was, and it had begun to pain me like a wound.

III

As the winter went on, I began to be more and more uneasy about her; I did not think she looked at me with the same fondness as before.

Sometimes when we drove to dances she did not sit with me. She would sit with Alex or even, sometimes, out of spite as I thought, with Blackie Johnson, beyond the front glass screen. She was always gay and talkative and high-spirited and full of expressive friendliness with us all. I did not recognize then that all these things were part of her growing. I thought it was her way of taking her love away from me; I was hurt because she did not belong to me alone any longer. And because I was hurt I began to grow jealous of her. I could not bear it if she looked at Alex with friendliness, or if she teased Tom in his presence so that Alex too would show in his own expression the slightest fear that she was doing it to taunt him too. I had forgotten how much a prisoner she had been: how exciting and unbalancing and lovely it must have been for her, that winter, to live a life broadening to full freedom with young people like us. I wanted her only for myself, exactly as I always longed, hungrily and painfully, in the appalling drabness of an Evensford winter, for the intensified tenderness, the warmth and the loveliness, of a summer day.

Then I noticed that she began to get bored with the dances. "They are all the same," she would say. "It's always just us, and we just dance with each other. It's all got terribly respectable and stuffy."

Then I began to think that perhaps her boredoom with the

dances was really only the expression of her boredom with me. I thought that slowly and inevitably she was growing away from me; that soon she would not want me any more. It did not occur to me that she could possibly be in love with Alex; that she might be attracted, even without really knowing it, to a man like Blackie.

Then one evening I ran into Alex as he came off the London train. I thought he seemed taut and strung up and tired. There was always a fine, stretched pallor about his face, a high-strung tension about the thin cheekbones and the long, elegant chin that gave him an appearance of handsome nervousness. But that night his eyes were smoky and hollowed and exhausted and he said to me:

"You weren't meeting the train, were you? I mean, you didn't come down specially or anything? — You know — ?"

I began to say that it was all by chance I happened to be there, but he interrupted.

"For Christ's sake let's get a drink," he said. "Let's go down to The Prince Albert."

He coughed several times, his breath catching the night air. He swung his briefcase from hand to hand. Then as we reached The Prince Albert, the only hotel in Evensford, a double-winged Edwardian house of red brick with long lace curtains and rows of winter palms in the lobby, and a tarnished smell of liquor and train smoke in all the rooms, he said several times:

"In the lounge, in the lounge. It's quieter there."

In the lounge I sat down by the fire and he rang the bell, twice, impatiently, for the waiter.

"Beer," he said. "Beer. I'll have beer. And in a tankard — I hate it in a glass. Bring it in a tankard. I can't drink it in a glass. Bring it in a tankard."

Perhaps I looked startled at this, because he turned on me sharply, protesting, as if I had said something:

"It's cooler like that. It tastes different. Altogether different — "

When the tankard came, set down by a waiter who looked slightly puzzled and startled too, Alex shouted after him:

"And a double gin, too. I'll have a double gin. I'll have a chaser," and then gripped the tankard with both hands, so that his knuckles shone as bare and polished almost as the silvered pewter.

"I'm damn glad to see you," he said. "Damn glad I ran into you — "

In my affection for him — and it remained, through everything that happened afterwards, the same affection, only rarefied by events — I felt that perhaps all this had gone far enough.

"What's got into you?" I said.

"Ever hear of a place called Milton Posnett?" he said.

"No."

"Nor has anyone else," he said. "Except Lydia."

The waiter came with the gin and Alex said: "Bring me some lemon in it. I like lemon in it. Bring Mr. Richardson one, too," and then, when the waiter had gone:

"It's some dead-alive hole out in Huntingdonshire. We're going to dance there."

"What dance?"

"It's just a hop. A village hop. A bob-a-time Saturday-night shindy. I know one thing — I'll not take my mother there."

I did not speak. I could not see what so simple a thing had to do with his attitude of complex nervousness. He sat quiet for a few moments, his body screwed up, his face down almost to the level of the table, above the tankard. I waited; he did not speak either, and I said:

"What's all this about? Who told you?"

"She did," he said. "Lydia. It's her idea." He looked at me

with pitiful embarrassment. "That's what I wanted to say — what I wanted — I took her out to dinner last night."

He looked so pained about this simple fact that I did not know what to say.

"Place on the Great North Road," he said. "Eaton-something — Blackie took us. Eaton-something — Eaton — "

"Eatanswill?" I said.

"What?" he said. "What? No — that wasn't it," and the bitter, sickly joke was lost on him.

"She telephoned me," he said. "It was her idea," as if he thought this brought the improbability of the whole thing into reasonable line with truth. "She wanted to talk about something. This dance thing. She's tired of it. She's fed up. She thinks it's got awfully stuffy — "

"Perhaps it has."

"She wants to go somewhere new. For a change. You know? — sort of — " He looked at me with gin-smoky, fuddled eyes. "So when we were coming home she suddenly pulled the partition and said to Blackie: 'Blackie, you know all the places. Where could we go? Somewhere different? For fun? Somewhere we don't have to dress — where we could let go.' And then he suggested this place. It's some bloody awful hole — you know what those villages are — I think he comes from there."

Again I could not see what there was to be troubled about in this simple thing. Again he looked at me painfully with mute, fuddled eyes.

"Perhaps she's right," I said. "We can't go on doing the same old round for ever."

"It isn't that," he said. "Have another drink? I'm going to have another one. Waiter!"

The waiter did not come, and after that, for some minutes, Alex forgot him. Then what he said next, sucking the words with fumbling lips out of the tankard, seemed very amusing and I laughed.

[114]

"It isn't that," he said. "I think she's flirting with Blackie."

"How many did you have in London?" I said.

"A few, a few," he said. "Not many." I laughed again, and he seemed acutely pained:

"What's so funny about it? When you look at him he's bloody handsome — in his way."

"That doesn't mean it's her way."

"No? You can never tell," he said. "You can never be sure. They get attracted by people you loathe. You wonder how the hell they can — you can never be sure."

I asked him if there was anything that could possibly make him sure, and he said:

"She made me kiss her good night in front of him. Deliberately — "

I felt sick. "Let's go home," I said.

"Deliberately," he said.

I said I thought he had had enough. I added that I thought I had had enough myself. The trivial obsessions of a half-drunk, even a friend, did not seem very amusing. He called again for the waiter. Then he got up and rammed a blundering forefinger several times into the bell. It rang insistently far away in the bar and he said:

"She sees something in him — I can tell by the way she looks at him."

"She's excitable and impulsive," I said. "That's all."

"I'll knock the bastard down if he even looks at her," he said.

I suddenly felt sick with fear and doubt and uneasiness that all he was saying might be true. The arrival of the waiter made me get up. Alex was staring into the pier glass above the fireplace and the waiter asked me if anyone had rung. I said it was all a mistake. We were sorry to have bothered him. We were going home.

"Home be damned," Alex said. "Two more. Two more, waiter. Let's have two more."

[115   ]

"I'm going," I said.

I walked angrily out of the hotel, blundering and groping in the darkening night air beyond the lighted steps. Alex ran after me.

"Don't go off in a bloody huff," he said.

"I'm not," I said.

He waved his hands expansively and uncertainly in air.

"It's a bad habit of yours," he said. He laughed with wry, shaky good-humor. "Going off in a huff. Storming out like an offended bloody old cockatoo."

"You're sozzled," I said.

"Bad habit," he said. "Terrible weakness."

He laughed again and I caught a glimpse of his face, half-drunk, careless, taut but amusing and lovable under the grim light of a gaslamp. My annoyance with him vanished suddenly and I laughed too.

"I'm sorry I stormed out," I said.

"Bad habit," he said. "Something you'll have to grow out of."

"I flare up," I said. "I feel something flare up inside me."

"Eh?" he said. "Feel what?" He laughed again and then, with a sudden grave mannerism that might have been a mockery of himself if I had not noticed that his teeth were gripping hard together, pulling his mouth into a bloodless line, he shook hands.

"Don't know what I should do without you," he said.

His hand was cold. He stood for a long time in the street, holding my hand, gripping it with wiry fingers. He said several times how good it had been to talk and how he felt better because of it. His eyes were uneasy in their bright depression of fatigue under the street gaslamp. He might have been ill except for the constant twisted smile on his mouth and once as he waved his hands in a more exaggerated show of relief and affection for me he staggered and almost fell down.

I wished very often afterwards that he had fallen down. We might then have had a good laugh together. We might have seen the funny side of something that, in the narrowed magnification that youth brought to it, seemed to him only intensely muddled and taut and tragic.

Instead he suddenly turned and looked at me, very curiously, the smile gone from his face, leaving the eyes once again smokily troubled.

"I keep getting a feeling something bloody awful is going to happen," he said.

"Who to?" I said.

"That's it," he said. "I haven't the least idea."

As we walked the rest of the way home he did not speak of it again. He did not speak of Lydia either. But that night I lay awake for a long time looking into the mild winter night sky, very bright with stars over the jetties, the alleyways and the dark roofs of the town, troubled and sleepless, thinking of what he had said to me.

"I keep getting a feeling something bloody awful is going to happen," he had said, and I knew that the worst that could happen to me, then or in the future, was that either the love I felt for him or the love I felt for Lydia, or even both of them, might somehow be taken away.

The following evening, when I went up to the Aspen house, I knew how stupid I had been to think of all this.

"If that's our Mr. Richardson," Miss Bertie called, "bring him in at once. I want to scold him severely."

The voice sailed with dry and starchy assertiveness along the main corridor of the house as I entered with Lydia. Unless we were dancing or I had an invitation to dinner I went up to the house soon after eight o'clock. The Aspens dined at seven; I would join them afterwards for coffee. If it were not raining Lydia came down the long drive to meet me, and that evening she came down with her coat slung sleevelessly over her shoulders. She ran the last twenty yards or so down the slope of the avenue, running into my arms to kiss me, and I said:

"You had dinner with Alex. I know. You didn't tell me."

"He rang up suddenly and asked me," she said. I did not comment on this. "It wasn't anything. Are you jealous?"

"Yes," I said.

"Good — I wondered if you would be."

She laughed softly and then said something about my having to get used to sharing her with people and that the world, after all, wasn't composed simply of ourselves. I suddenly felt oddly uncertain about everything and she seemed to sense it and pulled me against her. "You're so sweet," she said, "and I do love you." Then she drew her mouth warmly across the side of my face. "Let's stand a minute — I want you to hold me."

I stood with my back to a lime tree, holding her against me. As I pulled her to me she put up her arms and her coat, sleevelessly draped about her shoulders, fell off, and I felt all the hollowed shape of her body in its dress, hard and soft, warm and strenuous, pressed against me. The night was profoundly still and quiet and unwintry again, and she said:

"Shall I tell you a wonderful, marvelous, exciting, terrific thing?"

"What?" I said.

"They're going to talk to you about my birthday," she said. "And then next week they're going to London, looking for a present for me. They're going for two days."

"Well?" I said.

"You poor simple — it means we can be in the house alone together — you and I," she said.

A flare of excitement, dispelling all the fear I had, went

[118]

through me fiercely. "It'll be all right. Don't worry. I'll arrange it all," she said.

It was because of this — and there was a wonderful feeling of personal sweetness, lovely and tender and almost naïve, in the way she told it to me — that I put Alex, Blackie and all the vacuous, dreary thoughts I had had about them the previous evening completely behind me.

"Give me one of those long kisses of yours — do you know its a year since I first kissed you, and then I had to make you?" she said. "And then we must go."

I kissed her for a long time and then, on the way up to the house, she stopped and said one more thing:

"What would you say I ought to do for my party?"

"What do you mean?"

"Well, it's *my* party. It's *I* who am twenty-one — it's nobody else — it isn't you or Aunt Bertie or anybody, is it? What do you think?" she said.

I told her I thought she ought to have the kind of party she wanted, and she threw her arms about me, with a sort of whispered shriek of delight.

"Exactly!" she said. "Of course! Oh! I'll love you for ever for saying that. I'll love you all the time they've gone away — "

Up in the house, in the drawing room, Miss Juliana had her neck swathed in flannel and pins and sat in a rather mopey fashion, sucking honey from a teaspoon, before the fire. I thought she cringed a little, putting her hand to her face to touch its tender nerves, as Miss Bertie greeted me with sharp and friendly firmness:

"Come along in, Mr. Richardson, and let me scold you! You promised to come and give your opinion about the ixias, and that was a week ago."

Miss Bertie was always having difficulties with freesias or cyclamen or amaryllis or some other flower of which she felt

I knew the secret; she thought all her gardeners had wool in their heads and wood in their fingers. "They're so awfully hidebound, you see, so fixed," she would say to me, "you would think it was *their* garden, *their* conservatory." It was I who had spoken to her of the delicious many-colored ixias that would make a change, as I told her, from the everlasting bowls of narcissus and daffodils.

"What about the ixias?" I said.

"The ixias do not like us," she said. "They sniff and sulk. They reject us."

"Perhaps the gardeners don't like them," I said.

"Possibly there is something in that."

I began to say something about affection breeding affection, even in plants, when she said:

"Oh! That's altogether too profound for me. It's far more likely someone has been overdosing them with dung-water." She fussed and laughed her way across the drawing room. "Anyway, we shall go and have a look at them. You go on ahead and put on the light for me."

In the delicious night humidity of the conservatory, all heavily and delicately fragrant with hyacinth and narcissus and small cowsliplike primula among ferns, I could not see that the ixias had much wrong with them except perhaps a touch of fly on the thin, gleaming leaves.

"It's a little early for them, perhaps," I said. "They need only the gentlest forcing —" But I could see suddenly that, after all, the flowers were really a secondary thing. She was not really listening. Suddenly she gave one of her henlike fluffings that always preceded some pronouncement of her intentions and said:

"Mr. Richardson, there was really something else I wanted to ask you — do you mind? — What do you feel about Lydia's party? — Say with utmost frankness what you feel."

I made a pretence of thinking for a moment or two about

it; and then I said I thought that, since it was her own party, she ought to have the party she herself wanted.

"You really feel that? Did she say that to you?"

"No," I said.

"It makes no difference if she did. The point is she wants a rather large party — she wants to have dancing on the lawn in the evening for the whole town, and a great many people, and so on. How does that strike you?"

Then I remembered how Lydia had so often said that she was getting bored with dances; and it made me say:

"I think every girl wants to have something wonderful on that day. There's nothing quite so big and exciting for her again — except when she's married — "

She played sadly with the leaf of a narcissus.

"I remember my own twenty-first," she said. "My birthday is on the thirteenth of August and my father thought it was fitting to have grouse, with a claret of '53, I think it was. The grouse was bloody and" — she suddenly looked at me with a kind of melancholy mischief, rather wistfully — "and I'm bound to say the claret was bloody too."

In that moment I felt that I liked Miss Bertie very much.

"After that we were allowed to play bezique," she said. "You never played bezique, I suppose?" She made a sour little face. "With grown-ups?"

I said I had never played bezique. I did not even know what bezique was. But she made it sound like a complaint of the liver; and then she said:

"That's all I wanted to ask you." She smiled, and it was that same curious expansive smile that all the Aspens, even Rollo, sometimes gave, quite enchanting and yet disenchanting too.

"I think we'll give her the party she wants, won't we?" she said.

"It ought to be very lovely in May," I said.

"You never know," she said, "it might be the last nice thing, really nice thing, we could give her" — and with that she turned out the light above the flowers.

When we got back to the drawing room she gave me a glass of port, pouring it out for me herself. Lydia, who also had one, looked very pleased about something and then puzzled for a moment as I lifted my glass and said:

"Well, here's to bezique and no grouse" — a remark that seemed to bring some life back to Juliana, who sat gaping and gray as an old landed fish in her chair. She had been rather croaky and poorly all that winter and the eyelid she turned and, as it were, unpeeled at me, was yellow at the edge.

"What have you two been hatching up besides flowers?" she said.

"I thought you were going to bed," Bertie said to her.

"Not yet," she said.

Afterwards I fancied Lydia had, perhaps, been wearing both of them down about the party, and that Juliana, the weaker, had been the first to crumple up. But now a brightness began to assert itself in Juliana and she actually said:

"I rather think I'll have a glass of port, too."

"Its congestive," Miss Bertie said.

"Then, let it be congestive," Juliana said. "My belly has had nothing inside it all day."

Then Miss Bertie suddenly turned to me and, as if it were the newest possible subject between us, said:

"Mr. Richardson, my sister and I wanted to ask you something" — she looked quite grave and flat-faced — "it was the question of Lydia's party. For her twenty-first — what sort of party do *you* think she ought to have?"

By that time I knew my one-sentence piece so well that I actually hesitated.

"Be quite frank and say what you feel. Speak with the utmost frankness."

[122]

Lydia gulped nervously at her port, and I said:

"I think she ought to have exactly the kind of party she wants to have."

Miss Bertie wagged her jowls — they did not quite form a dewlap, but they had a certain doglike floppiness that made her facial expressions sometimes seem convulsive, giving the impression that she was laughing when she really wasn't — and then said:

"Thank you — that's just exactly what we were thinking too."

Lydia gave a shriek of joy. She threw her arms round Miss Bertie, calling her the dear pet. Miss Juliana put up pretty, ill, protective fingers, murmuring nervous warnings about things being catching, and then let Lydia kiss her on the hair.

"Oh! I could kiss you all," Lydia said, and then looked swiftly about her and said to me — "You too — "

And suddenly she did kiss me, lightly, with a shy, sisterly sort of art.

"Well!" Miss Bertie said. She began to jog up and down like the bonnet of an old motor car, laughing. Then Miss Juliana gave a croaked, congested giggle, and Miss Bertie said:

"What about *us?*"

I then kissed Miss Bertie's dog-like, semi-dewlapped mouth, feeling the crisp brush of her moustache as we blundered together. Then I made for Miss Juliana, who croaked: "Not me! You'll catch your death!" and Lydia said:

"Oh! Aunt Juley, let him. He kisses beautifully" — and Miss Bertie said:

"Oh! so it *wasn't* the first time!" — and we all laughed with great relief and gaiety together.

These twitterings, so trivial and timid, seem stupid now; perhaps the sisters were not, after all, as obtuse as they sometimes seemed; perhaps in their old-fashioned diffidence they had their own way of doing things. At any rate, we began to discuss the party Lydia wanted. The air was clear at last.

She knew, as I discovered later, perfectly well what she wanted. But that night she spoke of first one thing, and then another, as if they were surprise packets, quite unexpected.

"Oh, yes! And then the band on the terrace, and everyone dancing on the front lawn."

There was first of all, it seemed, to be a reception in the house for invited guests. "And champagne!" she said. "We must have champagne — I liked it so much at the New Year's party. It always reminds me of that."

Then the grounds would be open — they had not been open since the Coronation of George V, a date I often remembered because it was for many years the one and only time I had ever seen the Aspen house, except that I had not even the vaguest recollection of strings of fairy-lights seen from the wicker hood of the family pram — and then the town would come in for dancing, which Lydia would start at nine o'clock, I hoped with me of course, although as a matter of fact she did not do so.

At ten the invited guests would have supper in the house — we did not work out all these details that first evening: Lydia let many of them fall out like casual afterthoughts, sometimes weeks afterwards — and there would be large, cold buffets, with perhaps a speech or two.

"And *all* the town must come," Lydia said. "Everybody. We want everybody. We must put it in the papers."

"That means your horrid Mr. Bretherton," Miss Juliana said.

"Oh! He'll get drunk," I said.

"I think *I* shall get drunk," Lydia said.

"Lydia!" they said.

"Well, Rollo will," she said, "if nobody else does — and

[124]

probably Alex will, if somebody teases him enough — won't he?" she said to me.

"I shouldn't tease Alex," I said.

"I think it's such fun to see the look on his face," she said.

"Don't tease him," I said.

"No?" she said. "All right — then I'll be serious with him — how does that suit you?"

There was just one more thing she wanted. She thought of the old people. Many old people, she thought, would not be able to come unless they were fetched in cars.

"Knight could fetch some of them in the Daimler, and Mr. Johnson" — she did not once mention Blackie — "could fetch some in his car."

The Aspen sisters thought it a nice idea; it touched them, in these days when the young, as they often said, were getting indifferent and disrespectful and even callous about their elders, to think that she had been thoughtful enough to remember them.

Then Miss Bertie said — and I thought it seemed to point so conclusively to the end of the proceedings that I got up, at last, to go — "All we need is a fine day."

"It should be lovely," I said. "Maytime — nearly the end of May — nearly June."

"Maytime — the springtime, the only pretty ringtime," she said, and her floppy face became alight with the most touching pleasure. "I think it will be wonderful — I'm sure it will."

Lydia came to the front door to say good night to me, and we stood for a few moments on the dark porch outside.

"Clever man," she said.

I did not think I had been very clever about anything, and I did not know when or how.

"Clever," she said. "You've got those bright blue eyes and they see right through people, don't they?"

I was not, as a matter of fact, ever more obtuse in my life. But it warmed and pleased me to hear her say these things, and especially:

"I like the others — Alex and Tom and all of them, but you're the one with character. You're the deep one, aren't you?" She said these last words in a whisper; and then also in a whisper: "Good night, darling. I'll love you every minute — and next week every second." And with wonderful tenderness she kissed me good night in the dark winter air.

On the way down through the park, in the avenue, I met Rollo. He began shouting:

"Here! Who the devil is that? Who the blazes are you — ?" And then he saw me. "O! Hullo, Richardson. So plum awful dark I couldn't see. I thought it was some damn poacher. We've had a hell of a lot of it this winter."

"Knight was telling me."

"They're getting confounded cheeky with it, too. Plum awful. Bloody soon we'll have to have chains on the pheasants."

"Knight was telling me they came one night in a van."

"It's true," he said. "Gang of damn shoemaking chaps, factory blokes. Can't leave a thing alone that isn't theirs. Damn Bolshies — everybody nowadays is a damn Bolshie."

"This has always been a poaching town," I said. "Back to the old days — "

"I don't know what it used to be like," he said, "but it's plum awful now." Streaks of whiskied breath went past me on the mild air. He straightened his flattish, broad-checked cap, swinging his short Malacca cane at the dark. "You know what I'm beginning to think?"

I waited to hear.

"I think the whole bloody show is going to pieces," he said. "That's what. There soon won't be any people left like us."

IV

IT did not really occur to me until long afterwards that Alex might have been in love with her; I did not properly grasp that his anger at Blackie, his drunkenness or his moods were all part of his complexity about denying it to himself, to me and, because of me, to Lydia herself. Even after the dance at Milton Posnett I was so completely obsessed by fondness for him that I could not even begin to see these things.

The dance at Milton Posnett was the last before Lent that year. I had hoped, once or twice, that Lydia had forgotten about it, but sooner or later she always brought it up again. But I had learned, at least, one thing: that it was stupid with her, as with children, to say Don't or No or Must you? It was better to give way to her, sooner rather than later, on the assumption that very soon she would forget what it was you had had to give away.

Milton Posnett turned out to be a scrubby riverside village in Huntingdonshire, low on the edge of fens. High rows of black elms grew on either side of the yellow stucco schoolhouse, where the dance was. All of us were strangers there — except, as it turned out, Blackie — and when we went into the low schoolroom, still hung with its scarlet and white and green and gold festoons and even a little dusty tinsel from Christmas, I thought there was a sort of glazed hostility, blank rather than in any way aggressive, in the eyes of the big-boned country boys who were hauling their girls about the dusty floor. A four-piece band of men in red top hats was playing a slow, lugubrious foxtrot, and there was a stumping of village feet that was like a barracks-room parade.

Alex took one morose look at all this. He had occasional fits of depression that coincided with attacks of catarrh, so that a kind of despondent ferocity developed in him, and then he said:

"I'm going to get a drink. I've got to have a drink before I can face *that*." He was breathing heavily.

The girls were changing their shoes and brushing their hair in what I imagined was the infants' cloakroom; there was a smell of dust and face powder and sweat and, oddly enough, of spilt ink-bottles everywhere; and in a sudden fit of depression I followed Alex into the street under the elms outside.

"I can't think whatever possessed us to come here," I said.

"Can't you?" he said. The catarrh had already brought an unlovable, bellicose look of resentful pain to his eyes. "Blackie comes from here — that's why."

I think I was mystified by that, but not troubled. Then Alex said:

"Come on — we're going to have a couple of blinders before the pubs close. My head thumps like a press."

"You go," I said. "I think I'll go back — I'll come along later."

"All right," he said. "I'll order a few up for you in case they call time."

When I got back to the schoolroom Lydia was dancing with Tom, and Nancy was waiting for me. Mrs. Sanderson had not come with us that night. Alex had decided that village hops in schoolrooms had nothing to offer her smart and dignified elegance. He had brought as his partner a girl named Nora Jepson, a thin, smooth-haired, serpentine girl whose dancing had about it a shining felicity that was thrilling and uncanny. It was my impression that Nora never wore anything but shoes and stockings and a georgette dress. Her figure was as lithe and plain as a boy's. She danced with a tense feline beauty that looked voluptuous but that was, in fact, passionately academic. She was one of those people who dance for dancing's sake — which was perhaps, after all, why Alex had brought her, since all evening he did not dance with her once and he must have known she would not care.

The band played in deadly off-rhythms and across the floor village boys clamped about, raising dust, like horses.

"This is pretty awful," I said.

"Oh? I think it's rather nice," Nancy said. "Don't be so uppish. It's just an ordinary Saturday village dance — the sort we always went to before Lydia came. I think it's good for us. We were all getting so far up in the air I thought we were never coming down."

I clenched her about the corsets and swung her across the floor, impotent with annoyance, and she said:

"Lydia's waving to you and you're not looking. Wave."

Turning, I saw Lydia.

"Don't gape," Nancy said. "We've all gaped — try to be different, do."

Lydia was wearing a long silk dress of black and scarlet that reached down to the floor. It was low in the bodice and had no sleeves. A broad black band at the waistline pulled across her body perfectly smooth and flat, giving the impression that she was wearing only a scarlet skirt and a scarlet blouse, leaving the middle of her body a stretch of bare, black skin. I had never seen this dress before; she seemed to have chosen it a fraction, perhaps a size, too small for her. For some reason — perhaps because the bodice was so low and her bare shoulders so high and arched — it gave the impression that she was taller than she was. It seemed to make her stand out, tall and aristocratic and rather dashing, above all the others in the room.

She waved the tips of her fingers at me above Tom's shoulder, and I waved in reply.

"Well, what do you think of it?" Nancy said.

"I think it's wonderful."

"You would."

"It's the nicest thing she's ever had on," I said. "It suits her."

"She brought it to show off," Nancy said. "Really, you men are all alike. You never even begin to see why women do things, do you?"

"That's because they try to blind us with the things they do," I said.

She snorted at me. Her pleasant, padded bosom heaved as she took a deep, resentful breath.

"I don't know whether that's clever or not," she said. "I shall have to think it out."

At this moment the dance ended, and Lydia began clapping her hands, twice as loud as anyone else, throwing back her head. When she did so, her black hair fell loosely away, and she clapped her hands above it.

"She makes me feel so small when I look at her," Nancy said. "So terribly small and ordinary. I don't know quite why — "

"That's because you never begin to see why women do things," I said.

She was not very pleased with me for saying that and when I turned to her again, after staring a second or two longer at Lydia, she was making excuses and going away to the cloakroom.

Only a moment later Lydia left Tom and came sweeping and sliding across the half-empty floor to me. When she came I could feel a flicker of wallflower faces, all round the room, that was like the white flutter of the pages of a book.

"Darling!" she said in a loud voice — it was a kind of throaty, half-suppressed scream, and I saw one or two village men gawp as if her entire dress had fallen away — "Where's Nancy? Where's Alex? Where's everybody?"

She laughed and held up her face to me and said: "Come on — let's have this one!" And over my shoulder she called something to the band about playing another tune.

They too were gawping at her. They were not ready to play, but suddenly she clapped her hands again in that extravagant way that made almost a loop above her head, and the band started up. We had been twice round the floor, I think, before it occurred to me that no one else was going to dance that number. She realized it too and threw back her head, laughing. This gesture of hers — it was something new and she was pleased with the neat extravagance of it, as if it had been something she had perfected after a lot of practice — threw the middle of her body forward against me. I was stirred and embarrassed, and I think a little baffled, and as we turned across the empty floor she said:

"Everybody staring?"

"Everybody," I said.

Suddenly I felt nothing but embarrassment. I was cold and contracted with the stupidity of dancing out there alone.

"Come on, it's awful, let's cut it," I said. "Lydia, let's get off the floor — "

"Oh! Don't be so conventional" — she bit her lips. She seemed to want a stronger word, and abruptly it came — "Don't be so plebeian — "

"I'm not," I said. "And anyway, it's the wrong word."

"Oh! Words, words, words, you and your words," she said. "Don't you ever feel? — feelings, feelings — don't you ever have feelings?"

I think, in that moment, I realized two things about her. The first was that she was growing not exactly tired but impatient of me. The second I did not really grasp for a long time, although the beginnings of it were there as she turned and snapped at me about my feelings or the feelings she suspected I never had. It was the idea that she was one of those people who, as they rush into maturity, really think less and less and less. Thought is driven out by a growing automatism of instinct and feeling and blood. More and more, half-consciously, blood drives and governs and pushes them along.

But she hardly gave me time for more than a flicker of both these things to cross my mind. She took a swift look round the room and said:

"Is Alex there? Where's Alex?"

Feelings of which she had no kind of suspicion whipped through me as she said that. I felt a mixture of unhappiness and impatience and impotence and a small corrupting bitterness against a friend I loved very much. It was on the tip of my tongue to make one of the swift, lashing remarks that hurt Nancy so much, but I managed to hold it back, and I said:

"Alex's got one of his attacks. He's stuffed with catarrh and he's gone to have a drink or two."

"He mustn't do that," she said. "Go and find him and tell him to come dancing. Tell him to come down on the floor and forget his self-pity."

"Whatever gave you the idea of self-pity?" I said.

"Well, isn't it?" she said. "Everybody knows how sorry men are for themselves if they get half a pinprick or a snoffle. By this time he's full of gin and self-pity."

I tried to think of something to say.

"And if it comes to that, so are you," she said. "I can feel it by that injured look in your eyes" — and I noticed the word "feel" again, and it hurt me more than anything she said.

Finally that long, awful dance came to an end. When we walked off the floor like two entertainers, facing a wallflower square of staring, gawping faces, everybody was dumb and I was miserable and tired.

And then in a second she dispelled it all. She took my arm in the sweetest possible fashion and said quietly:

"Be a dear and fetch Alex. It isn't nice to bring a girl to a dance and then spend all the time drinking. Is it? And you know how Alex is."

"All right," I said.

She puckered her face at me, delightfully; her voice was soft. "And don't be short with me. Don't be angry."

"I'm not angry," I said.

I went away to find Alex. It was exactly as she had said: Alex, glaring and catarrhal and miserable, half blind with the soggy encrustation of his wretched complaint, sat sorrily drinking at the bar. She was also, in a way, right about me. That night there was a good deal of self-pity in both of us, and it did us a little good to exchange it over a drink or two.

"Lydia sent a message," I said. It was not quite true; but I think perhaps I had an idea it would cheer him up. "She wants you to come and dance with her."

"Down the hatch!" Alex said. "Barman, this is Mr. Richardson." The barman said good evening, and Alex said: "Take another one for yourself, barman. Have another. Cheers."

"Not just now, thank you, sir."

"Well, here's looking at you!" Alex said. It was impossible to tell whether he was three-parts drunk or merely fogged by a sort of catarrhal cloud. "What was that about Lydia?"

"She sent a special message for you to come and dance with her."

He knotted one hand painfully across his forehead.

"It'll do you good," I said. "It'll take you out of yourself."

"You danced with her?"

"Yes," I said. "She's wearing a terrific dress. She's got them all stunned down there. She's on top form."

"Blackie there?"

"Oh! For Christ's sake shut up about Blackie," I said. I was very tired of Alex's stubborn notion that Blackie was a kind of evil ghost sent to haunt us all.

"Drink up," I said. "You're keeping Lydia waiting."

I don't know why I kept up the myth that Lydia was waiting. Having started it, I could do nothing else, I suppose, but pretend that it was true. Then, because Alex was stubborn and because I was tired of the complexity of self-pity and catarrh and what I thought was an obsession about Blackie, I even began to magnify it.

"It'll soon be midnight and the damn dance will be over and you'll never have had one dance with her," I said. "She'll be furious. Come on, Alex, let's get back — "

"Let's have another bloody good round," he said. "Eh? Barman!"

"Never mind that," I said. "Lydia wants you. She's waiting."

In this way, at last, I got him out of the bar. I don't think he was drunk. Self-pity and catarrh and talk and gin had stiffened and confused his mood. He was trying to understand something that oppressed him. He blew his nose a lot as we walked down the village street, and once he shook his head violently and said:

"Do you know, old boy, I can hardly hear."

"You don't need to hear," I said. "Girls are there to be looked at."

At the door of the schoolroom I pushed him in towards the streamered lights. "Go and find her," I said, "before it's too late." He stumbled in, vague and half blind. I had to keep it up to the end, and I followed him.

The first thing I saw was that Lydia was dancing with Blackie. I felt a sour, griping sensation in my throat as I

[134]

first saw her, tall, dark and scarlet, head thrown back, waltzing round with him. Then I looked at Alex. His mouth was parted a little as he tried to catch his breath. It gave him the cruelly afflicted, groping look of someone who could neither hear nor see very clearly.

I stood like this through the dance, waiting, watching the two of them through my blurred and growing confusion. I felt sick. In part I hated myself. When the dance ended I saw Alex move a step forward — "they're all alike to me," he had said once, when on some occasion or other I had been too shy to ask a strange girl to dance with me, "mow in, old boy, one's just like another" — and then at that moment Lydia began clapping her hands. It was that same loud, extravagant overhead gesture I had seen her use earlier in the evening. She flaunted rather than clapped her hands, tossing her hair back from her face once or twice with a lovely, haughty sort of flick at the same time.

By the time I looked at Alex again the band had started the same dance a second time. I noticed now that Lydia and Blackie were not really dancing the orthodox steps of the waltz; they were walking it in the slow, sidling fashion that was popular in those days.

By now I could look at neither them nor Alex any more, and I went outside. There were no stars. The air had a rawness as it came in across misty fields from dark, low fenlands. I suppose I walked up and down, under the elms in the schoolyard, for about five minutes, feeling all the time more cold and more stupid, before suddenly I heard a girl scream.

Afterwards, I was never sure if it was Lydia who screamed, but when I got back into the hall Alex was hitting Blackie for the second time. It was exactly the sort of punch you would expect from a man like Alex, part drunk, part miserable, part frenzied. He seemed to strike sightlessly, with both hands. One blow hit Blackie in the mouth, and then Blackie, with an odd twist of surprise on his face, hit Alex. Then Alex rushed in again and fell down. Then as he scrambled up he clutched Blackie wildly about the body. Something about that rush of his must have hurt Blackie, because suddenly he clenched both fists and began beating them down on Alex's head like hammers.

I shouted and rushed across the floor. Two or three girls screamed, running towards the cloakroom. I heard Alex snorting with breathless pain. A table fell over, smashing several glasses. And a girl screamed: "Glass! glass! glass! Mind the glass!" and the leader of the dance band stood up in a chair, yelling. In the center of the floor there was a tangle of men's bodies where Alex and Blackie had fallen down together, with more men fighting on top of them, shouting and tugging to wrench them free.

I got hold of Lydia's arm and pulled her away. She seemed, I think, the calmest person there — not perhaps really calm, but stiffened and transfixed. She seemed as if fascinated by the sheer pointlessness of Alex and Blackie kicking and struggling there on the floor. Tom was there too, and I shouted to him:

"Take Lydia, Tom, and find Nancy and Nora. I'll go back and get Alex."

By the time I got back to the floor Alex and Blackie had been separated. It was all over. There was a great deal of glaring and dusting of trousers, and Alex was quivering terribly all over as he gasped for his catarrh-choked breath. He shouted some pointless remark at Blackie, who shouted another back, but at that same moment the dance band started up again, very loudly, drowning everything, and I dragged Alex away.

Outside the schoolhouse Lydia and Nancy and Nora Jepson were waiting with Tom. I think I murmured something to Alex about his being an awful damn fool to have hit Blackie, and then I said, "Let's get home — even if you have to drive the car yourself." But he did not answer.

Nor, for some time, did anyone else speak. Nancy was crying a little; Nora Jepson stood with a hurt, wistfully sick look on her face — she went into the sanatorium later and then married a young doctor there after he had finally cured her by patient after-care — and she must have wondered why on earth she had ever been dragged along. I wondered greatly myself; and then I wondered still more as I stood there, confused and panting, and staring at Lydia, whose face was still transfixed with excitement, as if she were enjoying it all.

Someone, at this moment, blundered out of the schoolroom, banging his hands on the thighs of his trousers. It was Blackie; but whether he was aggressive or apologetic or furious or repentant I never had time to discover. Because at the same moment Lydia, with an awful cry, broke down.

"Oh, Tom! Oh, Tom!" she said, and she rushed to him and put her arms about him. "I've had enough of this. Oh, Tom dear — take me home."

And Tom, with that same curious bewildered look on his face as I had seen on it at the ice a year before, took her into his arms without a word.

V

ALEX'S simple cure for the vacuum of Evensford's Sundays was to stay in bed all day. And it was typical of him that on the Sunday following the dance at Milton Posnett he was up by nine o'clock, perhaps for the first time on a Sunday for many years, dressing himself in the tasteful dove-gray suit of narrow herringbone that fitted him so well, with the white-spotted crimson tie, the handkerchief peeping from the breast pocket, and the red-enameled cuff links, a present from his mother, sparkling on the pale-blue shirt-cuffs that revealed themselves just the necessary three eighths of an inch below his sleeves. Alex loved dressing well and he hated getting up; he dressed slowly and meticulously and then infuriated his friends, both male and female, by keeping them waiting. But that morning he was at the Aspen house by ten-fifteen, asking for Lydia, so that he might apologize.

And it was typical of her — in several ways, only one of which I grasped at the time — that she was sweet with him. He had gone to see her in the remorseful, barren mood of a man who had done something unpardonable in drink and could not remember if it were worse than, or only as bad as, he feared. It was characteristic of her that she made him feel that it was neither. I think she was really expecting him. It was what she must have felt would happen; and it was what she really wanted.

It gave her, too, another opportunity of bringing Alex and Blackie together.

"Come on," she said, "if you're going to apologize to me then Blackie is going to apologize to you. It was six of one and half a dozen of the other."

"And so," Alex said to me, "we went to see Blackie."

"What happened?" I said.

"At first he wouldn't apologize." There was something so inherently gentlemanly in Alex that I think he had probably been shocked by that. Men to whom you apologized, even with reluctance, in cold blood, or in bad grace, ought naturally to have the decency to apologize back, even if they still hated you — otherwise they were rotten.

"Not even to her?" I said.

[138]

"The funny thing is I think he was shy," he said.

"A drink was called for," I said.

It was a casual and pointless remark, but Alex said:

"As a matter of fact, we had one. And that was damned interesting. We went over to The Prince Albert at twelve o'clock."

"And you put your hand deep in your pocket and all was well — "

"No," he said. "No. Not quite like that."

A curious, puzzled seriousness had begun creeping into his voice. He began to ruckle the veins of his brows. "As a matter of fact, I felt damn sorry for him — you know, that *isn't* his mother. He lost her — Old Johnson married again."

I said I couldn't see what that had to do with Alex, Blackie, Lydia or myself; and he said:

"Old Johnson's dying — pneumonia and complication with the arm — did you know?"

The thought of Old Johnson dying shocked me. I could not speak; and Alex, in his bemused, serious way, went on:

"Blackie says the second wife has gradually been milking the old man of all he's got — there'll be nothing left for him. He'll probably have to wind the business up. He's been trying to get the old man to reorganize it on modern lines for years, but the old man couldn't see it. And now there'll be damn little left to organize."

"It's wonderful what a drink will do," I said.

"Well, we did have several," Alex said. "Lydia insisted on buying several."

He paused again, looking troubled, and then said:

"You know, I don't know that Blackie is quite such a bad egg. I think we misjudged the bloke. He looks miserable and difficult, but I think he's really worried to death. After all, it's a bit too much to see what's really yours being taken away from you."

"How many drinks did you have?" I said.

"You know," he said, "I think you'll grow up to be a damn cynic or something perishing awful like that. I'm only trying to see it from Blackie's point of view."

"I suppose so," I said.

"You see, the bloke *has* got the right ideas. The horse-and-wagonette age *is* over. The future *is* with cars and motor-bikes and road transport. Nobody can deny that."

I was not very interested in cars, but I did not deny it.

'You know," Alex said, "I wouldn't mind that garage business — as a sort of spec. There's money there. It needs three or four thousand putting into it, and then in a few years — main road and everything, more and more cars."

"Is that Blackie's idea?"

"Oh, no — Oh! God, no," Alex said. "That's what I think. After all, there are only two other garages in Evensford and one of those is kept by that shyster Pratt — after all, Evensford is growing, and in a year or two — "

Alex, behind the well-dressed and casual and sometimes catarrhal air of someone who was a little elegant for a small town and not very strong, was really very shrewd. At seventeen he had been given by his father a single-storied warehouse and fifty bundles of fivepence-a-foot goatskin and *glacé* kid and a few feet of orange and crimson calf that no one would buy. In five years he had built himself a prosperous and expanding little business as a factor, employing a dozen people and a series of attractive office girls who all left him, in turn, because of broken hearts.

Just then, as I now remember it, I suddenly thought of Lydia's attitude to all this.

"Wasn't she bored?" I said.

"Oh, no. On the contrary," Alex said. "Not a bit. She was fascinated. We talked about it the whole way home."

I seem to remember saying something about being glad

that the whole affair had ended so amicably. Perhaps I had misjudged Blackie; I did not know till afterwards. Perhaps he was, as Alex said, really a terribly self-conscious person, very shy. I was not interested. Neither cars nor business, leather nor money excited me very much. While other people slaved over stitching machines or clicking boards or tanning vats I preferred, for reasons that baffled most of them except Alex and Tom and Nancy and, I suppose, Lydia, to roam the Aspen park or the fields beyond Busketts and attach what now seems perhaps an overserious importance, but that was then an exultant and beautiful and precious one, to things like the arrival of the first primrose. I was apt to go off into dreams about these things and I was probably dreaming when Alex said:

"I think she's sorry for him. I think she probably twigged instinctively about things being a bit rough for him long before I did. Women do that, don't they? They think in another way."

"They don't think. They feel," I said.

"Do they? I suppose they do," Alex said. "Anyway, one thing's certain. The set isn't going to break up. I would have felt a damn stinker if it had broken up because of what I'd done."

"It was my fault," I said.

"Don't start that," he said. "It's all over now."

"Except," I said, "that Blackie didn't apologize."

"He was shy. He was tongue-tied. And anyway, Lydia did for him," he said. There was a sudden renewal of excitement about her in his face as he said this, "And that makes it even as far as I'm concerned."

So, in this way — it was almost springtime now and already on evenings of pale green twilight there was a brittle-sweet heartbreaking singing of thrushes that carried on into darkness — we kept together until Lydia's birthday in the last week of May. But before the birthday — it was perhaps a week before, because I remember there had been some controversy about the cutting of the horse chestnuts in the churchyard and how in the end they were not cut that year but were specially exquisite and rich in the warm May weather — a curious and unexpected thing happened.

It did not cause anything, and I do not think it had any effect on any of us except myself. It seemed to be purely an incidental thing and I did not speak of it. But it was, even so, the last thing in the world I should have thought of happening, and it helped me to see things as I should not have seen them otherwise.

In the first week of May that year we moved into another house; we left the thundering presses of the factory terrace and went to live in a pleasant square-bayed villa with a garden of apples and raspberries at the side. It seemed an extraordinarily large and opulent affair after the neighborhood of Joe Pendleton, the tarred back fences and the pigeons. I was glad, because it seemed to indicate that we were rising in the world; I was glad, too, because I was able to take a week off for the flitting and then spend the last part of it walking about the countryside.

I was coming home one afternoon from behind Busketts — a gated footpath ran between cow-rubbed hedges of hawthorn and then dipped across fields and finally broke out into the Evensford Corporation rubbish dump and became a cinder-track winding through gas-tarred back yards — when I heard Nancy's voice calling me from the plum orchard that lay partly up the hill behind the farm.

"I've got something to ask you," she called.

She was wearing a white summer dress, probably her first that year, because I could see how neatly and sharply the ironing creases showed on the sleeves above her elbows, and when I went over to her she said:

"Stranger again. Where do you get to all the time?"

Perhaps the thing that slightly irritated me about Nancy, more than anything else, was this rather tart passion for asking questions to which she perfectly well knew the answer.

"Anyway, I'm awfully glad to have seen you, because Tom wants to know what you're going to wear for the party. The great birthday."

"It hadn't occurred to me."

"You need somebody to look after you," she said. "You just can't turn up in anything."

"I don't propose to," I said. "I shall wear whatever Tom and Alex wear."

"Yes," she said, "and that's exactly what Tom wants to know. What *shall* he wear?"

I was glad when she ended this rather pointless conversation by asking me in to tea.

"How many lumps? I always forget. And do cut the curd-tart yourself. Cut it. Take a good piece for yourself — take a real man's piece," she said.

We sat on one of the window seats, in the long room that faced the garden, to have tea. The window seats were painted white. Above them the casement windows were open, so that when she sat by one of them, leaning her head back in the corner, there were small stirrings of breeze in her blonde, light-textured hair. She looked very attractive that day, in something the way a brushed and soft-eyed domestic animal looks attractive, in rather the way a light-haired dog lies on a carpet, wanting to be stroked.

We talked of the beautiful weather.

"More tea? More to eat?" I think I had four cups of tea; I had been out since morning, walking, with nothing but sandwiches, and I was hungry and thirsty. "I've had my bedroom done up — they've made a wonderful job of it. It's plain white, with crimson — but when you've finished tea I'm going to take you up and you can see it yourself."

We fluttered like this through tea, and then after tea — the unexpected incident of which I have spoken had nothing to do with Nancy; it was simply Nancy who was the cause of it — we went upstairs. Her room was composed of two attics thrown together on the south side of the house. Two casement windows looked across the Busketts' fields, all green that day with rising corn and glittering yellow with buttercup and knotted with ropelike hedges of hawthorn, and she sat on the window seat of one of them and said:

"You can see Souldrop Church from here. And the ventilators in the tunnel at Long Lays."

She sat there looking sideways. Her pale, golden neck arched itself and turned, tender and fleshy in the May sunshine. Her room was pure white and fresh, with curtains on which were loose designs of scarlet peony. I could smell strong new paint in the air. She said, "Come and sit beside me," patting the white-and-scarlet cushions on the window seat. "You're so far away — " And finally I went and sat beside her, staring, too, across the fields.

"It's the nicest view in the world," she said. "I love it — every springtime I love it more."

I loved it very much too: not simply for what it was but because this, I knew, was the kind of land that Evensford had taken away from us. It had taken the pattern of white hawthorn, the gold and the white, the dark steely brown of ploughed earth and the green of corn, and had left us ash heaps. In place of primrose spinneys of nightingales we had been given back yards of gas-tarred fencing and croaking hens. For these reasons alone, what we looked at that day, across the Busketts' fields, in the May sunlight, was trebly precious to both of us, and presently she said:

"There's a nightingale down in the spinney there — he's singing all day long now. You can hear him now — hark! — you can hear him, there he is — "

She turned her head sharply to listen. The nightingale gave a startling pellucid whistle, thin and piercing and exquisite, down in the oak spinney; and I suddenly leaned across and kissed Nancy on the lips at the very moment the high note flew to its complete pitch across the still afternoon.

It was not a very long kiss; it was pleasant and I did not mean it seriously. She was quiet and she did not move her body to respond. I remember how Alex had once said that the moment you kissed Nancy you began to think of some other girl; and I had hardly touched her lips before I began to think of Lydia.

"Why did you do that?" she said.

At first I did not say anything. If I had been honest I should have told her, simply, perhaps laughingly, that I loved her because, like Tom, she was part of the view.

Instead I touched her face with my mouth and laughed. "It was just the first kiss of summer," I said.

"Why did you do it?" she said.

When I look back I wonder sometimes if what I said in answer, or rather perhaps what I didn't say, was not of more importance than anything else that ever happened between us. I said simply:

"Because I like you. You know that."

There are girls who would have shrieked at that, or perhaps, in fury, have slapped me across the face. Nancy did not do anything but stare down at her hands.

I stared too for some moments at the fine golden hairs of her arms glinting in the sunshine and then I said:

"How's Tom? I haven't seen the old — "

"He's all right," she said.

"What about the exam?" I said. "Did he ever take it?"

"He takes it in July," she said. "He gets worried about it and thinks he'll never pass."

"He'll pass," I said, and then she glanced down at the oak-spinney again and said:

"I wake in the night and listen to that nightingale. And then I start thinking and I can't get to sleep again."

So much depends on the course of small conversations that, at the time, do not seem to mean very much, and I did not ask her why she could not sleep and what kept her thinking so much as she listened to the nightingale.

"I ought to be going," I said.

"If you must go I'll walk as far as the stile with you," she said. "It's so beautiful out-of-doors."

We walked down from the farm through fields of buttercup and rising moon daisy, in a strong, golden May light, through air clotted with the scent of great hawthorns.

At the road, just before I turned to say good-by, I saw the empty shell of a thrush egg, about the size of a blue-enameled thimble, lying in the grass. I picked it up and held it in the palm of my hand and said:

"It's wonderful how strong they are. There's a theory that if you drop one from fifty feet on to grass it won't break — "

"It's because it's so light," she said.

"I suppose so," I said.

"Sometimes the most fragile things don't break," she said. She bent down to the ditch and picked a cowslip and twisted it in her fingers.

I tossed the eggshell away and as it fell into pillowy sprays of hawthorn, hanging there like a speckled blue petal, she said:

"How's Lydia? I forgot to ask you."

"She's very well," I said.

"She sent me a sweet letter about the birthday party. She's getting very excited. Apparently everybody is coming — "

"Everybody," I said. "As far as I can gather. Well, I must go — "

"So must I," she said. "Good-by." And I smiled at her brown, clear-eyed face and said good-by. And then, at the very last moment, as if she did not want me to go, she stopped and threaded the cowslip into my buttonhole.

Those insignificant little things — the tea, the conversation on the window sill, the thrush's egg held for a second or two in my hand and then tossed away, the cowslip threaded into my buttonhole — cannot possibly seem of very great importance, even together. But they were responsible, really, for what happened a few minutes later. Together they delayed me just long enough to make it possible. Without them it could not have happened.

It takes about half an hour to walk from the last gate at Busketts to the center of the town; and I had been walking, I suppose, about twenty minutes when a car slowed up alongside the curb. If I had walked on the other side of the street I should have been on the high causeway, eight feet up, and no driver would have bothered. But now a gray-haired man of about sixty, with a strong Northern accent, leaned out of the driver's window and said:

"Excuse me — would you mind telling me is this the town with the church that has the Strainer arch?"

"This is the town," I said.

"Thank you very much," he said. "Is it far to the church?"

"Not far," I said. I began pointing ahead, giving directions. "About half a mile." And then he said:

"It's warm, isn't it? Hop in — if you're going that way, I'll be glad to drop you."

He flicked the door of the car open and I got in, and inside three minutes — in those three minutes he managed to do all the talking, told me his name, which I forget, his business, which I rather fancy was in wool, and how keen he was on church architecture and brass-rubbings and that sort of thing—we were at the church. It is a wonderfully fine church at Evensford. A great spire of soft gray limestone with corner embellishments of chocolate-red ironstone rises up for two hundred and seventy feet from a churchyard of black yews and horse chestnuts and an apostolic row of twelve pollard elms.

At the church steps I got out of the car. I thanked him for bringing me down. "Not at all," he said, "thank you." Then I told him that if he could not get in at the main west door of the church he would probably find the small south one unlocked. He got out of the car, too. I walked up the western steps with him towards the churchyard. The horse chestnuts were all in heavy blossom, littering the steps with fallen pink-white petals. I remember him remarking that it was like a wedding. "That's a wonderful spire," he said. He stood for a moment or two longer looking up at it in admiration, before at last he lifted his hand and thanked me again and went away.

I felt rather proud of Evensford church at that moment; and I suppose I must have stood there, staring up at the gray-and-chocolate pattern of the great spire, for two or three minutes longer, before suddenly, on the south side of the church — there used to be a fine white acacia there, but they have cut it down now for the reason that they always cut things down in Evensford, that is, no reason at all — I saw Lydia come out of the south door and walk round towards the eastern end.

She was wearing something I had not seen before. It was a light-gray costume with black velvet revers. I hurried up the steps and went after her.

"Lydia!" I called. By the time I got round to the south side of the church she was just going round by the last corner buttress on the eastern end. "Lydia!" I called after her. "Lydia — "

She seemed to hesitate for a second before going round the corner. But it was not until I got round the corner, running to catch her up, that she stopped and waited for me.

"Lydia — " And then I stopped too.

For what seemed to me about five minutes I stood painfully staring at the woman in the gray suit with the black velvet revers. She was wearing large clip-on earrings of pearl. In one gray-gloved hand she was carrying a large black *glacé* hand-bag, and her hat, which she had taken off, in the other. I must have looked incredibly, idiotically startled.

Then she smiled. It was not quite the way Lydia smiled, abruptly, with wonderful, beautifying expansiveness, but it was very pleasant and very friendly.

"I'm afraid you've made a mistake," she said.

"I'm terribly sorry — I'm most terribly sorry," I began to say.

Then she smiled again, more generous and more amused this time.

"I'm Lydia's mother," she said.

I have no idea how long I stood there, under the church wall, staring and trying to think of something to say. But presently she laughed.

"Don't look so alarmed," she said. "I'm not a ghost. I haven't come to haunt anybody."

I still could not think of anything to say. The only possible thing, it seemed to me, was to apologize, and I began at last to say, "I'm terribly sorry, Mrs. Aspen," but she cut me short.

"I'll tell you what I am, though," she said. "I'm thirsty. If you want to apologize really nicely, you can take me and get me a drink somewhere."

There was just time to walk down to The Prince Albert before the bar opened at six o'clock. Heat lay thickly along the south-sloping back streets and when we went into the lounge, all fern and palm and molting deer heads and carved barometers and pier glasses, she gave a big sigh and took off the jacket of her costume and laid it across the back of her chair.

It was then that I saw how much like Lydia she really was. Her eyes seemed to me just as brilliant and intensely pellucid in their dark reflections. Only her mouth was different. It had crept, as it were, inwards, tightening until it was really too small and too narrow a bud for the rest of her expansive, powdered face.

When the waiter came and I asked her what she would like, she said:

"Personally, if it's all the same to you, I'm going to have a very large whisky and soda." She looked up at the waiter and smiled, and he in turn looked down at her and smiled too. "And when I say very large I mean very large," she said, "don't I?"

"Yes, madam," he said.

"I was in here to lunch," she said, in a voice loud enough for him to hear as he went out of the door. "He knows me now."

When the waiter came back with her glass she looked at it and then at him and said: "That's more like it. That's better" — and held three of her fingers against the side.

"So you know Lydia," she said.

"Yes," I said.

"Tell me about her."

I think I repeated four or five conventional statements of the kind that people always do; and then she smiled.

"Is she good-looking?" she said. "Very pretty?"

"She's very handsome," I said.

"Just how I was," she said. "I was a terribly gawky thing until I was nineteen and then suddenly" — she did a queer little wriggle with her hands — "in and out in all the correct places."

Perhaps I was staring at her merely in the hope of being able to think of something to say; perhaps I was sliding off into one of my daydreams, thinking of Lydia; but suddenly she said:

"You've got the most unbelievably blue eyes, haven't you?"

"So they tell me."

"Awfully bright and awfully penetrating."

"That's what Lydia says."

"Are you fond of her?" she said. I said yes, as simply as I could.

"Oh! That's nice." She laid her left hand with gentle impulsiveness on one of mine. "Oh! That's awfully sweet. I think that's wonderful. I think we have to have a drink on that, don't we?"

So we drank to that, at first with one drink and then a second; and then, although we had no fresh excuse, we had a third, for which she paid with a note from her large black handbag, afterwards holding up the bag against the light so that she could see her face in the mirror inside.

"What does my face look like to you? Ghastly?"

She evidently did not expect an answer, and I did not give one. She patted her face about with a powder puff and bared her teeth, shaping her lips again with lipstick that spread on the teeth small carmine stains.

"Tell me," she said, "about the family."

I repeated, as flatly as I could, a few conventional things about the family.

"What about that bastard Rollo?"

"Well — " I said.

"Perhaps that was an unfortunate word," she said. She gave a last suck at her finished lips. "Eh? Unfortunate?"

I said that perhaps it was.

"You do agree with people so, don't you?" she said. "Do you always agree with people like that? Do you agree with Lydia?"

"Mostly," I said.

"That's probably because she's indulgent and generous to you," she said. "I'm sure if she's anything like me she has a generous nature."

"The path of wisdom is supposed to be the path of excess," I said. It was a phrase Alex and I sometimes bandied about, thinking it profound.

"Oh! Steady on," she said. "I can't cope with that stuff. I'm a whisky-and-soda girl. Not champagne. Lower the standard a bit — give a girl a chance."

Laughing, she choked a little over her whisky. "I believe you're a bit of a character with those eyes of yours, aren't you?" she said.

"I should find it hard to be a character with anybody else's," I said, and that phrase too seemed to amuse her very much. She rocked from side to side with uneasy laughter, spilling part of her whisky down the front of her blouse.

"A drink certainly does liven *you* up, doesn't it?" she said. "Always does the opposite to me. I get all blank and cozy and warm — just like a warming pan ready for the bed." I thought this rather a good phrase and I smiled. "What are you smiling at?" she said. "I suppose you wonder why I'm here?"

I did wonder.

"A little business with the family solicitor," she said, "that's all. Once a year. Papers to sign — and that sort of thing. I don't always come down."

She stopped speaking and took a long drink of whisky, staring down at last into the glass. The whisky seemed to flow back almost at once in a fresh spate of words that were, to me, surprisingly touching because they were not bitter:

"You called me Mrs. Aspen up there, and it quite shocked

[152   ]

me. First time for years. I always go by my maiden name since we were separated. I've never been part of the family, because I really never married into it. I suppose there was too much difference in our ages — Elliot and me — anyway, it was one of those things, and there you are."

I am easily sorry for people, and there may, perhaps, have been some sort of preoccupied expression of pity on my face to show that I was touched by what I had heard, because she said:

"You're terribly sympathetic. I talk too much, don't I?"

"No," I said.

"That means I do," she said, "but I don't care. I saw all about the birthday in one of the papers. I hope she'll have a nice birthday. I hope it'll be nice. Will you be there?"

I told her everybody would be there.

"All except me," she said. "I shan't be there. But you might think of me if you can spare a moment, will you?"

I promised to think of her. All this time, as she grew warmer, drowsier and more unthinking, more and more like some cozy, inanimate object or, as she said herself, like a warming pan ready for the bed. I caught inflections of her voice that, deep and throaty and disturbing, were so like Lydia's that if it had been dark I felt I might have reached out and touched her hands.

"Well, I must push off," she said. "What time would there be a train?"

I looked at the mantel clock and said: "The next is at seven-thirteen. You've got eighteen minutes."

"Does that connect?"

"Where for?" I said.

"London."

"Yes," I said, "they all connect for London. Sooner or later."

She laughed. "Just got time to have another," she said.

[153]

Then, not laughing, but rather wearily looking at me from eyes that had begun to puff a little underneath with red-striped, snail-like bags, "One-eyed hole, isn't it?"

I supposed she meant the town, and I said yes, it was a one-eyed hole.

"What sort of life does the girl lead?" she said. "Wrapped up? Cotton-wool — you know?"

"No. They like her to be free," I said. "They've been very good about that. They didn't want her to grow up like — "

"Like me," she said. "That's what they didn't want her to grow up like."

In this moment much of what had been sometimes a little confused about that winter evening at the Aspen house, when I had first met Lydia, became more clear. There had been, that night, among all the flusterings over onion soup and port and the talk of skating, more than a little fear.

Ten minutes later I took her to the station. We had two or three minutes to wait on the platform, and I thought, as she stood first on one foot and then on another, that she seemed uneasy and worried and more than a little tired. Even when she stopped moving from one foot to another she wavered a little and could not stand quite still. Then suddenly she put her hand on one of mine, as she had done in the hotel, and said:

"You won't say anything about this? I don't want anything said about this."

"No," I said.

"Now, no monkey business," she said. She turned on me a pair of eyes that were quite fierce in their black determination. "I mean what I say. When I say I don't want anything, I mean I don't want anything." That too was exactly like Lydia. "Keep it to yourself," she said. "See? I know what towns like this are."

I knew too; and I squeezed her hand.

[154]

"You're rather a dear. You're rather sweet," she said, and I was flattered.

At that moment the train came in. There was a good deal of shouting and banging, with a big blast of steam as the engine came under the bridge, and at this moment she chose to say:

"You know, I think I could rather — "

What it was she was going to say I never knew. Steam and banging doors and porters' barrows drowned the rest of her words. A moment or two later I had opened a door for her and she was standing inside the carriage, leaning out of the window, to say good-by.

"Nice to meet you," she said. "God bless."

She started to take off her gloves. Then she took off her hat and threw it onto the rack, revealing a mass of hair as dark as Lydia's. The hat fell off the rack and her eyes bulged, I thought for a moment with possible tears, as she picked it up and said:

"There goes my Sunday best. Never have another."

I hoped she would not cry; and, to my great relief, she did not cry. She put a hand in one of mine instead. "It's been, well — you know — " She brushed her other hand once or twice through her hair — "Well, you know — rather nice. God bless," and then the train began to move away.

"Good-by," I said.

"Good-by," she said. "Good-by — "

At the last moment she laughed weakly, with trembling mouth. Her gray glove blew a final waving kiss at me.

I never saw her again; but I was glad that I had seen her, because later, indirectly, in a way I did not grasp to its fullness at the time, the sight of that drowsy, uneasy, tearless face helped to enlarge my understanding.

VI

THERE was a moment on the evening of Lydia's birthday, about nine o'clock, on the steps of the terrace, when I thought she was going to lead off the dance with me, in front of what seemed to be the whole of Evensford waiting on the lawns below. To my relief she led off with Rollo instead.

It was like summer that evening; the air was beautifully soft and mild. Under the light of the house and the terrace, where festoons of colored lamps were burning, the faces of people glowed like flowers against a dark background of full-leafed trees broken by chestnuts still in full blossom and laburnums that had already spilled into lemon tassels of flower. I think someone that day, or perhaps the previous day, had cut an early field of clover just beyond the outskirts of the park. All evening the fragrance of it hung over us, still and delicate, as we danced on the lawns. There was a great scent of lilac too, and gradually, as the evening went on, the smell of crushed grass bruised under the feet of dancers. As this smell of bruised grass grew thicker and thicker I felt more and more excited.

Earlier in the day, as I went up to the house, about an hour before the party began, I met the Aspen doctor walking down the drive. He was a dryish man, with the French-sounding name of Morat, who was really Scotch.

"Is it Miss Juliana again?" I said.

He said he was awfully afraid so; and when I asked him what was wrong with her, he said:

"Her heart. The old regulator isn't set quite fast enough."

I said that she always gave the impression of being a woman of terrific vitality.

"Women are deceptive," he said. He looked at me with humorless sagacity. "You think they're this, and you think they're that, and all the time they're the damn t'other."

"Will she be well enough for the party?"

"What party she has she'll have in bed," he said, "and if she doesn't she'll have it in a box."

He walked away; and then, ten yards off, turned and said:

"By the way, Old Johnson died this morning. You knew him, didn't you? Been expecting it — " And I said how sorry I was.

When Miss Juliana came downstairs at precisely six o'clock that evening, dressed in a long silk dress of fuchsia purple, her favorite color, with a large double necklace of deep violet amethysts set in pinchbeck to match, she looked rosy and assertive. She seemed in every way totally unlike a woman whose heart is tired.

"You may take me round the garden," she said — I had arrived early because I wanted to see Lydia before it all began — "Bertie and Lydia are still dressing. Where are your friends? Aren't we supposed to begin at six? What do you think the weather is going to do?"

I had learned, now, the trick of not answering these vitally ejected questions. She took my arm. Slowly we walked into the gardens, where clumps of yellow and purple and coppery-golden iris were in bloom. She herself smelled of violets. A large white marquee with scallopings of scarlet and a scarlet flag had been erected on the far side of the front lawn, between two cedar trees. Lilac was in bloom, pale and dark and pure white, on all sides of us, and she said:

"The sweetest thing happened. The gardener's apprentice boy brought strawberries for Lydia. No one knew of it — he did it all himself. Kept it quite secret. Wasn't that wonderfully sweet? Don't you think so? Don't you think she has nice

[157]

friends? The drawing room is full of presents. Quite wonderful ones."

She gave me no time to answer; I got no further than "Yes" before she went on:

"That's greatly because of you, isn't it? It's been simply wonderful the way she's grown up. Don't you think so?"

We were now at the far end of the paved garden, where the roses began. A sour convulsion leapt up through my throat, leaving me for more than a minute in speechless constriction; but at last I said:

"Miss Aspen, there was something I wanted to ask you."

"Yes, yes," she said, "ask on. I don't see buds on the roses there, do I? Do I see buds? — she almost let go my hand, peering among wine-brown rose leaves, almost sizzling her words through her large protuberant teeth — "Yes, buds on them! — look! — and would you believe it, already *greenfly* — !"

"Miss Aspen," I said, "I wanted to ask if I might marry Lydia."

She did not seem to be listening. She turned on me a face so remarkably flattened by indifference that it was more stupefying to me than any anger could have been.

"My dear boy, I thought you'd already asked her."

"Oh, no. I wanted — "

"Then why on earth did she come and talk to me for an hour last night with mountains of wretched innuendoes?"

I began to feel there was something wrong with my brain. Pulses of bewilderment and excitement rocked my head as she said:

"The child talked and talked and talked. Have you any money?"

I almost said eighteen pounds fifteen, but I told her: "A little. Very little," instead.

"There you are then. That's exactly what I mean. Why else should she come and talk to me in half-riddles about women

[158]

marrying men without money, if it wasn't because of you? When are you going to ask her?"

I was aware of the beginnings of a sort of nebulous delirium at the back of my head.

"You should ask her tonight," she said. "Then we could announce it. Don't you feel that? Isn't that what you'd like? I think we should go straight back and ask Bertie, and then you can ask Lydia, can't you? Don't you feel that? Don't you agree?"

She seemed to be very excited. I do not remember now, at this distance, much of what I felt as we went back through the gardens to the house. It had something of the blind delirium of a race. I only now remember her saying:

"You must speak to Bertie. Now — without delay. Plunge forward" — I remember that precise expression because she said it as she half-stumbled up the steps of the iris garden and it made her give a great, sharp, almost portentous, drawing-in of her breath — "and while you speak to Bertie I will have a word with Lydia myself — "

Then, as we came to within sight of the main terrace, she looked up and said:

"Ah! Arrivals. Isn't that your nice Mr. Holland and his sister? I can't see very well. Isn't that them? Isn't that the town clerk's wife, too? — Mrs. Fitzgerald and her sister — ?"

We went on to the terrace and were immersed, a few moments later, in a pool of friends.

When I look back it is not difficult to see that displays of volcanic and fluttering fire like hers were the product of a mind that was also forgetful. There was, as I see it now, a kind of endearing flippancy about her. All these warm tangents and gravitations of her temperament were the result of sickness; perhaps the heart telegraphed its own nervous pulse warnings to the brain. I know now that if I met her again I should not take her so seriously; the heart may have been tired and I am sure it was warm and true, but it was also untrustworthy, from no fault of its own. Now I should be amused by her only for what she was, a sweet but sick eccentric. But that day I was too young, too excited and too obliviously single-minded to know all this; and I felt that all she said was true.

Partly because of this, perhaps entirely because of it, the first words that Lydia said to me, when we met five minutes later, had no real effect on me:

"Where's Blackie? Have you seen Blackie? He's supposed to be bringing people up —"

"His father died today," I said. "It may be difficult —"

"Difficult? Why should it be difficult? They've got their living to earn just the same, haven't they?"

"Did you get my present?" I said, I had sent her a pair of garnet earrings, set in a three-quarter oval, that were like soft, dark raspberries. In order to do so I had sold my bicycle. I felt the garnets would somehow go well with her high color, her temperament, and her black, thick hair.

"Of course I did," she said. "You're a very darling person and I like them and thank you."

"I hoped you'd wear them."

"Not at the party," she said. "They come unscrewed and get lost and you know how it is —"

A vague delirium was still beating at the back of my head.

"Will you put them on later?" I said. I stood there, feeling my head rock and not knowing quite what I was saying or what impulses were driving me. "Alone somewhere? — for me? Because I want to see them and I want you and I've got something to say to you."

"What a speech," she said.

As I stood staring at her, in what I think could only have been a lost and hungry and desperate sort of fashion, because I wanted her so much, she laughed and said:

"No: I won't put them on."

"No? Why not?" I felt my brain ready to flare up in a final shot of delirious anger. Then she laughed again and bent her head.

"Because you can put them on for me," she said.

I felt wonderfully happy then, and a moment later we were once again immersed in a crowd of friends.

For almost all the rest of that evening — and perhaps I should not have expected otherwise, since the gardens were so crowded and the day was so much her own — it was never possible to be alone with her. All evening an orchestra played for dancing and it was a wonderfully gay, crushed and, in the end, rather noisy party. There is something wonderful about the thin sound of a string orchestra on a summery night in the open air; there is really a sort of starriness about the sound. Now and then somebody would send over to the orchestra, down below the terrace, asking them specially to play something, a waltz or a foxtrot, and once Alex's mother sent across for a minuet of Mozart. All evening there hung over us the warm scent of drying clover, and because of it all I was caught up again, tangled and lost, in the most trembling, bemusing web of happiness.

Some time after supper Alex started to get charmingly, intelligently drunk. An exaggerated and ironic gaiety came over him. And suddenly I heard Lydia saying to him:

"Alex, dear, will you do something for me?"

"No," Alex said. "You have a whole orchestra of second fiddles down there — ask them."

"Alex — please."

"No."

"Alex, you nice person" — she was wearing a long dance frock of pale clematis-mauve silk with small gold spots on it, and now she drew herself up and touched his arm and looked him in the face — "not even if I let you kiss me?"

"No," he said. He bowed with affectionate irony, staggering a little. "I get precisely the same effect, dear lady, from a glass of champagne — "

"All right," she said. It was easy to see that it was all light-hearted and unangered and unimportant. "I'll ask Tom."

"In that case, I hope you'll kiss Tom?" Alex said. "No favoritism."

"I expect I shall," she said. "If Tom can bear the pain."

Tom, I think, was very happy too that night; and presently when Lydia took his arm and they went away together I saw her head close to him as they crossed the terrace, and she was whispering into his ear.

Tom owned an old Morris-Oxford coupé that he shared with Nancy. It always seemed to me that the exhaust was cracked because, from cold, it exploded like a gas engine. Five minutes after Lydia had walked across the terrace with Tom I heard the car start, firing its gunshots down the avenue.

At that moment I was dancing with Nancy, "That's Tom, isn't it?" she said. "Where on earth could Tom be going?"

"He's probably running an errand for Lydia," I said. "I saw her take him off, that's all."

"I think he'd jump in the river if she asked him," she said. I shrugged my shoulders and she turned on me with great scorn. "And don't shrug like that. So would you."

"Let Tom take care of himself," I said, "and let me take care of you."

She said something about my being in rather a bright mood, and then:

"By the way, has Alex's mother spoken to you? It seems there's a wonderful dance on midsummer night at Ashby — she wants us all to go."

And then, very suddenly: "I can't think for the life of me where Tom's got to."

I felt once again that Tom was perfectly capable of taking care of himself. But I did not know until some long time afterwards, until he told me himself, where he had gone to, suddenly, that evening of the party.

Lydia had sent him with a note to Blackie Johnson. A strange driver had turned up with the limousine, bringing relays of elderly people who could not walk. He was simply a man hired for the day. There was no sign of Blackie. It was supremely typical of her to ask Tom to take that note — Alex having refused — and it was equally typical of him that he took it without question.

When he got to Johnson's garage the only light in the place was a naked gas flare hung over the sink in the kitchen. He heard a sound of voices quarreling inside. He stood for a moment or two in the yard before knocking at the door. Then he knocked several times and got no answer. It seemed an odd time for people to be quarreling, he thought, with Johnson dead in the house, and then the voices grew so loud that presently he could pick up the voice of Blackie shouting at his stepmother. It seemed they were quarreling as to where they were going to bury Old Johnson. Then Tom heard Blackie shout, "He'll be with his folks, that's where he'll be. Where *you* can't rob the damn grave" — and then Tom knocked on the door again, more loudly. To his astonishment it was yanked open at once and Blackie Johnson stood there, bare to the waist, his face streaked with shaving soap, and a naked razor in his hand, glaring out into the dark at Tom:

"How much longer are you going to stand there hammering?" he said. "Who is it? — Oh, it's you."

Tom, not saying a word, gave Blackie the note and then stood there, waiting. Lydia had told him expressly to wait for an answer. Behind, in the kitchen, the stepmother began crying, and Blackie, slitting open the envelope with the razor so that a mess of beard-blackened soap smeared itself like lard along the edge, shouted for her to shut up. She went on crying, not exactly crying but whimpering, dryly and stutteringly, Tom said, as if trying to make herself cry. Then Blackie stepped a pace or two back into the kitchen so that he could read the note more easily under the gaslight. The soapy razor, naked, stuck out from the hand that Blackie leaned against the door, and the big chest, a mass of bear-skin-glittering hair from throat to navel waving over a dark-golden pack of muscle, heaved for a moment or two out of sight. Then the woman cried again, annoying Blackie a second time, so that he shouted that if she didn't shut up he'd do something he'd be sorry for. There was a smell of old grease and car oil and burning gas and Tom felt sick. It revolted him to feel that death was in the house and that people were quarreling over the dead; and as he stood there, dumb and shocked in his absolute decency and impotently horrified by it all, I think that probably his ultimate feelings about Lydia began to take shape. A dark, ugly flare of something threw up, in paradoxical relief, the slow, beautiful beginnings of his final emotions about her. It was strange that it needed something exactly like that — something of quite incidental ugliness and revulsion to project, at last, in recognizable clarity, feelings that were to break down, ultimately, all his diffidence and fear.

But I did not deduce any of this until he spoke of it much later, under the pressure of another circumstance. It is quite possible that he was not even partially aware of it himself. All he saw that night was Blackie reading the note under the gaslight, the razor sticking out, the black chest naked and glinting; all he heard was the quarreling, the whimpering, the bawling about under the same roof as the dead, and then, at last, Blackie Johnson crackling Lydia's stiff notepaper like an eggshell in his hand and saying, before he shut the door:

"No answer. Tell her no answer."

He told me afterwards that he stood for some time outside, in the old yard with its wagonettes and landaus and its curious straw-oil odor of two worlds, afraid to go back. He was afraid partly because he felt he saw some terrible menace in the quarreling and the naked razor, partly because of an idea, typical of his utterly simple decency, that he had failed Lydia, even though he loathed what he had seen and what she had asked him to do.

And finally when he did go back it was perhaps lucky that he could not find her. By that time I had found her myself, and was alone with her in a room upstairs.

Many of the spare upstairs rooms in the Aspen house were being used that evening as cloakrooms; but in the room where we went, one story above, it was dark and comparatively quiet, and no one bothered us. There were still, even then, gas fittings in several of the upper rooms, mostly of brass-scrolled mantel-lights with globes of colored glass, but we did not need any light in the room because, from the terraces below, the lights of the party shone up in a greenish-golden glow through the windows.

It was nearly midnight before I managed to get her there. We stood by the lighted window and she took the earrings, in their maroon leather box, from where she had hidden them between her breasts. I could feel the box warm from her body as I held it in my hands. Afterwards I used to think how odd it was that I stood there, trembling and tenuous with excitement, aching and fired and nervously happy, while almost at the same time Tom stood watching Blackie, razor in hand, reading the note she had sent him. But I did not know of this at that time. I simply took the earrings from their box. Then, because I could not very well hold box and earrings at the same time, I put the box back between her breasts, touching the crest of them for a moment at the same time.

"I said you could put the earrings on," she said. "Nothing else. Don't be greedy — anyway, it's no time for lingering here."

"I think it's the perfect time," I said. She looked so dark and lovely in the semishadowiness of the terrace lights from below that I kissed her suddenly and for a long time.

"That's all," she said. "Now put the earrings on and let's go down."

I did not want to go down; and I was determined, at last, that nothing would make me. As I put the earrings on I trembled and fumbled a little, and then, in a rather hot and clumsy gesture, kissed them both, and she said:

"I believe you're the smallest bit tiddly. It's the champagne — "

I held her tightly against me, making her body press itself forward from the waist.

"This is the same room where we came once," I said. "That Sunday — do you remember? — the Sunday you didn't go to church?" And she said, in a rather shortish voice, that she remembered.

Down inside me I felt that a well of feeling had been unlocked. As it came rushing up through my body I heard the orchestra across the lawn lightly beginning a new dance, and I felt once again the same starry sort of beauty in the sound of strings in the half-dark air.

Presently she moved restlessly in my arms and I could see the earrings shining, dark rose-rich blobs, as she moved. She said something about not holding her there any longer and how late it was and how we ought to go down. At that moment I thought she seemed more wonderful than ever; and then as she moved with final restlessness by the window I could bear it no longer and I said:

"I've got something to ask you. I've asked Juley, but I haven't asked Bertie yet." Now at last when I said it my voice seemed flat and strained. "Would you marry me?"

She did not answer for a moment; she looked sideways, with deep black eyes, through the window. Across the lawns people were calling "Good night" to each other. I could hear their voices rising after a silence of the strings.

Then she said: "No."

"Lydia — "

"I don't think I could," she said.

From the back of my head delirium began to pound at me again.

"Oh, but my God," I said. "You've got to. I want you so much — you've got to — "

"I haven't got to do anything."

I could not speak. Outside, across the lawn, the orchestra did not begin again. In the silence I stood there still holding her. I looked at her face, but she did not look at me, and I stared down at the small earring box between her breasts. The orchestra still did not begin again, and presently I said what I suppose everybody says at these times:

"Will you think it over? Will you think about it?"

"Of course I shall think about it," she said. "It's the first time — "

"Don't you love me any more?" I said.

"Love you?" she said. "I don't know."

"Would you kiss me?" I said.

She lifted her lips and I felt I achieved something, sterile though it was, as I kissed their unresponsive flatness. Then at last, down below, the orchestra started up again, making her break away.

"Let me go now," she said.

"Don't go," I said. "Lydia, please don't go — "

I held her for a few moments longer; then it occurred to

me what the orchestra were playing. People were singing too.

"For she's a jolly good fellow — for she's a jolly good fellow — which nobody can deny — "

"Let me go," she said. "Let me go — they're singing for me."

I opened my arms, letting her go. She sprang away from me, shaking her hair. With bitterness I said:

"You're twenty-one now. You can please yourself now, of course — it's all yours."

She went out of the room, not speaking. I heard her running downstairs. I stood by the window and did not go after her. Down below, from across the lawns, people were crowding up towards the terrace, singing and laughing and calling her name. I could see their faces in the terrace lights, like greenish flowers upturned.

"For she's a jolly good fellow," they were singing. I felt myself trying to grasp at something that, like the smell of clover, was beautiful but not tangible; it was sweet and young and in the darkness it was floating away. "For she's a jolly good fellow — which nobody can deny — "

PART THREE

PART THREE

I

I was never certain if Juliana ever spoke to Lydia; it could have made no difference if she had. Three mornings later, on the last day of May, she woke, sat up and reached out across the bed, presumably for the knob of the old-fashioned bellpull above the commode. Her hand never reached the bell. The maid, bringing in her early-morning tea ten minutes later, found her, one arm still outstretched, dead where she lay.

The two Aspen sisters strike me sometimes as having been like two trees that grow up too closely together; the stronger seems to overshadow the weaker, taking strength and light away. Then the weaker falls down; then suddenly it seems as if, after all, it was the weaker that really gave protection to the strong; and presently, exposed and bared, the strong too falls down. Miss Bertie, in the same way, never recovered from the death of her sister. What I had taken, or mistaken, for strength and clarity and firmness, as against the rhetorical flutterings and the beautifying ugliness of the large, long-toothed mouth, were really only comparative virtues. When the object of comparison had gone Miss Bertie seemed just as irresolute, just as vague and, as it turned out, just as helpless as Juliana had been.

Presently, for this reason, a change came over Rollo: perhaps not so much a change as a shifting of attitude. He came

suddenly forward out of an obscurity in which his sisters, together, had been able to keep him. Again it was a question of
qualities that were comparative. He had seemed like a weak
and futile person, with all the vacuities of the inbred, simply because the sisters, so monolithic and garrulous and
dominant in their different ways, had kept him overshadowed. He was a man too who had spent his inheritance. He
had been forced to eat, over the years, in the form of a strict
and meager monthly allowance, a great deal of humble pie.
If he had never seemed to resent this it may possibly have
been because he hoped that, in due course, death would help
him. The sisters would leave him something. If they did not
leave him something then one of them would leave it to the
other; and in due course it would come to him. This must
have been the reasoning that had kept him, over the years,
so evidently cowed and subdued, the family weakling, shooting his pheasants, railing against shoemaker poachers, totting
steadily at his whisky and keeping his friend in Corporation
Street: a man who had made up his mind, in a simple way,
that he had little to do but wait, reasonably behave himself
and hope to survive.

Then Lydia came. There had never been a sign that he dis-
liked her; or even that he openly resented her. He mostly
behaved with decent avuncular attention, bantering and
chaffing her sometimes with semiaristocratic fatuities, mostly
in such things as hiding love-notes from me by slipping them
between two pieces of toast in the huge Victorian silver rack
at breakfast and then solemnly offering her toast and laughing like a braying camel when the note dropped out. All
these seemed like the natural pleasantries of a man of limited
if not backward mind.

This is how I saw him. It was typical of Lydia that she saw
him in quite another way. When, after the death of Juliana,
he seemed to emerge from futile obscurity, stronger and

[172]

larger, I was surprised. But Lydia was not. "This," she said, "is what he's been waiting for."

After the death of her aunt, Lydia too emerged; she stepped into another stage of her growing-up. Now, as I look back, I am amazed to think that I did not see that she and Rollo were, in a number of things, rather like each other. Both were persons of feeling who really did not think about their actions. If I did not recognize these qualities then it can only have been because I was stupefied by affection for Lydia and biased, as it turned out, by dislike of Rollo.

For a short time after the death of Juliana I did not notice anything of this. Then I became aware of a series of pin-pricks, little jabs of unsubtle sarcasm, whenever Rollo met me.

He had evidently labored heavily on things like "Ha, here comes the fair and dashing suitor — how's the suiting going, old boy?" and "How are things in the world of the light fantastic? — all fair in love and war still, I suppose, eh?" And then, about three weeks after Juliana's death, as I met him one day across the park:

"Hullo, old sport." I felt the hairs in the nape of my neck tingle fiercely as he called me this. "How's the rivalry? — How's the old suitor bearing up under the competition?"

This seemed to me hardly worth answering, but I said:

"What rivalry and what competition?"

"What?" he said. "You mean they keep it from you?"

I did not ask what had been kept from me, and he said:

"Oh! My error. My error."

At this point I tried to go. He said something about not rushing off in such a plum-awful hurry and he lifted very slightly the barrel of the gun he was carrying.

"Damn pity you don't shoot, old boy. Hell of a lot of vermin about. Never had so much. Eat up the ears of corn

[173]

and all that, you know. Mustn't let them eat up the ears of corn, must we?"

I said something about a few ears more or less not mattering very much, and he said:

"Just where you're wrong, old boy, just where you're wrong. The corn's got little ears and the little pigs've got big ears" — I could not think what on earth he was driving at — "and when you get too many ears after too many ears — " Even he seemed to get entangled, now, with his stumbling subtleties and finally gave up with the profound remark:

"Ah! well, everything comes to him who waits, they say, don't they?"

"In that case I won't wait," I said.

"Oh?" he said. "No? Damn pity." He laughed with a curious hardness not meant to show amusement. "Well, I suppose love won't wait, either, will it? No?"

"No," I said.

"No, but it pursues pretty damn hard sometimes, doesn't it?" he said, and in the face of that cutting subtlety, much too profound for me, I walked away.

Later that same day I walked in the garden with Miss Bertie. She confused, I noticed, the names of two species of viburnum, now coming into flower on the walls in rosettes of sterile ivory, that she ought to have known. She stood too for a long time before a plant of Mexican orange blossom, filling the June air with too-thick scent, and finally pointed at it a confused and laboring finger:

"What *is* this plant?" she said. "For the life of me I can't remember — names have begun to go clean out of my head."

As we walked vaguely on together she mentioned Juliana several times by name. She said she found the days unbearably hot. It was really a day of clear, breezy warmth, not at all oppressive, but I felt her grunting beside me in spasmodic struggles to get her breath. Her tendency to mention Juliana by name increased as we walked on; and all at once I grasped that she was under the illusion that Juliana was not dead. It even occurred to me that she thought I was Juliana, because suddenly she said:

"Did you hear Lydia and Rollo having words again after breakfast? They were at it again last night too — it's awfully distressing, that sort of thing, I can't bear it. We never had it before and I can't bear it now."

I did not know what to say, and she went on:

"He brought the most monstrous accusations about all sorts of things. Well — not exactly accusations. He taunts her. He's begun to be unbearably sarcastic."

Out of her obscure reflections she suddenly emerged clear-headed. She stopped on the path, realizing who I was.

"I want to ask you something," she said. Her voice was slow and deliberate. She gazed straight at me with eyes of tired, pellucid gray. "Have you asked Lydia to marry you?"

"Yes," I said.

"And what did she say?"

I told her what Lydia had said. She looked down at her feet while listening to me. Her hands, larger than Miss Juliana's, were knotty with bulbous, slate-colored veins as they wrapped themselves about the crook of her stick.

"Are you going to ask her again?"

"Don't you wish me to?" I said.

"I wish you to very much."

I was not sure if I wanted to ask her again; I was proud and I dreaded the notion that she would hurt me. So I did not speak, and that made Miss Bertie say, in one of those moments of tactfulness that can be more wounding than pure bluntness:

"If I were you I should ask her again — before it's too late," she said.

I could not speak. Her face widened with distressing brightness as she said:

"I've just remembered the name of that shrub. It's hibiscus something or other. It's that nice white hibiscus. Odd how you sometimes can't grasp these things — "

"Yes," I said. I did not tell her that it was not hibiscus.

"That's it," she said. "Hibiscus. It's so maddening when a simple thing like that eludes you. It's the most maddening thing in the world not to be able to grasp a thing you know all the time."

Her eyes sought waterily to focus themselves on distances of burning chestnut flower and oak across the park. Her mouth opened to gasp at air drenched with the thick sweetness of summer.

"It's awful how sometimes," she began and then stopped. "Shall we go back?"

We went back.

Three days later the six of us — Tom and Nancy, Alex and his mother, Lydia and myself — danced together for the last time.

The great house at Ashby is not quite a castle; its grandeur is in its remoteness. Nothing stands to molest or overlook or embarrass it in more than a thousand acres of unbroken pasture. The road runs through it through a series of iron swing gates, across bare open fields. It is — or was then — a great self-contained unit of husbandry and servility and wealth and earthly splendor where beef grew easily fat and cream came plentifully as water to larder and table, and where peaches ripened to perfect beauty on walls of yellowing stone, above which the level eyes of two hundred windows stared blindly out, across fat sleepy pastures, towards a world it could not see and did not need.

The night we danced there all the gates across the fields were open, each with a coach lantern on the side posts. Cars with their headlights threaded across the dusk of midsummer fields like lethargic processions of gliding fireflies. Even from the first four gates there was no sign of the house and it was only when we came suddenly round a bend in the road by the fifth gate that all of us saw the colossal lighted rectangle blazing out across the fields, all its lawns bathed in golden electric light, and Nancy cried out:

"Oh, it's like an island! Exactly like an island you see from a ship at sea." The house seemed to float in tiers of illuminated decks on dark water. "Oh! Stop. Lydia — ask him to stop. Just for a moment so that we can see — "

Lydia leaned forward, pushing back the sliding glass division of the limousine. "Stop a moment, will you?" Her voice was level and quiet. I saw Blackie's face turn, quiet too, with deference, above the dashlight.

"Yes, Miss Aspen," he said.

I had never heard him call her Miss Aspen before. He sat patient, unaloof, his hand on the wheel. Nancy, excited, said again how like a ship the house was, and Mrs. Sanderson said if only the evening was as lovely it would be the most wonderful think we had ever done together.

We sat for some seconds longer staring at the lighted house. I suddenly felt all my frustrated happiness with Lydia begin to reignite itself in a series of exciting little fires, creating one large tender illumination, about the tiers of glowing windows. There seemed, I felt, to be a spell on things, and then Alex said:

"Car coming up. We'd better move on."

"You can drive on now," Lydia said through the open division.

"Yes, miss," Blackie said.

I caught the glow of her face in the dashlight. At the house, in the large, long central hall already crowded with people, I could not wait to dance with her. She danced quietly, almost reticently. She did not speak to me much, and I was glad.

The spell of elation, begun by Nancy in her first excitement at seeing the great lighted house across the fields, lasted through three dances before I realized they had gone. Lydia seemed to wake too and said:

"Don't you think you should dance with Nancy? The poor girl is sitting out there like a flopped wallflower."

I did not want to dance with Nancy.

"Be a dear and go and dance with her," Lydia said.

"The dance after the next," I said.

"After this one. Will you? Don't make her unhappy."

I swung her round, feeling the smooth curve of her thigh against me. "You will, won't you?" she said. As she lifted her face at me the eyes were shadowless.

"Don't make her unhappy," she said again. "She was so excited when she saw that house — I could have cried for her. Have the next dance with her, will you? For me?"

"Only for you," I said. "Not for Nancy."

"That sounds selfish," she said. "It's not like you to be selfish."

"I didn't mean to be selfish."

"Then don't be," she said. "It doesn't suit you."

All the delicate, distant fires I had seen at the house windows seemed again to prance about in my head, firing and illuminating me with happiness. It was like being back, I thought, in the summer of the year before, in the summerhouse across the park, lost among birch and bracken, in a world of mown hay and sunlight and partridge chickens hiding in grass. Everything then had seemed to have on it a bloom of simplicity; there had been no complication to upset us as we discovered each other. Now the bloom, like the spell of the house, seemed to have redescended on us, and I said:

"All right. Just for you. And because I love you."

"You mustn't love me."

"I shall love you till my bones rot," I said.

"It's sweet to hear you say it, but all the same you mustn't. Spare a little for Nancy."

She said this with a gentle cooing sort of delicacy, smiling up at me.

"You're much happier if you make other people happy," he said.

"That sounds like a text hung on a bedroom wall."

"Well, it isn't. It's true, and I discovered it."

"How?" Elated, I mocked her a little, but there was no response.

"Never mind how," was all she said. "Just go and dance with Nancy."

But when at the end of the dance I went to find Nancy it was only to discover her eating strawberry ice cream with Alex, and she danced the next one with him. Over his shoulder Alex said something about having a private word with me afterwards, and I heard Nancy say, "Oh! shut up and dance. You and your private words. You're always jawing, you two." So I danced with Mrs. Sanderson, who said:

"To what do I owe this immense, sudden, free-gratis-and-for-nothing honor?"

I had neglected her too. "I'm sorry," I said.

"I really had no chance," she said. "I've been chased all evening by a master of fox hounds who actually called me a little vixen — "

"Heaven, this is a tango," I said.

"Now I know why your feet are crossed like knitting needles — would you rather sit out?"

"Please," I said.

The tango was something I had never mastered. After I had found her a glass of claret cup we walked outside, into a crescent-shaped anteroom where guests were standing about in groups, eating supper.

"Not in here," she said. "There's my vixen friend."

We sat eventually on a long seat of petit point needlework at the foot of the main staircase. The petit point is clear in my mind because, all the time we talked, she ran her left hand flatly across it, over and over again, as if she were apprehensive about something.

Then suddenly she said: "I suppose you heard about Blackie?"

I had not heard about Blackie; and perhaps a little peremptorily I said: "What about Blackie?"

"You mean you didn't hear about the fire?"

How exactly like me it was, I thought, not to hear about a fire.

"He had a fire in the back stables this week. All the old landaus and wagonettes and things were burned. All those old wooden stables and things went up like touchwood. He lost nearly everything except the limousine."

"And no insurance," I said. I felt a spasm of regret at the destruction, at last, of all that was left of Old Johnson's charming, straw-stuffed world. "There never is."

"No, there wasn't," she said.

I did not say much; I was less sorry for Blackie than for the memory of Johnson and the charred world of landaus and brakes and the Schneider sleeping under the martins' nests. Then she ran her hand across the petit point and said:

"I'd like another drink — would you? Find something that's recognizably alcoholic — this is neither claret nor cup."

I went out and came back with champagne, which she welcomed. She drank it rather quickly and said:

"I'm a bit worried about something — Lydia has lent him money to start up again."

"Good God," I said. I felt a little sick.

"The trouble is I feel partly responsible." Now that she had begun to tell me what was in her mind her hands were motionless, tightly clasping her glass. "You see she came to

[180]

Alex and asked his advice about it. That was sensible enough. And Alex said 'Yes.' But I think he did it more because of — "

She stopped; she drank and stared into her glass. She had always seemed to me a woman of such poise and self-possession that now, when she looked uncertain and troubled, it was doubly striking. For a moment she looked extraordinarily like Alex, drawn and strained and knotted up in one of his moods of entanglement and disentanglement, and then she said:

"Is it true you asked her to marry you and she said no?"

"Yes," I said. "Anyway, what's once or twice in our rough island story? What's once between friends — ?"

"I didn't know a thing about this until Alex told me," she said. "You mean you're going to ask her again?"

"Why not?" I said. Perhaps I thought that I ought to express myself in terms that were casual and adult. "I think women probably like being asked several times. It makes them feel desirable and flattered."

It was that sentence which seemed to disconcert her, I thought, more than all the rest. She suddenly drank the rest of her champagne and stood up.

"Let's go outside," she said.

She gave me her arm and we went outside. In the courtyard — it was one of those centralized courtyards of grass, enclosed on three sides by the house and on the fourth by a balustrade, beyond which steps led to the garden — the night was very warm, almost hot, with molten stars. I remembered that it was midsummer. She put one of her hands affectionately on mine as we walked up and down.

We stopped at last and leaned on the balustrade. From the house I could hear once again the starry sounds of strings, climbing away on scales into darkness.

"Look," Mrs. Sanderson said, "I'm going to say something that will probably hurt you terribly — "

"I don't think you could possibly hurt me," I said. I smiled, and I did not think she could.

"I think Alex is going to ask her," she said.

For some seconds I stood there laughing. It seemed to me like a piece of perfect midsummer madness that Alex, inconsistent, excitable, charmingly unreliable and volatile, should ask any girl to marry him.

"Is it funny? Don't you think he's serious?" she said.

"Of course not. He never is."

She stood staring across dark summer fields, apparently thinking before she spoke again.

"He didn't come to bed last night," she said. "He took the hammock and stayed at the bottom of the garden all night, under the apple trees."

"There's no better cure for love than a good hammock," I said.

"Oh! Please," she said. She laughed very briefly. "If that's all you think of my worries about you we'd better go back again."

I said I thought so too, and I turned to go.

"One moment," she said. She caught my hand and drew me back to her.

"You're not to speak of this to Alex," she said.

"All right," I said. "In any case he wouldn't remember — "

"I must say I hope not," she said. She smiled and then, very suddenly, but not clumsily, she kissed me on the lips. "You were very sweet about it. I don't like to see people hurt and I'm glad you weren't."

"Of course not," I said. "It's midsummer and everybody expects a little madness."

That conversation with Mrs. Sanderson amused and elated me; it seemed to me to belong to the mood that had made

Nancy stop the car and cry out that the great lighted house, rising in isolation across dark fields, was like an island sighted from a ship at sea.

When I went back into the house through the two large central rooms for Lydia she was not there; and nor, I noticed after a time, was Alex. I remember how that amused me too. The thought of Alex offering Lydia a proposal went through me with such amused swiftness that I actually caught myself laughing out loud, and then, heard a voice behind me saying:

"You might share your jokes occasionally. Even if you can't share yourself. What's so dreadfully funny?"

Nancy stood there, and I said: "Some day I'll tell you. Where's Lydia?"

"Oh, don't worry. I've been keeping an eye on her for you," she said. "She's outside."

"I must find her," I said. Then as I moved away she called after me:

"And not alone, either. In case you'd like to know."

"That's what's so funny," I said.

When I walked outside, through the courtyard, and then along the opposite, southern wing of the house, it was some time before I recognized, along a path, beyond the garden lights strung about pergolas of roses, the color of Lydia's dress. It was the same pale mauve dress she had worn at her birthday party.

"Lydia," I said, "is that you?"

She stood up suddenly. I think I had some sort of irresponsible idea of teasing her about Alex, and I remember being very amused for three or four seconds longer by the idea of Alex making his proposal out there, in an aura of midsummer madness and starlight and roses. Then I saw that it was not Alex with her, but Blackie.

I stopped on the path. I had never been angry with her

[183]

before — annoyed sometimes, very near anger, cut by spasms of miserable vexation and sometimes profoundly bewildered and profoundly hurt, but never more. Now I was blackened by a rush of anger that went through me like a blast of flame. I felt for a second or two extinguished by it; I could not see. I made some sort of blinded turn on the path, everything inside me acrid and seared and blackened out, and began to go back.

I heard her running after me. I did not stop and she called, quite quietly:

"Please. Not like that. Don't go. Not like that, please."

She ran the last five or six steps, catching up with me. She called me several times by name. Level with me at last, she stood in front of me and said:

"There's no reason at all to run away like that. That's silly."

I did not answer.

"Just come back with me."

I did not answer.

"I'm simply talking a little business with Blackie," she said. "That's all. He needs help — "

"So do we all," I said.

"If you're going to take that impossible, childish, jealous attitude, there's no point in explaining," she said, "is there? Not that we need to explain — "

"We?" I said. "We?"

"Yes, Mr. Richardson," Blackie said. "We."

The three of us stood there on the path. I knew in my heart that I was behaving with terrible foolishness; I had an idiotic idea that she had somehow finally rejected me in favor of Blackie. In blind anger I lashed out and seized on this and made it an excuse to yell:

"I don't know what the bloody hell you have to do with this, anyway."

"It was just business." His voice was quite restrained and decent and quiet.

"Oh, yes! Oh, yes! Oh, yes!" I said.

"Miss Aspen was kind enough to offer some help," he said. "She offered it yesterday and I said I would think it over and give my answer — "

"In the dark, in the garden, in the bloody romantic summer night?"

"I don't think that's quite fair, Mr. Richardson," he said, and I cut back:

"Who's talking about being fair?"

"Quite obviously not you," she said, and in a new blind rush of anger I turned on her and half shouted:

"Anyone would think the offer was terribly secret or something. Anyone would think you'd asked him to marry you."

"And supposing I had?"

I shouted "And have you?" and she said:

"Even if I had it could be no possible concern of yours."

I turned and walked furiously up the path. All the spell of the evening receded, smothered in waves of galling blackness. In the monstrous confusion and pain I blundered into the house and came at once on Alex.

"Good God, you stand there like death," he said.

"I'm going," I said. "I'm walking home."

"Now look, now look," he said. "A drink is all you need. What's happened now?"

With incredible and inexcusable stupidity I said:

"Lydia's in the garden with Blackie. I found them there. She talked about marrying him — "

He stood motionless, his face very white. In a few momentously idiotic sentences I had hurt him more than I had been hurt myself. His lips began groping for words which eventually he found with sickening quietness:

[185]

"That couldn't be true, could it? That simply couldn't be true."

"Why couldn't it?" I said. "You said yourself you saw it coming on —"

"Good God," he said. "It couldn't be true."

"I heard her say it myself," I said.

He did not speak again. I listened to the band thumping and drumming in the other room. A few moments later we stood at the refreshment bar and a man with a cheerful orange mustache, of the type of an army major, said:

"Damn good anchovy toast. Just whipped a fresh lot up from somewhere," and I saw Alex take a piece and crush it into his mouth.

I took one too. A savage, salty rawness of anchovy over sweet wine seared my tongue, and I choked a little as I heard a voice behind me say:

"So this is where you are."

The voice of Nancy seemed to me, at that moment, smug in its arched restraint. She said in a lecturing sort of way how gentlemanly and how like us it was to leave everybody flat. I felt my impossible anger against Lydia turn still more impossibly towards her. The joy that had been on everything finally died completely. And then perhaps because neither of us said anything she said:

"You're a pair. One is as bad as the other. You're big in conceit and little in everything else —"

"I'm going, Alex," I said. "Good night."

"Now look," Alex said. "You know what I told you. That's a bad habit of yours. Walking out —"

"Oh! Let him go," Nancy said.

"Thank you," I said. "Alex will dance with you." I felt inside me a final festering burst of monstrous bitterness. "My dancing days are over."

* * *

I suddenly turned, looked past her and walked out.

Alex did not follow me. I walked through the courtyard and then on through the grassy freshness of fields. The coach lamps were still burning on the side posts of the open gates. Once I looked back at the house and there, exactly as before, it was shiplike and splendid on a dark sea of pasture. It looked not only beautiful and comforting and inviolable but also — during the war a regiment of paratroops succeeded waves of deathwatch infantry battalions as its occupants, leaving it finally gutted and scarred and empty, and now it is a home for delinquent girls — as if it must remain like that for ever.

Out on the road I felt calmer; the night air was beautiful, silent and still warm. A few cars passed me and once, about a mile on towards the river, one of them drew up beside me and the man with the joyful orange mustache put his head out of the window and said: "Any more for the jolly old Skylark?" and I was aware of a mass of penguin dress fronts entangled by colored skeins of girls. I thanked them and refused. There was much laughter. "Lover of the open air!" the orange mustache said. "Home, James —"

I did not feel like a lover of anything, least of all myself, that night; but if anything was remotely worth loving it was possibly the open air. It was already morning as I came down to the river. White summer mists in flat, powdery pockets lay here and there on broad curves of water. I sat on the bridge, a narrow, hunchbacked bridge built of stone with triangular bays down either side of it, and stared down at the river. A few fish were rising even then, and I could hear an occasional fishlike flap of water against the buttresses. Two meadows away a night goods train came slowly clanking out of the half-dark countryside, halting finally by a signal, blowing steam. The signal against it did not change and all at once the steam was shut off, leaving nothing but a great stillness after the echoes had died away, meadow folded damply into meadow across miles of windless summer night air.

Out of this stillness I heard, eventually, the noise of a car. It seemed to be coming rather fast. I stood in one of the triangular bridge bays to let it pass. It came out of the fading morning darkness over the humpback, pulling up with a squeal of brakes on the crest of the bridge.

Alex was riding on the footboard. He let out a zipping yell, more like a cheer, as he saw me standing there.

"Good old boy! The lost is found — hop on! You'll find it cooler on the dashboard."

From inside the car there was a strained silence of five sober faces as Alex fell off the car and embraced me drunkenly.

"Hop on! — thought we'd lost you — Everybody said you'd take the Cotteshall road — good old boy, come on!"

"I'm walking home," I said.

"You said that before — that's damn silly."

"I'm walking," I said.

With gay, tipsy arms Alex tried to drag the coat off my back.

"Hop in — jolly good old boy — glad we found you — "

At this moment the back window of the car went down.

"Please get in." It was Mrs. Sanderson's voice, cool, restrained, deadly sober. "I think we've all had enough of this. You've had us worried stiff."

"I don't see why," I said.

She waited. The train whistled across the meadow.

"Are you coming?" she said.

"No."

"It's not like you to be stubborn," she said. Then I saw Nancy lean forward and say:

"Of course it's like him to be stubborn. It's exactly like him. He's the stubbornest person in the world when he sets his mind to a thing."

[188]

Four or five yards down the bridge Alex struck an attitude, one foot on the triangular step of the bay, the other on the low parapet. "The boy stood on the burning deck — !"

"If you're not coming I think we'd better go," Mrs. Sanderson said. "Are you coming?"

"No," I said.

"Leave him," Nancy said. "He'll get over it. He's in one of those moods. He thinks he's too good for us all."

"Clever of you to recognize it at last," I said.

After this witless remark Mrs. Sanderson wound up the window. For one prolonged moment, before Blackie revved up his engine, I hated everything. I hated myself, I hated the yelling fatuity of Alex's pose on the bridge parapet; I hated the cold, sober faces in the taxi; I hated the voice of Nancy telling me the truth about myself. The train tooted its whistle across the meadow. I hated it all and I wanted to go on in loneliness, alone.

At this moment the front window of the car went down. "Won't you come?"

It was Lydia speaking. Her voice was very soft; she had not spoken to me in that soft, fond way for a long time.

"No," I said.

"I wish you would," she said. "It would be better."

I could hear her voice coming with a deep disturbance of tenderness from the depth of her throat. I caught a glimpse of the upper part of her dress, pale mauve in the dashlight. From the bridge Alex yelled something incomprehensible, but exactly as if she and I were alone she took no notice of it and simply said: "It would make me very happy — in fact, it would make all of us very happy — "

I did not answer. I knew that I had taken up a position I could not sustain. It seemed to me I heard someone, Nancy I thought, crying in the back of the car. But I only stood stubborn, transfixed, hateful while Lydia said:

"For the last time. Please."

"No," I said. "There's one thing I'll do though — I'll give you the chance of getting out and walking with me."

"I can't do that," she said.

In answer I made another witless remark, born out of my impossible attitude: "There's no such word as can't — you *could* —"

"It so happens I don't want to," she said. The weeping of someone in the back of the car became, in that moment, my own weeping, cruel, private, lonely, desolate inside me. "I've made up my mind about it. It's all made up. I don't suppose you understand it, and I don't blame you. But that's how it is — so please will you —"

She never finished speaking that sentence. Alex slipped at that moment on the parapet, yelling as he did so. I heard the scrape of his dance shoes on stone. I turned just in time to see him slipping down on his buttocks over the bridge. It seemed like the action of a man who had simply grown tired of standing and was going to sit down. For one second he actually did sit down — and then his body straightened out and fell.

"Alex!" I yelled. "Alex —"

I heard him strike his head on the upper arch of the bridge as he fell. His white evening scarf fell off. The splash of his body striking the water was flat and uncontrolled. When I ran forward I saw him float down, under the arch, downstream, to the other side.

Some seconds later I saw Tom poised for a moment in his white dress shirt on the bridge. I heard Nancy scream: "I knew something would happen — I knew it would —" and then she shrieked incoherently, running pointlessly up and down.

This shriek was answered, exactly like an echo, by the train waiting for its signal across the meadow. Then I saw Blackie running. I jumped the end parapet of the bridge, landing on the towpath, and began running too. From there I saw Blackie dive. For a few moments I heard two bodies swimming without seeing them. Then I saw two pairs of detached white sleeves thrashing dark water between islands of reeds and I heard Tom yelling what sounded like:

"Just where you are — just there — mind the weed — "

Suddenly all my latent childhood terror of the river came back. I saw Tom come up and dive again. Then Blackie dived. I could not see Alex. On the bridge Nancy kept running up and down, hysterical, until Lydia and Mrs. Sanderson caught her and made her quiet. Beyond them a faint light began to appear in the sky. The arches of the bridge were ovals of paling gray.

At last Tom came up. Nancy saw him and began screaming his name. "Tom! Tom! Tom! T–om — !" in a long wail of terror. I saw him shake his thick, wet, blond hair, roping it back with his hands. He trod water. No one else appeared on the water, and suddenly he went thrashing over, perpendicular, in another dive. Then across the fields the train tooted its whistle again and the sound of it woke me and I began to run down the towpath.

I remember not bothering to unlatch the towpath gate, but vaulting it. I heard what I thought were the wheels of the train cranking. The sound clacked hollow across the fields. Then I knew it was the fall of the signal I had heard. Steam squeezed in a long hiss across the meadows and one by one the truck buffers hit each other, irregular chock against chock, until the train was pulled straight and began to move away.

By the time I turned and vaulted the gate again I could see Tom swimming in to the bank, bringing somebody with him. I fell down the bank and we lashed together in shallow water, above a shelf of reeds. I dragged somebody through the reeds, half out of water, and I saw that it was Blackie. Tom was drawing his breath in long, grating gasps. He took a single

[191]

wild look at Blackie as I pulled him through the reeds. He seemed surprised, as I was, that it was not Alex. Then he dived again in a long spoon-curved sort of action that took him half across the river.

From the bridge Lydia ran down and we laid Blackie on his face. He was sick, spewing water in coughs on the grass. She did not speak a word. Across on the line the signal flapped back to danger behind the receding train. Blackie turned slowly on his face, the hairy pack of his chest muscles black and wet and faintly shining in the growing daylight, and I heard the train drawing farther and farther away.

A patch of floating mist in the river seemed to grow white. It was really Tom, struggling to free himself of his shirt before he made another dive. On the bridge Nancy screamed his name again, "Tom! Tom! T–om!" in a long wail, and then went on screaming it at each successive dive.

Then I saw him appear in a new place. He was clinging to a buttress of the bridge. He was hanging on, alone, against the current. It was not strong but his own strength was going, and I saw the river beating him, pulling his body out from the tips of his fingers. Lydia called:

"There's a rope in the car," and I rushed up to the bridge. The car tow-rope had a hook on it and I paid it out over the parapet to Tom. I felt it tauten as he held it. Then I caught a new sound. It was the engine of the car, still running, the exhaust puttering softly like sobbing breath.

Something hit me in the face, and then hit me again, on either cheek, and then afterwards so many times that I lost count of it. It was Nancy. She struck me over and over again until I could only go on holding the rope and bow my head and let her hit me just as she would.

I think it was Mrs. Sanderson who finally stopped her and took her away. In a stunned fashion I walked along the bridge, feeling the rope taut as Tom held it. I knew by that time that there would be no Alex. Mrs. Sanderson did not cry. The last sounds of the goods train climbing slowly through the valley met the sounds of returning echoes and then faded away. Blackie lay on the bank and coughed for breath, sick and spitting, and Nancy cried piteously, alone now, against a gate in a field beyond the bridge, weeping: "Tom, oh! Tom — Oh! Tom — my God, what have we done?"

I pulled Tom by the rope through the reed shelf. He crawled up the bank and lay on his face beside Blackie. Rising pale gray mist left the black skin of water as clear and still as if no one had touched it.

I turned Tom on his back and knelt by him and wiped water from his face. The light of the sky was growing clearer every moment. The under arcs of stone cast sharp ovals of white on the water. The sound of the receding train had ceased entirely, and as weeping hatred went through me I began to shake all over again, asking myself, as Nancy did, for God's sake what had we done? Then Tom staggered to his feet and said:

"One more try — I think I could get him," and then, with a cry of exhaustion, fell down.

Some time later the light in the east came to full strength. Sun threw yellow patches on a river that was not black any longer, and I realized, very slowly, that we had just begun the longest day of the year.

II

PERHAPS I ought not to have been surprised that Bretherton came to see me two days later. In the summer evening he stood on the doorstep, notebook sticking from his pocket, small, pink-lidded eyes blinking like a pig that wakes in a glare of sun.

"Thought you might be able to do us a good turn — give us a line on things."

I had neither a good turn to do nor a line to give, that day, on anything in the world.

"You know — personal stuff. Do you think he did do it?" They were still dredging, that day, for Alex's body; the river had always been quick to take people but equally slow to give them up again. "Any reason — ? You know?"

I did not know. Alex was dead and a great part of myself — that day I felt almost all — was dead with him. But Bretherton took my silence as tacit acquiescence to the idea that Alex had killed himself.

"You know — strickly" — As he said "strickly" he took his pencil from his breast pocket. "Strickly between our two selves. In confidence — under the Old Pals' Act."

I had nothing to give him under the Old Pals' Act either. I stared past him and said:

"It might just as well have been an Act of God. It probably was."

"You know, you'd have made a good reporter if you'd cut out the idealism," he said. "You've always been too idealistic. Not how did it happen? — strickly — ?"

I had nothing to say.

"You were there," he said, "you ought to be able to describe it, didn't you? That was a wonderful effort of young Holland's — we're playing that up. Did you go in?"

"I don't swim. I'm too idealistic," I said.

"No need to come the old mild and bitter if you are," Bretherton said.

"I don't know anything," I said. I began to shut him out, suppressing some further words about the Old Pals' Act, a good turn and strickly between ourselves. "It'll all be in the records, Mr. Bretherton," I said, "all you want to know — "

"Yes, that's all right. But I wanted to get the human side — "

I shut him out at last. I had nothing to tell; I could not explain. I could not explain that Alex had been killed not so much by a fall from a bridge as by an accumulative process of little things, of which some were gay, some stupid, some accidental, but all of small importance in themselves. Perhaps he had died on the icy evening when Lydia had first taken notice of Blackie; or on the occasions when she had led him on, or had appeared to lead him on, exactly as she had sometimes led on Tom and myself. Perhaps then, perhaps later. Perhaps on some other occasion. I didn't know. He might even have died under the Old Pals' Act, under the pressure of our own affection for each other, in our secret loyalties. We had been very good pals: that might have been it. If we had not been very good pals we should never have talked, as young men do, in terms of starlight and solemnity and bravado and fun and all that self-centered sort of holiness that is so wonderful when you are young. Everywhere there was a confusion of reasons. We shouldn't have been idealistic. We should have known better. Lydia could have killed him. His mother could have killed him because in her generous and charming way she had treated him with too much indulgence, giving him too much money, letting him drink too much. It didn't matter. I myself could have killed him, and I believe that Nancy, like myself, thought I had.

I went slowly through a summer without affection; I invented a sort of sterile and loveless vacuum for myself. When I walked it was always out of the town on the east side, where we lived, and never south, towards Busketts, or southwest, towards Lydia and the Aspens, or towards the station, behind which the Sandersons lived in their Edwardian villa in a cul-de-sac of poplar trees that screened the branch-line trains. I did not want anybody; I had given up my job. The summer was very hot and whenever I could I used to stuff sandwiches into my pocket and walk, mostly across fields, by path and green lane, into country I did not know. I was away early in the morning and back after the factories closed at night. It was suffocating and hot in the streets about the factories that summer, and the ploughed lands about Evensford, on heavy yellow clay, began to dry up. By late July clergymen had started the usual business, in churches, of offering prayers for rain. There was no rain, and by August the tips of the elms on the high clay land were scorched yellow, then brown and dry. Corn began to catch fire by railway tracks. Sheep stood under long hawthorn umbrellas, sheltering from the glare of an otherwise treeless countryside, panting in the bony hollow way they have under the distress of heat, painfully convulsed and shuddering, snatching for breath. In beanfields you could hear the splintering crack of exploding pods, burnt black by heat, and one of the commonest sights was the water-carts hauling slowly across simmering horizons, to and fro from the brooks, carrying water about the farms.

One August afternoon I was coming home across fields to east of Evensford, about three miles away, where a country of open land for a brief space suddenly closes in, tightened up by a range of small fox coverts, the last before the ash tracks of the town began. This is the country where, ten years later, they carved an airfield with bulldozing ruthlessness through every fox covert and farm and pond and pigsty until nothing but a gray circus, with a perimeter five miles long, a trapeze of radio towers and landing lights, and a herd of black, flying elephants, remained above the steeple of a tiny church below. But that day war was still a long way off, and there was only heat to trouble me.

I had become so transfixed and stupid about solitariness that I had even invented a system, a sort of game, rather as children do when they play hop-scotch on pavements, of avoiding roads wherever I could. If I stepped on a road it was, as in the game, a black mark against myself. It gave me a little excitement to make long detours so that I did not touch a road. It set me problems in physical complexity against all the complexity inside myself. It kept me from going mad, and through it I discovered new country.

That afternoon I was walking across a farmstead — a small stone house with a few blackthorn hovels and a railed garden lay below — when I heard the clank of a water-cart across the baked clayfield behind me and a voice yelled across the sizzling air:

"What do you think you're doing on this land?"

The water-cart was spotted bright red, almost camouflaged, with areas of fresh lead paint. A fair-haired man bare to the waist stood up on it, tightening the reins. The horse had ash boughs stuck into its bridle. Suddenly I caught from the man, in the brilliant glare of sun, a flash of pale-blue eyes.

"Where do you think you're going?" he shouted.

I started to move across to him; and then he jumped down; and I knew by the jump of the body who he was.

"Tom," I said. "Tom — "

I remember how we stood there, staring at each other and shaking hands. Tears started to well up inside me and I saw his mouth shaking as he smiled.

"Did you know it was me?" I said. "Or do you — "

"I knew all the time," he said. "I saw you the other day, but you were too far away. I'd know by that walk of yours."

"You're a long way from Busketts," I said.

"This is my farm," he said. "Dad bought it for me — to set up on my own. Only sixty acres, but it's got water and the house."

"You live here?" I said.

"In the house," he said. "Come on down and see."

We sat for a long time in the stone kitchen of the house, drinking cups of ice-cold water from a well that came up under the scullery floor. Sun-withered hollyhocks, pale rose, turned by heat to a florid purple, covered the kitchen window. A few hens pecked beyond the threshold, scratching in the neglected flower-bed outside. The stone-dark coolness of the house after the blaze of heat was exactly like the shock of a frozen hand across my neck. It made me draw my breath. And once again I could have cried as I sat there listening to Tom telling me of the farm, his one horse, his six heifers, how it had been too late that summer to start crops, how he cooked for himself, how at last he was free and independent, how Nancy came over once or twice a week to tidy up the place and perhaps cook an extra meal or a cake or a pie for him, and how so far he was working it singlehanded, seven days a week, all alone.

"And where have you been?" he said.

"Nowhere."

"What are you doing?"

"Nothing," I said. "I gave up the job."

I felt icy water flow through my body. Feeling woke in me like a cold, moving pain. I had been nowhere and done nothing and felt nothing and had asked for nothing. Suddenly feeling was rushing back and I knew I could not hold it, and then he said:

"If you're not doing anything why don't you come up and give me a hand? — for a day or two — a week if you like."

Loneliness burst inside me like a fester. A suppuration of self-affliction poured through me, hot as the air outside. I could not say anything, but I must have nodded, because he said:

"That's absolutely wonderful. Nance will be thrilled to bits. I'll nip over and tell her tonight, and then — "

"Not for a day or two," I said. "Let me settle in."

"All right, all right, anything," he said. "When do you want to come?"

"Just when it suits you."

"It suits me as soon as you can throw some stuff together. Tonight if you like — we'll have a damn good supper of home-cured and four eggs — " and for the first time since Alex had died we laughed together.

That evening we drove into Evensford and fetched my things. In one of the hovels behind the farm Tom had a brand-new Ford. "Nance bothered me to sell her the old one when I came over here," he told me. "She has to have something to run about in." We drove back through dusty hedgerows at a gentle pace. "Another week and this one'll be run in."

From that day, for the rest of the summer, I felt rather like the car. I felt as if I were running myself in, gently working back to living. Of Tom's sixty acres, four fields were grass. They were small fields bounded by hedgerows of mighty hawthorn, with trunks like rubbed mahogany under which the six heifers panted all day in shade. In the fifth field, a crop of barley, the only crop that year on the place, about five acres left by the previous tenant, was flaring white on the small hillside. Tom had begun to mow it by hand, and when I arrived we started tackling it together. That field too was bounded by big, neglected hedges of hawthorn, and heat lay compressed in it, over the blinding patch of barley, like the breath of a bakehouse oven. We worked stripped to the waist. Tom worked with a scythe and I followed him with rake and bonds, making sheaves. Sometimes when I bent down and stood sharply up again the field seemed to rock about me, dazzling, pitching slantwise, almost melting away under hard blue sky. We used to start work at five and then have breakfast, in the old-fashioned way, about nine. We always had thick rashers of home-cured bacon and fatty fried eggs and new bread and gallons of strong, milky tea. We ate like wolves and soon the blisters on my shoulders skinned, raw and sharp, like peeled pink onions. After breakfast we took cold tea into the field and worked on till noon. In the afternoons we carried water for the cattle, fetching it in the red-scabbed water-cart from the brook, the Biddy brook, that ran over the road down the hill. Pale pink willow herb and flowering cresses and water-dock had almost choked the narrow gullies of water under the white footbridge, and every day the depth of water seemed a little less. Every day I stood in the brook, without even taking off my boots and socks, and made a new water-dip among the weeds and cresses, handing buckets up to Tom on the cart. The coldness of water running over my feet was very like the first cold shock of well-water in the cool kitchen after the heat of the afternoon when I had first met Tom. It did more than cool my body; it acted exactly like a compress on my injured mind.

Sometimes at this point the brook, from liquefied deposits of iron, ran very red, staining cress roots as I pulled them out a kind of rusty scarlet, and one afternoon the redness clotted on my socks and boots and the legs of my trousers, and when I hauled myself up on the bridge Tom laughed at me from the cart and said:

"Now you look a rare bloody mess," and I laughed too and said:

"I feel wonderful."

About the fourth or fifth afternoon — I am not sure which, because the days melted into each other — I came into the kitchen, naked to the waist, in boots still squelching pads of water from the brook. I had come to put the kettle on the paraffin burner for tea. As I came into the kitchen I could hear the sound of the burner. Then I could see that already the cloth was laid.

Then Nancy's voice called from the scullery, "That you, Tom?" And she came into the kitchen, carrying a pink glass jug of milk in her hands. It was one of those transparent jugs that turn the milk, in a fascinating way, a pure, light pink. She stood absolutely still, clasping it in her hands. I could see her fingers pink through the upper glass of the jug. Then the milky, fleshy cheek of her face turned almost the same color, flushing up to bright, pale eyes.

"Where did *you* come from?"

"I live here," I said.

"I think Tom might have told me."

She put the jug down on the table. She turned quickly and went out of the kitchen; and turning she saw my red, wet boots and the watery pads they had made on the floor bricks.

"And where have you been? You're plastered up to your neck."

She did not wait for answer to that; I stood at the scullery door, looking in. The scullery had an open square-foot of window shaded by the branches of an elderberry. The odor of elderberry was strong and dark, and Nancy moved pale and big between narrow, shady walls about the singing paraffin stove and the fat, brown teapot.

"How do you like your tea?" she said.

"Strong and black," I said.

The kettle spouted steam; she forgot the heat of the handle

and burnt the tips of her fingers, sucking them. "Damn," she said. She picked up the kettle by the fringe of her apron. She poured water into the teapot and said:

"It's hotter than ever today, don't you think? I was going to cook a few things when the sun went down a bit — "

"Curd tarts?" I said.

"Whistle and they'll come to you," she said. She pushed past me with kettle and teapot. "I've got something else to do besides make milk turn sour."

It was on the tip of my tongue to be what she always called clever in answer to that, but I checked myself in time.

"The sun would curdle it for you," I said, "in no time — "

"I'm going to bake bread," she said. "Think yourselves lucky I've got time for that."

The three of us had tea together and once or twice Nancy snapped: "Sparing with the milk, Tom. It's all we've got." That meal, with Nancy between us, was not quite the same as we were accustomed to, and some of my confidence receded. I began to feel tightened and defensive once more, resisting affection.

"We're going to paint the kitchen out on Sunday," Tom said. "It's wonderful what difference this bloke makes. We'll have the barley all down tomorrow."

"You both look as if a wash would do you good, the pair of you — "

"We bathe every night, don't we?" Tom said, and winked at me.

"Every night."

"I'll believe it when I see it," she said.

"Well, you can," Tom said. His happiness at my being there had been, I think, greater than my own; he looked all the time wonderfully bright, almost glowing with happiness. "We'll have the old bath tin here on the floor — penny a look — "

"I don't think *that's* very funny," she said.

My defensiveness increased as tea went on. I was glad when it was over. We had hens to feed; water and swede-tops to give to the heifers; a bait to find for the horse. I had not often been so happy as I was that late summer, with Tom, the horse, the fields and the six heifers. Already the heifers had begun to know me and would come forward from under the hawthorn shade to lick my hands.

That evening the heifers stirred under the hedge before I reached them, and something a tone brighter than sepia-yellow elm leaves broke from the hawthorns and trotted in the glare of sunlight up the field. I stood watching a fox, old, rusty-yellow, big as an airedale, lope across a series of rabbit warrens on the brown hill. He turned once and looked round at me, hesitated, haughty, cool and old, so that I felt almost that if I had whistled him he would have come back. Then he jumped a rabbit hole, shook himself and trotted away towards the coverts, like an old, rank, yellow dog, until I lost him in the high sere grasses.

When I went back to the house a bowl of milk was souring in the sun on the window sill overlooking the garden. Tom and I had started to dig in the garden every evening after supper, and I had visions, when rain came again, of planting flowers.

"There's a fox about, Tom," I said.

"I know — I've seen him — we've got to get the old roger, somehow."

"He's all foxes in one," I said. "You should have seen the way — "

"He's been here since the Middle Ages," Tom said. "He lay in the barley one day, washing himself like a dog. I bet if you called him Sir Roger he'd answer."

After that we called him Sir Roger; we used to wait for him in the henyard, under the hovels, every night; we even took the gun to bed with us, so that we could fire at him from the upstairs windows.

Before supper that night we washed. We had lived on a staple and increasingly monotonous diet of bacon and eggs, varied by bread and cheese or bread and jam. That night Nancy cooked us roast sirloin, with beans and new potatoes and a lot of excellent gravy, with a dessert of tarts. There was a refreshing smell of peasmint in the air. The meat, roasted in the old range, with coal, was crisped at the edges, and you could taste the delicious, fire-burnt, crusty juiciness of it on the long red slices. I remember how I carved the meat that night and how I tried to carve it thinly. The knife was not very sharp and Tom rubbed it up on the doorstep. He said what an extraordinary thing it was that so few people could carve, and then I remembered how once, at the Aspen house, I had carved for the old ladies when Rollo was not there. The thought of it made me remember Lydia and I went off, suddenly, not knowing it, into a daydream of thoughts about her. I had tried not to think of her. Now I wondered if she would marry anyone, Blackie for instance, and how much she thought of me and if she was happy. The knife was poised in air, with a slice of beef still on it, and a little blood dripped down, without my knowing it, onto the tablecloth. My impression of her was so vivid that I felt I could see her and feel her in the fading summer evening air. Then suddenly the beef flopped off the knife, falling with a wet splash onto the dish below.

"Thank you," Tom said. "Thank you indeed. Thank you most kindly." He peered down at his empty place. He had been holding his plate in air for quite some time. "Nothing like having the food thrown at you."

"Good God," I said.

"Well, who was it?" Nancy said.

"I'm terribly sorry," I said. "I was thinking of the fox."

After that I paid more attention to the beef, and gradually, in a series of pretended refusals and pretended hints that it would eat just as nice if not nicer cold, we finished it up. Tom had brought in some beer, and between beer and beef and plum-fat slices of curd tart I began to feel blown and hot and sleepy.

I said presently I hoped they would not mind if I crept up to bed, and Tom said: "Good grief, man, who wants bed after that lot? You'll never sleep. Let's have a whack at old Sir Roger."

"One wants to go to bed, one wants to go fox hunting," Nancy said. "What's the other one want to do? What about the washing up? You've left two days' already."

"Oh, I suppose so," Tom said.

"Tom and I will do it," I said.

"*You* and I will do it," she said. "Tom can get in wood for tomorrow."

"I'll just have one pipe and a squint for Sir Roger," Tom said. He had begun to smoke a pipe, a new thing for him, and the only time he ever showed uneasiness was when he filled it and packed it tight and lit it and relit it over and over again.

So Nancy and I washed up, which I suppose was what she wanted, by the light of a tiny oil lamp that made movement vague and yet heightened by the enormity of wall-shadow in the little scullery.

My dislike of washing up and my blown sleepiness brought me to the edge of a drugged doze; so that I did not pay much attention when she said:

"Did you see Tom's new car? What did you think of it?"

I said it was nice, and that I liked it.

"Did he tell you how he got it?" she said.

"He said you bought the old one, and — "

"She made him buy it — didn't he tell you that?"

"No," I said. "Who did?"

"Lydia. She made him do it," she said.

I dried a number of forks and spoons without knowing it, until I held seven or eight together in my hands.

"Put the cutlery in the box," Nancy said. "You didn't hear what I said, did you?"

"You said Lydia made him buy the car."

"After that."

I had to admit to a vacuum after that.

"She twisted round him until he bought the car from Blackie. She almost got old Miss Aspen to buy one. It's all to get business, and they say — "

"Is she married?"

"No. What makes you ask that?"

I did not answer. I not only did not want to hear what they said; I did not propose to believe what they said, moreover, even if they said it.

"Tom saw a lot of her when he was buying the car," she said. "She was up at the house every Sunday."

If my summer had been loveless it had also been free of the acerbity of female minds. I did not like Nancy much at that moment, and I might have liked her even less if she had not, a second later, almost changed the subject.

"They say there's been a fearful battle going on up there. Did you know?"

I said I did not know. "And up where?" I said.

"At the Aspens'. Old Miss Aspen isn't capable any more. She's gone to pieces and never gets up. So Rollo is trying to edge Lydia out, and Lydia is trying to edge Rollo out. He's drinking it away on one side and Heaven knows what's happening to it on the other. She's probably drinking it away too. It's going to rack and ruin. They've been selling land. There were awful death duties on Miss Juliana's will — and now there's the slump."

The slump? I had not heard of the slump before. I had

been aware only of missing a charming, clovered world of vine-houses and acacias and partridge chickens and roses of opulent grace on warm house walls, an oasis of lime and chestnut and grass where Lydia and I had discovered each other, and I did not believe in even the rumor of its change and decay.

"And who says she's drinking?" I said.

"Well, I didn't actually say that."

With extreme care I polished the blade of a knife on the cloth, making it glitter and cast large bloomlike shadows on the walls.

"Whenever women dislike other women they start making them drink," I said, "or they give them babies."

"It's the men who give them babies," she said coldly. "If that isn't too biological for you."

I think I said I had advanced as far as that, and then: "I suppose you'll be telling me next she's going to have a baby?"

"Not that I know of," she said. "But would it surprise you?"

"Not since she's a woman," I said.

She seemed to think desperately for an answer to that, and she said aggressively:

"I don't think anything would surprise me when you consider who her mother was."

"And who," I said, "was her mother?"

She faltered and said:

"Well, I mean, everybody knows. She's dead now, I think, but everybody knows. They say — "

"I suppose you never met her," I said.

"No," she said. "But I don't see that that matters."

I thought of the gray-gloved hand blowing a good-by kiss to me from the window of Evensford's little train; I thought of the tearless face that was almost tearful and I did not answer.

"No, I never met her," she said. "But that's where she gets it from — Lydia I mean. You've got to get it from somewhere, haven't you?"

There was nothing I had to say.

"Of course you don't see it," she said. "But you mark my words — she'll go like her mother one day. She'll go that way too."

"And which way," I said, "was that?"

She pursed her lips and in answer she used the words that my father always used to describe any aspect, in Evensford, of decline and decay: the paths to the grave, the whisky bottle, the race course, the other woman and, not least, the sanatorium. They were all ominously and terribly embraced in them.

"Wrong way," she said. "That's the way she'll go. You see. Wrong way."

That was the end of almost all we had to say to each other that evening. It was curious that we did not, at any time, ever really dislike each other. It was simply that her nature, which ought to have been so soft and milky and appeasing in order to match her gracious and pleasant body, seemed to grow petty when confronted with mine and with anything Lydia had to do with mine. Without intention we started grating furiously on each other. Possibly we suffered — if there is such a thing — from a sort of immutual affection. More and more we conducted conversations in cooling phases, so that always, in the end, we stood frozen against each other, without words.

So perhaps I should not have been surprised when, as she said good night to us, she asked:

"Could you two bear it if I came over and cooked dinner for you on Sunday? You'll get nothing otherwise if you're painting."

We said we should like it, and she said:

"And what would the gentlemen like to eat? Then I can get the butcher to bring it over."

We decided there was nothing better than roast beef again, preferably more than ever, and this time with Yorkshire pudding and possibly yellow plum pie, preferably with cream from Busketts. She made some remark about people giving their orders and knowing what was best, and then said:

"And don't let me come up here at twelve o'clock and find you still in bed. Get the place painted. It's my birthday in three weeks and then we could have a little housewarming party."

August burned into September until the shorn lobes of grassland were the color of the fox we were always stalking but could not catch and the only green was in the great sprays of hawthorn and the water weeds about the brook. When the barley was finished we carried it and stacked it in the yard. It was our only crop, and the land on which it had grown was fissured like the cracked dry basin of a pond, still too hard for ploughing.

There was nothing we could do but turn to the house, and in the last week of August we painted it through. Then we began on the outside. Before we started it looked something like a gray stone box sunk, under a crust of crumbling tile, in a wilderness of elderberry and shriveling hollyhock and gooseberry and vast clumps of horse-radish and rambler rose. We went through everything with scythes and mattocks and even crowbars for the horse-radish, like slaughterers. Under a tangled mattress of fading rambler rose the front fence fell down, and when we put it up again I thinned out the ramblers and tied them back, in fresh, long fans. We did not think the front door had been opened for fifty years. Its bolts were so rusted that when we opened it at last we stepped out into high, wiry, mildewed tunnels of honeysuckle and rambler, impenetrably interlocked, black with the birds' nests of past summers and brittle with the tinder of dead branches. When we removed it all we saw that the door had a small fanlight in the shape of a quartered orange above it, and at the foot of it boot-scrapers in the form of ancient fenders. We painted the door, the fence and the windows white. The house began to have eyes and seemed, presently, larger than it was. This illusion of size sprang also from the cleared garden, the square foreapron of bare earth on which I planned to have, in autumn, clumps of wallflowers and tulip and winter stock. Tom kidded me a good deal about the flowers. There wouldn't be time on a farm, he said, for things like that.

A clutter among the hens brought me out one evening, while it was still light, to see old Sir Roger standing between the house and the barley stack with a dripping pullet in his mouth. He looked like an old yellowish dog singed by fire. He stood for fully half a minute sneering back at me, and I made as if to throw something at him, giving a great, rambling sort of yell:

"Tom! — Sir Roger — !"

He moved off then at a slow lope, the hen still in his mouth like a blooded rag, and before I yelled again for Tom the big, yellow body was sliding up the hedgerow. By the time Tom came out of the house, running with an extraordinary softness I did not understand, the fox was nothing but a snip of alternate dark and yellow shadow beyond the hawthorns.

We raced after him up the field. After a few yards I noticed that Tom was slipping on the bare, dry grass. He had been changing his boots when he heard my yell and was running now in his stockinged feet. It was rather comic to see him slipping and floundering up the slope, swearing "You blasted old Roger — you damned saucy old bastard, you — " But by the time we reached the crest of the field, where a cart track wound between hedges of blackberry and thorn up to the coverts, there was nothing to be seen. We had lost him for the fifth or sixth time and Tom, opening the gate and walking some distance up the track, shouted into the evening silence:

"We'll get you! — you wait, you old devil — you damned old Roger, you — " And then turned to me and said:

"Come on, we'll get him up at the covert — that's the only place we'll get him. We can follow the blood."

I reminded him of the stockings and he laughed, remembering it too, and we turned back.

"I get so concentrated on that damn thing," he said, "one of these days I'll forget my head."

The following week it was Nancy's birthday. There was a difference in age of only about eleven months between Tom and Nancy, and it seemed to me sometimes that they were more than brother and sister. They were like two persons out of the same pure, blond world, with the same buttery hair, the eyes of the same earnest blue transparence, the same untreacherous, unsubtle minds. And since they had been reared, actually, in the same cradle, it was perhaps not surprising that they sometimes thought alike, wanted the same things and felt for each other with intuitive tenderness.

It seems clear to me now that it could only have been for this reason that she invited Lydia to her birthday: not necessarily because she wanted it herself but because she knew, intuitively, even more than he did, that Tom wanted her.

I should, I suppose, never have guessed that. He had not told me yet of the night when, so shocked and so sickened, so puzzled and so decent, he had heard Blackie and his stepmother quarreling in the house of the dead about how they should bury the dead. Nor should I ever have guessed, at least in precisely the eventual terms, another thing.

A great change had come over Lydia; and I want to tell why.

III

THE evening of Nancy's birthday, a Saturday, was a purple umbrella of storm, under which long westerly crevices of somber and brilliant ocher marked a black horizon that seemed slowly to be elevated, like a mountainside, until it merged into a mass of boiling thundercloud. All above the fox coverts, under a sky panting continuously with pale yellow sheet lightning, you could see the conical larches, burnt by summer heat, bronze in the high, bright flashes.

It was not an evening, after all, to eat hot roast sirloin and baked potatoes and well-larded pies of sizzling yellow plums; and I was in my shirtsleeves, without a tie, as Tom drove into Evensford to fetch Lydia, leaving me to help Nancy. The little house was suffocating with storm and fire and roasting beef and crackling pudding and the smell of table candles, which I had to light early because of the storm. It was perhaps not a very good evening for drinking Burgundy either, but I had bought a bottle as a present for Nancy, and she wanted us to drink it. There were still a few pale yellow roses on the house wall and I ran out, at the last moment, just before darkness fell, to gather what I could and put them on the table. I uncorked the bottle of Burgundy and set it there too, between the candles and the roses, and there was a delicate fire on it and on the still dry petals.

Whenever I was alone with Nancy I grew slightly on edge, not precisely nervous, but defensive, and the back of my neck would start tingling. That evening I felt not only defensive, but strained and nervous inside. The bleak thought of rejection by Lydia came back and oppressed me. I kept forcing myself towards a notion that I did not want her. I felt I had made the impossible mistake of thinking that one of the virtues of love was permanence. Now I tried to persuade myself not only that it was not permanent but that it was best that it never should be.

The way out of this was flippancy. Already, as I arranged the roses and uncorked the wine and listened for the rain that seemed so long in coming, I had fired off one or two casual sparks of what I thought was bright conversation to Nancy, lost in vapors of beef and gravy in the scullery.

Presently she came out into the kitchen, wiping her hands on her apron, and said: "You're far too bright tonight." I did not feel bright; I was conscious only of straining all the time against myself, and I said:

"It's just the storm. It's the electricity in the air."

She took me by the sleeves of my shirt, and the back of my neck started tingling.

"Look," she said. "Listen to me." She looked steadily into my face. "I want to ask you something."

"I've already kissed you once," I said, too brightly. "I've already blessed your declining years — "

"I'm not asking for favors and I'm not asking people to burst themselves with wit, either," she said. "Just simmer down and listen."

"I am unsimmered," I said, and I felt bleak again.

"All I want you to do is to promise to behave yourself," she said.

I said if she supposed I was going to behave myself in any other way than a perfectly natural one she was much mistaken.

"I don't know what that means," she said. "I just want you to behave" — she hesitated, trying to select some more exact, incisive word, and at last she found, for some reason, the word balance — "with some sort of balance," she said, "otherwise the party will get lopsided and somebody will start feeling out in the cold, and you know how it is — "

"Naturally." I added some remark about feeling out in the cold in a storm temperature of about eighty degrees, and she said:

"I've arranged it so that Tom is partnering Lydia. That's what I want you to bear in mind."

"Why didn't you say so in the first place?" I said.

"Because — " she said, and then she stopped, turning her head. "That's the car now — I saw the headlights as they turned the bend."

I felt I wanted to go out into the garden and remain there, watching the growing storm. But then I heard rain begin falling, at first in big, floppy, countable drops, and then in a sudden running hiss, with a sound like one of the pots in the scullery boiling over. A magical sweetness of dusty earth freshened by rain floated, a few seconds later, through the open door. As I breathed it I felt it turn sharply, inside me, into a dull, beating ache.

Then I saw car lights flashing on the barley stack and across sliding thunder rain and on the stones of the yard. There was a banging of car doors and then Tom and Lydia came running out of the rain, under the shelter of a mackintosh he had thrown over their heads.

They came running into the doorway at a crouch, heads down against the rain, shaking the dripping mackintosh, laughing.

Flares of excitement beat at the ache inside me as Lydia lifted the mackintosh from her black hair and shook it free.

"By Jove, that was a dash," Tom said.

I stood staring at Lydia. A few drops of rain had settled on her face. She looked at me in return and did not wipe them away.

"Hullo," she said. I felt, for some reason, a long way off. Her voice was very quiet. "How are you?"

"I'm very well," I said. "Thank you."

She looked at me calmly and clearly.

"You look very well," she said.

I was perplexed that I did not ask her how she was.

Then Nancy called from the scullery: "I'll be with you in a minute, Lydia dear. There's a light upstairs if you care to go — "

"I'm all right, I'm quite happy," Lydia said.

"Get her a glass of sherry, you two," Nancy called. "I don't want the gravy to go lumpy."

"That's my job," I said. A prolonged torment of nervousness went through me as I fumbled about among bottles and glasses. Rain poured with splendid summer savagery outside, drowning the sound of my sloppings as I poured sherry into glasses.

"Bless you all," Lydia said. "It's nice to see everybody." Her voice was deeper, cooler, more adult than it had been. "And that goes specially for you, Nancy," she called into the kitchen. "Bless you, dear, and a happy birthday." I drank, nursing a private sense of roving despair.

"What a night," Tom said. "Old boy, think that tomorrow we might start ploughing — "

As we sat at dinner rain beat with a great, warm spout of savagery on the roof of the house and summer lightning continued to pour pale yellow sheets on the hill where the coverts were. I carved the meat, trying once again to carve it thinly and this time not to dream. Tom poured the wine and we toasted Nancy. The air was dripping with thunder heat and the heat of cooking, and the candlelight cast enormous shadows about us in engrossing confusion on our newly painted walls.

It was probably not until this time that I noticed that

[215]

Lydia was wearing black. Except for the first evening I had met her I had not seen her in black before. It was a very simple dress, with plain, long, tight sleeves and a close halfway bodice that fitted her well and showed her breast. It had on it a wide collar, oval and coffee-colored, that relieved the blackness and gave it a pleasant dignity. Occasionally she had been rather loud, sometimes a bit wild, as at Milton Posnett, in her dresses, but now I thought she looked reticent and mature and womanish and cool. The last of adolescence had gone out of her. She looked, for some reason, older than any of us, and as if she could make up her mind, at last, about what she knew she wanted.

She admired the little farmhouse very much that night. She kept arching her neck and asking questions about it, looking about her at the groping, engrossing shadows roaming on white walls and simple brickwork and low, black beams.

"And you two did it," she said. "I call it wonderful. Just you two — you men."

"Men," I said drearily, "are sometimes capable of odd flashes of achievement. Here and there — "

"I want to see it all," she said. "Tom — you must take me all over."

So after dinner Tom took her over the house. He had fitted up an inspection lamp from a battery on the landing, and he carried it from room to room. Rain beat with thundery violence on the house, hissing across the yard. I made coffee, and Nancy, in the scullery, piled the dishes.

When the coffee was ready I went to the foot of the stairs, calling Lydia and Tom. There was no answer. And then I saw the inspection lamp cable trailing up into the attics. I did not wait. She was determined, that night, to see every inch of the house, and Tom, equally determined and fussy as a house-proud hen, must have shown her every brick and sill and board of it.

"I think it's the sweetest place," she said, when they came down again, and her eyes were shining. "You really feel you could live here — you feel it when you come inside." And then Tom showed her the photographs we had taken, before and after the renovation, and she was absorbed, her head close to his, as the pictures passed from hand to hand.

"Just listen to that rain," Nancy would say. "Just listen."

We drank a lot of coffee and talked and listened to the rain. About ten o'clock a gap seemed to open in the hot sky just above the house, letting down an obliterating, solid deluge.

Tom actually leapt up in the center of the room as the spout of rain hit the house. "A cloudburst," he said, "that's what they call a cloudburst — you'll never get home in this."

"That's all right," Nancy said. "Who's worrying about that? You've got spare beds and Lydia and I can sleep together."

Rain struck the house with the power of a mountain torrent, so that for some seconds we could not hear ourselves speak. Then it became cut off, like a tap, and only the distances roared with watery echoes.

"I'll make more coffee," I said.

When I came back from the scullery from making coffee, Tom was not there.

"Where's Tom?" I said.

"He's gone to telephone from next door," Nancy said. "He's gone to tell Mother and Lydia's people we're going to stay the night."

"If he can slosh all the way up to McKechnies," I said, "he could just as easily have driven the car."

"Really, men are dense sometimes," Nancy said.

I began to pour more coffee.

"Not for me," Nancy said. "I'm going to make up the bed — no, stay where you are, Lydia. I can do it."

So Lydia and I, a moment later, were left alone together,

and I started trembling. She was sitting on the floor, leaning back against a chair, holding her coffee cup in her lap. Only the table candles were still burning, and her neck was ivory in the black dress. All about the house, hissing and weaving, the lessening rain spun a web of sound that was more like a heightened and oppressive form of silence in which we had nothing to say to each other. I looked at her body and felt as I had done on the evening I had first met her: poised on a knife edge, insecure, trembling, icy and yet burning inside.

For about a minute she did not look at me, and I began trembling even more. At last I could not bear it any longer, and got up and took the empty coffee cup from her. She lifted her face for a second or two, holding it there, remarkably cool and unexcited and yet exciting me.

Suddenly I bent down and kissed her. With my mouth I pressed her face against the chair. She lifted her hands, pushing them against my shoulders, very lightly and gently holding me back. I felt her lips, slightly hard at first, gradually relax and take me into them, a little acquiescent as I thought, and more tender.

When I drew away she looked at me. Her eyes were indecipherably dark in the candlelight and I could not tell what she was thinking.

Then I began asking her when she was going to see me again. She seemed to think about it for some moments, letting her head fall softly to one side. "Please," I said, and she smiled in a sort of absent way and looked beyond me.

"No more," she said.

I felt a shock of misery go through me.

"Just because you kiss people it doesn't mean that you love them. That isn't love," she said.

"It isn't very long since you did love me," I said.

"Isn't it?" she said. And I knew suddenly that to her it already seemed very long.

[218]

When she opened her mouth to say something else I began kissing her again, and what she had to say never came. I pressed her down in the chair and ran my hands over her hair and breast and face.

"Now you know how I feel about you," I said.

"No," she said. "That's it, you see. I don't."

It was like lying down and being trampled on.

Ineptly and flatly I said: "How is it you don't know? Tell me — "

"I know I just don't, that's all. It isn't why or how or anything of that. It's something you know without thinking and you can't explain." And then she said something that was the key to the whole affair:

"People do all sorts of odd things and they never know why."

What I said next was bound to come sooner or later, and I said it with marked, even bitterness:

"Don't tell me you've found out why with someone else. Perhaps with Blackie?"

She remained very quiet and calm.

"I felt terribly sorry for Blackie," she said.

"Sorry?"

"I know you don't see it like I do and probably you never will," she said. "But then you're not me and I'm not you, and how could you?"

"Don't ask me to tell you why," she said after a moment. "It was something I felt and I can't explain."

I felt too miserable to say anything, and she said: "Don't be bitter. I'm not the first girl to think she loved people and make a fool of herself a few times before she found the right one," she said. "There's nothing very odd, is there, in that?"

"Nothing odd," I said.

"Well — "

[219]

"Only something miserably and damnably and rottenly painful for those who don't happen to be the right ones," I said.

She did not answer that. She let her head fall sideways, staring past the candlelight with inexpressible contemplation of some distant point or thought or conclusion that I could not share.

A few moments later Nancy came downstairs, and then almost immediately Tom came back.

"Had a bit of a job to get through," he told us. "Some lines down somewhere. McKechnie says there's a tree down too on the Caldecott road."

"I think it's as well we stayed," Nancy said. "Anyway, we can all sleep late tomorrow and then have the beef cold for lunch, with baked potatoes and horse-radish sauce."

"Just like Nance," Tom said, "to shut the stable door when the horse-radish has bolted."

"Tom's suddenly very witty," she said.

"That," I said, "is because he's very happy" — a remark that, profound as I thought it was, nobody seemed to understand.

It was after midnight when we went to bed. As we said good night to each other I saw all the reality of my remark about happiness and wit come to life wonderfully in Tom's face. His eyes were transparently tireless and shining. In them was a glow, a maturer, brighter version of the expression I had first seen on the day I had taken Lydia skating. It had seemed to indicate, then, a transfixed, bewildered state of wonder. Now the eyes were vivid and awake with joy.

It was past midnight when he preceded her, solemnly courteous, up the stairs, carrying candles, to show her to her room.

"I've put her in the room next to you, after all," Nancy said. "The bed in my room isn't very big for two."

I said something about there being times when small beds were preferable, and she said:

"Shut up. Don't forget we've got Presbyterian neighbors. They're probably spying now."

"It was one of my jokes," I said.

"We didn't have many tonight, did we?" she said. "It was Tom who was on form."

"Yes," I said. "Did I behave?"

She picked up the final candle to go up to bed.

"How should I know?" she said. "I wasn't here for the important part of the time."

I let the rain hiss my answer.

In bed I lay listening to the church clock, across the fields, striking hollow quarters through the steaming rain. My mind, fired and wakened by too much coffee, raced brilliantly and desperately about, thinking of Lydia and Tom and even Alex in a sequence of bright distortions. Tom and I slept on two iron hospital-like beds that creaked like loose metallic corsets as we turned from side to side, and after a time I heard Tom tossing and turning about, sleepless as I was.

"Awake?" he said, and I said "Yes," and damned the coffee.

He sat up in bed. Rain, lessening a little now, was falling in a gentle autumnal stream over dark fields and I could see a little far distant lightning still panting across the sky above the bronzy coverts.

"We had a nice evening," Tom said. "Well, more than nice — wonderful."

"Very nice," I said. "Lydia loved the house, didn't she?"

"She loved it," he said.

The air was humid and I threw back the clothes, stretching out, listening to the dying rain.

"Not raining so fast now," Tom said.

"No, not so fast," I said.

[221]

For a few moments he did not speak again. Then he said something else about the rain, and I replied. We went through a series of these deadlocks. I knew then that he was trying to tell me something. He moved several times nervously about the bed. Presently he got out of bed to open one of the windows, which we had closed against the rain. I heard him breathing the cooler, rain-washed air. He said he thought the rain was stopping now and how wonderful the air always was after the rain.

He started to speak several times. There is nothing like the complexity of a straightforward mind that finds it cannot express itself in a straightforward way. He made several more false starts, and then got as far as "That night she asked Alex to do something for her — at her twenty-first. I never forgot that. Do you remember?"

I said I remembered, and then he began. He unwound it from inside himself in a series of tortured repetitions. He went over and over it: like a man trying to get a speech right. He spoke in humble confusion about his feelings as he had driven down to the garage with the note for Blackie — how he had not wanted to go, how he wished Alex had gone, how he wished to God something had come up to get him out of it. Then he came to the scene there — the two people quarreling with, as it seemed to him, such brutal disrespect over Old Johnson, dead upstairs, and Blackie with soap-gray razor, big and dark, and offensive under the gaslight. He must have gone over this scene again and again, re-enacting it for himself in the light of later and torturous reflection, reliving it under the high glare of his own conclusions, his outrage and his troubled decency. All the time he had wanted to be sick. He was sick with the odor of grease and gaslight and petrol fume. He was sick at something brutally casual, at something of revolting physical grossness that he could only feel and could not describe. "God, you couldn't begin to think — you

[222]

couldn't bear it," he said several times. "You couldn't bear it, I tell you — "

I thought the sky began to turn copper-colored as we lay and talked there. For a few moments there seemed to be no sound of rain. Then he got out of bed and went to the window and said:

"The sky's clearing — I think it's stopped. Yes — there's a star."

In the growing, darkish, coppery light he moved about the bedroom, finding his slippers and his dressing gown. He said:

"I'm going down for a drink of milk. Perhaps it'll soothe the coffee down. Do you want some?"

I said no, and he went quietly downstairs, shutting the door after him. Through the window I saw one star after another reveal itself in a breaking sky. I lay watching them and thought of Tom and what he had said and how, at last, I felt I understood him. I thought of Lydia and what she had said, earlier, about love and the inconsequent business of love and how there were a great many things, some of them important to yourself and some of them monstrously impossible and silly to other people, for which you could not give any explanation. Stars began to brighten all over the lighter, rain-swept sky. All the eaves of the house dripped coolly into sloppy puddles in the yard. I thought a long way back to the day when Lydia had first skated, when Tom had first seen her and she had not even remembered his name. It was impossible to guess how tortuously and how far he had traveled round before he had reached the point of knowing consciously that he wanted her. She in turn had seemed desperately to try to gain one object, and now, at last, had succeeded only in gaining, as people so often do, another she had tried to avoid.

I lay there for a long time, watching a sky from which all cloud and rain and lightning had departed, leaving the entire, sparkling, naked range of stars. When at last Tom did not seem to come back I got out of bed and went and stood at the window, leaning on the lowered sash, staring across the fields.

From below Tom's voice, and then Lydia's, came from the yard. I saw a stream of light from the kitchen swing out to the barley stack, and I heard Tom say:

"You see — all over. Every star in the sky out now." And then: "It's drying already. It just ran through the cracks like a drain. Careful just here — "

Footsteps, voices, then the figures of Tom and Lydia went across the yard. I stood for a moment or two longer, looking down. From the yard I caught the words "Tom," and then something else, and then something about "ploughing perhaps on Monday." Tom's voice threaded nervously into air alone, babbling on as he had done in bed, confused and groping.

I saw it at last silenced by an upward gesture of her arms. He seemed to stand stunned and then she began to kiss him. He had probably never kissed a woman before except perhaps at a party, in fun, at a dance or in some stupid game at Christmas time. Now he was in love, for the first, the most miraculous time. I walked away from the window and lay down on the bed. I stared up at the stars again and thought of him, stunned, joyous, blown explosively out of himself by the force of a new and tender wonder.

"All the stars are out," I heard him say again. "Every single star."

IV

Tom's neighbors were a family of Presbyterian Scots named McKechnie; they owned a farm of three hundred acres up the hill. In the beginning they had been, as neighbors are in the beginning, very friendly. McKechnie, a man of sixty or so, had something of the appearance of a thin cylinder of freckled steel gone rusty at the top. The McKechnie boys and the McKechnie girls, seven of them, were cylinders of comparable appearance, all stiff, all dry, all freckled, all rusty at the head.

Every Sunday the McKechnies did a regimental march to church in Evensford. Since there was no Presbyterian worshiping place in Evensford they had joined a chapel, the fearsome Succoth, that gave the nearest pattern of a tomblike ideal. In summer they trailed across field-paths, the girls white-gloved, the men in squarish bowler hats; in winter they marched by road. They did not cook at the McKechnie house on Sundays. There were stories of midday dinners of cold pork, faggot and bread and jam, with only streams of long, cold prayer and cold water to wash them down. The McKechnies brought even to the Nonconformity of Evensford an essay in Sabbatarianism the severity of which it had no hope of matching. Even Evensford cooked and ate on Sundays. With the halo of the chapel pew went, just as deeply revered, the halo of the oven: roast beef and hymn book were equally sanctified. Only the McKechnies, spare and cylindrical, with their strange eyes of sandy-green, their vivid rustiness and their fleshless essay in self-denial, stood mirthlessly apart from a day that Evensford, both in belly and spirit, really enjoyed.

The friendliness of the McKechnies on weekdays was entirely the opposite of this. Mrs. McKechnie became a pale but jovial-feathered hen sending down to Tom, in the afternoons, plates of still warm girdle-scones. McKechnie lent him tools, promised a pup from a coming litter of sheep dogs and threw open to Tom, without prompting, the entire three hundred acres of shooting from the house with its drawn Venetian blinds of dark cocoa color up to the coverts on the hill. The McKechnie sons went to endless and selfless trouble, even once or twice at night, to bring us veterinary help when the six heifers had forty-eight hours of mild poisoning from a temporary pollution of the brook. "And if ever ye find ye can't manage, Tom," Mrs. McKechnie would say, "just shout and one of the girls'll be only too glad to come over."

One of the girls was Pheley. I thought at first her name was Phebey, but when the final entanglements of accent were cleared away it plainly emerged as Pheley, perhaps a diminutive of Ophelia: we never knew. Pheley, cast in the freckled-rusty-cylindrical mold of all McKechnies, was twenty-eight. Her figure seemed to have various spoonlike knobs stuck about it, like bony afterthoughts. In sunlight her eyes were a pale, sharp green. In other lights they were sandy, with irradiations of mild, streaked emerald. She had a habit of saying "Ye never will!" or "Ye never do!" as other people say "There, now" or "Fancy." Her voice had a light, piercing astringence, a sort of overeager gristliness, and her skin the pale, embarrassing candescence of the sandy-haired.

It was Pheley who brought down to Tom her mother's plates of still warm girdle-scones. At first it was only scones, with honey to put in them; then it was oatcakes and currant biscuits and shortbread and damson pie. Tom, in the weeks before I joined him, was not ungrateful for these things. They saved his cooking, varied the monotonies of his cheese and eggs and bacon. It came, at first, as a pleasant surprise

[226]

to him, an act of unsolicited neighborliness that touched him. Then, alone there at the farm, lonely at times, oppressed by the death of Alex and miserable, as I afterwards knew, because I had abandoned him, he began to expect them. He began to look forward to the figure of Pheley coming down the hill.

"Well, here I am again. The old nuisance. Always turning up like a bad penny. Well, we had a wee bit stuff left over — "

Soon she began to come every afternoon; she began to focus on Tom, during the hot weeks of August, the ferocious concentrations of a burning glass. Through the pallid eyes, deceptively emotionless as marbles, poured a white heat of narrowed interest that must have throbbed under the colorless candescent skin like fever. She started to linger about the house. She stretched her long, gaunt, red-haired figure, with its uneasy afterthoughts prodding under the blouse like her own clenched knuckles, in his chairs. She gave him ardent help with buckets and horse and heifer feed and said: "Take the load off your poor feet while I rinse the tea things — Ah! Ye're awful, the breakfast things too. Didn't you have *any* dinner? You know you could have dinner with us."

Presently the McKechnies invited him home. In the four or five weeks before I joined him he went up to the Venetian-blinded house, stuffed inside with manorial fumed oak, two or three times a week for supper. He walked over the farm with McKechnie. He was intensely anxious to succeed up there, in his own small, neglected farm, by himself. He wanted to set out alone, severed from his father, from his family, as a sort of Benjamin hitherto overshadowed by big brothers. McKechnie was a good farmer, and Tom, I think, felt that he could learn much from a man who had so succeeded on a comparable piece of neighboring soil. So he was glad of McKechnie. He drank in a great deal of McKechnie's advice, generously and gladly given, about the peculiarity of land that is so strong that it grows wheat like dark reeds but so harsh, in misuse, under rain, that it becomes savagely temperamental and intractably ruinous to people who work it stupidly and weakly.

So McKechnie would say: "Ye'll never grow barley on that bit. That's a mistake. Never do that again. Bring your barley up yon hill. There. That's your barley land, boy. Keep your wheat down at the bottom. It's terrible strong land there. Catch it right, and ye're made. Catch it wrong, and I doubt if prayer'll ever put it right from now till Doomsday."

Tom became intensely grateful for advice of this kind. Even when he didn't go to supper he got into the habit of walking across, in the evenings, to the McKechnie land. The two farms shared for a short distance a cart track that led, finally, up to the coverts. It was a mass of sloe and camomile and silver weed, with hare tracks running across from one field to another, and some distance along it a pile of wurzels, sprouting pink-violet from a summer of clamping, stood unused by a gateway.

"It'll do your heifers no harm to eat a bit of water for a change. Roots are another way of feeding water — just come up and help yourself any time ye want them. The gate's unlocked at the end."

If McKechnie was not there, Tom could talk to the sons; and if there were no sons Pheley was always waiting.

One evening, after about a month of this, Pheley met him on the hill. There was no one at home, she said, and she wanted to walk back with him. She seemed rather upset. If each of the McKechnie girls had been dressed as men and each of the McKechnie sons dressed as women, it would hardly have been possible to tell that a mistake had been made. Except for her thin, narrow, soprano voice, Pheley was very like a tall, pinafored boy.

That evening, as they walked down between alleys of

ripening sloe bushes, under a brilliant July sunset that seemed to inflame every McKechnie hair until it was a virulent shade of red ocher, she asked him if he saw anything different about her.

And Tom, in exactly the way typical of himself and of most men, said "No. I don't think so."

She turned, strained and nervous and drawn, and said:

"Nothing? You mean you don't see anything changed at all?"

And Tom said, with that honest innocence of his: "No. You look just the same as ever, as far as I can see" — a remark that would have annoyed most women but that must have gone through Pheley like a sting of agony.

Then she stopped. "Take a look at me, Tom," she said. "Will you take a good long look at me?"

Tom took a good long look at Pheley. He could see nothing different. She stared at him, all fiery and sandy-eyed, with a blazing impression of being overstrung about something and on the verge of tears.

Then suddenly she whipped off her hat.

"Good God," Tom said.

"Now you see," Pheley said; and he saw that she had cut her hair.

Perhaps it seems ridiculous to recall, at this distance, the heartburning intensity of days when girls were constantly whipping off their hats and saying to young men, with grief or triumph or some other high emotion, "There! I went out and had it off." And some poor stunned fellow would stand there trying to frame out of his incoherence a word of enthusiasm for a transformation that had reduced his lover to the level of a newly barbered boy. It seems impossible now that homes were being torn apart by great rifts of anger and shock because fathers returned from offices to find daughters bobbed and shriven, with trembling mothers standing ready to placate and pacify men who grieved impotently for locks and curls they felt they would never see again.

When Tom looked at Pheley he was reminded of a girl he had known, at school, who had had her hair cut off because of ringworm; and how, for him, she had never really become a girl again.

"Well," Pheley said. She spoke with a sort of doomlike abandon for which her high, astringent voice was not fitted. "It's done now. Whether anybody likes it or not. It's done now."

It seemed to Tom that there was nothing much to make a fuss about. He could not see much difference, as far as attraction went, between a long-haired Pheley and one who seemed to be wearing a red stage-wig. Then she rose in pure blasphemy.

"Grief, there's been hell to pay."

Tom did not know what to answer; she had a curious, naked look of unreality, all red and stagy and slightly embarrassing, as she stood there doubly fired by the setting sun.

Then wild, pressed, sandy-shot tears started springing from her red-rimmed eyes, and she said, whimpering:

"He whipped me."

Tom stood terribly stunned. He had not grasped that the cutting off of Pheley's hair might be, to McKechnie, a sin second only in outrage to something like a damnation of the Holy Ghost.

"He came upstairs and whipped me."

She hung her head, a grown woman of twenty-eight, beaten and turned child, crying desperately. For some moments Tom experienced a terrible sorrow for her. It was all so monstrous and infamously typical of narrow sectarian prejudice that he did not think for one moment it had anything to do with himself.

"Don't cry," was all he could think of saying. "You musn't cry."

She stood there crying a little longer, and then he took her to the house. He made a pot of tea, and they sat at the kitchen table, drinking it. Tears had reddened and enlarged the almost hairless lids of her eyes until they were as puffed and swollen as her mouth.

After a time she spoke, tremblingly, of her awful discontent. He began to get some idea of the monstrous iron that bound the McKechnie household. No cooking on Sundays, no music, no jokes, not even much talking, no papers, no reading except of sectarian things. A prayer meeting once a week and often, especially in winter, twice or three times; a long, dry, scouring word to the Lord before breakfast every day. A hardness, an enamel of twice-fired prejudice and precept, held the family, the eldest son, a man of forty, in a kind of isolated and awful fealty. Pheley had never been to a dance, a cinema, a theater, a public house or a public place where music was played. She did not know what these things were like. An inculcated horror of them bound her like a fear of disease. It not only seemed monstrously outdated and unreal to Tom but about as fatuous: a fatuity that left him shocked and disbelieving and amazed.

Pheley poured all this out to him and he listened. She drank tea slowly, dazed, as if her lips were bruised, and once or twice she stirred uneasily, with a corresponding tightening of her lips, in her chair.

After a time Tom asked her if she felt better, and she said: "Except for my back."

Tom grasped the meaning of this slowly. Her earlier remark about beating had shocked him, but he had not thought of it as being so harshly literal as that. He took it to mean a boxed ear, a few slaps of a hand about the head perhaps, not more.

"Your back?" he said. And she got up from her chair and said:

"I'll show you."

She reached over her shoulder and undid the clasps of her dress and spread the panels of it outward with her two hands. She wore even then an old-fashioned camisole instead of a slip, and something had ripped it down the center. Underneath it the flesh was so much like pale alabaster that where the strokes of beating had cut into it the lines seemed raised and crusted, already more blue than red. They might have been laid there with a hot and accurate bar.

When she sat down at the table, her shoulders naked, she started weeping again. Tom felt a wave of sickness that was exactly as sour and mortifying as the one he had felt when hearing Blackie Johnson and his mother quarreling over the dead. The two things belonged to the same strange world of monstrous impossibilities. They did not happen. They were odious incongruities in a life that had never given him anything but decency and happiness and an immortal trust in the decency of others. He believed in that as profoundly as McKechnie believed in whatever God it was he believed in — and after that Tom didn't think it was much of a God — and he came as near to hating McKechnie as he had ever hated anyone at all.

It was like him, too, to be practical.

"You must put something on that," he said. "Some ointment, some hound's-tongue or something — "

Pheley smiled a little between her crying.

"You don't quite grasp it yet, do you?" she said. She looked more than ever like a pasty, red-eyed doll with an ill-fitting crop of stiff, sandy hair. Tom did not know what he had failed to grasp and she said:

"You don't get it. If I'm beaten I must bear it. I mustn't heal it. It must heal itself. If you deserve the affliction you

[232]

musn't anoint the affliction. Otherwise it has no value. Now do you get what I mean?"

Slowly Tom, shocked again, got what she meant. She cried again, this time, as on most of the others, not through pain but through the humiliation of being a grown woman, bludgeoned by chastisements she must have known were archaic and monstrous and which she found it hard to explain. Her face became a smudged and desolate mass of tear-marks that stained the pale auburn skin like a rash. She broke down a little, biting the fingers of both hands in order to quieten her tears, and then put her head at last on Tom's shoulder.

"We'll see about this," Tom said. "I'll get ointment to-morrow. You can come down in the afternoon and put it on."

She stayed a little longer, and then gave a curious secrecy to it all by saying:

"I'd better go now. Otherwise they'll be looking for me and they'll find the two of us here together. They'll think it has something to do with you."

It did not occur to Tom that it had anything to do with him. Nor did it occur to him, even remotely until some long time afterwards, that the cutting of Pheley's hair and the beating of her back might be two things by which Pheley and McKechnie might try to hold him to something, as it were to a promise, a solemn imputation of affection, he had never intended should be there.

When I first met Pheley we were down in the barley field; and in her first words there was a sharp, thin-lipped hostility.

"Oh! Who's the friend?"

She was quick to notice my small hands, inadequate and much stabbed by barley ears.

"Ye'll have to learn to make the sheaves half-size," she said, "won't you?"

"I'll make them twice as big," I said, "and then you can lift them."

"Ye never will!" she said.

One afternoon she brought us, with the girdle-scones, a large blue can of tea. As we stood drinking it she took up the rake and began raking up big rustling rolls of barley. She had very long, freckled and, as it were, red-nosed arms that went right round the sheaf in a pale, sinewy, expert lock. She made a dozen of these sheaves in, as it seemed, no time at all, leaving them like fat, lolloping sheep among my rows of skinny lambs.

"That'll give ye some idea," she said, and the point of this was not lost on me.

But the point of it was lost, that day, every other day and even for some time after she had cut her hair, on Tom. He accepted her simply as the pointed expression of the McKechnie character. It did not occur to him that she was any more than another boy, flat, angular, several years older than himself, who wanted to show a decent and generous neighborliness to a newcomer.

To me, at first, she was a sexless barb that irritated.

"Ah! Here comes the friend," she would say.

"And here," I got to answer, "comes the enemy."

In this way we tried unsuccessfully to hate each other off the place.

By the time we had the party for Nancy's birthday Tom had grown to accept her as something awkward on the landscape that had to be tolerated. Her high voice, crowlike, cawed at us through the afternoons. Tom paid his dutiful calls to the farmhouse in the evenings, taking back a washed tea can, using the telephone, asking advice from McKechnie. Whenever and wherever he went, Pheley was there.

Once he saw it in an amused light. "I was having a look

[234]

round for Sir Roger," he said, "and I damn near had a shot at something red. It was a McKechnie!"

After that I used to say: "Here she comes, Tom. Here's your vixen."

When Tom went up to use the telephone on the night of Nancy's birthday most of the McKechnies had gone to bed; but Pheley, her mother and father and an elder sister named Flora, married to a consol-operator in an Evensford factory who had deserted after six months, were still in the parlor, waiting for the storm to subside.

The McKechnies had electricity in the house. Naked bulbs were suspended at economic points from opaque white shades, of the kind used in offices, so that a harsh glare pierced here and there the ecclesiastical fumed-oak gloom. That night, as Tom was telephoning, the entire system fused, plunging the house in darkness.

Tom called that it was probably nothing to worry about — perhaps a transmitter had been struck by the storm somewhere — and the two McKechnie girls, Pheley and Flora, went groping upstairs for candles.

By the time they came down again Tom had finished telephoning, and it was Flora, not Pheley, who said:

"I see there's a light in your house, Tom. Upstairs."

"Oh! It's Nancy making up the beds," Tom said. "She and Miss Aspen are going to stay the night." He treated it all very naturally and casually and then said:

"If you showed me the fusebox I could find out what's wrong for you before I go back. It might not be a transmitter — there's always the chance it's a fuse."

Halfway down the whitewashed cellar steps Tom was shown the fusebox by McKechnie, who stood on an upper step, holding a candle so that Tom could see. The main house fuse had blown. In the two minutes it took Tom to mend it McKechnie said:

"Who did you say was staying the night with you?"

"My sister and her friend."

"Just the three of ye?"

Tom said I was there too, and McKechnie asked:

"Richardson? Would it be someone I knew?"

"Probably not," Tom said. "Used to work on the county paper. You know — the offices in Evensford High Street."

"Ah! Yes," McKechnie said. "I know. I used to see the light in there on Sundays. Always burning away there after we came from chapel."

A moment later Tom plugged in the fuse. The naked economic bulbs flared harshly about the gloom. At the foot of the stairs Pheley, a delighted, candle-bathed, eager figure, stood overwhelmed at Tom's swift excellence with fuses.

"Ah! Tom, ye're so quick. That would have taken Ian or Jamie half an hour or more — "

"Take your candle and go to bed," McKechnie said. His voice too was like a switch, snapping out all conversation. "You too, Flora. It's after ten." And the two sisters, wordless except for almost inaudible good nights, cowed as recalcitrant children, turned and went after their petering candles upstairs.

Tom said "Good night" and then remembered the telephone and asked if he could pay for the call.

"Y'owe me nothing," McKechnie said. "Good night."

For a few eager days Tom was lost in a world that contained nothing but Lydia. I withdrew myself from it with unobtrusive excuses that I do not think he even heard. It was late September. The countryside had begun to be embalmed in soft, eggshell light, under skies of drowsing turquoise, with delicate settling night mist that began to give back to the grasslands a first renewal of green. It was warm and cloudless by day and during my absence Lydia came up to spend a whole day at the farm with Tom. They cooked lunch

[236]

together and afterwards sowed grass seed in a rectangular plot in the front garden, beyond the porch. "This will be our lawn," Lydia said, "this is where we shall sit — we shall get the sun here all afternoon."

Lunch had been a howling failure. "Literally howling," Tom said. "I never laughed so much for years."

The meal was to have consisted, it seemed, of fried steak and potatoes, with tinned apricots and cream. I doubt if Lydia had ever cooked a meal in her life. She put the frying pan on the oil burner, flopped the steak in, without fat, and hoped that presently God, or someone else, would announce it ready. While it heated she got herself absorbed with Tom in the other room. I think he was still too shy to make advances, and a blinding flash from the oil stove, ten minutes later, could have done nothing to help him. He flew into the scullery and discovered that a sort of dry explosion had blown the frying pan from the stove. There was a horrible odor of blue-flamed steak and Tom said something about the outlook for young farmers' wives, to say nothing of young farmers, was not very rosy, and Lydia said "It's nothing but your beastly stove" — and chased him with the frying pan.

The chase with the frying pan added much to the loveliness of the day. Tom laughed so much that he could not run more than fifty yards across the paddock. At one point Lydia lost a shoe and Tom called back at her "There was an old woman came hippety-hop" — and she threw the frying pan at him and then fell down. After this Tom chased her back to the house, where they finished up with boiled eggs and bread and butter. They laughed so much over these too that they could hardly eat them. "I think we must have given them fifty minutes," Tom said, and I did not ask why.

In the afternoon they sowed grass seed and lay for a long time in the sun. Later they took the water cart to the brook and Lydia, taking my place, stood in the stream and filled the buckets. She tucked her skirts into her knickers, Tom said, as if she didn't care a damn for him or for anyone else, and she took off her shoes and stockings. Sooner or later it was inevitable that she started throwing water at Tom. They started to laugh again too, and on the green and stony stream bed she slipped and sat down. As she sat there, telling him rather drolly how cool it was to feel the water about the nice parts of herself, he cried with laughing. "And now what do I do while everything hangs out to dry?" she said. And when Tom drove back up the hill, seeing the road through a simmering veil of laughing tears, Lydia sat on the water cart, wringing water from her skirt and knickers so that it ran down her bare legs and thighs in such noisy streams that they laughed about that too.

It was perhaps here, as they came up the hill, perhaps earlier, as they shrieked after each other with the frying pan across the paddock, that one of the McKechnie sons saw them fooling together.

Back at the house Lydia stripped, put on an old mackintosh of Tom's and hung all her wet garments on a line in the stackyard. "Just like a proper old washing day," Tom said. "They took years to dry" — and once again I did not ask him why.

Nothing could have been happier than his face as he told me all this next morning, when I came back.

He kept laughing, and then, as he reached some point where he did not want me to go further with him, he would suddenly stop and choke back his words, going off into some unnarratable private dream. I was glad of all this; there was something wonderfully touching about seeing him rise excitedly out of his shell of shyness, and if I did not shout with laughter too it was usually because an occasional dream of my own kept insistently returning to trouble me in spite of anything I could do to hold it back. I was haunted, briefly, sharply and sometimes in a peculiar, elusive way still harder to bear, by a small recollection of partridge chickens running among summer ferns, by the sound of fingers scratching at a counterpane in a hot bedroom and a voice sobbing to me convulsively.

I had previously thought I had got over these things. It now appeared that I had not got over them; and because of it, that day, I had something of my own to tell Tom.

"Going away?" he said. "Where?"

"London," I told him. "I've got a bit of a job there."

"Job — ? What sort of job?"

"Books — sort of — "

"Books again," Tom said. "Always the old books. Just like you."

"Always the old books," I said.

"I shall hate it without you," Tom said, "but I'm damn glad. You know what I mean?"

I said I knew what he meant, and we laughed together.

"Anyway, we'll have a good bust-up one night before you go — a good old send-off," he said. "With some more of that wine."

That week Tom began to put the plough into the barley stubble. The land was still iron-hard, and because he was busy there and because we now had an extra horse I went down with the water cart, that afternoon, alone. It was light, dreamy weather and I stayed down at the bridge for nearly an hour, talking with an old turkey-cock named Sturman about the way the summer had baked us up. "Rare weather," he kept saying, and went off into some reminiscence of how the stream had dried up completely in the summer of '87.

By the time I got back it was four o'clock. I drove the water cart into the stackyard and left it there. And then, as I crossed to the house, I saw Tom leaning on the paddock

[239]

gate staring heavily across the field. Down on the near corner of the barley stubble the plow horse was browsing the hedge.

"Tired out from yesterday," I said. "That's what comes of running after girls with frying pans — among other things."

He turned slowly to look at me from the gate with a face that was white and expressionless. There was no kind of emotion in him. He stared at me blank and stunned.

"Good God, you look dicky," I said, and then I saw his gun at his side.

"I can't believe it," he said, "the oddest damn thing happened when you were gone — "

He stared up the field, telling me of what had happened. About half an hour after I had gone Sir Roger had loped up the hawthorn hedge, not fifty yards away. Tom had got into the habit of taking the gun with him almost wherever he went, and it lay that afternoon under the hedge at the end of a furrow.

He ran up towards the McKechnie land, seventy or eighty yards behind the fox, with the gun in his hand. The fox, as always, did not seem to hurry. Once he stopped and dallied and leered back. By the time Tom got to the gate leading into the track the fox was not more than fifty yards away.

"I'd have got him if it hadn't been for the gate," Tom said.

The gate was padlocked. Then Tom saw McKechnie coming down the track. Tom yelled something about the fox but McKechnie came straight on, as if he did not hear. Then he began shouting at Tom, in a throttled, shaking voice.

"Here, I want you, I want you! — ye're the one I'm looking for — "

Somewhere beyond the sloe bushes the fox lost himself, and McKechnie came shaking and strutting down the track.

"Dinna run off — I want ye, I want ye — !"

Tom stopped in the track and waited. There was something inexplicably hostile about the action of McKechnie as he came stumbling on, panting.

"Dinna run off — ye needna think ye can get away like that." He glared at Tom with a vast, holy sort of outrage, his eyes glittering and reddening with excitement. "I want you — I've got one plain, simple, straightforward question to ask ye, young man."

Tom simply stared, too staggered even to ask what question it was. And when it came it stunned him.

"I want to ask ye this, young man." And Tom said afterwards it had a sort of throttled staginess about it, so that even then he could not think of it as real. "What are your intentions towards Pheley? — my daughter?"

The pole-ax effect of this blow lasted until I saw Tom at the gate. "We had a terrible row," he kept saying, "a terrible row — I thought he was going to hit me — "

It was all so stupidly in the monotonous McKechnie fashion that I began to laugh.

"Pheley," I said. "Pheley. What have you done to Pheley?"

"I can't even look at her," he said.

I could understand that; no one could look into those stripped, hairless, green-sandy, awful eyes.

"You came into it too," he said. I laughed again at that.

"Me? What have *I* done to Pheley?"

"You all come into it. Nancy, Lydia — he raved about you all."

"The bloody old fool," I said. "Come and have a cup of tea and forget it."

"You might have thought I'd violated her," he said as we went into the house. "Either her or the Kingdom of Heaven — "

"Good grief," I said, "think of Heaven populated with the McKechnies."

Some of the trouble went out of his face, leaving me, if

anything, the more furious of the two of us. I had strong views about bigotry and parsimony and conventions and the high discount charged by small-town moralities on happiness, and I kept urging him angrily to treat it for what it was, to forget it, to let Pheley and the McKechnies, in general, go to hell.

But suddenly the tea we sat drinking at the table reminded him of something. He hit the table with both hands.

"Good God, it was the day she came down here about her hair."

Then he told me of the hair, the beating, the rage, the tears and the way he had listened.

"That still doesn't alter it," I said. "The bigots will wreck your life if you let them. Don't let them. Forget it and let them go — "

That evening a more fatuous and in a sense more terrible thing happened.

About seven o'clock there was a knock at the door. When I went to answer it — Tom and I had been having a drink together, and I had just been saying that if he couldn't forget it one way he'd better forget it another, and drink was as good a way as any — Pheley stood there, with her sister Flora, the deserted one, behind her.

"I've come to see Tom," she said.

I hesitated.

"We've both come to see him," Flora said.

"Tom's down in Evensford," I said.

"Oh?" Flora said. "His car appears to be in the garage" — after that it was not much use pretending, and Tom came out of the kitchen to the door. He was white again, his blue eyes terribly troubled.

"Well?" he said.

Flora said that it was a nice thing when people started by telling lies, and Pheley said in a grim, hollow whisper:

"I've got a few things I want to say to you."

"I'll buzz off, Tom," I said.

"No, you don't," Flora said. "You're in this too. And if the pair of you don't mind, so am I."

The monstrous thought did not strike me until afterwards that she had come as a witness. She began to put on her sinister, deserted voice:

"We're going to have this out," she said. "I've had some of this before."

We had it out. An evening of pallid lamplight flamed with idiotic words. Nothing plausible or logical or conclusive or of plain sense emerged in anything that anybody said. But two festering texts ran through it all, suppurating hate:

"This is what they do to you if you give them a chance," Flora said. "And what else can you expect of people who begin by lying and end by blaspheming?"

"Good God," I said.

"There you are!" she said, pulsing and sour and triumphant.

After this I withdrew from the contest, pouring myself a drink. She crowed "And drink too — " and I walked out into the garden saying: "Excuse me. Before I either say or do something I shall regret forever."

"It's already been said! It's already been done!" she screeched.

For some time I walked about the field. Nothing so stupid had ever happened to us. Then I thought of Pheley's hair, the way she had cut it off, and the way her father had beaten her; and suddenly I knew what, under the sexless, sterile, pale-eyed face, she evidently felt for Tom. That seemed, incredible as it was, to alter everything. I saw it suddenly from their point of view: how Pheley had committed the next worst thing, perhaps, to adultery, and had been whipped for it; and how, for both outrages, Tom was the cause.

[243]

I went back into the house in time to hear Flora saying: "And girls riding about undressed on carts. And running about half naked like madwomen."

"I think this is finished," I said. "We're going to bed."

"With whom?" she screeched.

I held open the kitchen door. "Good night," I began saying. "Unless you'd like to search upstairs — "

"We'd know who we'd find!" she said.

"I'm surprised," I said.

"I don't know why you should be!" she said. "She was one of yours — "

At this point I knew that, at last, old rumors, old hatreds, old jealousies, old gossip had, as they always do in little towns, caught up with me. No answer was needed, and Pheley began crying on the threshold.

"Is that your last answer?" she said to Tom. I stood utterly flabbergasted. There had never seemed any question to which Tom had been compelled to give an answer. He stood hopelessly staring. He was knocked out by the impact of this stupid appeal, and she took it for his last dumb, iron refusal of her. "You didn't treat me like that when we sat there that afternoon," she cried bitterly, "did you?"

Tom was too stunned to answer, and she took it as his utter rejection.

"All right," she said, "then you must be responsible for what happens."

"Come on, Pheley!" Flora said. "He knows it now!"

Alone in the house with Tom I took two more drinks and raged about the room in a sad state of mocking bitterness. "You must be responsible for what happens, you must be responsible for what happens!" I mouthed. "They always say that. They say it to get under your skin. They say it when they know they're beaten. They say it when they know they can't get anything except through conscience and tears — "

[244]

"God," Tom said. He held his face in his hand. "My head hurts. I can't think. I don't know where I am."

Two nights later a voice called me, at home, on the telephone my father had proudly had installed. It wheezed bronchially several times, with smoky autumn phlegm, before I recognized it.

"Do you know a girl named Pheley McKechnie?" it asked. It was Bretherton.

"No."

"I thought you did."

"No."

"Isn't she a friend of young Holland's?"

"Not that I know of," I said.

Bretherton, wheezing again, seemed puzzled by these answers, and I said:

"Was there any reason for asking me?"

"No," he said. "No. None at all."

"You should never do things without a reason," I said: a remark that, in the past, had been one of his favorite sticks with which to beat me.

Half an hour later, walking down to catch the evening post, I saw the newsboys with their placards leaning by the walls of "The Rose and Miter," in High Street, where in the old days the potato-oven used to stand.

"*Local Girl Missing*," they said, in the daubed violet ink Bretherton used for swift sensation. "*Inquiries widespread*."

I bought a paper and went to see Tom. Pheley had been missing since the previous afternoon. As I waited for the bus to take me out of the town, Bretherton himself darted past, coughed into a charred stub of cigarette, his scarf unwinding pythonwise from his stumpy neck.

"Oh! You got the paper," he said. A few violet words about

Pheley were smudged across the stop-press column. "Got an idea it's going to be juicy."

"Is it?" I said.

On the last half mile of road between the bus stop and Tom's house Nancy came along in the old car and picked me up.

She had never heard of Pheley. "Pheley who?" she said.

I told her about Pheley; I tried to sketch in, casually as it were, with a triviality I did not feel, something of the monstrous scene of two days before. Then I told her what was in the paper, and she said:

"But it couldn't have anything to do with Tom?"

"Of course not," I said, and then I felt suddenly and impotently angry, muttering under my breath.

"What are you muttering about?" she said.

"Bigots," I said. "Crucifiers."

"Do you know *what* you're talking about?" she said.

"Yes," I said. "Perfectly."

And in a savage, bewildered silence we drove on to the farm.

In the yard Tom stood talking to the young Evensford policeman named Arthur Peck. Tom too had been at school with Arthur. I had heard that Arthur was joining the Metropolitan force and it seemed a good opportunity to say:

"I hear you're going to London, Arthur. I might see something of you there."

"Good," he said. "I heard you were going too."

It was wonderful how in Evensford your most private news had a way of escaping.

"Still play some tennis?" Arthur said.

"Sometimes."

"We might have a farewell game before we get lost in the big world," he said, and I said that perhaps we would.

During all this Tom did not speak a word.

Trying to keep up a casual lightheartedness about things, I did not look at his strained, rather tired face as I said:

"What's Tom been doing? Finding him out at last?"

"Finding him out," Arthur said. He had bicycled over. Now as he began to stoop down, snipping his bicycle clips on to his trousers, so that his legs looked pinched and his body top-heavy, he said: "Just inquiries. Checking through the village." He stood heavily on one pedal of his bicycle. "Nothing to worry about, Tom." He got on to his bicycle and began to wobble away, elephantine, reassuring:

"Get 'em every day. Run away one day and home the next. No place like home — "

Tom stood staring after him.

"Come on, Tom," I said, "the McKechnies drove her away. Let the McKechnies find her."

Not until a long time afterwards did I discover how right I was in this.

Nancy, out of some solemn, sisterly instinct, did not say much. She felt only that tea was necessary. She went into the house and filled the kettle and put it on the paraffin stove. Tom did not come in with us, and I looked out of the window and saw him wandering in the yard.

"He looks terrible," Nancy said. "Are you sure he didn't promise that girl? — I mean, was there anything — "

"Not a word," I said. "Nobody in his right senses would even look at her."

"He doesn't look in his right senses," she said. "Somehow." Brightly she went into the yard, calling to Tom that a cup of tea would do him all the good in the world.

He sat for some time nursing a cup in his hands, blowing troubled surface ripples across the tea.

"I didn't say anything, did I?" His eyes, turned up at me, were miserable with too-honest distress. "Did I? You know that — I told you everything — did I say a word?"

"Of course not," I said. "Even if you had — "

"But I *didn't* — " Now I could see that what really troubled him was an imputation that his intentions had not been utterly and supremely honest. He was quite childlike as he protested: "But I didn't — " Over and over again. "I never even gave them the slightest cause — "

"Now look," I said. "You've chewed it over and over all day. Now let it rest. The only thing now is to get hold of Lydia and all of us go over to The Old Swan for dinner or to the cinema or something, and forget the whole affair. Look at it rationally. It's got nothing to do with us — "

"Rationally?" he said, and he stared at me as if utterly mystified by the word.

To my relief Nancy said: "I think that's the soundest suggestion yet. We haven't all been out together for a long time — "

"It's exactly what we all need," I said. "And we can make it a farewell party."

"Farewell?"

"He's going away," Tom said.

"Who is going away?" she said to me.

"I am," I said. I had not told her I was going away, and she said, sharply:

"I suppose everybody else knew but me? I'm always the last to know."

Bretherton had a genius for uncommunicative late extras, and that night, as we drove home about ten o'clock, newsboys were running about the streets of Evensford trying to sell a few fresh-splodged violet words about Pheley that told us nothing at all. "Search for missing girl widens," the stop press said, and as if that were not quite enough: "Anxiety grows."

"I feel worried," Nancy said. We stood under a street light, reading the paper, waiting for Tom to come down from the dark after taking Lydia home. "When are you going away? You didn't tell me."

"The day after tomorrow."

"You do like to spring things on people," she said. "Must you go?"

"It's all fixed," I said.

"Couldn't you stay until this thing blows over?"

"It has nothing to do with me," I said. "It has nothing to do with Tom. It has nothing to do with you. I keep trying to tell you."

"I don't think Tom sees it quite like that," she said.

After Tom had driven away alone, with myself shouting after him, "Get a good night's rest. I'll be over tomorrow — " I went with Nancy to get her car from Wheeler's Garage, between the gates of the Aspen house and the church.

The garage mechanic who helped us get the car out saw Bretherton's late extra in my hand.

"Any news of the McKechnie girl?" he said. "She was in here yesterday afternoon."

"In here?"

"Wanted a taxi," he said.

"Where did she go?" I said.

"No idea. Hadn't a taxi in the place. Three trains to meet in Nenborough and one at Evensford. They say she took a bus to Nenborough in the end."

"So that," I said to Nancy, "is that," and I thought she seemed relieved as she said, "Can I drive you home? or drop you at the bottom of the hill?"

"Drop me at the hill," I said.

At the bottom of the hill, where old yards come sharply down between Evensford's earliest back-street Victorian factories, gaunt between gaunter rows of terraced dwellings of yellow brick turned black by furnace smoke, we sat for a few moments in the car, talking.

"This isn't what you intended for yourself, is it?" she said. "London? You don't belong there."

I said nobody could stop in Evensford for ever. "Even Pheley couldn't," I told her.

"Pheley must have had a reason for going," she said.

"Of course she did. She cut off her hair and her father thrashed her."

"You don't think she could be in love with Tom?" she said.

"I'd think anything," I said. "Women get the queerest ideas about things."

"So they do," she said. "I remember your telling me."

I spent the next morning cleaning up several pairs of shoes and pressing my two pairs of best trousers and packing most of my things, and it was midafternoon before I went over to the farm to see Tom.

When I got there I heard the raised voices of McKechnie and Jamie McKechnie, the eldest son, screeching with dry, tight anger in the yard.

"Because I'm tellin' ye — for the last time — I'm warnin' ye — " McKechnie's voice had the grating needle-shriek of an unoiled bearing — "if anything happens to that lassie — so much as one hair of her is hurt, I'll hold you responsible — before God I will."

"I'll tell ye more than that," Jamie said. "I'll give ye the kind o' thrashing you'll never forget — "

"Who thrashed Pheley?" I said — and McKechnie, startled, turned and shouted:

"And we want no interference from your blasphemin' gallivantin' friends!"

"Come on, Tom," I said. I took hold of his arm. It was stiff and rigid. "The McKechnies drove her away. Let the McKechnies find her — "

"What was that?" McKechnie yelled.

[250]

"Don't you swing that stick at me," I said.

He swung the stick at me. I remembered feeling it chip the bone of my arm, with a crack of pain, just above my elbow. Then I grabbed at the stick, trying to hold it, and he wrenched it like a long, lacerating cork through my clenched hands.

The next moment the four of us were fighting. I think McKechnie lashed at me twice more before Tom came in and hit him in the throat. I remember wishing Alex was there. Then McKechnie gripped me by both shoulders, his mouth open, spewing throttled grunts, as he tried to force me away. It was finally like a tangled and clumsy game of leap-frog in which we all fell down together across the threshold of the house door, shouting and choking and trying separately to hit each other. Then in the middle of it I heard, shrilly outside the tangle of our own voices, the voice of Flora McKechnie, coming through the gate of the yard on a scream of pain.

She screamed how the police were through on the wire and how the men were to go down to Evensford as soon as they could.

"They're going to drag the river!" she screamed. "They're going to drag the river!"

I remember how the four of us staggered separately about, speechless and panting.

Then Tom, terribly white, began to say, "I'm sorry — I'm awfully sorry about this, Mr. McKechnie," his voice broken and shaking. "I'm really most awfully sorry — perhaps I could do something to help — ?"

"You've done enough!" Flora screamed.

I spat blood several times from my mouth, feeling sick. I heard the last of McKechnie's words lacerating Tom:

"I'm tellin' ye — if they find anything down there ye'll

wish ye'd never drawn breath. And when it's all over ye'l
hate the day y' ever did."

It was five o'clock by the time I took a walk to the village
after telephoning for Nancy. Tom at last had the telephone
installed.

"And where is he now?" she said, when I told her what
had happened.

"He's all right," I said. "He's having a nap. I gather he
didn't sleep much last night."

"He's not spending another night out there by himself,"
she said. "He's coming home."

"You persuade him," I said.

"I'll bring Lydia," she said. "We'll persuade him together."

The coverts were beginning to turn gold-brown, like long
flat encrusted loaves, and I stopped several times to look at
them as I walked back across the fields. The day had been
dull and warm. Now the sky began lifting, clearing in time
for long rays of amber light to spread across the valley and
catch, with bright flames, the brown larches up the hill.

Every time I stopped I felt, for some reason, that I was
looking at them for the last time. When I came back, if ever
I came back, the coverts would be bare or snow would have
covered them or spring would be breaking. I did not think
much about Tom. I thought for a long time about Lydia:
about how we had skated and danced together, about how I
had often misjudged her and forgiven her in the end. I
thought of her with tenderness, perhaps a little sentimentally;
I had given up trying to be dispassionate about her. It was
no use denying that I was going away because of her, and
that because of her I was not coming back.

Flat white saucers of mist were beginning to gather along
the brook as I came back to the farm. Tom was not in the

yard or the kitchen. When I went upstairs I found him asleep, with all his clothes and boots on, lying across his bed. I covered him over with a blanket from the other bed and then pulled the curtains and he did not stir.

By the time I had put out a little corn and fresh water for the hens I heard Nancy's Ford driving up the hill. It had grown, if anything, noisier than ever since she had driven it; and I went out to meet her and tell her not to bring it into the yard because of waking Tom.

Nancy went into the house, but Lydia sat in the car for some moments while I talked of Tom. She kept inclining her head, as if listening for something. She said at last how quiet it was. I listened too, and all I could hear was the bony tap of hen-beaks hammering at the last grains of corn in the enamel bowl across the yard.

"When do you go?" she said.

"Tomorrow," I said.

I tried not to look at her face. She was not wearing a hat. The wind in the open car had blown her hair about, and now she sat looking into the driving mirror, pressing the parting of her hair into shape with her fingers.

"You must give me your address," she said.

Presently she got out of the car. As I held the door her skirt was pulled up and across her legs, and I saw the full curve of them before she pulled it back with her hands. She saw me look at her, and I thought a flash of something warm went through her eyes as she said:

"You ought to shut the hens up, if Tom can't do it. Shall I come and help you?"

As we shut the hens in the barn, driving them back beyond the old inner partitions that had once been cowstalls and then bolting them in, so that they were safer, there was a moment when we stood together, listening to the hens rustling down among dry straw, before locking the outer door for the night.

"Will you be away long?" she said.

"All winter."

"I wish you weren't going," she said. "It's been nice, with the four of us — "

"I needn't go," I said. I did not want to go; I felt empty with loneliness and the thought of going.

"It will do you good to go," she said. "You are the sort of person who expands through friends. You will meet wonderful new people and in the end you'll like it better."

We went into the house. Tom was not awake and when I went up to look at him again he was lying on his side, the blanket drawn up round his face, breathing heavily.

"He'll sleep all night," I said.

"What are we going to do?" Nancy said. "Wake him — or let him sleep on?"

"Let him sleep," I said.

"Perhaps it's better," she said. "I'll sleep here myself and get him something to eat if he wakes."

As we sat there waiting for Tom to wake I could feel the hush of his sleeping spreading gradually over the house. We did not speak once of Pheley and finally Nancy said:

"I think we might as well have supper. I'll make sandwiches, and we can have some coffee — "

"If you don't mind," I said, "I must go. I'll walk back. I'd like the walk."

"Oh! please," she said. "You'll miss saying good-by to Tom."

I said I could ring Tom in the morning and she said, rather curtly:

"Oh! Well, if you must. What about you, Lydia? Will you stay? — I didn't want to leave the house."

"I think I ought to go too," Lydia said.

"It's a long way to walk," Nancy said.

"Not if we take the footpath." I stood up to go. Her curtness gave a strained aloof look to her face.

"I don't mind either way," Lydia said. "I must just get my gloves from the car."

We all listened again for a few moments for a sound from Tom, but nothing happened. Then Lydia went to get her gloves from the car.

A moment later Nancy and I stood in the yard to say good-by.

"It's all starlight now," she said. She lifted her face to the mild, luminous October sky, held it there for a moment and then looked at me.

"Don't forget us," she said.

"When I forget — " my mind searched amiably for some quotation I wanted about forgetfulness, but I could not grasp it, and I said: "You know, the quotation — when I forget thee or — "

"Oh! You and your quoting," she said.

"Well," I said, "it doesn't matter. Give Tom my love when he wakes — "

"And me?" she said.

"You too," I said. "Good-by."

I kissed her lightly on the lips and she said, very softly: "Good-by. Take good care of yourself. Come back."

"Tell Tom not to worry," I said. "He'll feel better about things when he's slept on them. You always do."

"Do you?" she said, and then Lydia came back, swinging the black kid gloves she had left in the car.

As Lydia and I walked down the hill together I said, "Fields or road? It's starlight," and she said, "Fields, I think. It's so long since I went that way."

So we walked home by field-path, high on the ridge of the valley, under a full sowing of stars that seemed to be reflected

below in the lights of Evensford and the towns beyond the
river. Dew was rising heavily in the fields. It lay wet on the
bars of gates and stiles as we came to them. Sometimes patches
of white mist floated motionless in hollows, and once as we
walked through one, thirty or forty yards long, I walked in
front of her to find the path and she called out: "I can't see a
thing — where are you?" and I said, "Here," holding out my
arms so that she could touch me. "It was just blank," she said,
"I thought I'd lost you," and when we came at last to clear
starlight she took my arm and we walked the rest of the way
like that, together.

I don't remember much of what we said as we walked home
that night, but when we reached the gates of the park I asked:
"May I walk up with you? It's so long since I did."
"Of course you may," she said. "Come in and see Aunt
Bertie too."
"I'd just like to walk up with you, that's all," I said.
Chestnut leaves were already beginning to turn and fall
and as we walked up the avenue I could hear them floating
dryly down through the silence, bouncing light and shriveled
against boughs as they fell. A sweetish, humid smell of autumn rose damply from the spinney about the brook. A few
rooks stirred in high still green elms and suddenly I remembered all my days there. The snow, the springtimes, the
clovered summers came rushing back to me with pain.
"I think this is as far as I'll go," I said. I stopped under the
limes, two hundred yards from where the avenue forked to
skirt the terraces of the house.
She stopped too and turned to me. She began to say something about wishing me luck. I saw her lips parted to frame
her words. She had thrown back the collar of her coat because
the air was warm for walking, and I saw the triangle of her
throat pale under the black edges of it and between the blackness of her hair. Then she stopped speaking and looked at me.

She seemed to look at me for a long time, and then she came close to me and I was kissing her.

As I kissed her she moved her mouth with uneasy tenderness, trying to break away from me. Then I held her head with my hands, pressing it hard against me, and would not let her go.

At last I let her go, and she held my face in both hands, looking at me.

"Have I been bad to you?"

"Yes."

She smiled softly and I said: "But then you warned me you would be. Only you didn't say with whom."

"Don't be so serious," she said. "You're always so terribly serious."

I did not answer.

"If it comes to that you've been bad with Nancy," she said, "and perhaps Tom has been bad with Pheley."

"Not in the same way."

"How could it be the same?" she said. "It would all be so easy if all the things you meant to do were the things that happened."

I heard a shower of limes spurt with a sort of damp shudder from a tree along the avenue. When it ceased the park lay still under deep mild starlight, and I said:

"Do you mean it with Tom? Because I hope you do."

"I do mean it," she said.

"I'll never forgive you if you don't mean it."

"I do mean it," she said.

She looked at me with beautifully clear candid eyes that seemed to be full of the calmest gentleness.

"Don't worry," she said. "I'll be good to Tom."

"You'd better be," I said, "because I love you both. More than anyone I ever knew. Except Alex."

She smiled again. A shower of leaves fell from the limes.

Across the park an owl let out a long soft-blown hoot that quivered away beyond the farthest trees.

"You'd better go before the owls get you," she said.

"Be careful the owls don't get *you*," I said.

She laughed very softly.

"I've a queer feeling they will, some day," she said, and while her lips were still parted to frame the words I kissed her again with a long dry empty pain, for the last time.

I was still reading in bed at midnight when the telephone rang.

"Is it you?" Nancy said. I remember feeling slightly vexed at being fetched downstairs at midnight by Nancy. "Were you asleep? Did I wake you?"

I said no, she hadn't woken me. "Where are you?" I said. "What's the matter?"

I thought she gave a fluttery sob into the telephone. "Tom's not in the house," she said. "He hasn't been here for an hour. He isn't with you, is he?"

No, I said, he wasn't with me. I spoke shortly. It occurred to me with some annoyance that she was using Tom as an excuse to talk to me.

"Where do you suppose he can be?" she said. "He was still asleep when I went to bed — and then I woke up and had a queer feeling he wasn't there — "

Tom had always been one of those people who can freeze into sudden wakefulness in the night. He could go downstairs and drink milk or even, in summertime, wander in pajamas in the garden, eating and thinking. I remembered too that he was always getting up in the night because he imagined nervous flutterings among the hens or because he thought he heard Sir Roger.

"He probably thought he heard the fox," I said. "He always imagines he can."

"Would he take the gun?" she said. "Shall I look to see if he has taken the gun?"

"Go back to bed," I told her.

"Will you hang on a minute while I look to see if he's taken the gun?"

I said I would hang on. The telephone felt cold in my fingers; and I had rushed down without slippers and my feet too were cold. I heard Nancy's footsteps, hollow and diffused, running on the bare passage flags at the other end of the telephone.

There was a rattling of the telephone as she took it up again.

"The gun isn't there," she said.

"Then he's gone to have a pot at Sir Roger," I told her. "Just as I said."

She did not speak. The silence, uncanny in its abruptness after her nervous garrulity so late at night, gave me an impression that she was no longer there.

"Hullo?" I said. "Are you there?"

"Yes," she said. "I'm here." She paused again. "I thought you seemed annoyed because I rang you — "

"No, no. Of course not. Why should I be?"

"You sound annoyed now."

"It isn't that I'm annoyed at all," I said, and as I spoke I felt doubly annoyed. "It's just that — " I began to say something about her fussy protective instincts, but a sudden rattling came over the wire and she said:

"I didn't hear what you were saying — "

"I was just saying I wasn't annoyed but that my feet were getting cold, that's all," I said. "I ran down without my slippers."

"Then put them on," she said. "You'll catch your death. You do do the silliest things."

Back in bed I put the light out and tried to sleep. The coldness of my feet kept me awake and I lay listening to the bell-like strokes of Evensford church clock chiming the quarters until it was one o'clock. I lay troubled, at first, by the way I had spoken to Nancy. I began to feel I had spoken too sharply; I felt I had not been fair. Then because of being troubled by Nancy I began to be troubled also by her anxiety about Tom. Something behind all her fussiness about him made me think she was afraid. Earlier in the day I had been very logical and rather terse and not very patient about Pheley. Now I did not feel so logical. I was bothered by stupid recollections about the McKechnies that now, in the middle of the night, tended to grow haunting and magnified. I remembered what I had said about bigots and crucifiers. I remembered how Pheley had cried, that evening, that whatever happened to her would be the fault of Tom.

Suddenly I was terrified for Tom. Something started to jibber inside me. I felt the coldness of my feet run up and envelop the rest of my body.

I got up and fetched a bicycle and started to cycle out to the farm. There was no light on the bicycle. All the street lights were out. I took the back streets out of the town, on the northeast side. There would be no one in the streets on that side of the town, I thought, and then suddenly, on the outskirts, a policeman hailed me from a bakehouse door:

"Hey — just a minute — where's your light there?"

I got off my bicycle, waiting for the heavy footsteps running up the pavement.

"It's all right, Arthur," I said, "it's me."

"This is a damn fine time to be out," Arthur Peck said. "Biking to London now?"

He laughed, and all at once I felt it difficult to explain my jibbering mess of premonition and anxiety about Tom. I started to try to explain and Arthur said, "Well, it's a good

[260]

tale, but I don't know how it would sound to the magistrates. If I were you I'd buzz off back home."

"Otherwise — ?"

"Otherwise I'll put you down in the old book tomorrow morning — no front light, no rear light, found wandering at night, suspicious circumstances." He laughed — "Come on, I'll walk part of the way back with you."

We walked back through the streets together. I felt rather stupid; and then a little flat and arid from fears that had decayed. I did not know quite what to talk about, but I said at last how extraordinarily clear the night was, and how full of stars.

"I ought to have been a bloody astronomer," Arthur said. "I stand and look at them so much."

"Where's the next bakehouse?" I said.

"Horseman's, Denmark Street," he said. "They get nicely warmed up there about two o'clock. I generally have a round of new bread and cheese and a cup of cocoa there. Old Horseman's good to me. He's a good old stick."

I got a pleasant impression that it was nice for Arthur, alone, so late at night, to have someone to talk to; and as we went through the streets, with Evensford asleep all about us, I felt lulled by his friendliness into a state where I was no longer troubled. Then Arthur remembered how, as a boy, he used to sell hot-cross buns for old Horseman, starting at six o'clock on cold Good Friday mornings, and I said: "I sold hot-cross buns once. For old Welsh. I got up at five. I couldn't sleep I was so excited. I made three and fourpence — "

Arthur laughed and said that they were the days. He said Evensford wasn't a bad town, either, and asked me if I should miss it? Stars shone over rows of gray packed roofs with crisp autumnal brilliance, and I said, "Yes, I suppose so," and a whole piece of my life seemed suddenly to go dead behind me and break away.

At the corner of Denmark Street we stopped and there was a wonderful smell of new baked bread in the dark air.

"That's the smell," Arthur said. "I know it's nearly morning now."

We talked for a few moments longer and I watched the quivering filaments of stars. Then we exchanged addresses and Arthur said that we must meet in London for a drink or a cup of coffee. I said we would, and the smell of new bread grew warmer and sweeter in the night air. Gaslight from the bakehouse windows fell on the dry pavement outside in a long, green bar, and a glow of rosy crimson joined it as old Horseman opened the furnace door and stoked the fire. I listened to the shovel scraping harshly on the bricks of the bakehouse floor and saw the glow of crimson and green fuse and rediffuse and separate, leaving one clear, pure tone of green when the door was closed. The glow of the bakehouse fire, warm and red and beautiful, and so swiftly extinguished, seemed suddenly like all my life in Evensford. The girlishness of Lydia, the love and the beauty and the springtimes and the secret moments of them, too fine and too exquisite and often too serious, fused into a single large collective flame of happiness that was suddenly cut off by darkness. I knew that it would not happen again. I knew that it would not reawaken itself. I was not even sure that I wanted it to reawaken, now or ever. I had no longer the feeling of trying desperately to grasp at something that was floating away; I wanted it to go; I knew that I could not bear it again if it came. Like the sweetness of new bread on the cool dark air it could only torment the hunger it made.

Then Arthur stood with his hand on the big brass knob of the bakehouse door. I heard it slip in his fingers. It had always been too big for me to hold as a child and it had always slipped through my fingers in exactly that way. Sometimes I used to stand there knocking softly, unable to get my small hands about the big slippery knob, asking to be let in, to be let in please, because I wanted a loaf of bread for my mother, until after a long time old Horseman would open the door with floury hands and let me through.

"Well," Arthur said, "off you get. I'll be seeing something of you. Good-by." He shook hands. "I expect Evensford will be here if ever we want to come back."

"If ever we want to."

"I bet it won't have changed at all if we don't come back for twenty years. You see. Towns like Evensford never do."

"There'll be different people," I said.

"No, there won't," Arthur said. "You see."

"Different ideas."

"No," Arthur said. "You see. Towns like Evensford never change."

"Well, it'll be different in one way."

"How?" Arthur said. "I bet it never will. How will it be?"

"It won't have us," I said.

We laughed at that, and then said good-by again, shaking hands for the last time. The knob of the bakehouse door twisted properly at last and the door opened. I felt the warm, deep glow of the ovens, the sweetness of bread, the flouriness, the yeast and the smell of fire.

"Come in, Arthur," I heard old Horseman say. "You're late tonight. It's after two."

I walked slowly home, pushing the bicycle. I stood in the garden for a few moments, under the fading, bronzy pear trees, glad of solid people like Arthur Peck, of the comforting sweetness of new bread in bakehouses. I stared at the stars for the last time, thinking of Tom and Lydia, with tenderness, without malice, and with a feeling that everything about us all was tranquilized.

"Good-by, Lydia," I said.

*　　*　　*

Next morning at eight o'clock my father came to wake me.

"There's someone to see you," he said. "A policeman. I fancy it's that boy you went to school with — only he's grown so much I hardly know."

"Arthur Peck," I said.

I dressed and went downstairs. It seemed strange that Arthur should be standing on the far side of the garden, wiping and continually rewiping the sweat from the inside of his helmet with long strokes of his hand.

"We're always saying good-by," I said. "What's up?"

He stood still, wetting his lips. There is always something curiously undressed about a policeman without his helmet, and now I saw that he had unfastened the collar of his tunic too.

"What is it, Arthur?" I said.

It seemed to take him fully a minute, wetting and rewetting his lips, staring at me and then staring away again, to tell me that Tom was dead.

He began to say something about "An accident — we're pretty sure it was an accident. Shot himself getting over a gate — after a fox or something, his sister said. It's one of those things that could happen to anybody — climbing over a gate at night with a gun — "

I stood thinking of Nancy. I knew that it was not one of those things that could happen to anybody. I heard her voice crying to me over the telephone. I stared down at the orange-bronzy leaves of the pear trees falling on the wet October grass, aware of nothing inside myself except the recollection of her voice trying to tell me how frightened she was.

"Thank you for coming, Arthur," I said. "It was very good of you to come."

Three days later Pheley McKechnie came back to Evensford; and I left, the next afternoon, by the London train.

PART FOUR

I

I<small>T</small> was more than two years later when I came back to Evensford, in a wintry springtime of long cold evenings and days of dusty dry winds that stripped young buds from trees already backward and slow in breaking. "This is the year we don't have any blossom," my father said. Our few apple trees were fixed in a cycle of alternate sterile and fruiting years. "There's just one sprig on the Lord Derbys. That's all."

Evensford is a town of narrow and late development, of no tradition and a single industry, with its people confined for livelihood by the shoes they make and the leather they tan. It is something like a gray beehive in which every worker has his own cell of concentration for a single-minded purpose, exactly like an instinctive and brainless bee. For these reasons the slump had hit it very hard.

They always used to say, in Evensford, that there was nothing like leather and that everyone had to have a pair of shoes; but that spring it began to seem possible that perhaps a million people had suddenly decided to wear shoes no longer. I arrived home when the town was carrying a load of four thousand unemployed; when the three tanneries were shut down by the river; when factories were working, if they were working at all, three days or two days or even one day a week, and when every little while it seemed that my father came home with news of another smash. "Nichol's have gone. Oakley's have gone. They say Williamson's haven't a pair on the books. They say Green and Porter can't last much longer." The streets were melancholy with three-men bands of shuffling heroes with strips of medal ribbons pinned on narrow chests. Back doors were haunted by slow-footed men carrying suitcases of cheap fiber that opened to reveal meager wardrobes of hanging shoelaces and cards of buttons and rolls of cheap pink and blue ribbon for threading through ladies' underwear. Over the streets, on the cold long, light evenings, there hung that smell of burnt leather I hated so much, a yellow-gray cloud of smoke from grates that burned no coal. There was no joy in Evensford. "It has been an awful winter," my father said. "There is a lot of distress."

It was typical of him, and indeed typical of Evensford, that he had decided, in his modest and generous way, to do something about all this. There was not much, in a practical way, that he could do; but he was very fond of singing and he had formed, that winter, a little choir.

"There are fifteen of us," he explained to me. "Ten basses and five tenors. Part of the old Orpheus. It's always difficult to get the tenors, as you know. But we're knitting together a bit now and it's going very well. We sing at hospitals and places and concerts for charities and relief funds and aftercare and that sort of thing. We go to the sanatorium a lot. We feel it gives a lot of pleasure to people — anyway it makes us very happy."

I was very restless in the long cold smoky twilights of a backward springtime.

"Why don't you come and sing with us?" my father said. "I think you'd like it."

"You know I can't read a note," I said.

"It doesn't matter about reading," he said. "Charlie MacIntosh doesn't read. Will Purvis doesn't read. They're two of the best men we've got. It doesn't matter about reading — your ear is good. And so is your voice. I've always said what a good voice you had."

"It's been ages since I sang a note," I said. Nor, in fact, did I feel like singing.

"So it has for all of us. You get back into it very quickly."

Much of my restlessness rose, that spring, from an inability to decide what I wanted to do. I suffered, I felt, from a kind of mental cramp. But if there was one thing about which it was not difficult to make up my mind it was the question of singing part songs at charity concerts or about the beds of hospitals.

"Well, as you like," my father said. "But I think you'd find it would take you out of yourself."

It was impossible to tell him that it was not out of myself that I wanted to be taken; and he went on with his singing for another week or two of that backward spring, without me.

Then one day he said: "I wish you'd do something for me if you haven't anything on tonight."

I said I would if I possibly could.

"We want somebody to give out the sheet music when we sing at the sanatorium tonight. Peggy Whitworth always does it, but he fell down this morning and broke his leg."

"That's a bad blow for you," I said.

"Oh, it was only his wooden one," he said — and I think he said this because he was aware of my restlessness and with the idea of cheering me up.

But as he said it I was not cheered; I could only feel impatient with myself that I did not share his generous simplicity. A great deal of myself was not merely cramped; it was depressingly complicated. What I wanted for myself was not clear, and much of what I felt about it seemed to twist back inside me, impossibly knotted.

"Couldn't you get someone else?" I said.

"I think you'd like it up there," he said. "They give us a beautiful ham supper with coffee afterwards. It's all very gay and cheerful. It would do you good to see their faces."

He looked out of the window, into a garden of apple trees lightly sprigged with blossomless leaves.

"I think it's turned much warmer," he said. "I think we shall probably sing out of doors this evening. In that case you needn't come inside if you didn't want to."

I still hesitated and he said:

"It's a beautiful garden there. Full of flowers. Full of daffodils."

"All right," I said. "So long as you don't ask me to sing."

"It's a curious thing," he said, "you feel you *want* to sing when you see their faces. It makes you feel glad to be alive."

In the gardens of the sanatorium my father and his friends made a semicircle and sang, unaccompanied, a program of songs. It was true, as my father had said, that the air had turned much warmer. The soft May evening became filled with a scent of daffodils. There was a slight astringent odor, too, of something clinical and dry on the long glass-verandaed terrace where rows of patients sat or lay in their beds, intent and listening. The daffodils were scattered in broad streams of yellow and white about grass lawns on which, in a wide line, a series of open white huts contained other patients from whom, at the end of each song, came the sound of a distant, delicate clapping.

The choir sang "There Was a Jolly Fisherman" and "Oh! My Love Is Like a Red, Red Rose" and then "Sweet and Low" and then several comic songs and then "Believe Me If All Those Endearing Young Charms." These were the songs I had heard my father sing ever since I was a child. There is something very beautiful and touching, as Miss Aspen had once said, about the sound of men's voices harmonizing softly in the open air, and I felt the evening begin to draw out, tense and fine and overdelicate, like a nervous string. Then, as I collected the sheets of one song and began to give out another, a young man beckoned me from his bed on the terrace outside the ward. When I went to him he said:

"Do you suppose they could sing 'The Golden Vanity'? — You know, it's about the boy and the lowland, the lowland, they left him in the lowland sea — that's a fine song. I like that song."

"I'll ask them," I said. "Is there something else you'd like if they can't sing that one?"

"No," he said. "That's the song. They sang it last time."

Then as I moved away to ask my father about the song I saw a thin strange girl stir on a bed. She gave me a bare quick smile as I looked at her.

"Hullo," she said.

"Hullo," I said to her, and there was nothing about her face that I thought I could remember.

Presently the choir sang the song called "The Golden Vanity," the song about the boy left in the lowland sea, and the sound of it seemed to drift about the garden in melancholy and beautiful waves. There was a great deal of applause for that song; it was a great favorite. By the time it was finished, the daffodils were motionless in a sunless air that had calmed down completely. Then the matron of the sanatorium made a speech of thanks and my father replied, saying how much they all liked coming there. Once again he made the joke about Peggy Whitworth's broken leg, and there were ripples of laughter along the terraces. Then there was a rattling of plates and cups. Nurses in snowy uniforms rustled as they handed round cups of coffee drawn from a large urn and plates of ham sandwiches and sausage rolls.

As I took a ham sandwich from a young bright nurse, I remembered something and said:

"The girl in the end bed — could you tell me who she is?"

"The end bed? — over there?" she said. "That's Nora Jepson."

I remembered then, and I went and sat on Nora's bed.

"Hullo," she said. "You didn't know me, did you?"

"Not just for that moment," I said.

"I thought you didn't."

"I didn't know you were here," I said. "I've been away so long — "

"I've been here nearly six months," she said. "I'll probably be out by the end of the summer. What are you doing now?"

"Not much," I said.

"No dancing?"

She laughed with sudden thin brightness. She had always been a spare and sinuous girl, too fine-drawn, and now, as she lay in bed, a little excited at talking to me, I thought she looked much the same as ever, perhaps even a little less strained then when I had seen her before.

"My dancing days are over," I said.

She looked thoughtful for a moment.

"That was my trouble," she said. "Too much dancing. I know now. They have dances here sometimes — one Saturday a month — for the nearly cured ones. It's friendly and nice, but I can't bear it. I put my head under the clothes so I can't hear the band — "

"You were the great one for dancing," I said. "You used to float — positively float — "

"That's because there was nothing on me," she said. "I was worn away. Dr. Baird said my bones were hollow when I came in here. Like a bird's. Do you know Dr. Baird?"

"No," I said.

"He's the young one. He's been wonderful to me. Here's Mrs. Montague coming — you know her, don't you? She does the therapy side — "

"She taught me in school," I said.

Mrs. Montague, a tallish, sallow-skinned, spare woman of sixty, with rimless spectacles, who had taught me as a child, came up to the bed with strips of flowered petit point in her hands, saying, as I stood up:

"It was nice of you to come. Your father is very proud that you came," and then, "Don't you think she's wonderful, this Nora of ours? Doesn't she look fine?"

"She's marvelous," I said.

"You'd think she was more than that if you'd seen her when she came in here. She was ready to float away." She laughed, showing pleasant, gold-stopped teeth. "We know who's responsible too, don't we?" she said. "I must float, too — "

She walked away and then, seven or eight yards up the ward, dropped some of her pieces of petit point. I ran after her to pick them up and she said:

"Not too much talking. They all incline to think they're better than they are. It's warm, too, this evening — it's that muggy May weather that's so difficult for them. Please come again, won't you?"

When I went back to Nora Jepson, leaning over the foot of the bed to say that it was time for me to go, she said she was sorry she had gabbled on so long and kept me.

"I've made you miss all the sandwiches," she said.

I said it didn't matter, and she said:

"Come and see me again, won't you? I want to introduce you to Dr. Baird. He's a great reader. He loves to talk to people. You won't forget, will you?"

I promised, as I moved away, that I wouldn't forget; and then suddenly she called me back, saying:

"Forget — forget — I'm the one that's forgetting. I knew I had something to tell you."

"What was it?" I said.

She turned her face sideways on the pillow. There was a smile on her face as she looked up at me.

[273]

"There's a friend of yours here — that's what. She came in after Christmas."

"A friend?" I said.

"An old dancing friend."

I stood still, wondering, looking down at her face on the pillow. "Who is it?" I said, and she gave me once again, lightly, the quick bare smile.

"Lydia," she said. "Lydia's in here."

As I walked across the lawn and under the still almost leafless walnut trees where the daffodils made large motionless yellow sheaves about the boles I felt myself shaking. The scent of daffodils floated sweet and warm in the still air and there was a smell of bruised grass from the lawn that was fragrant and sappy. A blackbird was still singing, bursting and throaty and exquisite, in the first touch of twilight, and after the long cold spell of dry and gritty winds it seemed possible, almost, that summer had come.

Dark and unsurprised, Lydia lay flat on a bed in one of the open huts and looked at me.

"I heard you were home," she said.

"Lydia," I said. I sat down by the bed, trying to find her hands. They were under the bedsheets and she kept them there.

"I didn't know you were ill — "

"You're not supposed to touch me. You're not even supposed to be here."

"I'm not the only one," I said. "For God's sake how did you get here?"

"Who told you I was here, anyway? Nora did, didn't she?"

"How did you get here?" I said.

When she smiled her teeth were bared in the spontaneous way that made her so unexpectedly beautiful.

"Nora and I did it together," she said. "We went on a long

binge — nearly two years of it. We did it together — every night. Until we couldn't any longer."

I asked her why, and the word was dryly shaken from me with the most pointless emptiness.

"Because of a lot of things."

She looked past me remotely.

"What did you suppose it could be?" she said. She stirred her hands under the sheet, still keeping them there. "You didn't come and see me before you went. You didn't even come to the funeral, did you?"

I had always been filled with oppressive horror of the paraphernalia of death. "No," I told her. "I couldn't come."

"You didn't even come to see me."

"I felt you didn't want me," I said.

"We all wanted you," she said.

I sat for some moments staring with perpendicular blindness at the bed. There was no sound except the blackbird singing in the walnut tree outside. I listened for some time to the unbearable sweetness of it and Lydia said:

"He sings all day now. He wakes me in the morning and I lie here and listen to him before they bring my breakfast."

If I had nothing to say it was simply because whatever I could think of saying was inadequate and deprived of all possible emotion except a stifling pain.

"We had a terrible binge, Nora and I," she said. I let her talk for some moments, staring down at my hands as I listened:

"We just burnt ourselves out — she's a terrific person when you get her going, Nora. She's got tremendous vitality. We tried to keep up with each other, but she lasted just a bit longer than I did. Now Dr. Baird says she'll be out by the summer — anyway, soon."

She had learned the trick of lying absolutely relaxed and

[275]

prostrate, her hands covered, her head quite still as she talked.

"I don't believe you're listening," she said.

"I'm listening," I said. I had really been thinking of something Nancy had said, long ago, about Lydia going the way of her mother.

"Don't look so far away, then," she said. She smiled again with a spasm of unexpected loveliness. "There's no need to be so gloomy — I'm not going to die." She paused for a moment, looking horizontally, from under her long dark lashes, down the bed. "I very nearly did, though — "

When I had nothing to say to this either she went on:

"I always said the owls would get me one day. They very nearly did this time. I went down and down, right to the bottom, right down beyond everything, where nobody was — just nobody — Oh! Do you have to sit such miles and miles away from me — ?"

When I turned my face and looked at her again I saw that she was crying. Because she lay so flat the tears did not fall away from her face. They made two pools in the dark sockets of her eyes, separate at first, and then joining together. Then for the first time she lifted her hands from under the coverlet. They were terribly like two casts of colorless plaster as she lifted them free and said:

"Don't be frightened — you won't catch anything. Come and hold me for a minute — what there is of me."

I could not tell her how frightened I was as I held her there, as gently as possible, on the bed, and as I held her she said several times, very quietly:

"There was no one there. I was down in a place where there was nobody at all but me. There was nobody there to be with me."

I felt myself sink down and become submerged, for a few moments, in the dark crater of her awful loneliness.

"You're the first one I ever told about that," she said. "I never spoke about that before."

I kissed her face, and she said:

"This won't do at all. If Dr. Baird or Nurse Simpson finds you here you'll get six months. They'll never let me have another visitor. You'll have to go — really you will. Good-by, now."

I could not even frame the word; I pressed my lips against her face instead.

"Good-by," she said. "Come and see me again another day. Will you?"

"Yes," I said.

"Often? — promise. I shall hate you if you don't."

That old expression of hers lifted me up a little.

"If you were nice to Dr. Baird," she said, "he might let you come in any day. See if you can get Nora to introduce you. He's very sweet on Nora."

I stood up, letting go her hands, and she slipped them down under the coverlet.

"I'll bring you some flowers," I said.

"Oh, will you?" she said. Her eyes sparkled under dispersing tears, with a flash of gaiety I did not share. "Oh, that would be nice — that's just like you. You were always the great one for flowers."

I smiled and looked at her and raised my hand in good-by.

"Thank you for coming," she said.

When I went to take her the flowers, a bunch of copper-yellow irises that were like stiff torches, two days later, it began to rain with warm Maytime thunderiness as I went up the hill. The gatekeeper took my name and telephoned it through to the matron's office, while I stood in the doorway of his small entrance lodge, waiting for the answer. An avenue of sycamores led up from the lodge gates to the main buildings. As I stood there rain began to drip warmly and heavily through the green-flowered leaves, splashing fatly and softly on to the gravel, on the knotting branches of lilacs and on the formal beds of yellow tulips below. I waited a long time for the answer, and at last the gatekeeper said:

"She's asleep. It really isn't visiting day. They say you could come back later, or you could leave the flowers."

I left the flowers. After I had left them I walked up and down the road outside, listening to the blackbirds whistling continuously in the high, rain-soaked branches of surrounding trees, and thinking of her lying asleep there, in the thundery greenness of the afternoon, alone, in the rain.

Some days later my father said to me: "What did you think of the visit to the sanatorium? How did you like it? I saw you talking to quite a lot of people there."

I said I had enjoyed it very much, and he smiled and said:

"I'll bet you could never guess where we're singing next Tuesday?"

"No," I said, "where?"

"It's quite a little honor," he said, "at least we feel it is." He looked enigmatical and pleased with himself.

"Well, I'll tell you," he said at last, "we're going to sing for Miss Aspen — Oh! No, not your Miss Aspen. The old lady — up at the house, next Tuesday, at seven. Don't you think that's a bit of a feather in our caps?"

I said I thought it was, and he said:

"Perhaps you'd like to come? It would give you a chance to see the house again." Then before I could answer he went on:

"They say the old lady is going downhill fast. She doesn't get up now. She's a poor thing, they say. And Rollo — "

He stopped, and I said: "What about Rollo?"

"They struck his name off the Liberal Club last month," my father said, almost as if it were a disgrace comparable to being barred from the gates of Heaven. "He's been banned from The Prince Albert, too. They say he's soaking every penny of the place away."

With these remarks I felt I was really back, at last, in the narrow aisles of Evensford, where disgrace could go no deeper than expulsion from the Liberal Club, a shabby fifteen-roomed Victorian villa in which a few boot manufacturers and leather men and shopkeepers earnestly played cribbage and solo-whist and snooker on an ancient table over thimbles of whisky for stakes of sixpence a time; where banishment from public-house bars for drunkenness was a sin even worse than the one of ever going there in the first place. Indeed Rollo had been so guilty of flouting canons of behavior in a sphere my father thought reprehensible in itself that he seemed quite sorry for him.

"It's a great shame to see a man like that going down," he said. "Soaking it all away. After all, the Aspens are some-body."

"Well," I said, "it'll take him some time. There's plenty to soak away."

"Is there?" my father said. The question was so direct that it startled me. "That's what everybody has always thought, of course. That has always been the popular idea."

I thought of what had always seemed to me the immutable opulence of the Aspen house in its park of great trees. The fact of its richness, more impressive because it lay like an oasis in the center of Evensford's red-brick municipal mess of factory and chapel, of leather and Nonconformity, was something I had grown up to regard as inviolate, almost as unquestionable as things like the Commandments and the Royal Household.

"They say they lost a good deal in the crash," my father said. "But then, so did everybody. George Baker of the Evens-ford Shoe Company died in February, and his will was in the *Shoe and Leather News* this week. His father left him forty thousand when he died in 1916, and George was a director for forty years. But what do you think he left after all? He lived in that great big house in Park Way, and everybody thought he was the wealthiest man we had in Evensford."

Before I had time to give my opinions on this my father said:

"Seven thousand. That's all. I tell you it stunned people here. They thought he was one of those quarter-of-a-million men. And then look at William Allen Parker, of Parker, Groome & Fletcher — there's another man. The biggest people in the district. I remember when they had a Russian Army contract for two million. And you know what that meant. He had a stroke while inspecting the stitching-room one day last January. At one time they talked of giving him a knighthood."

My father paused for a moment and then informed me in shocked tones:

"A bare four thousand. That's all. Hardly enough to pay the duties."

I knew that the fortunes of his fellow men were, in that town of narrow and single-purposed interests, like creeds; and that when they were assaulted or threatened it was a painful and momentous thing.

"It isn't always the people who look as if they've got it," he said. "Often the opposite. Look at Luther Edward Jolly. He wore the same straw hat for forty years to my knowledge, and picked up stub-ends in the gutter. The biggest skinflint in the whole Jolly family, and that's saying something. You remember what he left," my father said, as if I were intimately acquainted with the balance sheets of every Evensford family — "a hundred and thirty-eight thousand."

"The Aspens have been here for at least five hundred years," I said.

"I grant that," he said, "but you know what they say —

the longer you're here, the longer you have to spend it." And he added sternly: "And let me tell you that drink is one of the surest ways — "

But on the following Tuesday, when I followed my father and his choir through the gates of the park, I did not think there seemed much change under the great belt of flowering chestnuts, all alight with blossom and noisy with the croak of nesting rooks, or along the avenue of limes, where fragile drifts of blue anemone were fading to pale green seed among deepening grasses, and where, too, thicker larger drifts of narcissus were withering at last among opening lilac trees. It seemed to me the same as ever. The joy of it came rushing back to me, borne on the floweriness of Maytime.

But you could not judge, as my father said, from outward appearances, and there was nothing like the rush of Maytime for giving an appearance of eternal lushness. The grass was as thick as ever; the narcissus had never been so beautiful. Warm rains, after the long, late spell of drying wind, had brought splashes of milkiness to the hawthorns all about the park, and there was already a touch of fiery blueness in the tips of cedar trees.

It was only when we gathered on the terrace, in preparation for singing under the windows of the bedroom where Miss Bertie lay, that I noticed how the conservatory had neither flower nor fern in it. I remembered its humid, exotic sweetness. I remembered the smell of water dripping from watered ferns, the odor of hot iron from the pipes and the crackle of the stove. It was empty now.

A maid with the customary old-fashioned winged apron showed us to the terrace, saying to my father, "I'll tell Mr. Rollo you're here," and I began to sort out the part-sheets as we waited.

I think we waited fifteen or twenty minutes for Rollo. When he came at last he had the unbalanced, dusty, button-

eyed appearance of a molting bird stuffed and somehow re-
animated and brought from behind the glass of its case. He
stood blinking for some moments with his small dark eyes
bloodshot and dazed. Then he said several times:

"Frightful business."

Then he changed this to "plum awful — heavy batch of
letters to get away. Plum awful — how are you?" and began
to shake hands.

The veins of his face were a series of entangled purplish
knots among which the rest of his features were larger knots
of fierier, looser flesh. His lips were like a pair of swollen
blood blisters that dribbled, as he spoke, an occasional tear.
He hovered among us with repetitive, fumbling courtesies,
shaking hands, and then shaking hands again. The sleeves of
his straw-colored Donegal jacket had evidently become frayed
at the edges and had now been shortened and bound with
strips of leather. From out of them his hands protruded with
semicrippled rheumatoid gropings, red in the vein, crooked
and knuckled like dead birds' claws as they sought to grasp
our own.

"I call it damn decent of you chaps to come," he said,
"damn decent," and his voice had the liquefied lip-entangled
clumsiness of someone who is toothless. He grinned several
times as if to show that this was not the case, and his tongue
licked at his lips with vague directionless stabs that ended
in flutters of wet red laughter.

"Well, fire away," he said at last, "fire the first jolly old
shot — what's it to be?"

"Whatever you think Miss Aspen would like, sir," my
father said.

"Oh, any damn thing," Rollo said. "Loud, though — she's
getting cheesy in the ears up there."

"Very good, sir," my father said. "I suggest we sing a few
of the things that we like ourselves — and then perhaps you

could go up and ask her if there is anything she would specially like us to do?"

"Good idea," Rollo said. "Damn good idea."

He staggered away through the French windows of the small drawing room. Afterwards, my father said to me: "I felt very sorry for him — it's painful to see a man come down in that way."

It was a bright mild evening, full of late bird-song from the spinneys, and the men sang beautifully. I sat on the wall at the end of the terrace, watching and listening as they sang the songs I knew. Miss Bertie's room was at the corner of the house, in one of those hexagonal brick bays built on like the section of an enormous saltcellar. Tea roses of pale gold, falling from loose extended sprays, unpruned and untied, were breaking into color from trelliswork of green laths between the window bays.

The men sang "Early One Morning" and "The Oak and the Ash" and then "Sweet and Low," their favorite, and several others. During this time Rollo did not appear again. There was a clatter, once, of a very young maid clumsily setting down plates and glasses in a porch at the other end of the terrace. Apart from this, there was no sign from the house that anyone could be listening. I began to be haunted by an impression that the house was empty that all the life of it had died away, and that the men were singing to themselves.

After the sixth or seventh piece there was still no sign of Rollo. The men had a rest while I went to look into the open windows of the smaller drawing room. But there was nothing there except a mass of furniture covered with dust sheets, and when I got back to the choir my father said:

"Perhaps you could find one of the maids and ask her instead."

I went into the house by the side door. The long passage

[283]

between the big main rooms was haunted by Rollo's three black Labrador bitches asleep among molting leopard rugs. A pungent dog-smell sprang nauseously from fainter odors of wax and paraffin. There was no sign of Rollo, and after I had called his name once or twice, the Aspens' old maid, Lily, came out of the kitchen recesses to answer me.

"Oh, it's you Mr. Richardson," she said. "I'm afraid I don't know where Mr. Rollo is."

Lily, a skinny gray-haired woman of sixty in a butterfly apron, as solid a part of the Aspen house as the newel post of the stairs, stared at me with grim density.

"Perhaps you would run up and ask Miss Bertie if she's enjoying the singing," I said, "and if there's anything special she'd like to hear?"

Awkward and hesitating, Lily stood there plucking at the front of her apron with her skinny red hands.

"Perhaps she has a favorite song?" I said.

The line of Lily's mouth compressed itself so hard that it almost vanished as she bit into her lips.

"It doesn't matter if she hasn't," I said. "It's just that they would like to sing some little thing to make her happy."

"Happy? Who? — Miss Bertie?" she said, and I thought there was a snarling break in her voice that was very near to tears.

As I stood awkwardly wondering what to say I swallowed an intense and nauseous breath of dog odors. There was a glint of black muscles upheaved and floundering among leopard rugs.

"Go on, you big slommacking great brutes," she said. She slapped skinny angry hands at the Labradors, each of which slowly lifted a ponderous carcass, dumbly staring back at her. "Go on, you great ugly things — move yourselves. Mortaring in on my clean floors — "

[284]

Ponderous and old and flabby, the Labradors waddled ten or twelve paces, collapsing deflated on the porch.

"Would you go up?" I said.

"Me?" she said. From the compressed tight lips there was again the old tearful snarl. "I'm not allowed up there — "

I saw her teeth grating with agitation at her drawn lips. Her eyes held hints of inexplicable disasters.

"I haven't been in the room for three months," she said. "Nearly four — come Whitsun. Never been in. Never been near."

To my dismay the tears broke from their snarling stranglehold. As they began to fall down her bony face she grabbed piteously at her apron, hiding herself in a starchy nunlike shield under which her voice shook with beating sobs.

"I'm not wanted here, I'm not wanted, I'm not wanted," she said.

I said something tactful about being sure that she was wanted, but there were only tense agitations from behind the apron in answer.

"Haven't you any idea where Rollo is?" I said. "Perhaps he could go up instead."

"No," she said, "no. Why should I know? I don't belong here. I'm not part of it. It isn't the same as when you used to come. They were the nice days — "

A Labrador rose from the porch and made up its mind to pad slowly back into the house, swinging a bloated belly of enlarged rose-black teats.

She heard it and from under the apron she released a tear-broken face, rushing forward with hatred:

"Get out! Get out, you big slommacking brute! They drive my life scatty — they drive it scatty!" she said. "They drive it scatty!"

The Labrador gave a slow bronchial cough, as if about to spit, and sank on the threshold.

[285]

I said it did not matter about the song, after all, but she scrubbed a bony hand across her tears and said:

"I thought they sang so nice. It was so nice. It seems wonderful to have somebody here again — somebody else besides her and Rollo and dogs — dogs, dogs, nothing but dogs. The big, ugly, dirty brutes — "

She stopped suddenly. She seemed to think of something, and said:

"You could go up if you like. You go up and ask her. She wouldn't mind — "

"No," I said. "It doesn't matter."

"She wouldn't mind. She often used to talk about you — take and go up," she said.

I hesitated for a few moments; and then a nauseous odor of bloated dog-flesh blew in from the porch and a skinny face stared in renewed pathetic appeal from the crackling wing of an apron; and finally I said:

"All right. Perhaps you wouldn't mind telling my father that I've gone up to ask her what she would like," I said.

"I'll tell him," she said. "You know which room it is?"

I heard her launch a final and hateful attack on the prostrate Labradors as she beat her way across the threshold. I went slowly upstairs. I remembered the bitter draft of snow-wind in the hall on the first night I had ever been in the house, the room that scorched and froze at the same time, the girl whose effect on me was to make me feel that I was poised on the edge of a knife. And the smell of the upstairs landing, closed and stuffy and sun-stale and free of the odors of dogs from below, made me remember the summer afternoons.

When I knocked on Miss Bertie's bedroom door a voice of unrecognizable pitch, compressed and piercing, called back at me:

"Who is that? Who is it?"

"I've come to — "

"Will you say who it is, please?"

"It's Mr. Richardson," I said.

"Who? Mr. Who did you say? Mr. Who?"

"May I come in, Miss Aspen?"

"Will you say who it is, please?"

I opened the door; I held it ajar six inches or so, and said, levelly:

"Miss Aspen, I have come from the choir to ask you if there is anything you wish them to sing. It's Richardson. Lydia's friend."

She gave a hollow bleat of surprise.

"May I come in?" I said.

"You may not," she said. "You may certainly not."

I held the door a few inches ajar; I just could see, inside, the lower end of a sepulchral brass bedstead hung with patterned shawls.

"The choir would be delighted," I began to say, but she cut me off at once:

"How is Lydia? You saw her, didn't you?"

"Yes," I said. "I saw her. She's very well, I think — "

"You think? You think?"

"I'm sure she is," I said. And with querulous sharpness she snapped:

"Who sent you up here? Who told you you might come? Lily? — was it Lily?"

"My father was most anxious to put in a piece that you specially wanted," I said. "If you'd tell me — "

In a persecuted, trembling voice she said:

"It was Lily, wasn't it? Why is she here still? She was to have gone — I told her to go — "

"Have you enjoyed the singing, Miss Aspen?" I said.

"Yes, I've enjoyed it. I've enjoyed it. It was very kind of — it was kind — it was very kind."

She lapsed into a silence in which, presently, I caught the

break of semiexhausted breathing. In the background I could hear the voices of men talking to each other on the terrace below; and then, in the further background, the call of birds in the still evening across the park. In another month the clovered smell of drying grass would rise from the maze of swathes and drench the air about the place with the sweetness of high summer, but all I could smell as I stood there was the fustiness of a bedroom that had not been opened for a long time, the dry sour odor of someone old in the decay of self-imprisonment, and drifting in again, up the stairs, the rank whiff of bitches from the hall below.

I waited a little longer, listening to the grating croak of her recaptured breath. I looked at the gray peelings, imprinted with bright turquoise stars of dampness, of the yellow wallpaper above the fireplace, and then I said:

"I must go now, Miss Aspen. Was there any song you wanted them to sing?"

She did not answer. For some moments it was so quiet that I could hear the piercing note of a swallow, fine-drawn and delicate, scratching the evening air outside.

"Miss Aspen," I said, "was there a song?"

Her voice sounded far away, a little as if smothered by something, as she answered:

"No. There is nothing I want," she said. I waited, and she went on: "I was never very strong in music. I don't know any songs."

"Thank you," I said. "Good-by, Miss Aspen."

She did not say good-by; but for one moment, as I closed the door, her voice lifted itself a fraction for the last time.

"Tell your father it was very good of him to come."

I went downstairs, pursued by impressions of an intense loneliness that remained with me during and for some time after the singing of the final song. I told my father she preferred above all the song called "The Golden Vanity." The men sang it with great feeling, with a splendid air of melancholy tenderness that flowed about the decaying terraces in the evening air.

When it was all over Lily hobbled out on to the terrace, bringing us cups of coffee. The younger maid served us with cake and cheese. There was no sign of Rollo. Several times Lily said how beautiful the singing was and how it was almost like old times to have us there, and my father said how everyone had enjoyed it and how he hoped it was satisfactory.

"Well, shall we go?" he said to me at last. "Are you going to walk down with us?"

"No," I said. "I'll walk home the other way. Across the park."

By the time I reached the top of the park, where the path went through the spinneys near the summerhouse, the sun had gone down. I stopped and looked back at the long slope of grass, greenish-gold and burnished already with buttercup and smoldering with sorrel-flower. Hawthorns, like solid crests of foam washed into hollows of grass, shone even brighter in the darkening evening air than the separate high flames of chestnuts. A flight of homing pigeons, flying over from the town, cloud-gray and hardly distinguishable in the receding light, flew across spaces between trees of yellow oak-flower, and somewhere down by the house a thrush, in a high-spun continuous thread of notes, was still singing brilliantly.

I looked for a long time at the house, red and big and unshapely with its additions of cupola and bay and pepperbox. I felt suddenly as if I were seeing it for the first time. It seemed all at once impossible and outdated, and as I stood thinking of the people in it, a drunk, a querulous lonely woman bitten with a decay of persecutions, a tearful maid and the bloated Labradors, I remembered some words of Rollo's, "There soon won't be any people like us," and then some

[289]

others of Miss Aspen's, "After all, it may be the last thing of any consequence we shall be able to give her."

I remembered too how she had persisted that Evensford was not on the map. It had taken me a long time, aided by the stench of three bloated dogs among the molting leopard rugs and a song or two of my father's sung under the bedroom windows of a woman who had no song to ask for, to grasp that it was not the town, but the house, that really had no existence there.

II

Summer began to unfold with a green splendor that affected even Evensford. Glistening white crops of moon daisies appeared on railway cuttings that drove into the town through colonies of slate-topped terraces and black-tarred fowl huts, in the flat riverside district whose cathedral was the gasworks. In occasional oases, at street corners, laburnums blossomed, yellow and brilliant against old wintry congealments of brown leather-dust on factory windows. There came a brief flowering of snowball trees, pure and sterile, in shady chapel yards.

About the sanatorium a circular forest of full-leaved oak and walnut and lime and even beech, a rare tree on that cold clay soil, threw a green screen that cut off, as in the Aspen park, all sight of Evensford making another oasis where it was possible to believe you were shut away in the pure light of open country.

The sanatorium was very full that summer. There is a certain long narrowness of jaw in a typical Evensford face that seems to put one face in every three into the category of incipient illness. All through the slump the surgeries of Evensford doctors were always crowded with men coughing over knotted mufflers, and with young girls who, like Lydia and Nora Jepson, were coming to the end of lost races against gaiety. There were too many people with transfixed bright eyes in Evensford that summer and with skins that seemed to carry just under the surface a haunting glow that gave them a strange transparency.

In all this a compensating passion for living showed itself, mostly in a love of flowers that was not only typical but very touching, and after the long difficult winter there was a keen hungriness in the narrow faces of workless men taking small white terriers for long walks into the morning countryside of waking summer and coming back, in the early evening, carrying bunches of marsh marigold and bluebell and the first pink sprigs of honeysuckle and hedge rose. There were always streams of people climbing the short hill to the sanatorium on visiting days, and on Sundays especially, carrying bunches of flowers plucked from gardens and allotments or from woods and fields. There were always taxis bringing elderly relatives from a distance, or young factory girls, sprightly and beautiful and vibrant because the race for gaiety was just beginning, arriving to visit other girls who had lost the race and were now lying in a private world beyond a screen of trees, troubled and subdued but not always sad, thinking it over and wondering why.

When I went to see Lydia for the second time that spring I was one of a long stream of Sunday-afternoon visitors carrying flowers.

"She has another visitor," the nurse who met me said. "But it will be all right. She is the sort of person who responds to people. We like her to have them when she can."

All across the grounds of the sanatorium there was an irresistibly beautiful fragrance of lilac, sweet in the late hot May afternoon, that reminded me of the Aspen park. There was still a miraculous singing of blackbirds in high walnut trees and a wonderful freshness in the tender broken overtones of many greens that had still not been merged to the single, darker tone of summer.

When I got to Lydia's hut, Blackie Johnson was sitting in the chair by the bed. He was holding a bunch of flaming orange marigolds in one big stiff hand.

"Hullo, there you are!" Lydia said. "How nice — what a lot of people — everybody coming to see me all at once!"

She was sitting propped up by pillows. She did not look very thin, but there was a rosiness about her skin, under the dark hair, that seemed unreal and puffy.

Blackie rose with stiff and diffident heaviness to shake me by the hand.

"Hullo, Mr. Richardson," he said, "how are you?"

He stared at me in a crushed, stupefied sort of way, almost as if in self-imposed humility.

"Hullo, Blackie," I said.

"You're not to call him Blackie," Lydia said. "His real name is Bert. You have to call people by their proper names."

"I'm sorry," I said.

"That's all right, Mr. Richardson," he said. "Everybody still calls me Blackie."

"Then they mustn't," she said. "I'm going to convert them."

Blackie gave a curious embarrassed smile, the sort of smile that seems so often to be sheer pain on the faces of big muscular men, and then changed his bunch of flowers from one hand to another. His blue serge suit was too tight for the solid muscular pack of his body, and there were already marks across his thick neck where the starched edges of his collar had rubbed against the flesh.

"Oh, more flowers!" Lydia said. "Irises — yellow ones! Do you remember how they always grew on the other side of the rose garden? Aunt Bertie always loved them. Did you see Aunt Bertie? You see, I know where you've been — !"

"Yes, I saw her," I said.

"How is she? — She wrote me a long letter about the singing."

"She's well," I said. "I think she's well."

"You think?" she said. "Well, isn't she? You saw her, didn't you?"

"No," I said. "I talked to her through a door."

"Oh, well, don't stand up there nursing your flowers. Put the flowers somewhere and come and sit on the bed and talk to me."

"I'll put them in your water jug," I said.

"No," she said, "Bert will put them in. Bert can do it. Put them in, Bert, won't you? And the marigolds too" — and then, as Blackie rose with queer subdued obedience to take my flowers and his own to the water jug on the washstand in the corner: "What was that horror Rollo doing? On a blinder again?"

"I think so," I said.

"You think so?" she said. "You mean he was. Why do you always have to say you think so?"

"Thinking is a thing I go in for sometimes," I said.

She laughed and said that was exactly like me. Blackie fumbled awkwardly with the flowers. Then she reminded me, in a rather forced voice and with a tense gesture on her face, that I hadn't kissed her. So I kissed her, in the briefest and most formal way I could, on one cheek, and she said:

"Now sit down, both of you, and in a few minutes they'll bring us tea. No, they won't! — because I didn't know you were coming," she said to me, "and now they'll only bring it for two. We'll have to tell them — Bert, you'll have to go and tell them. Find Nurse Simpson — "

Blackie, coming stiffly from the business of trying to arrange the flowers in the water jug, looked, in his tight dark serge, with his choking collar, like a manservant waiting to take an order.

"Find Nurse Simpson," Lydia said, "there's dear. She's the nice one with the frizzy hair — you know her, don't you, the frizzy blonde? Tell her it's tea for three now, not two."

Blackie left the hut and began to walk, on bright creaking black shoes, down the path between the huts. But after seven or eight paces she called him back:

"Bert! — wait a minute. It would be nice if we could get Nora over. Ask Nora if she'd come over. She came on Wednesday — they allow her now. It would be like old times if Nora came. Wouldn't it?" she said to me.

I did not answer. I did not think it could possibly be like old times, then or ever, and I was glad when she said:

"He's comic, isn't he? I think he's enormously comic. He comes every Wednesday and every Sunday. He has done — all through — all the time — "

"It's very nice of him," I said.

"I know. It isn't that. It's the way he does it. He just sits here in his best suit and stares and sometimes we have the most awful job to make any sort of conversation."

I sat thinking of the big muscle-packed aggressive Blackie lying with a spanner in his hand under a car in Johnson's yard, and she echoed my thoughts by saying:

"Isn't it awfully queer sometimes how people change?"

"Very queer," I said.

"You wouldn't think he was the same person, would you? Not in the least the same person. As soon as he heard I was ill he started to come and see me — except the first few weeks when Dr. Baird wouldn't let me have anybody."

She screwed up her eyes and asked me how you could account for that, and I said:

"You encouraged him. That's how."

She lowered her voice to answer me:

"I didn't encourage him. I've done all I can not to encourage him. What have I ever done to encourage him?"

I sat thinking. The thing that had not changed about her was her hunger for people, her impulsive thirst for company.

"After all," I said, "you lent him money."

"That's the point," she said. "I didn't. I offered to lend him something and he wouldn't take it. That was the trouble that night at Ashby. He was too proud — too proud or too shy or something. I was so sorry for him when his father died and he had the fire. I wanted to help him."

She began to search under her pillow for something; she could not find it and she said:

"That was all we were talking about that night at Ashby. When you stormed out and went home and wouldn't wait — "

She broke off, and in her silence I could feel, even though she did not intend it, a suspense of accusation — "if only you'd waited. You see, you're so impatient. You won't wait to have things explained. You storm away and then things happen — "

She broke off again to search under her pillow, and I said:

"What are you looking for? Can I — "

"My comb." Her distraction at something in the past was consumed by her small distraction at not finding the comb. "I must have a look at myself before Nora comes. Nora's a stunner. You wouldn't think so, with that long, thin body, would you? But she can break them all."

"Your comb's on the dressing table," I said, "and your brush too," and as I reached over to get them for her she said:

[295]

"I tried to get Bert interested in her, but he wouldn't look. In the end she'll probably have Dr. Baird — "

She stopped talking at last. The quality of overexcitement in her voice and her eyes became transferred to her hands. She unfastened them nervously and began to brush her hair. She said only once, "You see, my hair comes out — in handfuls," and she held straggling, dark strands of it for me to see. Her hair, as she slowly brushed it down over her shoulders, reminded me of the first time I had ever seen her, looking so impossibly young that she had succeeded in cheating me, and then she finished looping back her hair and said:

"Throw the pieces outside. The birds will fetch them. I lie here and watch them. They fetch them for their nests. That's a thought, isn't it?"

It seemed to me rather a nice thought; but I had no time to answer her before Blackie came back, bringing Nora and Dr. Baird.

"I'll give you strict injunctions, all of you," said Baird, a fair Anglo-Scot with an athletic presence and a strength that revealed itself most notably in hairy, antiseptic, commanding hands, "she's to stay half an hour. Not a second longer."

"Oh! Dr. Baird," Lydia said. "This is a gathering of old flames — !"

"Then damp the flames down," Baird said, "or put them out altogether."

From this remark a brightness developed that lasted through tea. Perhaps its real cause lay in Nora, who had now begun a series of progressively extended walks every day in the grounds and who said, several times:

"The most wonderful thing of all is to have a dress on — and stockings — it's marvelous to feel you're a girl again. Not just a stick of bone in a bed."

Through all this I saw Blackie staring at Lydia: steadfastly, hopefully, with patience, like a dog trained out of a puppyhood of snarling resentments into a calm obedience that had the same touching, inexpressible canine devotion.

Even when he was shaken out of this by Nora saying that she gained seven or eight pounds in weight and demonstrating, by holding her frock to midway up her thighs, how the shape of her legs was coming back, fuller and nicer even than before, I felt he looked at her less for herself than because he saw in her body the approaching pattern of Lydia's. I felt he longed for the day when she too would walk in the grounds, in the sun, and hold up her dress to show that the grace of her body was coming back.

"I'm getting terrific," Nora said. "I can even do a twirl with my skirts." She revealed glimpses of pale underwear and thighs of slim delicacy like pale mushroom stalks under the pink gills of her dress.

"Wait till *I* get up," Lydia said. Through dark fixed eyes, she gave the impression of having been pushed a little out of the picture. "Just wait till *I* stand there — "

"You've got to go carefully," Blackie said. His voice had the methodical solemnity of a man who has created a creed for himself. I heard it so often afterwards that it came to have a pitiful, bludgeoning profundity. "You know you've got to go carefully. We can't have you going back."

"Oh, she won't go back!" Nora said gaily. "Who ever thinks of her going back?"

"She's got to go very carefully," Blackie said.

"If we'd been careful, Lydia, we shouldn't have been here," Nora said, "and then I shouldn't have know how lovely it is to feel I've got nice legs again."

"Nor should we," I said, and Blackie, absorbed in his creed of care, was the only one who did not laugh at the joke I made.

Punctually to the half-hour, Dr. Baird rejoined us.

"It's time, little girl," he said. "Come on."

"She's a big girl. She's been showing us where, too — she's been dancing!" Lydia said. "Nora! — do it again for Dr. Baird — !"

Blackie put a check on this excitement by suddenly starting to say good-by to each of us in turn, formally shaking hands, saying, "Good afternoon, Miss Jepson. Good afternoon, Doctor. Good afternoon, Mr. Richardson," and finally:

"Good-by, Miss Aspen."

"He *will* call me Miss Aspen!" she said.

"You play rugby?" Dr. Baird said. "You ought to play rugby, man, with that pack of weight on you."

"No," Blackie said. "I'm afraid not, Doctor."

"He used to play motor bikes," Lydia said, "but he's given that up."

"Nobody plays rugby in this damned town," Baird said. "I can't get a damned soul interested — "

"I must go now," Blackie said. "Good afternoon, all."

"Good-by, Bert," Lydia said. "It was so nice of you to come."

Afterwards, when the three of them had gone, she looked at me and said:

"It was nice of you, too. Come again, won't you?"

"Not if you'd rather I didn't," I said.

"Of course I want you to come."

"I didn't know Blackie came, and if you'd rather there weren't the two of us — "

"Oh, he's just my watchdog," she said. "Did you see the way he sits and looks at me?"

"Yes," I said.

She laughed. "He reminds me more than anything in the world of a watchdog. It's wonderful how people change, isn't it?"

"Not everybody changes," I said, and I stooped to kiss her good-by.

[298]

This time she turned her lips to me. As they brushed my face there was a dry flakiness about them, and for a single unbearable moment I wanted to hold them there, deeply and for a long time, but she whispered:

"Off you go, now. Nurse Simpson will be chasing you. She's severe. You will come again, won't you?"

I smiled. "And still she wished for company," I said.

"What's that?" she said. "One of your quotations?"

"Good-by," I said.

She looked suddenly tired from exertions of overgaiety and conversation. As she lay back on the pillows she gave me a distant smile.

"You haven't changed at all," she said. "I don't think you have."

Some minutes later I went into a world of departing visitors, dispersing either on foot or by taxi, to hear Blackie Johnson, at the sanatorium gates, politely and stolidly refusing two anxious elderly fares who wanted to catch the down-express to Leicester.

"I'm very sorry," Blackie said. "I've got another job."

The old Chrysler limousine was standing in the road, with Blackie solid and Sundayfied in the driving seat. As he saw me he called:

"Here you are, Mr. Richardson. Thought you were never coming. Jump in."

Mystified, I got into the front seat. He leaned over and shut the quaking upholstered door with a bang.

"I hoped I'd catch you," he said. He grated in the clutch and the Chrysler growled heavily down the hill. "Is there somewhere I can take you? Can I run you home?"

"I wasn't going anywhere," I said.

"Do you mind if I run you round in the country for half an hour?" he said. "If you can spare the time? There's some-

[299]

thing — " He broke off, fumbling at the gears, big and nervous, unable to frame the words for a situation that was clearly the greatest trouble to him.

We drove on for some miles in silence, out of the town, into bright sunlight, past trooping Sunday walkers, and gradually into lanes of rising wheat behind hedgerows of emerald and snowy may-cloud. The air was humid behind the closed glass of the Chrysler, and at last he partly opened a window and said:

"What do you make of her, Mr. Richardson? What do you think of her?"

"I think she looks well," I said.

"Do you?" he said in agitation. "You do really?"

"I think so — "

"I don't know what to make of her," he said. "Sometimes — "

He pulled up the car with harsh abruptness in a side lane along which children had strewn, in broken sheaves, numberless naked bluebells, the blanched white sockets limp in the hot sun. He opened the window a little wider. I could smell the rising summer in the scent of grass, in the clotted vanilla of masses of hawthorn and in the sweetness of bluebells still alive in small oak copses.

"You think she's all right?" he said. "I keep trying to get hold of Dr. Baird to ask him — but you know how they are — doctors — "

"Well, if Nora's anything to go by — "

"Nora's different," he said. "Nora's not the same. You can't go by Nora."

"Baird seems confident," I said.

He sat staring down the road. A cuckoo, breaking from a copse, called its way over dark-green sunlit wheatfields, pursued by another. I watched them for some time, out of sight, before Blackie said:

"The first time I saw her I couldn't sleep all night — I couldn't get to sleep for thinking of her. She couldn't speak to me that time. They let me have three minutes with her, with a nurse there — that's all — and she couldn't speak to me."

I stared down the road, not speaking. It seemed to me that he had waited a long time for the chance to lift a private, troubled load of something off his chest, and now that he had begun he could not stop himself:

"You didn't see her then, Mr. Richardson," he said. "You didn't see her before that, either. You didn't see it all coming on, last winter and last summer and the winter before that. After Mr. Holland — that's when it started — after that — "

I let him go on, staring through the dusty windscreen of the car at golden clarified sunlight steeping like warm liquid the wheatfields, the copses and the high hedgerows of hawthorn. His voice unwound itself from light coils of recollection that hurt him as distinctly as if he had been unraveling a tortured knot of veins inside himself.

He somehow extracted from this tangled mess of his own pain the story of the two winters and the summer, of the long binge about which she had spoken. Several times he got it, as Tom had had a habit of doing under extreme emotion, in disorder, backwards, turned in on itself, hopelessly repetitive, so that he had to start again. I didn't interfere with him; I suppose he talked for about an hour. He spoke of Nora sometimes, but never of Lydia: only, with an awful sort of respect that had the effect of making his distraction about her more troubled and sometimes most poignant, of Miss Aspen. It was Miss Aspen ordering the car every night, Miss Aspen crazy to go to new places, to try new dances, to go farther and farther, later and later, and more and more often. It was Miss Aspen, wild and hungry for company, who would never stop and never tire. Through it all ran the word "business," like the beat of an unnecessary justification.

"I was very glad of the business, Mr. Richardson, when it started I was very glad of the business. She had tried to be very kind to me before that — you remember that, don't you? She tried to put business in my way — she tried to lend me money, and all that. I couldn't see it then — I'm a bit pig-headed. It takes me a long time to see a thing like that. Then when I did see it I was sorry. I wished I hadn't acted like that. But I didn't see her. I didn't get a chance to explain. And then she rang me up one day and it started and I was glad of the business. I was very glad of the business."

From time to time he would break off, saying: "I wish I hadn't done it now. I wish to God I'd never started it."

All through the two winters and the summer there would hardly be a night, except Sundays, when she and Nora did not hire the car. Besides the dances there were a number of clubs, opened mostly by dubious colonels and their wives or mistresses up and down the river, offering some sort of food and drink and high-pitched company and a brittle, searing brand of fun. They found them all, beat their way hungrily through them, exhausted them and went farther away for others. He did not say much about men. He supposed there must have been men, in the same way as there was a good deal of drink and rowdiness and such idiocies, popular at the time, as games of stripping down to brassières on dance floors. But the thing that stuck in his mind, troubling him most, was the deadliness. An awful deadliness. There was no joy in it: only a deadly, awful pointlessness. The two girls went through everything with the same wearing hunger. They even brought it to a thoughtless brand of insolence, leaving him alone in the car for five and six and seven hours at a time, until three or four o'clock in the morning, which in summer meant the break of day.

Then one day he found he had had enough of this; after several months of it he was getting worn out himself. Most nights he managed to get a little sleep in the car, but it was never enough and always, next day, he began to feel frowsy and brainless and incapable of doing the work he wanted. His business — "I'm not all that hot on it, anyway. I'm no businessman" — began to fall off. His accounts fell behind and got into a mess. Then one night, after crawling home for hours in a river-fog and narrowly missing the river at one point, he found he was really frightened. A queer idea of impending disaster stuck itself into his head and he could not get it out. It haunted him all next day, and that same evening he said to her:

"Miss Aspen, I'm afraid I can't take you any more. I'm afraid I shall have to give it up."

She didn't answer that — there was no protest or anger or remonstration or question about it at all. But that night, when she at last came out of one of the dubious colonels' clubs, he saw her stagger about sightlessly in the lights of his car, half-supported by Nora, until she suddenly lurched and fell down.

He wasn't shocked by the fact of seeing her drunk. He picked her up in his arms, and it was more as if she were sleeping. He even felt a sense of relief about it. He tucked her up with rugs, beside Nora, who was in a state of stony suspense, at the back of the car. Then he drove carefully home. It was a little foggy again, in dangerous patches, but in places there were stars. Then as he drove his sense of disaster came back. He found himself appalled by the idea that she might have fallen and hurt herself or wandered stupidly about and got lost in the river.

"So I knew if she was going on with it I had to go on," he said. "I was frightened about her."

Later, after he had taken Nora home, he drove to the park

[303]

with Lydia. She was still asleep in the car when he stopped by the gates. He tried to wake her by gently calling her name. "Miss Aspen, Miss Aspen," he kept saying to her. "Miss Aspen, you'll have to wake up. We're home now — you'll have to wake yourself, Miss Aspen. Come on."

Like this he tried for about half an hour to coax her into wakefulness. Then he decided to drive the car across the park, to the house, and try to get her indoors and settle her for the rest of the night in a chair. He drove the Chrysler quietly to the door of the house. Then he shut off the engine — and it was the shutting off of the engine, at last, that woke her.

She stirred among the rugs and opened her eyes and looked at him, not knowing what had happened or where she was. She looked very confused and she touched his face. She asked him where had they been and where was Tom? Wasn't Tom with them? She had some sort of idea that they had left Tom behind somewhere, alone and forgotten.

It was when she touched his face again that she remembered. She began crying quietly, deeply, out of a terrible emptiness. She begged him to take her home. He said gently: "Miss Aspen, you are home. We're here. This is home," and she simply shook her head, crying desperately.

Finally he lifted her out of the car, still in the rugs, and took her into the house, picking his way with a torch from the car. She hid her face in her hands as he carried her, sobbing deeply, not speaking again until he laid her on a chair in the drawing room. He got an impression of her suffering from a strange gap in her memory. She seemed, too, to be trying to fill it, because she said:

"Where am I? Where have we been? Who was with us?" and she asked him again if Tom was there.

He shaded the torch with his hand, and her face seemed gray in the diffused light of it, only her eyes, as he said to me, yawning at him, black and lonely — "awfully lonely," he said several times, "awfully — terribly lonely."

Then he asked her, "Will you be all right, Miss Aspen, if I leave you here now? Do you think you'll be all right?"

Suddenly she sprang into a single bright moment of wakefulness and said:

"Yes. I'll be all right. You go now."

All the time his fear of leaving her was growing into the creed of anxiety that I had heard him state that afternoon. He was desperately frightened of leaving her there, in the dark house, alone, and he said again:

"You're sure you'll be all right, miss? You're sure?"

"I'm all right. Come for me tomorrow, won't you? You said you couldn't come for me again, didn't you?"

"I'll come for you," he said.

Then she leaned forward and kissed him on the face, thankfully, in a rather confused sort of way. "Just as if she thought I was somebody else," he said. Then she fell asleep again, and he quietly got himself out of the house by the aid of the torch.

"She frightened me that night," he said. "And I've been frightened ever since. That's why I wanted to ask you — you know — if you thought — "

A cuckoo flew with bubbling, throaty calls across the wheatfield, disappearing beyond the copses. In the still air I caught again a great breath of grass and hawthorn and bluebell and earth beating through new pulses of spring loveliness to the very edge of summer.

For some time I watched his hands clasp and unclasp themselves nervously on the driving wheel and then at last flick at the ignition key.

"You think she'll be all right?" he said.

He started the car almost involuntarily, and the sound of it startled a blackbird from the hedges and sent it squawking down the hedgerow with fear.

"Yes. She'll be all right," I said.

His hand seemed to quiver on the gear-lever as he let in the clutch.

"Because every time I go up there I'm frightened," he said. "I'm frightened she won't be there any more."

III

Bᴜᴛ whenever we went to see her she was there. She remained in the sanatorium all that summer, and in fact for the rest of the year, and I saw her whenever I could. Sometimes, in the beginning, on Sundays, because I knew that Blackie Johnson would be there, I stayed away from her, but whenever I did so she attacked me with not very serious reproaches that were part of her growing strength.

"You never know," she said, "I might be up when you come one day. And if I am I want you to be the first to see me. I want to do Nora's trick for you. I've got legs, too. You used to think they were rather nice ones."

"All of you was nice," I said.

"Oh! Don't say that," she said. "I think I shall cry if you say that."

"You were very nice," I said. "You were the first one — " And then I could not finish what I had to say.

"Don't reproach me," she said. "I can't bear it if you reproach me."

She looked at me piteously; and after that, as she struggled up and down through the confusing graph of growing strength, waiting for the time when they would let her walk, too gay sometimes and then too much in despair, I tried as much as possible not to see her alone. It seemed much simpler, and in a curious way much more inevitable, to have Blackie there.

Then I began to be aware of the fact that Blackie liked to have me there. His stiffness and his fear about her were lessened because of me. And gradually, as two people sometimes do who begin with violent dislikes of each other, we began to be friends. I knew I had misjudged him. I liked it when I found him there; I felt I began to understand him. He used to sit by the bedside on Sunday afternoons, all through the summer, in a dark-blue serge suit, sweating in the oppressively hot little hut, patient and tortured, awkwardly staring at her and waiting for her to get well. Except for discarding a waistcoat, he did not dress any differently all that summer. He wore his peaked blue chauffeur's cap and sometimes, out of pure habit, he brought his brown leather driving gloves with him. Then he would sit with the cap on his knees and the driving gloves in the cap, nervously playing with first one and then the other, unaware that he was doing so. I would see her go through phases of amusement, irritation, despair, vexation and even anger about this until she could stand it no longer. I would see her hands picking with rising disquiet at the coverlet until finally she would snap at it with desperate impatience, as if she felt like tearing it to rags, and say:

"For goodness' sake, Bert, stop playing with your hat and gloves and take your jacket off and be cool. It makes me boil to look at you."

Then he would put his hat and gloves on the floor. He would take off his jacket. With self-conscious care he would fold it up and put it on the hat. Then she would say: "Don't fold it like that. You'll crease it all up. Hang it on the chair," and he would hang it on the chair. Then he would sit back in the chair, hotter, more sweating, more awkward than ever from his exertions, and she would say:

"Can't you take your collar off? It's your collar that makes you so hot. It looks as if it's choking you."

"I'm all right," he would say. "I'm all right."

Then she would invite him to look at me.

"Why don't you dress sensibly like that?" she would say. "Just shirt and trousers and no tie? You'd be so much more comfortable."

"I'm comfortable," he would say. "I'm quite comfortable."

Into his starched Sunday collar his thick Adam's apple would beat like a gulping piston. Sweat would stream down from the black side-panels of his hair and soak, with bluish stains, into the armpits of his shirt. He would run a dark, hairy finger along the inner rim of his collar and painfully extract it, scooping sweat. And she would cry in despair:

"Oh! You're so stubborn! You do irritate me so!"

But he was not stubborn; and if he irritated her it was only because he was trying, desperately hard, to do exactly the opposite.

Then her nurse, the blonde Miss Simpson, muscular and candid, would bring tea on a hospital trolley. And Lydia would laugh at Blackie and say:

"Come on now. You can make yourself useful. You can pour."

He would make a slow, bungling, clattering mess of this. His big engineering hands, into which oil seemed to have soaked with a stain of permanent shadowy brown made more greasy by sweat, would grasp at cups and plates and teapots with the kind of excessive care that ends in shattering clumsiness. Lumps of sugar would be dropped into the tea from considerable height, like bombs. Tea would squab sordidly into saucers, from which he would drain it noisily back into cups.

Somehow, finally, he would get cups and plates distributed; and then would begin the business, really the performance, of having his own tea. He elaborately prepared for himself clumsy mountains of bread and jam. He balanced his cup on his knees and then set it on the floor; then took a vast mouthful of bread and jam and then a vaster drink of tea, washing it down, stirring and sucking and clattering loudly. Food and drink and china were pieces with which he made a series of terribly laborious moves, ended by her crying from the bed:

"Why don't you put your cup on the trolley, you poor man!"

Then at last she would turn to me:

"*You* pour me a cup, will you?"

And I would try to pour it not too efficiently, not too delicately, in order not to touch him with acuter embarrassments; but she would be sure to say:

"There you are — that's more like it. That's something *like* service — "

Then perhaps as I took away her cup she would press my arm and smile and say:

"Thank you. You're awfully sweet to me."

I knew that this would embarrass him, and I would try to play it off by mocking her:

"Does madam wish anything else?" I would say.

"You can put my pillows straight. Sit me up a little higher — "

She would let herself sink into the pillows a little, so that I could lift her up. She would make it necessary for me to put my arms under her body as I lifted her. Then she would laugh, or the scalloped front of her nightdress would fall away, showing her breast, or her hair would get tangled and she would make me reach for the mirror and her comb and

[309]

then hold the mirror in front of her so that she could comb her hair into place again.

Sometimes I would not be able to resist a desire to tilt the mirror or move it away, so that she could not see herself. Then she would slap my knuckles with the comb and say:

"Hold it still. I can't see myself! Hold it still, can't you? — I shall hate you — hold it still — !"

" 'Now hate me if thou wilt — ' "

"You're an awful torment. You always did torment me so, didn't you? I believe you love to torment me! Hold still — !"

"How can I if I'm trembling?"

"You idiot! — hold it *still* so that I can see myself — I can only see one side of myself — "

"Let's hope it's the right side — the nice, true, kind, right side," I would say, and we would laugh together in the small private world of former acquaintance, exclusive, unkindly, where he could not follow.

Exactly what pain this gave him I could not tell. He had already been so pained and frightened by the thought of her dying that it is possible it gave him no pain at all. He was so absorbed in the idea of her walking again that I do not think he ever noticed, with envy or malice or even unkindliness, all that summer, that she began to show her growing strength by growing fonder of me.

One Sunday I could not go to see her. The next week he was sitting in the limousine waiting for me, eager, relieved, touched by gratitude, when I walked up to the gates. He leapt out, scrambling together with cap and gloves a bunch of violent gaillardias that were like stabbing orange and crimson suns against the plain dark serge of his suit. He kept saying, as we walked into the gardens:

"I'm glad you could come. I'm glad you could come. It was queer last week without you. She didn't talk much — we had a job to find something to talk about. She always seems

[310]

brighter somehow when you're there. You know what to say to her."

It was humid, thundery weather after a spell of drought.

"No flowers this week?" he said.

"No," I said. "Not this week." I said the drought had parched everything up, and he said:

"That's what I found. I went all over the place to find something for her. I thought I was never going to find a thing for her — I couldn't think of coming without finding a flower or two to bring."

As we branched off towards the huts, out of shade into open sun, Dr. Baird bore down the path towards us, signaling with big, hairy hands:

"Not today, not today," he said. I felt a chilling sensation of sickness. Blackie stood spectral, hunched, pinned down, on the path. "Well, not the both of you. Just one, if you like. And then only for three minutes. That's all."

"What is it?" I said.

"No need for alarm," he said. "She was very naughty, that's all, the day before yesterday. She put herself back a week or two."

From Blackie there was no reaction but a spectral stare.

"Don't worry," Baird said. "We expect these things. They can't always get on. The weather isn't easy, either. Which one of you would like to go in?"

"He'll go," I said. "He has the flowers."

Blackie stood staring, shaking his head.

"No. I'll wait," he said. "I'll sit down somewhere — I don't like to see her if — it upsets me to see her — " And I knew that all his fear for her, blinding and inarticulate, had come back.

She was lying without a pillow, very flat, staring with dark eyes at the ceiling of the hut, when I went in. I stood over her with the flowers. They glowed more than ever like fiery suns in the shadow of the hut. The luminous figure of Nurse Simpson hovered in the doorway. My shadow fell on Lydia's face and I did not know what to say.

"It was nice of you to bring the flowers," she said. Her voice was empty. Her lips were crusty and colorless, without make-up, and I could not see her hands.

"Blackie sent them."

"Didn't you bring any?" Her voice seemed hurt.

"The drought has withered everything up," I said.

"Including me." She gave me a smile, small, prolonged, indeterminate, that was troubled. "Blackie always remembers, doesn't he?"

"He'd rather die than not remember," I said.

The pain of my idiotic words shot across her face before I could check them. She gave a little sob, and the nurse, swift and admonitory, bore down on me from the door. "I expected this. I expected this. No crying now," she said. "Come, now. We've had enough of tears."

"I'm very sorry," I said.

"You'd better go," she said.

"I'm terribly sorry." I laid Blackie's flowers awkwardly on the bed, from which the starched fins of the nurse's apron, turning stiffly, knocked them suddenly off. I picked them up again and laid them on a chair before I turned and went away.

When I got out into the sun I found myself trembling so much that I turned and walked back the long perimeter of open huts, farther into the gardens, away from Blackie. A few convalescent patients in deck chairs were sitting in the shade of trees; and one of them, a girl, rose and came across to me as I went past them.

"Nora," I said.

"I thought it was you," she said. "How is she?"

I stood confused by surges of relentless heat.

"Come and sit down in the shade," she said.

"No thanks," I said. "What happened to start all this?"

"Oh! It's a relapse — Dr. Baird says it's normal in this type of case."

"Anything that happens more than once is normal," I said. "Is that it?"

"You should ask Lydia that," she said.

There was something oddly enigmatical about this remark. It struck coldly through my confusion. When she left me after a few moments and went away to her deck chair under the trees, I walked slowly round the remainder of the path. There was no sign of Blackie, but from the direction of the huts the luminous, candid Nurse Simpson, came swiftly rustling.

"Is she all right, nurse?" I said.

She regarded me with blanched severity.

"You should never have come in. Dr. Baird should never have permitted it."

There was something withering about the word "permitted."

"I'm terribly sorry if I did anything that — "

"If you'd been sorry before it needn't have happened," she said.

I felt once more bludgeoned by waves of relentless heat that seemed to become part of my own stupidity. She looked at me with what I thought was harshness, and said:

"I suppose you wouldn't grasp what I meant by that."

"No," I said.

"She worked herself up into a state because you didn't come in last Sunday. That's what I meant. And now you come this Sunday and start it all over again."

I did not answer. I turned and walked down the avenue, in and out of stabbing August sunlight, a little sick from sunlight and not really thinking, to where Blackie was sitting in the front seat of the limousine, waiting for me.

"How was she?"

He leapt out of the car, distraught and eager, his face drawn.

"She's all right," I said. "She's rather tired, that's all."

"And the flowers?" he said. "What did she say to the flowers?"

There seemed, I thought, no choice between truth and anything less brutal that I could tell him. I could not tell him, partly because I was not sure of it myself, partly because I did not want to give him pain, that she really hardly noticed the flowers. I could not explain to him that she was touched and amused and charmed by his kindliness; but that it meant no more than that. I could not tell him, again partly because I was not really sure of it myself, partly because I was half afraid, that I thought her love for me was coming back. And what was worst of all, I could not tell him, because it rose from the deepest of my perplexities, creating entirely new bewilderment in me, that I did not know, now, if I had any love to offer in return.

I only knew that he stood there in solid, naïve eagerness, his face perplexed and troubled as he waited for me to answer and then alight, as I did answer, with the sort of joy I could not feel.

"She thought they were very lovely," I said.

"What did she say?"

"Not much. She was very tired."

He stood there mutely, hoping that I should be able to remember something she had said. I could not remember, but in a moment of acute pity for him, not knowing what else to say, I told him she had cried.

"Cried?" he said.

He seemed to leap across a final chasm of doubt. His face, softening, became immensely relieved and happy. I thought

I caught a glint of tears in his own eyes too, and I knew, at last, that torrid afternoon, I had somehow succeeded in saying the right thing to somebody. Out of my own perplexity I had somehow managed to conjure the things he wanted, above all, to hear.

"It was damn good of you to go in," he said. "I don't think I could have stood it by myself — I couldn't bear it, I know." He became aware, suddenly, of the realities of the afternoon. "Can I drop you somewhere, Mr. Richardson?"

"No thanks," I said. "I'll walk."

He got into the car and said: "See you next Sunday. You'll come, won't you?"

"I suppose so," I said. "Yes: I'll come."

"I appreciate that," he said. "I appreciate that. I can't tell you how I appreciate that — you know — I can't explain — "

In his gratitude he could not finish what he was saying. In his happiness he drove unexpectedly fast down the hill, blind with joy.

She got well very slowly. I had some idea that the summer would be good for her. I had forgotten that Evensford, lying in an enclosed segment of valley out of which there is no road downhill, produces in summer an enervating pressure of heat that saps the body and meshes the mind in a damp, exhausting net. The summer air cannot rise from the hollow. The streets, in dry years, are drab and dusty, blown about with gritty papers. In wet years rain streams down steep, tawdry yards, dark-stained with leather, over old, high causeways, into gullies and gutters of blue brick that add to the soft depressive vapors.

It was some time before it occurred to me — mistakenly — that it was because of this that she did not improve. She lay every Sunday in the little hut, prostrate and relapsed, staring at myself and Blackie. There began to be something transfixed, almost embalmed, about her.

Blackie brought to her all this time the same inarticulate, growing affection, the same continuous anxiety to see her well. He continued to pour the tea which a muscular and affronted Nurse Simpson brought to us on the trolley. He was always there with his flowers. When under some breath of encouragement from Lydia he found it possible to break into a few minutes of articulate response, the only think he would tell her about was the old Chrysler limousine: how he was taking it down, decoking it, fitting new rings, replacing shock absorbers, doing something about the crankshaft, treating the upholstery with some patent cleanser that would bring it up, as he said, like new, so that she would not know it again.

"Then I'm going to respray it," he said. "A nice blue, I thought. Do you think blue would be nice? I'm going to see to the windows too," he said once, "so that it won't be so drafty."

One Sunday he got carried away on a wave of rambling technicalities. He became lost for some time in the obscure mysteries of gaskets. There had been some curious leak in the packing or something that had baffled him. He shed his inarticulate shyness completely as he rambled about, explaining this to her in repetitive mechanical terms. For a week he had struggled to get it right, and now he went over it again and again with the awful laboriousness of enthusiasm she could not share.

As he talked I saw a dark skin of boredom close over her eyes, until at last she shut them. I saw her body stir several times, with scarcely perceptible restless writhings, on the bed. He went on without noticing this. I got bored too, until I grasped at length that he was speaking out of a vision amazingly enlarged by love for her. I grasped that he could not express the depth of himself except like this, in the only terms, the obscure, mechanical, boring terms, he knew: that his tenderness for her could release itself only through a tortured technical language of things like gaskets.

He crowned it all by saying: "Anyway, it'll all be finished in a fortnight — and then you'll be able to come for a drive." A curious hypnosis caught and held him in a suspense of anticipatory delight, and I knew that he was building a chariot for her.

She eventually turned on the bed and said to him, opening her eyes:

"I think you'll have to go now, Bert. I'm getting awfully tired."

He came out of the maze of his obscure enthusiasms with a shock. He realized with lacerating self-consciousness that he had tired her out with his rush of talking. He grabbed his cap, incapable of any other reaction but some stumbling remark that he had been a terrible fool.

"No you haven't. You've been very sweet," she said. "Only I'm very tired."

He mumbled again something about how sorry he was and how he hadn't meant to do all this, and then, in a renewed laceration of a fear that he might have set her back a week or two, blundered out of the hut before I could stop him.

"I ought to go too," I said.

"No," she said. "Stay with me. A little while."

I had got up in readiness to go. She held out her hand. I took it and she said:

"I was going to be walking by the summer, wasn't I? — but here I am. I don't get on very fast, do I? Not like Nora."

"Dr. Baird has been wonderful with Nora," I said.

"They'll probably be engaged," she said. "Did you know that?"

"No."

"They want to announce it at Christmas — or the New Year. There'll be a dance then. Nobody knows but Nora and me — "

"Not even Dr. Baird, I take it."

"Oh! He knows in a vague sort of way. He has a vague idea — sit down again. Don't go — I don't want you to go — "

"Blackie will be waiting. He always waits for me."

"Yes, but don't go yet. Not for a minute," she said. "Do you think he'll always come up to see me? — every Sunday, like that? As long as I'm here?"

"As long as you're here," I said.

She looked at me with a puzzled, reflective way. Her lips were momentarily parted, as if she were going to say something: to ask me a question, perhaps, about Blackie and his inevitable devoted comings and goings; or of something else that was on her mind, perhaps about myself.

She actually did begin to say, "Do you — " and then broke off. I thought for a moment, uneasy and a little troubled, that she was going to ask me if I loved her; and I knew, if she did so, that I should not know the answer.

But she said again, "Must you go?" and I said again that I must, because of Blackie.

"Won't you please kiss me before you go?" she said.

As I stooped and kissed her she caught my face lightly in her hands.

"That makes me feel better," she said.

She smiled quietly and I felt myself dry and anguished and unable to give a part of myself that was shut away from her. She needed a great deal of love from me that afternoon, and the pain of not being able to give it to her hurt me more than if I had given it and she had turned it away.

"You'd better go now," she said. "You were always the same. You were never in one place five minutes before you wanted to go to another."

[318]

When I went away and across the grounds it was not Blackie who was waiting for me at the near end of the avenue, but Dr. Baird.

He looked at the watch on his hairy wrist. "You're early away," he said, "aren't you?"

"I didn't know I was early," I said.

"There's no need to keep to the clock," he said, "if you don't want to. She's the sort of person who needs a little flexibility. She needs a little company."

I remembered, as he suddenly asked me to walk across the grounds with him, how he had made the same remark before. We walked for a few minutes across lawns where dark groups of rhododendrons were already budding a light yellow-green in the October sun.

"You could come up every day if you felt inclined," he said. "Every afternoon. She's at that stage — "

It seemed to me that there was a troubled ambiguity about what he said.

"Every afternoon?" I said. "Aren't you pleased with her?"

"It isn't that."

He went on to talk for some moments, guardedly, with professional reticence, and yet troubled, as if he were holding something back, about how it was not that, how they had got over the organic troubles, at least the worst of them, and how it was now a question —

"Wouldn't you tell me the truth?" I said. "Isn't she going to get out of this?"

He gave me a jolted sort of look that was piercing and unpleasant. Rather sharply he said:

"You don't seem to understand what's the matter with her — you don't seem to grasp that she's terribly lonely, do you?"

"I think so — "

"You think so, man. You ought to know. You ought to know that she's been down to the bottom of the pit — God, man, you ought to realize that she's got nobody but you and that taxi fellow. She's got nobody else in the world — don't you grasp that?"

It was as if I grasped it, I thought, for the first time.

"It's time you woke up to that, don't you think so?" he said. He gave me a series of piercing and condemnatory looks, searching my face, and when he stopped suddenly after saying, "You see, you — you could — " I knew what it was he was trying, with so much difficulty, to say. I knew that he was asking me to give her, in some way, an outward expression of love. He stood breaking into minute particles a young rhododendron leaf, cracking it with his fingers. There was a curious feeling in the air of a question he had not actually framed in words. A barrier of stubbornness, really a barrier against feelings unbearably broken, seemed to grow suddenly stiffer inside me. I remembered how I had been so much in love that I could not eat for happiness; and how I had been so much hurt when love had been taken away that I had wanted loneliness because it was the only bearable thing. I could not explain all this. I felt only a screen of protection rise and harden inside myself against the possible renewal of deeper, harsher pain.

Perhaps he saw that I was choked by difficulties I could not express. Perhaps he saw it simply as an example of some tiresome youthful obtuseness that needed sternly rebuking: I don't know. But suddenly he tossed the ripped fragments of rhododendron leaf into the air and said quite brutally:

"Look. I'll tell you this. I warn you. Clearly and plainly. If she doesn't get the thing she wants — if something doesn't happen soon — she won't be there when you come up one day. Good God, man — can't you see that it isn't simply a question of some bloody organic adjustment?"

Savagely he plucked another rhododendron leaf and began

to crush it in his fingers and then threw it down, apologizing:

"I'm sorry, old man. I blow up easily about these things. I'm most awfully sorry." He stuffed both hands with affecting awkwardness into his trouser pockets, kicking at the grass with his feet. "You can come up every day — whenever you like. Come and go. I'll tell the nurses. You can come and go when you like and stay as long as you like. Never mind about anybody or anything — will you?"

I hesitated. I thought of Blackie, so mutely bound up in love for her that he became articulate only through the disintegration of mechanical things, of his limousine, his gaskets. He had nothing to offer but that. I thought I saw him suddenly as a personification of myself as I had been: wonderfully in love with a cold, fragrant face in the snow, with a young body in a hot summer bedroom. I knew, because it had happened to me, the kind of laceration he would know if, one way or the other, she were taken away from him; and how, unlike me, he would never be able to explain it all and never know why.

This too was something I could not bear to happen, and I said:

"I'll come as often as I can."

"I'm glad we had this talk," he said, as if suddenly everything were straightened and simplified.

"Yes," I said.

"There's going to be a big dance here for the New Year. Let's see if we can work her up to that, shall we? Make it the sort of goal? — the dead line?"

The expression did not seem to me the happiest he could have used; but he was so pleased with the success of his talk that he did not notice it.

"You used to be awfully fond of dancing, I believe, didn't you? I think it's rather an idea to work her back to that, don't you?"

I said yes, and then as we walked back to the avenue I asked:

"There's just one other thing. Could she go for a drive? Johnson has his limousine. It's pretty warm. I think that would do her good."

"Drive? — of course, anything. Let's aim for the drive first and then the dancing," he said. His eyes were more cheerful and friendly with the exuberance of success. "Anything that's real and positive. Anything that's going to make the future real and living for her. The future — that's what we have to have in mind."

After that, as I promised, I saw her as often as I could. The autumn was long and soft, with days that cleared through pale apricot mists into delicate half-summery afternoons. She sat a good deal in the sun. A crop of walnuts fell into the damp lush grass about the huts, and the air was so quiet sometimes that we could hear the crack of squirrels' teeth gnawing them among bushes of faded fawn-feathered michaelmas daisy and lilacs that had already lost their leaves. I brought to her almost exactly the tenderness of the shortening afternoons: warm and gentle and restrained and remotely shot through by the feeling of the half-lost heat of summer. There was hardly a day with cloud. In Evensford itself some of the feeling of gauntness, the skeletonizing of faces imperiled by the exhausting summer and the slump, lifted, leaving a sharp bright pause before winter. It was possible, up there, above the town, as the leaves turned and rained down and made flat patterns of yellow and coppery orange and all the colors of November in the grass, to feel, as at the Aspen house, that the town did not exist, that you were far away in clear, undesecrated country.

By the end of November she could walk about the hut. On the last Sunday of the month Blackie and I walked for a short distance, one on each side of her, up and down the path outside. She wore a long crimson dressing gown and she kept saying:

"It's to hide my legs. They're so hideous — they're like matchsticks. I can't bear anyone to see them any more."

Blackie's wonder at all this was inexpressible — inexpressible, that is, except by some reference to the inevitable limousine.

"It's like new. You wouldn't know it. You wouldn't know it, you really wouldn't know it was the same job," he kept saying, with that unbearable lumbering repetitiveness of his. "Come down and see it, Mr. Richardson. I'm going to have it photographed. For the hire work. Come down and see it one day."

"Yes, do," Lydia said. "He's so proud of it. Go down."

So I went down on a day in early December to Blackie's garage, where I saw the car. They say that genius lets grass and weeds and moss and rust grow on the fabric of ordinary existence while it concentrates, in blind and sublime exclusion, on the single burnished jewel it is in process of creating.

With the old limousine Blackie had done the thing genius is supposed to do. It stood like a burnished and glittering hearse in a world of sordid dereliction. It seemed to flower, blue and chromium, from ghastly wastes of junk. All about it were still unobliterated scars of fire that had destroyed the landaus, the brakes and the old carriage shed. The yard was littered with the piled wreckage of cars bought for scrap and left to rust, as if dropped and crushed by tornados, where they were. There was a shabbiness, an oily, moldering junkyard decay over which town cats pursued each other like scrawny tigers in a jungle of felled and desolate chassis.

But in the center the limousine, in which Old Johnson had so often tucked us up like a coachman at dances, stood refurbished and pristine.

Blackie touched it continually with his hands. Affectionately, with pride, brushing off the prints of his fingers with the sleeve of his jacket, he said:

"Never know it, would you?" He said this, I think, thirty or forty times. "Look at the inside, Mr. Richardson. Like new. You'd never know. I'd like the old dad to see it. He'd never know it. He'd have a shock."

The processes of this single-minded pride in a miracle of transformation began to wear so hard on me that I was relieved, at last, when he invited me into the house to have a cup of tea.

We drank it in the kitchen, on a bare deal table uncleared since breakfast, from a gray-blue enamel teapot and two saucerless cups, his own without a handle. His stepmother had died earlier that year, and he kept explaining:

"Mrs. Meadows comes in from next door sometimes — does me up a bit. But it's not as if there was anybody here all the time. But I'll get round to it a bit better now — now I've done the job."

A smell of gas from old burners lingered acridly on air already clogged with the odors of stale grease and of petrol from the pump outside.

"It's not a bad old place," he said. "Good position, too. Cars come by in hundreds. In a week thousands of cars come by — at the end of the town too, where you can catch them. Where you want to be."

By the time I had finished my tea the dream had encroached again:

"Just one thing I forgot to show you," he said. He dragged me joyfully back to the furbished chariot. It was to be photographed that afternoon, and as we went into the yard he held his hands out several times, flatly, to the sky, afraid of rain.

"There you are," he said. He opened the back door, revealing an interior of spotless spaciousness in which, by each side window, were chromium goblets I had not noticed before.

"For flowers," he said, and I knew that that was the peak, the crown of it all.

Before Lydia rode out in this chariot — he was going to turn down flat, he kept saying, every other job that came along, simply because he wanted her to be the first to ride in it — Miss Aspen died. A *cortège,* consisting of Rollo, alone, florid as if rawly bruised, in a solitary family coach, and then a few dignitaries of the town in other coaches, went through a smoky December silence of factory streets to a cemetery shabby with wet chrysanthemums. There were many wreaths. I saw Bretherton, coughing, mackintoshed, greasy-hatted, scrambling and treading about them, scribbling his notes for a piece about the last of Evensford's aristocracy. Behind the tones of the burial service came a continuous cough, hard and harsh, of factory engines, and above the flowers a smell of leather hung in the air.

Lydia took the death of her aunt very quietly. In a meditative way that offered me the first notion that the Aspen sisters had been like two trees, overshadowing, protecting, and keeping each other up, she said:

"She never had anybody to prop her up again. She never got over that." And then: "Now there's only Rollo and me. And there very nearly wasn't me."

A week later the weather turned very cold, and the valley was covered with snow.

IV

For four days snowless dusty winds blew up the valley, dark with ice, freezing shallow furrowed tongues of water about the marshlands. The last of the leaves were down. The sky held its snow away from us, in a northern bank, gray like a blight, and then gradually the wind began to fall away. As it fell it left a sky solid with iron-colored cloud that thickened without movement and was very quiet, without the whipping of dust among the blown fish papers and the last shriveled leaves of Evensford's gutters.

Snow began to fall on the morning of the day we were to take Lydia for her first outing. It fell for about two hours, in a thick, silent, flurried storm that transfigured everything by noon. Then suddenly it stopped; the sky had across it a pale yellow rent that folded back and became a lofty tender blue. By one o'clock the sun was shining. There was a great sparkling everywhere of blue-white branches and patterned fences and high-crowned shrubs in street gardens, everything transformed. It was suddenly no longer cold, and on a thin smooth layer of snow the sun was dazzling.

When we drove away from the sanatorium about two o'clock, out into the country, there was almost a touch of reverence about the departure, largely because Blackie was so overwhelmed by it that he could hardly speak to us. He seemed to become invested, that day, with some of the old courtesies of his father. He stood by the limousine with folded rugs on his arms, decent and awed and solid and immensely proud.

He insisted that Lydia and I should sit at the back of the car, and he tucked us up there, as his father used to do, with elaborate care, under four or five rugs, fussing continually.

"You're sure you're all right? You're sure you don't feel any cold? Tell me if you feel any cold. You make her tell me if she's cold, won't you, Mr. Richardson?" he said, "because the one thing she mustn't do is to get cold."

"I can feel the sun through the glass already," she said.

From somewhere he had managed to find a bunch or two of violets, which he had arranged in the chromium tubes by the

[326]

back windows of the limousine. The scent of them was lovely in the air, and with it was a delicate softness of the perfume she was using and the powder she had put on her face.

"Now where would you like to go?" he said. Even his smile had a sort of stiffness about it. "You tell me where. I won't drive fast. You needn't have any fear. The snow won't hurt — there's nothing to worry about with the snow. Where would you like me to take you?"

"Just anywhere," she said. "Just go anywhere. If we see something we like very much we can stop — "

"All right," he said, "I'll drive steady out into the country. You needn't worry. And don't get cold. You're sure you've got enough rugs? Don't get cold."

The sun was warm on the glass of the limousine as we drove away into a countryside light with fresh-fallen snow, under trees that dropped, through the warmer afternoon air, floating bobs of whiteness in shaken little blizzards that gradually left everywhere a clearer skeleton of branches. Bullocks blew snowy steam above yellow piles of hay in farmyards. There was a wonderful diffusion of snowlight on the shining car, the violets, and the red silk scarf one of the nurses had lent Lydia to tie over her head.

"Warm enough?" Blackie pushed back the glass division behind the driver's seat and in proud anxiety looked back at us. "Not feeling cold, Mr. Richardson, is she?"

"You're not cold?" I said to her, "are you?"

"Feel of me," she said, and I put my hand under the rug and felt of her hands. They were very warm, and as I touched them she caught my own and would not let me draw them away.

"She's melting already," I said. He laughed with a wonderful satisfaction as he closed the glass division and left us alone again and shut away.

"What made you say that?" she said. "Because that's how I

feel — melting and warm after being frozen up. Thawing out and living again. You don't know what it is to feel like that, do you?"

"No."

"It feels very wonderful," she said.

We passed flocks of gray geese that, as they snouted and burrowed about the snow, looked almost black-feathered against the glittering pure whiteness of otherwise deserted fields.

"It will soon be Christmas," she said. "If the geese escape they'll feel like I do — it isn't nice to be a goose, is it? or it wouldn't be if you knew you were one — what am I saying?" She laughed in gay, brittle tremors. "I was a goose, anyway. It wasn't nice and they nearly killed me."

I held her hands under the rug, letting her talk as she wanted.

"When you've nearly died once, it's funny how it doesn't frighten you so much again," she said. "Did you know that?"

I did not know that either.

"Well, it doesn't," she said. "I should have thought you'd have known. You were always so good at knowing how people felt — you had a way of guessing."

I could not answer; it seemed to me that I had made more mistaken guesses about her, perhaps, than anyone living.

"Anyway you hold my hand very nicely." She squeezed me impulsively, with a rush of tenderness, under the rug. "You do that very well."

We drove on at a dead slow pace into narrower lanes, between high-piled hedges of snow, where no other vehicles had been. Under the car wheels the snow crackled beautifully, with a sharp nutty sound.

"All we really need to make it perfect is a sleigh with horses and bells and that sort of thing," she said. "Then we could imagine — "

"You've got a chariot," I said. "You couldn't imagine anything nicer than that."

"What are you talking about?" she said. But Blackie at that moment pushed back the glass division and said:

"Tell me if you get tired, won't you? Tell me when you feel you've had enough and don't want to go any farther."

"Oh! We've hardly started — "

"You mustn't overdo it," he said.

We passed two small boys and a dog racing about a frozen pond, under a farm wall. I could hear the boys shouting and the dog, as it slithered over ice, barking excited and sharp in the still afternoon.

"There'll be skating," she said. "That would be wonderful — skating for Christmas. Everybody loves the idea of skating for Christmas. Everybody waits for it and it hardly ever comes."

We came to a small hill where the road made a passage between spinneys of oak and hazel above the valley of a brook. The delicate branches of hazel, fingered already with pale stiff catkins, were snowless under the high protective screen of oaks. Where the sun caught them the catkins were pale greenish-yellow, almost springlike, and I could see primrose leaves piercing a crust of snowy oak leaf under thin blue shadows. The hill was not very steep but Blackie put the car into lower gear, driving with a new excess of caution, so that we crept down into the valley at less than walking pace, the ghostly, glittering chariot making hardly a sound in the closed avenue of hazels.

Then we were clear of the woods and suddenly, delicate and transfigured and untouched, the valley of snow-meadows, with small lakes of frozen floodwater lying darker about it, was now there below us. It appeared so suddenly and was so beautiful, full in sun, the snow deep blue below the paler blue of sky and between the tawny-purple lips of frosty horizons, that she sat bolt upright in her seat and let go my hands.

"Oh! Stop — let's stop here! That's so lovely — "

He stopped the car immediately, gently, and then slid back the partition to ask:

"Nothing wrong, is there? You're all right? — not too cold?"

"Oh! There's ice by the brook," she said. "You can see where the birds have been across it — we ought to see if it bears — we really ought to see — "

"I'll go," he said, "I'll go."

He was out of the car instantly, plodding across snowy verges into the meadow where a small tributary brook ran and where, for a space of fifty or sixty yards, a patch of flood-water had frozen between dark islands of sedge.

"I'll try it too," I said. But suddenly she kept me back, holding my hand again, in a new rush of tenderness, under the rug. A wave of disturbed feeling, tender too but troubled and complicated by something she could not express, came over her face and remained there. She could not disentangle it; and suddenly, as if it were the scarf that were bothering her, she pulled it back from her face and let it fall away, leaving her hair free.

"Don't go," she said. "I wanted to ask you something — are you happy?"

"Yes," I said.

"Terribly happy? As happy as you ever were or could be or wanted to be — happy in that way?"

I could not look at her face. Out of the corner of my eye I watched Blackie, big and cautious, trying the edges of the ice pool with the toes of his shoes.

"I wanted to ask you that — because you seemed a little strange or something. I can't explain how it was — "

"It's been lovely," I said.

"I kept having a queer feeling that some part of you wasn't here," she said. "Do you know what I mean?"

From the meadow the sound of ice cracking and splintering came with a sort of thin exhilaration on the air. I looked out to see Blackie picking his way across the pool, arms outstretched; and as he saw me look he waved back at me.

"I think it bears," I said. "I'll go and see —"

"I'm coming too," she said. "Don't go without me."

I held her hand while she picked her way through the snowy grass of the roadside. Anxious, tormented that she was acting incautiously or stupidly or that she would fall and hurt herself, Blackie came running across the meadow, from the ice, to hold her by the other hand. She laughed, shaking her dark hair free from her face in the wintry sunlight; her neck was white with the upward reflection of snowlight as she lifted it. There was no other sound in the air but the crunch of shoes in snow and the delicate bubble of brook-water flowing away through fields between banks of snowy, frozen reed.

After we had reached the ice together she suddenly lifted her hands free from us and said:

"Let me go on alone. I want to do it alone." And we let her go forward, across the ice, by herself. I saw then how thin her legs were: thin, fleshless, almost straight, unsupple from long illness until now they were as clumsy as they had been on the first day I had taken her skating. She moved so unfreely and stiffly that, like Blackie, I was frightened for a moment or two she would fall down.

"Be careful! Are you all right? Let me come and help you."

"No," she said. "No. Don't come. I'm all right. I want to do it alone."

Like that she walked, almost crept, to the other side of the ice, fifty or sixty yards away. When she got there she turned and threw back her head, laughing, in the sun. Her hair was very dark against the background of snowfields, above the loop of crimson scarf, and she laughed again in a triumphant happy way and called:

"Come and fetch me, someone!" — and held out her hands.

Blackie did not move and I went with skating movements across the snow-crusted ice to fetch her. She came part of the way to meet me, her hands outstretched. Then as I met her she took my hands, crosswise, and we turned and came with a slow, skating motion to where Blackie, on the grass now, stood waiting, watching us, his face faintly concerned.

"Come on!" she said. "You too, Bert. Come on! — it's wonderful."

"I'm not sure it'll bear the three of us — "

"Oh! Of course — "

"It cracks too much," he said. "It cracks all over."

"If it cracks it bears," I said. "If it bends it breaks."

"I'm not so sure — it seems to bend a bit too," he said. And Lydia laughed so much at him standing there, hesitant and stiff and troubled, that eventually he crept on again and joined us.

After that we went across the ice several times together, holding hands, and at each turn he said: "Don't overdo it. Don't get tired," and then finally she said:

"The last time. By myself. Once more — and then we'll go."

We stood watching her again as she turned and moved about the ice alone. A sky of pale blue had begun to tone down, above the edges of the horizon, to a blur of rosy apricot that seemed gradually to stain all the upper boundaries of distant fields of snow. As I looked at it and looked at her face, shining and with her hair falling dark and disheveled and rather long from the thrown-back scarf, I remembered once again the afternoon I had first taken her skating. I remembered her awkwardness and her long awkward dress and the

[332]

self-consciousness it had all imposed on me; I remembered the rosy apricot of horizons, more bitter then with frost until they became a fierce bronzy orange above the tanneries about the freezing river; I remembered Tom and his appearance of staggered wonder, and then afterwards the weeks of skating, the walking home after darkness through streets of frozen snow under lighted shop windows and how she had wanted so much to know about each of them and how desperately and eagerly she had wanted to know about everything and everybody, myself most of all.

As I stood thinking of this she gave a cry across the ice and called:

"Here I come! Somebody catch me" — and partly in sheer obedience, partly out of fear, Blackie stepped forward on the ice and held out his hands, waiting for her.

She panted and laughed for a moment as he caught her, and then said:

"Oh! My legs are like jelly. They won't hold me — I think I'm going to fall down —" And she looked for a moment tremulous and a little scared as she rocked on her thin legs and staggered.

"You'd better carry her, Blackie," I said. And in a solemn, bewildered way in which there was no visible hint of whether he was suffering or glad or relieved or burning with wonder or anything else, he picked her up and carried her to the car.

We drove back slowly, in a world of snow freezing to branches under a sky deepening from blue to orange-rose and a final smoky-bronze. There was a great stillness everywhere. Snow no longer floated down through the white half-twilight from the trees. Her hands were warm under the rugs. Her body was quiet and relapsed and tired and she did not talk so much; but once she gave a great sigh from the recesses of the rugs and said:

"Skating! — that's something, isn't it? That means I'm

coming on, doesn't it? And soon I'll be dancing, too. Are you coming to the dance? — you are, aren't you?"

"If you want me to."

"Of course I want you to. I want it more than anything. You'll dance with me a lot, will you? Say you will."

"Yes."

"A lot? — all evening? — as long as my poor legs can hold me?"

"What about Blackie?" I said. "I think you should ask him too."

"I don't think he dances," she said, "but I'll ask him. Of course I will."

For the last mile Blackie switched on the sidelights of the car; and as we came into the avenue I saw them shining faintly through the twilight on passing tree trunks, on the gardens and on the snow. Then when he stopped the car and we got out I saw them shining on her scarf, her dark hair and her face as she stood there for a few moments to say good-by.

"Oh! I think I'm going to kiss you both," she said suddenly, "for taking me. Yes, I am — it was so lovely — so lovely, and thank you." And in what was for him a moment of intolerable and blinding surprise, obliterating everything else, she turned and took his face in her hands and kissed him.

She could not have conceived, as she did so, that she had set a final and irretrievable seal on all his feelings about her; that if they had been fluid and tortuous and merely latent she had suddenly done something to shape them with the stamp of her own. There was nothing in his face to indicate that this was so. He merely made a mutely agonized dart towards and into the back of the limousine. I heard him stumbling about there for some moments and while he did so she turned away from the car lights, kissing me on the lips.

"And good-by to you," she said.

"Good-by."

Her face was warm in the cold air as she put it up to me. Then she kissed me suddenly on the lips, for the second time.

"Good-by, darling," she said.

He came out from the car a moment later in a confused rush, carrying a rug in one hand and the hastily bunched violets in the other. He put the rug round her shoulders and she took the violets in her hands. In a voice of impossible, choking, self-conscious bewilderment he said:

"I nearly forgot them — I didn't want to do that — "

I let him take her into the building. As I stood waiting for him to come back I looked up, through snow branches, to the sky. It had no color except the green print of stars. There was no sound in the air. There was a strange frozen emptiness everywhere and I had the feeling, exactly as she had said, that some part of myself had severed itself from me and would never come back.

V

SOMETIMES as we danced together on the last evening of the year she would look up at me and say, "Couldn't you look at me sometimes? Just a bit? Must you always keep your head up there?" And I would smile at her in turn and apologize, trying lamely to show in my face some expression that seemed spontaneous. But the feeling that I had no love to give her and did not know why, that some part of myself had been driven away, perhaps destroyed forever, and now would not come back, was behind everything I did and felt and said. And it was made more difficult not only because I could not explain it. I knew that, in her excitement, she did not know it was there.

"I think not more than half a dozen dances," Baird had warned her, and she said promptly:

"And just for that you'll only get one of them."

"And none after midnight."

"I shall do exactly as I like," she said. "In any case, you'll be so busy with Nora you'll never know."

"My spies will be watching," he said.

But she took notice of him; and in a gay-colored room where dancers rustled through fallen streamers with a kind of long, dry whisper, we did not dance much. We shared a table with Baird and Nora. All the time Blackie was watchfully attendant in the blue serge suit he always wore on Sundays, a steadfast, bemused smile on his face as he drank the champagne Baird had been good enough to provide, and waited, like a dog waiting to be taken for a run, for his turn to dance with her.

There was a great happiness in his face whenever she threw him a crumb of conversation, and sometimes I actually thought his mouth, opening to smile at her, seemed to snap at whatever the morsel was, again exactly like a dog.

From time to time he wandered out to the men's room, and once he came back to tell us that snow was falling again. A few flakes melted starrily on his black hair and the shoulders of his jacket. Solemnly he spoke of the car as if it were an animate creature he had just watered and fed for the night, and she teased him delicately by saying:

"I believe you're frightened that car will run away."

"Oh no!" he said. "Oh no! It's all right. Dr. Baird let me put it in with his — "

"You and that car," she teased him. I saw the subdued shadow of a kind of pleasurable pain cross his face. "I daren't think what would happen if it ran away," she said. And

I knew that it was not the car of which he was afraid.

Then Baird came back, to say, with jocular pretence at severity:

"Is she behaving herself? Is she keeping her word?"

"She is indeed," she said. "After all, you're not the only one with spies. We've got spies on our side. Very faithful ones, too."

"And what do the spies report?"

"Three dances," I said.

"I'll take your word for it," he said. "How's the champagne?"

"We shall need another bottle for the great occasion," she said. "When is it to be?"

"In the supper interval."

"That gives us time for one more dance," she said to me.

"Don't overdo it," he said. "You know why."

As we danced I slipped away into bemusement again, involved in my own reflections. Suddenly I was aware of her looking up into my face, hearing her say:

"And do you know why?"

"Why what?" I said.

"Couldn't you come down to earth for a minute?" she said. "Just to help me?" And after I had made another pretence at spontaneity, with a smile, she said again:

"Do you know why I have to behave? Why I promised I would?" And then, before I could answer:

"Because if I'm good I can go out of here. Perhaps in a month. Anyway, very soon. Aren't you glad? Don't you think it's wonderful?"

I thought it was very wonderful, and I said I was very glad.

"Then act as if you were glad," she said. "What is it with you tonight?"

Quickly I said: "I was wondering how you would find it back at the house. With no one there but Rollo — "

"I'm not going back," she said. "I'm never going back there again. I don't want that big house and all that goes with it and doesn't go with it — I don't want it any more than you do."

"Where will you go?" I said.

"I wanted to ask you that," she said.

I said something about how I thought she ought perhaps to go away, for a change and a rest, a month perhaps of convalescence in the spring, somewhere by the sea.

"The sea?" she said. "Would you come with me too if I went to the sea?"

Before I could answer the band stopped playing. I saw Baird mounting the dais, smiling and raising his hands. I heard him begin to say, locking and unlocking his large muscular fingers with sudden nervousness, how he was not very much at speech-making and how there would now be an interval for supper, but before the interval there was something he wanted to say. His voice, pitched slightly high in its nervousness, quietened the last rustlings of feet among the fallen streamers about the floor. Then he spoke, with a sudden rush of feeling and a smile, of the future Mrs. Baird, and as Nora stepped beside him on the platform the room became swollen with high laughter and applause and people shouting. Then the band began to play "For they are jolly good fellows." And Lydia took my two hands with impulsive affection in hers, looking up into my face.

"She lived for that," she said. "All the time that's what she lived for — come on, let's be the first to drink to them."

At the table, as we held up our glasses and drank to Nora and Dr. Baird, saying over and over again that we wished them luck and how we hoped they'd be very happy, I thought I heard the occasional sniff of a nurse's tears among the laughter. It reminded me of the time when Lydia and Tom and Nancy and Alex and his mother and myself had danced

[338]

together, also on New Year's Eve, and had toasted each other and wished each other luck, also in champagne.

I came out of this recollection to hear Baird say:

"I hope you'll be the first to come and stay with us, you two."

Still half lost in the thought of Alex and how that night, in our headstrong stupidity, we had hated Blackie, I did not answer, and Lydia said:

"He means us, silly. You're not listening again."

"I am," I said. "I'm listening. Thank you very much, both of you."

"It'll be open house for you two." Baird said. "Any time — "

"Thank you," I said.

"You haven't kissed Nora," Lydia said. And in response I dutifully kissed Nora. Then Baird kissed Lydia. At this point somebody remembered Blackie, a slightly self-conscious odd-man-out, a dog waiting to be noticed when the rest of us thought fit. Lydia seemed struck too by that same appearance of watching hunger. A rush of pity came over her and with impulsive charm she took his face in her hands, kissing him.

"Oh! I want to kiss everybody," she said. "You too — all of you." And she pressed her lips against my face. "All of you — it's nice — I feel so happy."

I knew, presently, that I could bear no more of this. I felt I could not face any longer the affliction of a dilemma in which I could see, every time I looked up, the reflection in Blackie's face of the love for her I was incapable of giving. I could not stand any more the idea of being false to her.

As I made some excuse and went out, leaving her there with Nora and Dr. Baird and Blackie, I felt very much as I had done on the night Alex had died: stubborn and lonely and bewildered and incapable of dissuasion. I went into the men's room to wash my hands. A burly young man combing his hair at the wash basin asked me how my father was and if I remembered how nice, that warm May evening, the singing had been. "It put a lot of life into me," he said, "that singing. Do you remember? — I was the one who asked if they'd sing 'The Golden Vanity.' " As we talked for a few moments he smiled a lot into the mirror, very meticulous with the comb as he ran it through his hair. He said several times that they'd put two stone or more on him since he'd been in there, and then in a touching moment of private confession:

"I never thought I'd be able to look at my own face again. They gave me a mirror one day in bed, and there was somebody else staring at me. It wasn't me at all. It's a terrible thing when you look in a mirror and you see somebody you don't know." And then he added, as they all did, "I'll soon be out of here."

As I left him and went out, through the entrance corridors, on to the deserted terrace, I saw that it was still snowing. I stood watching the big flakes curling down through shafts of window light, into a world already deep and soft with snow. In the air there was a curious after-breath, gentle and almost warm, that snow seems to bring down with it after the coldness of cloud has been broken. Flakes that were soft and blown and shining made a line of wetness where they ended on the gleaming bricks of the terrace. Then as I stood watching them I felt rather like the young man in the washroom, looking into his mirror, startled by a reflection he did not know, troubled by being a stranger to himself.

I had been there five minutes or more when Lydia opened the glass entrance doors and came out to look for me.

"Oh! You're there," she said. "I somehow thought you were."

She came and stood beside me. She had put on a coat. The material was thick and blue, and she said, "It's one of the nurse's — she lent it me." And then I saw that it was not a coat. It was a cloak, and it reminded me suddenly, with its scarlet hood, of the one she had worn on the first Saturday we had skated together on the marshes.

"You're not cold, are you?" she said.

"It's quite warm with the snow," I said.

She touched my hands. "They're quite cold," she said. "Come into my cloak" — and she opened the cloak and folded me into it, close against the front of her body.

"How do you find me?" she said. She found one of my arms and drew it round her waist. "Smaller than I used to be? — not so much of me?"

In a flash of recollection that was more like a spasm of pain I remembered her body, soft and young and firm-breasted, as I had first seen it in the summerhouse in the park.

"Your waist is smaller," I said.

"You say nice things sometimes," she said. She brushed her lips to and fro across my face, gently, thoughtfully, as if to soothe me. "Except you didn't answer my question."

"What question?"

Her voice was muffled when she spoke again, half into the cloak:

"The question about the sea. Would you come with me to the sea?"

I watched the snow slowly graining with curling oblique lines the background of darkness beyond the lights of the terrace. Would I go with her to the sea? — I felt the question float away, losing itself in snow and darkness, dissolved among a thick slow white scramble of flakes. I knew that it was something that I was afraid to answer and that, presently I should have to answer, and then she said:

"Would you? Come with me, will you, please?"

I stared into the snow, trying to frame an answer. The flakes were quite soundless as they fell windlessly down on snow-covered grass, and yet I felt at the same time that I could hear, a long way off, a low-blown echo of them across the darkness.

"You will come with me, won't you?" she said. "You're not hesitating about something?"

"I can't come with you," I said.

She did not speak for a few moments. I felt her body quiver again before she finally said, with bewilderment:

"Why did you say that?"

"I can't come with you," I said.

I heard her drawing her breath with sharpness through her mouth.

"Do you mean you don't want to come with me?" she said. "You mean you don't want me?"

"It isn't that — "

"You do love me, don't you?" she said.

The directness of the question I had feared so long and did not want to answer struck something inside me that seemed to burst like a fester. I felt my entire body swamped by bitter surges of intolerable pain. I felt her begin to move away from me, in a short, stiffened struggle to be free, and then she quietened herself again and said:

"If you don't love me, please say so — I could understand it."

"How could you understand it?"

She did not speak for a moment or two. Across the snow I could hear, sharp and hollow, the barking of a dog, followed by the high yelp of another. The sound seemed to intensify a silence already so snowbound that everything was muted. I could not see a single light from the town. In this curious disembodied quietness the movement of her body turning to me seemed suddenly magnified. There was something reassuring in the enlarging disturbance of the cloak as she moved her hands underneath it and said:

[342]

"That was how I got in here. It was because of you and all the things I did to you — "

Across the snow the barking voices of the two dogs seemed to be joined by a third, and she said:

"Can you hear the dogs? It's Rollo. He lets them out every night. You can always hear them all across the fields. I listen to them sometimes when I lie awake — "

The ugly memory of the bloated Labradors crawling about the porch and the hall of the house came back to me with the strangest effect of beginning to clear the blurred and complicated distances inside myself. As the sound of barking across the snow increased and became a series of quarreling howls thrown to the empty fields I became unaware of her face. I felt I saw instead only the ugliness of Rollo, the dogs and the dying house. It was dying and I knew suddenly that I did not want her to be part of it, exactly as Tom had not wanted her to be part of a dreary gaslit kitchen where two people were quarreling over the dead. I could not bear the thought of her in either place.

What I saw too of myself seemed gradually no longer strange. The unrecognizable edges of a person distorted as much by fear of love as by lack of love began to reshape themselves into something that was acceptable at last. I had so often thought of her growing up from something awkward and lonely that it had not occurred to me that I too had been growing up, just as painfully, in that same way. It had not occurred to me that the pain of love might be part of its flowering. I had not grasped that the love I felt for Tom and Alex had so much to do with the love I felt for her. With inconceivable stupidity I had not given love to her simply out of fear of being hurt by its unacceptance; I had not grasped that I might have made her suffer.

"Would you forgive me?" she said, "for the awful, terrible things I did?"

[343]

Not answering, I remembered Bretherton. I had misjudged even Bretherton. "You've got to conquer yourself," Bretherton had said.

"Would you forgive me?"

The laceration of my misjudgments was so sharp that I could not answer.

"I thought of you every night when I lay there — at the bottom," she said. "After Tom had died. There was no one there and I wanted you."

"You know there is nothing to forgive," I said. "Except the things I did."

The slow breaking of her voice into tears seemed to wake me at last. Holding her, folding myself into the nurse's cloak, against her, I shut out the snow, the darkness, the raw night-barking of Rollo's dogs across the park. A flake or two of snow penetrated with the floating effect of frozen bubbles the aperture of the cloak, falling on my head and on her face as she lifted it up to me.

"Do you remember the snow last time?" she said. "How lovely it was after the winter? That lovely April weather?"

The cloak fell away from her face as she spoke to me. The sound of dogs quietened completely across the park.

"And will you come with me to the sea?" she said. She was not crying any longer.

"Yes," I said, and I kissed her face.

"It took me a long time to know how you felt," she said. "But I know now and I know what it meant for you."

Holding her, I felt I could hear the sound of the sea rising out of new distances. With happiness I remembered Tom and Alex, the winters and the summers, the young and the dead, the snow and the dancing.

Staring through the snow, I could feel already the warmth of the spring beyond it: the time of the blackbird and the lovely April weather.